About the Authors

Lynne Graham lives in Northern Ireland and has been a keen romance reader since her teens. Happily married, Lynne has five children. Her eldest is her only natural child. Her other children, who are every bit as dear to her heart, are adopted. The family has a variety of pets, and Lynne loves gardening, cooking, collecting all sorts and is crazy about every aspect of Christmas.

After reading a serialised Mills & Boon book in a magazine, **Penny Jordan** quickly became an avid fan! Her goal, when writing romance fiction, is to provide readers with an enjoyment and involvement similar to that she experienced from her early reading – Penny believes in the importance of love, including the benefits and happiness it brings. She works from home, in her kitchen, surrounded by four dogs and two cats, and welcomes interruptions from her friends and family.

Louisa Heaton is a married mother of four (including a set of twins) and lives on an island in Hampshire. When not wrangling her children, husband or countless animals, she can often be found walking her dogs along the beach muttering to herself, as she works out plot points. In her spare time, she reads a lot, or crochets. Usually when she ought to be doing something else!

D1464713

000003063279

Twins

Twins:
Twin Heirs

LYNNE GRAHAM

PENNY JORDAN

LOUISA HEATON

MIX
Paper from
responsible sources
FSC
FSC C007454

his book is produced from independently certified FSC™ paper
to ensure responsible forest management.

For more information visit www.harpercollins.co.uk/green

Printed and bound in Spain
by CPI, Barcelona

MILLS & BOON

First Published in Great Britain 2020
By Mills & Boon, an imprint of HarperCollins*Publishers*
1 London Bridge Street, London, SE1 9GF

TWINS: TWIN HEIRS © 2020 Harlequin Books S.A.

The Sheikh's Secret Babies © 2015 Lynne Graham
Marriage: To Claim His Twins © 2010 Penny Jordan
Pregnant with His Royal Twins © 2017 Louisa Heaton

ISBN: 978-0-263-29853-6

THE SHEIKH'S
SECRET BABIES

LYNNE GRAHAM

CHAPTER ONE

KING JAUL, who had recently acceded to the throne of Marwan on the death of his father, Lut, glanced across the date-palm-filled courtyard beyond his office. A beautiful brunette was playing ball there with her niece and nephew. Her name was Zaliha. Educated, elegant and as sweet-natured as she was well-born, she would make a wonderful queen, he knew. So why hadn't he broached the subject yet? he asked himself grimly.

Marwan was a Gulf state, small but oil-rich and deeply conservative. A single king was not expected to remain single for long. Government officials had made no secret of their eagerness for him to take a bride. A royal dynasty was not seen as secure until there was another heir in the offing and Jaul was an only child, the son of a man who had been an only child.

The newspapers were full of constant speculation. He could not be seen even talking to a young woman without rousing suspicions. His wide, sensual mouth compressed, uneasy memories surfacing of the wilder and more hot-headed young male he had once been. If he was honest with himself, he knew exactly why he was being indecisive about getting married. Moreover he was well aware that beautiful though Zaliha was, there was not the smallest spark of chemistry between them. But shouldn't that be what he wanted now? A marriage shorn of the wild attraction and excitement that had once led to his downfall?

A measured knock sounded on the door heralding the arrival of Bandar, who served as the royal family's senior legal adviser.

'My apologies if I'm a little early,' the little man with the balding head said earnestly, bowing with solemn dignity.

Jaul invited him to sit down and lounged back against his desk, restless at the prospect of an in-depth discussion of some obscure piece of constitutional law, which fascinated Bandar much more than it fascinated anyone else.

'This is a very delicate matter,' Bandar informed him uneasily. 'But it is my duty as your adviser to broach it with you.'

Wondering what on earth the older man could be referring to, Jaul studied him with unsullied assurance. 'There is nothing we cannot discuss—'

'Yet this is a matter which I first raised eighteen months ago with my predecessor, Yusuf, and he instructed me never to mention it again lest I caused offence,' Bandar told him awkwardly. 'If that is the case, please accept my apologies in advance.'

Yusuf had been his father's adviser and had retired after King Lut's passing, allowing Bandar to step into his place. Jaul's fine black brows were now drawing together while a mixture of curiosity and dismay assailed him as he wondered what murky, dark secret of his father's was about to be unleashed on him. What else could this *very* delicate matter concern?

'I am not easily offended and your role is to protect

me from legal issues,' Jaul responded. 'Naturally I respect that responsibility.'

'Then I will begin,' Bandar murmured ruefully. 'Two years ago, you married a young Englishwoman and, although that fact is known to very few people, it is surely past time that that situation is dealt with in the appropriate manner.'

It took a lot to silence Jaul, whose stubborn, passionate and outspoken nature was well known within palace circles, but that little speech seriously shook him. 'But there *was* no actual marriage,' Jaul countered tautly. 'I was informed that the ceremony was illegal because I did not obtain my father's permission beforehand.'

'I'm afraid that was a case of wishful thinking on your father's part. He wished the marriage to be illegal and Yusuf did not have the courage to tell him that it *was* legal...'

Jaul had lost colour beneath his healthy olive-tinted complexion, his very dark, long-lashed eyes telegraphing his astonishment at that revelation. 'It *was* a legal marriage?' he repeated in disbelief.

'There is nothing in our constitutional law which prohibits a Marwani Crown Prince from marrying his own choice of bride. You were twenty-six years old, scarcely a teenager and that marriage still stands because you have done nothing since to sever that tie.'

Wide, strong shoulders now rigid beneath the long cream linen thobe he wore, Jaul frowned, trying to calculate the sheer immensity of the wrecking ball that had suddenly crashed into his marital plans. He was already a married man. Indeed he was *still* a married man. As he had only lived with his bride for a few weeks before parting from her, what Bandar was now telling him naturally came as a severe shock. 'I did nothing to sever the tie because I was informed that the marriage itself was illegal and, therefore, void. Like a bad contract,' he admitted.

'Unhappily that is not the case.' Bandar sighed. 'To be free of the marriage you require a divorce under UK law *and* Marwani law.'

Jaul stalked over to the window beyond which Zaliha could still be seen entertaining her niece and nephew, but he was no longer remotely conscious of that view. 'I had no suspicion of this. I should have been informed of this situation months ago—'

'As I mentioned, Yusuf was my superior and he refused to allow me to raise the subject—'

'It is three months since my father passed away,' Jaul reminded him stiffly.

'I had to ensure my facts were correct before I could raise this matter with you. I have now discovered that in spite of your separation your wife has not sought a divorce either—'

Jaul froze, his lean, darkly handsome features clenching hard. 'Please do not refer to her as my wife,' he murmured flatly.

'Should I refer to the lady concerned as your queen?' Bandar pressed with even less tact. 'Because that is what Chrissie Whitaker is, whether she knows it or not. The wife of the King of Marwan is *always* granted the status of Queen.'

Jaul snatched in a ragged breath of restraint, lean brown hands closing slowly into fists of innate aggression. He had made one serious mistake in his life and it had come back to haunt him in the worst possible way at the worst possible time. He had married a gold-digger who had deserted him the first chance she got in return for cold, hard cash.

'Naturally I respect the fact that your father did not approve of the young woman but perhaps *now*—'

'No, my father was correct in his assessment of her character. She was unsuitable to be either my wife or my queen,' Jaul acknowledged grittily, a faint flare of colour accentuating the line of his spectacular high cheekbones as he forced out the lowering admission that stung his pride. 'I was a rebellious son, Bandar... but I learnt my lesson.'

'The lessons of youth are often hard, Bandar commented quietly, relieved that the current king was unlike his late parent, who had raged and taken umbrage at anyone who told him anything he did not want to hear.

Jaul was barely listening. In fact he was being bombarded by unwelcome memories that had escaped from the burial ground at the back of his mind where he kept such unsettling reminders firmly repressed. In his mind's eye he was seeing Chrissie walk away from him, her glorious silver-blonde hair blowing back in the breeze, her long, shapely legs fluid and graceful as a gazelle's.

But she had *always* been walking away from him, he recalled with cool cynicism. Right from the start, Chrissie had played a cool, clever, long-term game of seduction. Hot-blooded as he was and never before refused by a woman as he had been, she had challenged his ego with her much-vaunted indifference. It had taken a two-year-plus campaign for him to win her and she had only truly become his when he had surrendered and given her a wedding ring. Unsurprisingly during that long period of celibacy and frustration, Chrissie

Whitaker had become a sexual obsession whose allure Jaul had not been able to withstand.

The payback for his weakness had not been long in coming. They had had a flaming row when he'd left Oxford to fly back to Marwan without her and, extraordinarily, he had never seen her again after that day. At that point and perhaps most fortunately for him, fate had intervened to cut him free of his fixation with her. Following a serious accident, Jaul had surfaced in a hospital bed to find his father seated like a sentry beside him, his aged features heavy with grief and apprehension.

Before he had broken the bad news, King Lut had reached for his son's hand in a clumsy gesture of comfort for the first time in his life. Chrissie, Lut had then confided heavily, would *not* be coming to visit Jaul during his recovery. His marriage, Lut had declared, was illegal and Chrissie had accepted a financial pay-off as the price of forgetting that Jaul had ever figured in her life. King Lut had purchased her silence and discretion with a large sum of money that had evidently compensated her for her supposed loss of a husband while providing her with support for the future.

For a split second, Jaul recalled one of the most insane fantasies that had gripped him while he lay helpless in that hospital bed. Aware of his diplomatic immunity within the UK, he had actually dreamt about kidnapping Chrissie. Now in the present he shook his proud dark head slowly, utterly astonished at the tricks his mind had played on him while he had struggled to come to terms with the daunting fact that, not only was his wife *not* his wife, but also that given generous enough financial compensation she had no longer *wanted* to be his wife. Chrissie had been quite happy to ditch her Arab prince once she'd had the means to be rich without him. Only angry, bitter and vengeful thoughts had driven Jaul while he'd fought his injuries to get back on his feet.

'I need to know how you want this matter to be handled,' Bandar told him, shooting Jaul back to the present. 'With the assistance of our ambassador in London I have engaged the services of a highly placed legal firm to have divorce papers drawn up. After so long a separation they assure me that the divorce will be a mere formality. May I instruct the firm to make immediate contact with Chrissie Whitaker?'

'No...' Without warning, Jaul swung round, his lean bronzed features taut and forbidding. 'If she is not yet aware that we remain man and wife a third party should not be dealing with it. Informing her of that fact should be my responsibility.'

Bandar frowned, taken aback by that assurance. 'But, sir—'

'I owe her that much. After all, it was *my* father who misled her as to the legality of our marriage. Chrissie has a hot temper. I think a personal approach is more likely to lead to a speedy and successful conclusion. I will present her with the divorce papers.'

'I understand.' Bandar was nodding now, having followed his royal employer's reasoning. 'A diplomatic and discreet approach.'

'As you say,' Jaul conceded, marvelling at the tingle of the illicit thrill assailing him at the very thought of seeing Chrissie again. It felt neither diplomatic nor discreet. But then no woman had ever excited Jaul to that extent, either before or since. Of course now that he knew how mercenary and hard-hearted she was, that attraction would be absent, he reflected confidently. He was an intelligent man and no longer at the mercy of his hormones.

He had cracked down hard on that side of his nature as soon as he'd understood just how badly his libido could betray him. There had been a lesson writ large in that experience with Chrissie, a lesson Jaul had been quick to learn and put into practice. Never again would he place himself in a vulnerable position with a woman. This was the main reason he had decided to stop avoiding matrimony and take a wife as soon as possible.

His mood sobered by that acknowledgement and the impossibility of currently following through on that ambition, his lean dark features stiffened and his wide, sensual mouth curled with sudden distaste at the prospect of being forced to deal with Chrissie in a civilised manner. There was nothing remotely civilised about the way Chrissie made him feel… There never had been…

Her arms full of gifts and cards, Chrissie shouldered her way out of the front doors of the primary school where she taught the nursery class and walked to her car.

'Here, let me give you a hand…' A tall, well-built young man with brown hair and a ready smile moved to intercept her, lifting some of the presents from her arms to enable her to unlock her car. 'My word, you're popular with your class!'

'Didn't you get a load of stuff too?' Chrissie asked Danny, who taught Year Six and was in charge of games.

'Yes. Bottles of wine, designer cologne,' he proffered with amusement, flipping open her car boot so that she could pile the gifts in. 'Here in this privileged corner of middle-class London, the last day of term is like winning in a game show.'

Involuntarily, Chrissie smiled, her lovely face full of animation, turquoise-blue eyes alight with answering laughter. 'The gift-giving *has* got out of hand,' she agreed ruefully. 'The parents spend far too much money.'

Danny slammed shut the boot lid and leant back against it. 'So, what are your plans for the rest of the summer?'

'I'll be staying with my sister...doing a bit of travelling,' she confided a shade awkwardly.

'That's the sister who's married to the rich Italian?' Danny checked.

'I only have the one sibling,' Chrissie admitted, shaking her car keys in the hope he would take the hint and move out of her way.

Danny frowned. 'You know, you're only young once. Don't you ever want to take a break from your family and do something more daring on your own?'

With difficulty, Chrissie kept her smile in place. Two years earlier, she had gone down the daring route and what a disaster that had turned out to be! Now she played safe, stayed sensible and worked to eradicate the damage she had done to her relationship with her sister. She adored Lizzie, the sister five years her senior, and when Chrissie's life had gone wrong, Lizzie's disappointment, Lizzie's conviction that somehow she was responsible for the poor decisions Chrissie had made, had filled Chrissie with a guilt she had never quite managed to shake off.

'Lizzie loves you...she only wants to see you happy,' her brother-in-law, Cesare, had said to her once. 'If you would just trust her enough to tell her the whole story it would make her feel better.'

But Chrissie had never told anyone the whole story of her downfall. It had been a stupid short-sighted decision she had made and which she was still paying for. It was bad enough living with her mistakes but it would be even worse if she had to share the truth of them with others and see their opinion of her intelligence dive-bomb.

'Obviously, I'll be in Cornwall,' Danny reminded her as if she didn't already know. Everyone in the staff-room had been listening to Danny talk about his summer surfing plans for months.

'I hope you have a great time.' Chrissie eased past him to open her car door.

Danny closed his hand round her slender wrist to hold her back and looked down at her ruefully. 'I would have a better time if you agreed to come with me,' he admitted. 'Just mates, no need to lay anything else on the line. Last chance, Chrissie. Why not live a little and give it a go?'

Blue eyes flaring with pained annoyance, Chrissie jerked her wrist free. 'As I said, I've other plans—'

'Some guy did a right number on you, didn't he?' Danny remarked, his face red with discomfiture as he moved away a step and thrust his hands into his pockets. 'But all cats are not grey in the dark, Chrissie. If you still want a life, you have to reach out and take it.'

Breathing fast, Chrissie slid into the driver's seat of her car and closed the door. She *had* wanted a life, an entirely different life from the one she now had. She had dreamt of climbing the academic ranks by pursuing a doctorate and of the freedom that would be hers once she was fully qualified. But life, Chrissie had discovered, had a habit of stabbing you in the back when you least expected it, of forcing a sudden rethink just when you were on the apparent brink of success. Now she was in no position to reach out and take anything because she had responsibilities that restricted her independence and her liberty. To her way of thinking the most shameful aspect was that she couldn't get by without taking advantage of her sister's generosity. Yet it could all have been so very different, *had* she only made the right decisions...

Long before Chrissie had met Jaul, Lizzie and Chrissie had inherited a tiny Greek island from their late mother. Lizzie's husband, Cesare, had bought Lionos from the sisters for a small fortune. The sale of the island had taken place before Chrissie's twins were even conceived and so Chrissie had opted to put the majority of her share of the money into a trust that she could not access until her twenty-fifth birthday. At the time she had thought that that was a sensible idea—the amount of money involved had made her head spin and Chrissie had a secret fear that she might have inherited her mother's spendthrift ways. Francesca Whitaker had been extravagant and irresponsible with cash and Chrissie had wanted to carefully conserve her windfall for what she had assumed would be a more settled time in her life.

Now here she was, twenty-four years of age, and for the past year she had had to acknowledge that had she had the ability to use that money she had put away, she could, at least, have been financially independent. Instead, to enable her to follow a teaching career she'd had to share her sister's nanny, Sally, to look after her own children—affording Sally's services solely on her earnings as a teacher would have been impossible.

On the other hand, by following Cesare's advice, she had made *one* good decision when she had used some of the money to purchase a two-bedroom apartment before she put the rest of it away where it couldn't be touched. Furthermore she had bought the apartment outright, which meant she could afford to run a small car and at least contribute a healthy amount towards Sally's salary. Of course to hear Lizzie tell it, Chrissie was doing Cesare and Lizzie a favour by keeping Sally gainfully employed while they were abroad. In the same way, when her sister and her brother-in-law and their children flew into London for one of their frequent visits, Chrissie moved into their town house with them and stayed until they departed again because it was more convenient for everyone that way.

Now, laden with her carrier bags of gifts and cards, Chrissie unlocked the door of her ground-floor apartment.

Sally appeared in the kitchen doorway. 'Cup of tea?' she asked, a curvy brunette with a wide smile.

'I'd love one. No night out this evening?' Chrissie teased, for Sally had a very healthy social life and was usually rushing back to Lizzie's town house to dress up.

'Not tonight…not unless I want to go into an overdraft!' she joked, pulling a face.

Chrissie set her bags down and walked into the lounge. Two babies were playing with plastic bricks in the centre of the carpet. Both had a shock of blue-black curls and eyes so dark they were almost black. Tarif dropped his brick, crowed with delight and started to crawl eagerly towards her. Soraya laughed and, rarely as energetic as her brother, she lifted her arms high to be lifted.

'Hello, my darlings,' Chrissie said warmly, her face softening as she dropped to her knees to gather up Tarif before freeing up an arm to pull his sister close.

'Mum-mum,' Soraya said solemnly, a plump little hand touching her mother's cheek gently.

Tarif tugged her hair and planted a big, sloppy kiss on her cheek, nestling as close as he could get. And all the worries and little annoyances of the day fell from Chrissie in the same moment. Her twins had owned her heart from the day of their birth. She had been so worried that she wouldn't be able to cope with two babies but Lizzie had taken her home to the town house and showed her all the basics.

'You'll muddle through...we all do,' Lizzie had assured her.

But nobody had warned Chrissie that when she looked at her children she would be overwhelmed by her love for them. While she was pregnant she had tried to think of them as Jaul's children and she had deeply resented the position he had put her in. She hadn't felt ready to be a mother and had shrunk from the challenge of becoming a single parent. But once the twins were born, she only cared that her babies thrived and were happy.

'I took them to the park this afternoon. Tarif threw a real tantrum when I took him off the swings,' Sally confided. 'He was throwing himself about so much I had to lay him down until he got it out of his system. I was really surprised.'

'In the wrong mood, he's challenging,' Chrissie acknowledged ruefully. 'But Soraya's the exact same if you cross her. They like to test you out. They're quite volatile.'

Very much like their father, Chrissie reflected helplessly. An image of Jaul flashed into her head, long blue-black hair loose on his broad shoulders, brilliant dark eyes shimmering with anger. Hotter than hot, she thought numbly. Hot-tempered, hot-blooded, hot in bed, hot in every way there was. A snaking quiver of forbidden heat washed through her taut length. But Jaul had also been incredibly stubborn, impulsive and unpredictable.

'Are you feeling all right?' Sally asked, plucking the twins worriedly from their mother's loosened grasp. 'Sorry, you looked a bit pale and spaced out there for a moment.'

'I'm fine.' Chrissie flushed to the roots of her pale hair, scrambled up and hurried into the tiny kitchen to make the tea in Sally's place.

Sometimes the past just leapt up and smacked her in the face without warning. A memory would dart through her and time would freeze, catapulting her backwards. A stray word or a familiar smell or piece of music could rip her apart in the space of seconds, leaving her no hiding place from the backwash of old pain. If she hadn't loved Jaul, she would have got over him much more easily. But then she told herself that for the sake of her children she was glad that she had loved Jaul even if it hadn't lasted, even though he had used her and lied to her and probably cheated on her as well.

The money his father had offered her had been the bottom line, telling her everything she needed to know about the rogue male, who had told her they were married and would be together for ever. Jaul thought that money was the perfect solution to every problem, magically soothing hurt feelings and disappointed hopes. His immense wealth had provided him with a smooth escape route from all such tiresome complications. 'Together for ever' had come with a hidden qualification; 'together for ever' had only lasted until Jaul had become bored. Unhappily, it had never occurred to Chrissie when she was with him that one day she would be a tiresome complication in his life too.

'People expect me to be generous,' he had told her once.

'Just because you have it doesn't mean you have to splash it around,' Chrissie had countered. 'That's extravagant and wasteful and it looks like you're showing off.'

Jaul had sent her an outraged glance. 'I do *not* show off!'

Of course he had never had to show off to command attention. He was breathtakingly good-looking and guaranteed to turn female heads wherever he went and, if his looks didn't do it for him, his flash sports cars, phalanx of bodyguards and luxury lifestyle had made their own very effective impression.

Chrissie passed a mug of tea to Sally, who had settled the twins back on the floor to play.

'I've packed all their favourite toys and put them in my car. That'll be one less thing for you to worry about when you're packing up tomorrow,' Sally told her.

Slamming a door shut on the memories attacking her, Chrissie smiled at the brunette. 'Thanks but I've come to stay at the town house so often now that I reckon I could pack in my sleep. I can't wait to see Lizzie and the kids,' she confided.

'Max and Giana will be fascinated by the twins now they're more active,' Sally confided.

'Giana will be disgusted that they no longer stay where you put them.' Chrissie laughed, picturing her bossy little toddler niece, who treated Tarif and Soraya like large dolls and held tea parties for them. 'Or keep their hands off her toys.'

When Sally had gone, Chrissie fed the twins and put them in the bath before settling them into their cots for the night. While she read their nightly story to them, she was wondering where or indeed *if* she would have a job when the summer was over. She had only been teaching on a temporary contract, covering maternity leave, and permanent jobs were as scarce as hens' teeth. That concern still in mind, she went to bed early and slept fitfully.

The next day Chrissie got up on automatic pilot to feed and dress the twins before putting them down for their nap so that they would be fresh when they arrived with her sister and her family. She was running round tidying up, still clad in her comfortable sleep shorts and a tee, when the doorbell buzzed.

Curiosity had taken Jaul straight from the airport to the address Bandar had given him. Chrissie lived in an apartment block in an expensive residential area. His beautifully shaped mouth took on a sardonic slant. He might not have paid alimony to his estranged wife but the cash his father had given her had evidently ensured that she did not starve. Not that he would've wanted her to starve, he told himself piously, unsettled by the vengeful thoughts and raw reactions suddenly skimming through him at lightning speed. Two years ago, lying helpless in his hospital bed, when he'd thought of her turning to other men for amusement, he had burned with merciless, bitter aggression. But that time was past, he assured himself circumspectly. Now all he sought was to draw a quiet final line below the entire messy business of a marriage that should never have taken place.

Chrissie glanced through the peephole in her door and frowned. A tall dark-haired man was on the doorstep, his back turned to the door so that she couldn't see his face. She slipped on the security chain and opened the door. 'Yes?'

'Open the door,' he urged. 'It's Jaul.'

Her eyes flew wide in disbelief and she flung her head back, turquoise eyes frantically peering through the crack. She caught a glimpse of his gypsy-gold skin, a hard male jawline and then her gaze moved up to impatient dark eyes surrounded by lashes thick and dark enough to resemble eye liner and long enough to inspire feminine resentment. Unforgettable, he was unforgettable and her heart started thumping in the region of her throat, making it impossible for her to breathe or vocalise. In a flash, gut reaction took over and she snapped the front door firmly closed again, spinning round in shock to rest back against it because her legs were wobbling.

Jaul swore and hit the bell again twice in an impatient buzz.

Chrissie slid down the back of the door until she was in a heap at the foot of it and hugged her knees. It was Jaul…two years *too late*, it was Jaul. Anguish flooded her, a sharp, sharp pain of loss and grief that she had buried long ago in the need to move on and survive his betrayal. She couldn't believe that Jaul would just turn up like that, without any warning. But then he had disappeared without any warning, she reminded herself darkly.

The bell went again as though someone had a finger stuck to it and she flinched. Jaul was very impatient. She breathed in deep and slow, struggling to calm herself. What on earth was he doing here in London? How had he even found out her current address? And why would he come to see her after all this time? Had it anything to do with the fact that his father had died recently and he had inherited the throne? After his father's visit Chrissie had refused to allow herself to succumb to the morbid interest of checking out Jaul on the Internet. She had closed the door very firmly on that kind of curiosity but she had, quite accidentally in early spring, read a few lines in a newspaper about his father's sudden death.

'*Chrissie...*' he grated behind the door and his voice washed over her, accented and deep, unleashing a tide of memories she didn't want to relive.

She squashed those memories so fast that her head literally hurt as she sprang upright. No way was she hiding behind a door from the male who had torn her life apart!

CHAPTER TWO

CHRISSIE PEERED OUT from behind the curtain. Jaul was stationed on the pavement, his back turned to her again. Several men in dark suits, undoubtedly his protection unit, surrounded him. Her heart was still hammering so feverishly that her chest felt tight.

She had shut the door in Jaul's face, not the sort of welcome he was accustomed to receiving. He would be angry and when Jaul was angry he was dangerously unpredictable. Refusing to open the door had possibly not been her wisest move, Chrissie reasoned worriedly. As his imperious dark head began to turn she hid back behind the curtains and, second-guessing his next move, she returned to the front door and squared her slim shoulders. Loosening the chain she opened the door.

Jaul ground to a sudden halt with his hand still reaching out for the bell. Chrissie appeared in the doorway and he snatched in a ragged breath at the sight of the shorts and T-shirt that exposed every line of her long, slender legs and the sleek, pert curves of her breasts. Lashes swiftly veiling his gaze, he compressed his wide, sensual mouth. 'Chrissie…'

'What are you doing here?' Chrissie asked woodenly, inwardly amazed at how much the passage of time altered situations. Two years ago, had he finally shown up, she would have snatched him in and covered him with grateful, loving kisses. But that time was long gone. He had broken her heart, left her to sink or swim and had never once contacted her with an explanation or even an apology. That wounding silence had spoken the loudest truth of all: Jaul had never loved her, indeed could never have really cared for her in any genuine way. If he had he couldn't have walked away without once enquiring as to how she was.

'May I come in? I have to speak to you,' Jaul imparted in his rich velvety drawl.

'If you must.' Rigid-backed, Chrissie stepped aside. She was fighting not to look at him, not to personalise his appearance in any way. It was a mark of strength on her terms that she would see him again, deal with him and let him leave without any feelings whatsoever getting involved.

He was dressed much as she remembered in a soft leather jacket and jeans, casual and effortlessly elegant, his every physical movement a study of languorous grace. He stood six feet four inches in his sock soles, a fitting match for a girl of five feet nine, who liked high heels. Broad of shoulder, slim of hip, he had the long, powerful thighs of a horseman and the flat washboard stomach of a very fit and healthy male. Luxuriant blue-black hair brushed his shoulders, framing a lean-featured and wildly eye-catching face with a classic nose, high cheekbones and a shapely, sensual mouth. But it was his beautiful dark deep-set eyes that you noticed first and remembered longest, Chrissie reckoned, black as jet in some lights, bright as stars in a dark sky in others and pure tiger-gold enticement in the sun.

Something pulled taut at the apex of her thighs, leaving a melting sensation in its wake.

Chrissie only realised how much shock she was in when she saw the children's toys littering the lounge floor and realised in amazement that it had not once occurred to her that Jaul might be visiting to ask about the children. But how would he ever have found out about the twins when he had deserted her long before she'd even discovered that she was pregnant? And why would he show the slightest interest in the existence of illegitimate children by an ex-girlfriend? That was all she was now to him—an ex-girlfriend! He wouldn't *want* to know she had fallen pregnant. He wouldn't want to open up that can of worms, would he? Of course not. Her lush, full lips curled with scorn. Marwan wasn't the sort of country that would turn a comfortable blind eye to the immoral doings of its king. Of course, very possibly, his relationship with Chrissie might well fall into the forgivable 'youthful sowing of wild oats' category, she reasoned darkly.

Without a word, Chrissie bent down to scoop up the abandoned toys and toss them into the basket by the wall.

'You have children now?' Jaul prompted, watching her beautiful platinum-blonde hair slide like a veil of polished silk off her shoulder to screen her profile as she bent down. His riveted gaze rested on the gleaming curve of an upturned hip, a slender section of spine and the long, taut stretch of a svelte porcelain-pale thigh.

Slender thighs that he had parted, lain between, revelled between, night after night. He had never got enough of her. His muscles pulled taut to the point of rigidity, savage sexual heat zinging through him at speed and setting up a pounding pulse at his groin. His strong white teeth ground together, rage at his lack of control gaining on him.

Chrissie thought fast while she snatched up the last brick, grateful he couldn't see her face. It was a relief that he didn't know about the twins, a *huge* relief, she conceded, but it felt unreal for Jaul to ask whether or not she had children as though they were complete strangers.

'I've been babysitting…for a friend,' she lied as lightly as she could. 'Now, what can I help you with?'

Jaul picked up on the insolent note of that question immediately. That supposed politeness was pure honey-eyed Chrissie scorn and he knew it. A faint line of colour accentuated his exotic cheekbones while his dark eyes flashed as golden as the sun at midday. 'I have something to tell you that may come as a shock…'

Chrissie tilted her head to one side, eyes bright as a turquoise sea and luminous below soft brown lashes. 'I *lived* with you, Jaul. Nothing you do or say could shock me.'

Not after the way you abandoned me, but she swallowed that final assurance, too proud and too scared of losing face to risk throwing that in his teeth. But his apparent equanimity burned through her restraint like acid. It was offensive that he could approach her so casually after what he had done to her and utterly unforgivable that he should dare.

'The sooner you tell me, the sooner you can leave,' Chrissie quipped, dry-mouthed with the anger she was holding back.

Jaul breathed in deep and slow, fighting to master the stirring ache below his belt. It had simply been too long since he had had sex. He was a normal healthy male in need of release and there was nothing strange about the reality that proximity to Chrissie should awaken old familiar impulses. Somewhat soothed by that conviction, he settled grim dark eyes on her. 'I have only recently learned that our marriage was legal and that is why I am here.'

So great was Chrissie's incredulity at that news that she blinked and stumbled back against the bookcase behind her. 'But your father said it was illegal, that it had no standing in law, that—'

'My father was mistaken,' Jaul incised in a smooth tone of finality. 'My legal advisers insist that the ceremony *was* legal and, consequently, we are now in need of a divorce.'

Chrissie was deeply shaken by that announcement and her soft pink mouth opened a mere fraction of an inch. 'Oh, right,' she acknowledged while she played for time and tried to absorb the immensity of what he had just said. 'So, all this time we've been apart we've actually been legally married?'

'Yes,' Jaul conceded grudgingly.

'Well, fancy that,' Chrissie commented in apparent wonderment. 'Two years ago I was turned away from the door of the Marwani Embassy with the assurance that I was "delusional" even though our wedding ceremony took place there. Absolutely nobody was willing to see me, talk to me or even accept a letter for you…in fact I was threatened with the police if I didn't leave—'

'What on earth are you talking about? *When* were you at our embassy in London?' Jaul demanded curtly, standing straight and tall and betraying not a shade of discomfiture.

She stared at him, treacherously ensnared by his sheer physical magnetism. Her tummy flipped and a flock of butterflies broke loose inside her. Jaul had an electrifying combination of animal sex appeal, hauteur and command that stopped women dead in their tracks. So good-looking, so *very* good-looking he had grabbed her attention at first glance even though she had known he was a player and not to be trusted. Yet she had resisted him month after month until he had caught her at a vulnerable moment and then, sadly, she too had found those broad shoulders and that lying, seductive tongue irresistible.

'When, Chrissie?' he repeated doggedly.

'Oh, a little while after my *imaginary* husband disappeared into thin air,' Chrissie supplied. 'And then shortly after my final visit to the embassy, your father came to see me and explained and everything became clear.'

'I don't know what you hope to achieve by talking nonsense like this at a point when all either of us can want is a divorce.'

Chrissie elevated a very fine brow. 'I don't know, Jaul…do you think it could be anger motivating me after what you put me through?'

'Anger has no place here. We have lived apart for a long time. I want a divorce. This is a practical issue, nothing more,' Jaul delivered crushingly.

'You do know that I hate you?' Chrissie pressed shakily, a flicker of hysteria firing her that he could stand there evidently untouched as though nothing of any great import had ever happened between them. Yet once he had pursued her relentlessly and had sworn that he *loved* her and that only the security of marriage would satisfy him. There was nothing deader than an old love affair, a little voice cried plaintively inside her, and the proof of that old maxim stood in front of her.

Jaul was thinking of the woman who had left him lying unvisited in his hospital bed and he met her angry gaze with coldly contemptuous dark eyes. 'Why would I care?'

He didn't feel like Jaul any more; he had changed out of all recognition, Chrissie acknowledged numbly. He wanted a divorce; he *needed* a divorce. But she was still struggling to get her head around the astonishing fact that they had genuinely been married for over two years. 'Why did your father tell me that our marriage was illegal?'

His lean, strong face tautened. 'It was not a lie. He believed it to be illegal—'

'But that's not all he believed,' Chrissie whispered. 'He told me that you'd deliberately gone through that ceremony with me *knowing* it was illegal and that you could wriggle out of the commitment and walk away any time you wanted—'

'I refuse to believe that he would ever have said or even implied anything of that nature,' Jaul derided with an emphatic shake of his imperious dark head. 'He was an honourable man and a caring father—'

'Like hell he was!' Chrissie slammed back at him in sudden fury, goaded by that provocative statement into losing all self-control. 'I was thrown out of your apartment wearing only the clothes I was standing up in. I was treated like an illegal squatter and absolutely humiliated—'

'These grossly disrespectful lies gain you no ground with me. I will not listen to them,' Jaul spelt out, his beautiful, wilful mouth twisting. 'I know you for the woman you are. My father gave you five million pounds to get out of my life and you took it and I never heard from you again—'

'Well, admittedly I didn't get very far at the Marwani Embassy where women claiming to be your wife, illegal or otherwise, are treated like lunatics,' Chrissie parried flatly, declining to answer that accusation about the bank draft she had refused to use because it seemed Jaul wasn't prepared to listen or believe anything she said in her own defence.

Chrissie could never have accepted that hateful 'blood' money, intended to buy her discretion and silence and dissuade her from approaching the media to sell some sleazy story about her experiences with Jaul.

Jaul set his even white teeth together. 'I want you to leave the past where it belongs and concentrate on the important issue here...our *divorce*.'

Without warning, Chrissie's eyes sparkled like gold-dusted turquoises. 'You want a divorce to remarry, don't you?'

'Why I want it scarcely matters this long after the event,' Jaul fielded drily.

'You need my consent to get a divorce,' Chrissie assumed, walking past him back to the front door, thinking that this time around the ball was in her court and the power hers. Jaul expected her to be understanding and helpful and give him what he wanted. But why *should* she be understanding? She owed him nothing!

'Naturally...if it is to go through fast it has to be uncontested—'

'The answer is no,' Chrissie delivered, far from being in a cooperative frame of mind. She was bitter about the way he had treated her and stubbornly ready to make things difficult for him. 'If we're truly married and you now want a divorce, you'll have to *fight* me for it.'

Jaul stilled in the lounge doorway, dark eyes flashing bright as a flame. 'But that's ridiculous...why would you do something that stupid?'

'Because I can,' Chrissie replied, truthful to the last word. 'I won't willingly do anything which suits you and I know you want to keep all this on the down-low. After all, you never did own up publicly to the shame of marrying a foreigner, did you?'

'I believed the marriage was invalid!' Jaul shot back at her, lean brown hands coiling into fists. 'Why would I have talked about it?'

'Well, most guys would at least have talked about it to the woman who believed she was married to them,' Chrissie pointed out scornfully as she stretched out a hand to open the door. 'But you...what did you do? Oh, yes...you ran out on me and left your daddy to clear up the mess you left behind you!'

Sheer rage at that unjust condemnation engulfed Jaul so fast he was dizzy with it. He snapped long fingers round a slender wrist before she could open the door. Smouldering dark golden eyes raked her flushed and defiant face. 'You will *not* speak to me like that.'

Suppressing a spasm of dismay, Chrissie forced herself to laugh and her eyes sparkled with challenge. 'Message to Jaul—I can speak to you any way I like and there's not a darned thing you can do about it! You don't deserve anything better from me after the way you treated me...'

With a contemptuous flick of his long fingers, Jaul

relinquished his hold on her. Dark eyes still sparking like high-voltage wires, he scanned her with derision. 'Is this your way of trying to push the price up? You want me to *pay* you to set me free from this marriage?'

A genuine laugh fell from Chrissie's taut mouth. 'Oh, no, I've got plenty of money,' she told him blithely. 'I don't want a penny from you. I only want to make you sweat.'

Jaul no longer trusted his temper or his control. Nobody had spoken to him like that since he had last seen Chrissie and it was a salutary lesson. Their personalities had been on a collision course from day one. Both of them were strong-willed, obstinate and quick-tempered. They had had monumental fights and even more shattering reconciliations. In fact those reconciliations had been such sweet fantasies Jaul had never forgotten them and he got hot and hard even thinking about them, a recollection as unwelcome as it was dangerous.

His beautifully shaped mouth flattening the sultry curl tugging at the edges, fine ebony brows drawing together in a frown of censure, he breathed curtly, 'I can see there's no talking to you in the mood you're in—'

'I'm *not* in a mood!' Chrissie proclaimed furiously, catching an involuntary snatch of the spicy cologne he wore, her senses reeling at the sudden flood of familiarity that made her ache and hurt as if his betrayal were as recent as yesterday. It also reminded her of hot, sweaty nights and incredible passion, a thought which instantly infuriated her.

'I'll return later when you've had time to think over what I've told you,' he informed her with typical tenacity.

Chrissie bit back the admission that she would be staying at her sister's home for several days. That was her business, not his, and she had no intention of telling him anything likely to lead to his discovery that he was not only married but also a father. That would be setting the cat among the pigeons with a vengeance, she conceded worriedly, and it was not something she was prepared to risk without knowing where she stood.

The strained silence smouldered.

'A divorce is the only sensible option and I don't object to paying for the privilege,' Jaul grated between clenched teeth, out of all patience with her reluctance to discuss the issue. 'As my wife, estranged or otherwise, you're naturally entitled to my financial support—'

'I want nothing from you,' Chrissie repeated doggedly. 'Please leave.'

Long bronzed fingers bit into the edge of the door as Jaul fought a powerful impulse to say something, *anything*, that would stir her into a more natural reaction. What had happened to his bright and fearless Chrissie? He glanced at her in frustration. Her eyes were blank, her delicately pointed features empty of expression. Her entire attitude spelt out the message that he was the enemy and not to be trusted.

Without another word, Jaul walked out of the building, determined that he would not see her again. He had told her what he had to tell her. And now he would step back and let the lawyers handle the rest of it.

Chrissie got dressed in a feverish surge of activity. She flung clothes into a small case, carrying it and other pieces of baby paraphernalia out to the car. Her home had always been her sanctuary but now it felt violated by Jaul's visit and she no longer felt safe there. What if he had walked in and the twins had been present? Why did she imagine that he would have instantly recognised his own children when he had no reason to even suspect their existence? She was being hysterical and foolish, she told herself shamefacedly, but even so she could barely wait to get Tarif and Soraya strapped into their car seats and drive away from the apartment.

As she drove through the busy mid-morning traffic she had too much time to look back into the past. Memories she didn't want bombarded her. Indeed she could never think about her years at university without thinking of Jaul because he had always been there on the outskirts of her life, long unacknowledged but always noticed and never forgotten.

She had shared a tiny flat with another girl when in her second year at university. Nessa had been just a little man-mad, to the extent that Chrissie had tended to switch off when Nessa began talking about her latest lover. But even Nessa had gone into thrilled overdrive when she'd first met a prince. Chrissie had been less impressed, well aware that in some Eastern countries princes were ten a penny and not much more important. Jaul, however, had proved somewhat harder to overlook. He had flown Nessa to Paris in his private jet just for dinner and Nessa had been incoherent with excitement at the luxury of the experience.

Jaul had brought Nessa home the next day and had been in the flat when Chrissie had come home from the classes that her roommate had skipped. Chrissie still remembered her first glimpse of Jaul, his gypsy-dark skin and eyes brilliant as newly minted gold in sunlight, his lean, breathtakingly handsome face intent.

He had stared at Chrissie for the longest time and she hadn't been able to breathe or look away while Nessa gabbled incoherently about Paris and limousines. Jaul had taken his leave quickly.

'He was amazing in bed,' Nessa had confided as soon as he was gone, languorously rolling her eyes and quite uninhibited about admitting that she had slept with Jaul on the first date. 'Absolutely freakin' *amazing*!'

But for all that it had still been a one-night stand. Jaul had followed up by having flowers and a very pretty pair of diamond earrings delivered to Nessa, but he hadn't phoned again. Nessa had been disappointed but accepting, pointing out that, with all Jaul had to offer, he was sure to want to make the most of his freedom.

The next time Chrissie had seen Jaul she had been in the student union. She had noticed Jaul, naturally. She could scarcely have failed to notice his presence when he was surrounded by a quartet of suited sunglasses-wearing bodyguards and a crowd of giggling flirtatious blondes who, as she soon learnt, seemed to appear out of nowhere to engulf him wherever he went.

He had startled her by springing upright as she was passing his table and had insisted on acknowledging her when she would've passed on by without a word. Stiff with discomfiture, Chrissie had been cool, inordinately aware of the heat in his dark gaze and the jealous scrutiny of his female companions.

Back then Chrissie had been working two part-time jobs to survive at university because her family could not afford to help her out. One of Chrissie's jobs during term time had been stacking shelves in the library, the other waitressing at a local restaurant, but she had still found it a major challenge to meet her bills. Her father had still been a tenant farmer, whose ill-health had forced him into retirement while her older sister, Lizzie, had worked night and day to keep the farm going, while Chrissie continued her studies, but the knowledge that, without her, her family was having an even tougher struggle to survive had filled her with guilt.

But even as a child Chrissie had recognised that her late mother Francesca's chaotic life might have been less dysfunctional had she had a career to fall back on when her affairs with unsuitable men fell apart. A woman needed more than a basic education to survive and Chrissie had always been determined to build her life round a career rather than a man. Her mother's marriage to her father had been short-lived and the relationships that Francesca had got involved in afterwards had been destructive ones in which alcohol, infidelity, physical violence and other evils had prevailed. Shorn of her innocence at a very young age, Chrissie knew just how low a woman could be forced to sink to keep food on the table and it was a lesson she would never forget. No, Chrissie would never willingly put herself in a position where she had to depend on a man to keep her.

When Jaul had approached her in the library where she was stacking shelves one day a few weeks after their first meeting to ask for her help in finding a book, she had been polite and helpful as befitted a humble employee keen to keep her job.

'I'd like to take you out to dinner some evening,' he had murmured after she'd slotted the book into his lean brown hand.

He had the most stunning dark eyes, pure lustrous

jet enticement in his lean, darkly handsome face. In his
presence her mouth had run dry and her breathing had
fractured while she'd marvelled at the weird way she'd
kept on wanting to look at him, an urge so powerful it
had almost qualified as a *need*. Infuriated by the dizzy
way she was reacting, she'd thought instead of how he
had treated Nessa. Jaul had chased sexual conquest,
nothing more complex. Once the chase was over and
he had got what he wanted he'd lost interest and casual
sex with young women as uninhibited and adventurous as Nessa had suited him perfectly. He hadn't been
looking for a relationship with all the limits that would
have involved. He hadn't been offering friendship or
caring or fidelity.

'I'm sorry, no,' Chrissie had said woodenly.

'Why not?' Jaul had asked without hesitation.

'Between my studies and my two part-time jobs, I
have very little free time,' Chrissie had told him. 'And
when I do have it, I tend to go home and visit my family.'

'Lunch, then,' Jaul had suggested smoothly. 'Surely
you could lunch with me some day?'

'But I don't want to,' Chrissie had confessed abruptly,
backing off a step, feeling cornered and slightly intimidated by the sheer height and size of him in the narrow
space between the book stacks.

A fine ebony brow had quirked. 'I have offended
you in some way?'

'We just wouldn't suit,' Chrissie had countered between gritted teeth, her irritation rising at his refusal
to simply accept her negative response.

'In what way?'

'You're everything I don't like,' Chrissie had framed

in a sudden burst of frustration. 'You don't study, you party. You run around with a lot of different women. I'm not your type. I don't want to go to Paris for dinner! I don't want diamonds! I haven't the slightest intention of going to bed with you!'

'And if I didn't offer you Paris, diamonds or sex?'

'I'd probably end up trying to kill you because you're so blasted full of yourself!' Chrissie had shot at him in a rage. 'Why can't you just take no for an answer?'

Jaul had suddenly grinned, a shockingly charismatic grin that had made her tummy somersault. 'I wasn't brought up to take no for an answer.'

'With me, no *means* no!' Chrissie had told him angrily. 'Persistence only annoys me—'

'And I am very persistent as well as full of myself,' Jaul had acknowledged softly. 'It seems we are at an impasse—'

Chrissie had stabbed a finger to indicate the directional arrow pointing down to the nearest study area. 'You have your book—go study.'

And without another word she had walked away with her trolley, heading for the lift that would let her escape to the floor above.

CHAPTER THREE

CARRYING A TWIN in each arm, Chrissie was greeted by Sally at the front door of Cesare and Lizzie's home. Her nephew and niece, Max and Giana, clustered round the two women eager to see their cousins. Tarif whooped with excitement when he saw Max and opened his arms to the older boy.

'He *knows* me!' Max carolled in amazement.

'Once Tarif's walking, he'll plague the life out of you,' Chrissie quipped, passing over Tarif while Sally took charge of Soraya because Giana was too young to manage her.

An elegant and visibly pregnant blonde with green eyes and a ready smile came out of one of the rooms leading off the spacious hall. 'Chrissie...*lovely*. I wasn't expecting you until later,' Lizzie confided warmly.

The tears still burning behind Chrissie's eyes suddenly spilled over without warning. As she saw her big sister look at her in astonishment Chrissie swallowed back a sob and blundered into her sibling's outspread arms. *'Sorry.'*

'You don't need to apologise if something's upset you,' Lizzie insisted. 'What on earth has happened? You never cry—'

Fortunately Lizzie had not been exposed to Chrissie's grief two years earlier once it had finally dawned on her that Jaul was not returning to the UK. It had been a matter of pride to Chrissie that she should not distress her otherwise happy sister with the sad tale of how she had screwed up her own life. She had put a brave face on her abandonment and subsequent pregnancy, talking lightly and always unemotionally of a relationship that had broken down and a young man unwilling to acknowledge responsibility for the babies she'd carried.

'You don't need the creep...you don't need anyone but Cesare and me!' Lizzie had told her comfortingly and she had asked no further questions.

Now as Chrissie bit back the sobs clogging her throat she was faced with the reality that as she had never told her sister about Jaul, she had to do it now. Emotional turmoil had been building up inside her from the very moment Jaul had appeared at her front door. Her past had pierced the present and most painfully, for all the gloriously happy and agonisingly sad memories of Jaul she had packed away were now flooding through the gap in her defences and hurting her all over again.

'For goodness' sake,' Lizzie exclaimed, banding an arm round her taller sister to urge her into the drawing room with its comfortable blue sofas and sleek pale contemporary furniture.

Cesare was talking on his mobile by the window and he concluded the call, frowning with concern when he registered the tear-stained distress stamped on his sister-in-law's face.

'I was just about to tell you that my sisters are arriving this evening and expecting you to go out clubbing with them tomorrow night—'

Chrissie tried to force a smile because she got on like a house on fire with Cesare's younger sisters, Sofia and Maurizia, and the three women always went out together when they visited London. 'I might not be good company—'

Lizzie pressed her gently down onto a sofa. 'Tell me what's wrong—'

Chrissie groaned. 'I *can't*. I've been such an idiot otherwise I would've told you years ago. You won't believe how stupid I've been and now I don't know what to do—'

'Starting at the beginning usually helps,' Cesare incised.

'The twins' father has turned up,' Chrissie revealed tautly. 'And he says we need a divorce, which doesn't make sense after what his father—'

Cesare stopped dead to skim her an incredulous glance. 'You were *married* to the twins' father?'

'My goodness, I certainly didn't see that coming! *Married!*' Lizzie admitted in shock, sinking down on an ottoman near her sister. Chrissie felt guiltier than ever, looking back over the years to acknowledge that Lizzie had been a better mother to her than their own mother, even though Lizzie was only five years older than Chrissie.

'Right, the beginning,' Chrissie reminded herself in receipt of a wry appraisal from Cesare. 'Or you won't know what I'm talking about.'

And Chrissie tried with some difficulty to put into words how long she had known Jaul without ever getting to know him properly.

'But you never ever mentioned him,' Lizzie commented in a continuing tone of disbelief. 'You knew him all the time you were at uni and yet you never told me about him!'

Chrissie reddened fiercely, quite unable to describe how much of a silent role Jaul had played in her life long before she'd ever actually got involved with him. She had seen him on campus most days, occasionally speaking to him, occasionally avoiding him if he had been more than usually keen to press his interest in her. What she had never ever contrived to be with Jaul was indifferent. When he wasn't there, she had found herself looking for him. If a couple of days had gone by without a glimpse of him, she would be like someone starved of food and craving it and when he had reappeared she would study him with helpless intensity as if looking alone could revive her energies.

In many ways Jaul had been her most secret and private fantasy. She could never ever have explained their relationship to her sister without feeling mortified and she had been even more grateful that she had kept him quiet when, instead of getting to bring Jaul home to show him off along with her wedding ring, she had ended up coming home dumped and pregnant. Lizzie had been very hurt on Chrissie's behalf when their father had said he didn't want his unmarried pregnant daughter to visit, but Chrissie had felt much guiltier about upsetting and disappointing the sister she had always idolised, the big sister who had made so many sacrifices on her behalf. Having left school at sixteen to work on their father's farm, Lizzie had never got a further education or the chance to be young and carefree for even a few years.

'There was no need to mention Jaul. It was only during our last year at uni that we actually got involved,' Chrissie pointed out ruefully.

'And yet you *still* didn't mention him,' Cesare reminded her drily.

'I honestly assumed we wouldn't last. I thought we would be over and done again in five minutes. It was all so unexpected. I didn't think Jaul *did* serious and then everything somehow changed and I changed too... that's the only way I can describe it,' she mumbled uncomfortably.

'You fell in love with him,' Lizzie interpreted.

'Truly, madly and deeply and all that,' Chrissie joked heavily. 'We got married at the Marwani Embassy here and we had a civil ceremony as well.'

'But why such secrecy?' Cesare enquired.

'Jaul didn't want anyone knowing we had got married until he had had the chance to tell his father about us...which I don't think he was in any hurry to do.' Chrissie hesitated and then mentioned the argument that had taken place when a few weeks after the wedding Jaul had announced his intention of returning to Marwan alone without any reference to when he planned to return. 'I felt rejected.'

'Of course you did,' Lizzie said warmly, squeezing Chrissie's hand gently.

Chrissie told them about her fruitless visits to the Marwani Embassy and then the visit from Jaul's father, King Lut, that had followed. When she then repeated what the older man had told her, Cesare became undeniably angry.

'That was when you should've come to us for support and advice!'

'I still thought Jaul would come back to me. I didn't instantly accept everything that his father told me and I hadn't given up hope.'

'And then you discovered that you were pregnant,' Lizzie guessed.

'A couple of months had passed by then and I couldn't excuse Jaul's silence any longer. I realised that his father must have been telling me the truth.'

'But evidently he wasn't,' Cesare cut in, already thinking ahead. 'Does Jaul know about the twins?'

'No. I didn't tell him. And I told him I wouldn't give him a divorce just to annoy him,' Chrissie confided uncomfortably. 'That was pretty childish of me, wasn't it?'

'I'll put my lawyers on this,' Cesare informed her, compressing his well-shaped mouth. 'Jaul needs to be told about the twins asap. A man has the right to know his own children—'

'Even if he deserts his wife and never gets back in touch?' Lizzie protested emotively.

'*Sì*, even then,' Cesare murmured ruefully.

Chrissie told Cesare and Lizzie about her repeated visits to the Marwani Embassy and her continued and equally fruitless attempts to contact Jaul by phone. 'So, you see, I did try very hard to track him down.'

'But you still need to take a long-term view of this situation, Chrissie. Set aside the hostility. Concentrate on the children and the future and you won't go far wrong.'

'And you do owe Jaul *one* favour,' Lizzie said ruefully, startling Chrissie, who was dabbing her face dry and grateful the tear overflow had run its course. 'You have to go and see him and tell him about the twins before you bring in the lawyers—'

'For goodness' sake, I don't even know where he's staying!' Chrissie parried, aghast at that suggestion. 'In fact he might only have been passing through London.'

'Why does Chrissie owe Jaul another meeting?' Cesare enquired of his wife, equally in the dark on that score.

'He at least had the decency to tell her that they were still married himself, rather than from his lawyers,' Lizzie pointed out.' I don't think you owe him anything more, Chrissie, but I do think he deserves the chance to learn that he's a father from you and nobody else and in private.'

'I don't want to see him…don't even know if he's still here in London… I've got nothing to wear either!' Chrissie argued in an unashamed surge of protest, but behind it she knew she was caught because, like her older sister, she also had a sense of fair play.

Jaul had not been comfortable visiting her but, even so, he had done it because he knew it was the right thing to do. How could she be seen to do less?

Chrissie climbed out of the taxi that Lizzie had insisted she needed, pointing out that searching for a parking space while trying to identify the correct house was the last thing her sister needed in the mood she was in.

Not that finding the house where Jaul was staying had proved a problem, Chrissie acknowledged ruefully, shooting the vast monolith of a building in the most exclusive part of London a wry glance. Cesare's staff had come up with all the required information. With the kind of high-powered connections her brother-in-law enjoyed, tracking down Jaul had not proved that big a challenge while it had also provided her with extraneous information she had not required. For instance, the huge town house had formerly been an entire crescent of smaller dwellings and it had been purchased in the nineteen thirties and turned into a single dwelling by Jaul's grandfather to house the Marwani royal family and their numerous staff whenever they came to visit London. Apparently the family had made ridiculously few visits in the many years that had passed since then.

It had been an education for Chrissie to discover that this was one more fact she hadn't known about the man she had loved and married. Although they had visited London together, he had never once mentioned that his family owned a house there. In much the same way he had never mentioned that he was an only child destined to become a king. His Marwani background had always been a closed book to her from which he had offered her a glimpse of very few pages. In short she knew he had grown up without a mother, had attended a military school and had trained as a soldier in Saudi Arabia. When he'd signed up to study politics at Oxford University it had been his very first visit to the UK.

It shook Chrissie now to accept that Jaul was the sole ruler of his immensely rich country in the Arabian Gulf. She finally understood the arrogance and the authority that had often set her teeth on edge. Jaul had never been in any doubt of who he was and where he was going to end up. No doubt his marriage to Chrissie had just been a brief fun stop on his upwardly mobile royal life curve and had never ever been intended to last.

'Proceed with great caution,' Cesare had warned Chrissie once he had established the exact identity of the man whom she had married in such secrecy two years earlier.

That recollection had made Chrissie's skin turn clammy beneath the sleek turquoise shift dress she had borrowed from her sister's pre-pregnancy wardrobe. Her shrewd brother-in-law had pointed out that Jaul would have diplomatic immunity, that he was firm friends with several influential members of the British government and that he would have much greater power than most foreign non-resident husbands and fathers might have if it came to a custody battle. *Custody battle*—the very phrase struck terror into Chrissie's bones. Cesare assumed that Tarif—all adorable fourteen plump and energetic months of him—would now be heir to the throne of Marwan, which would make him a hugely important child on his father's terms. As Chrissie's fear grew in direct proportion to her anxious thoughts, her spine stiffened and her skin grew even chillier. On some craven, very basic level she didn't want to even try to be civilised; she simply wanted to snatch her kids from Lizzie's luxurious nursery and flee somewhere where Jaul couldn't ever find them again.

Instead, however, Chrissie reminded herself that she was supposed to be an adult and able to handle life's more difficult challenges. She mounted the front steps of the monstrous building with its imposing columns, portico and innumerable windows and pressed the doorbell.

Jaul was lunching in a dining room decorated in high 'desert' style circa nineteen thirty by his English grandmother and marvelling at her sheer lack of good taste. He didn't want to pretend he was in the desert and sit cross-legged like a sheep herder in front of a fake fire; he wanted a table and a chair. Mercifully his personal chef and other staff had travelled with him and the service and the food were exemplary. It didn't quite make up though for having to sleep in a bedroom decorated like a tent on a ginormous bed made of rough bamboo poles literally lashed together with ropes. Of course, he conceded wryly, the distractions of the extraordinary décor of the royal home in London served to keep his thoughts away from how Chrissie had looked in shorts with those impossibly long and perfect legs on full display.

Ghaffar, Jaul's PA, appeared in the doorway and bowed. 'A visitor has arrived to see you without an appointment—'

Jaul suppressed a groan and waved a dismissive hand. He was in London on a private visit and had no desire to make it anything else. 'Please make my apologies. I will see no one.'

'The woman's name is Whitaker—'

Jaul sprang upright with amazing alacrity. 'She is the single exception to the rule,' he incised.

Chrissie tapped her heels on the marble floor of the giant echoing hall full of what looked like a display of actual mummy cases from an Egyptian tomb. It was creepy and the lack of light made it even creepier. Staring at a two-headed god statue did nothing for her nervous tension, only ratcheting it up a degree or two and making the events of the past twenty-four hours all the more challenging to bear, never mind accept.

Without warning, Jaul appeared in a doorway and he seemed almost as strange to her bemused eyes, his tall, lean physique sheathed in an exquisitely cut light grey business suit. The only other time she had seen him in a suit had been on their wedding day and she stared, reckoning that that formality didn't detract an ounce from his dark, exotic appeal.

'Chrissie,' he said with a level of gravity that unnerved her, for it was a quality that she had only glimpsed in him at the worst moments of their relationship when he had proved how very serious he could be when she crossed him. 'I was not expecting you to come here.'

'Well, that makes two of us!' she admitted with an uneasy laugh that sounded raw in the echoing silence. 'But I had to see you in private and this was the most straightforward way of doing it.'

'You are welcome,' he breathed and he snapped his fingers and a servant came out of nowhere and thrust open another door while bowing and scraping. 'We will have tea and be...*polite*?'

Colour ran up to the roots of her pale, shining hair. To her horror, her throat developed a lump, emotion swishing through her again in an unwelcome and treacherous wave. Lustrous dark golden eyes rested on her and her heart started to go thumpety-thumpety-thump as if she had suffered a really bad fright. 'Yes...polite,' she agreed shakily, longing for the hostile, aggressive edge that had powered her earlier that morning when he had visited. Anger and antagonism had provided a blessed bumper between her and the maelstrom of emotions his appearance had awakened inside her.

'I would've phoned in advance of my arrival had I known your number,' Jaul breathed as if he knew exactly what she was thinking.

Mercifully he couldn't know, she thought wretchedly, searching his startlingly handsome features with an appreciation that felt terrifyingly familiar. So, he's a painting, a perfect painting, she acknowledged with self-loathing, but she didn't have to keep on noticing, did she?

'Perhaps we should exchange phone numbers now,' she suggested and he dug out his phone and took a note of hers while passing her a sleek business card. 'This feels so weird, Jaul...*all* of it.'

'Of course it does. Naturally we have both changed a great deal,' he fielded with a level of smooth assurance that made her want to slap him.

It was a welcome interruption when a knock sounded on the door and someone entered with a tray, followed by another person, who surged forward with a deep bow in Jaul's direction to yank out a small table and spread it with a cloth. A china stand loaded with miniature French fancies and tiny scones was put on display and the English tea was poured.

The sight shot Chrissie back in time to what she supposed had effectively been her first date with Jaul although she had not seen it as such at the time. He had taken her to an exclusive hotel for afternoon tea, a quintessentially English tradition he had naively assumed everyone followed. Feeling like a lady of the manor, she had very much enjoyed the experience.

'You *remembered*,' she told him without thinking about what she was saying.

But Jaul *hadn't* remembered. Afternoon tea had been his grandmother's routine and it was still served all these years on because the house had never benefitted from another mistress. The faintest colour scored his high cheekbones as he was shot back in time to recall that long-ago afternoon after he had finally persuaded Chrissie to see him as a normal educated male rather than a womanising party animal. She had been wearing a blue dress then as well. The dress had had tiny little flowers all over it and she had sat there, tense and shy with her beautiful hair falling to her waist, and he had been so *scared* of saying or doing the wrong thing and frightening her off again. Scared of what a woman might think for the one and only time in his life! He wanted to laugh at that recollection of his younger, less cynical self but now he was looking at Chrissie again, noting the silvery hair that was shoulder length now, the fined-down line of her perfect features, and other reactions were overwhelming him.

Images that Jaul had resisted for two years were suddenly leaping out of the box he had locked them in. Colliding with the bright turquoise eyes that he knew could turn feverish with longing for him, he went rigid recalling that incredibly erotic eagerness, nostrils flaring, dark eyes shimmering gold beneath his lush black lashes.

The atmosphere had become suffocating, Chrissie registered in dismay, shifting off one restive foot to the other. She met his intense gaze and froze, her temperature running cold and then hot until melted honey pooled low in her pelvis, an almost forgotten sensation from the past. But it was too late by then for her to draw back because Jaul was unexpectedly in front of her, close enough to touch and literally just grabbing her with two strong arms to weld her into sudden highly provocative contact with his lean, powerfully hard body. Air exploded into her lungs as she snatched in a startled breath.

'Chrissie...' Jaul husked, lean hands sliding down

her slender spine to tilt her hips into an even more intimate meeting.

And as she recognised and felt his erection below their clothes, the long, thick evidence of his need hard against her belly, an ache of near pain stirred between her own legs. Her head swam, clear thought forgotten, knees suddenly as weak as bendy twigs. He took her mouth with all the passion she had never forgotten, fiery and urgent and wildly demanding. She took fire from the kiss, which was like a flame hitting bone-dry hay, and the piercing arrow of bittersweet hunger travelled to the very core of her being. Her hands flew up to his broad shoulders and roved from the hard muscle there to the thick blue-black hair she had loved to bury her fingers in.

His tongue plunged between her parted lips and a shudder racked her in his arms, sudden wickedly strong need loosed inside her to run amok like bush fire. She wanted to rip his shirt off and run her hands down over his washboard abs. She wanted to drag him down to the rug below their feet and satisfy the hollow ache screaming at her feminine heart. It was powerful, it was seductive and she could no more have resisted that savagely strong hunger than she could have resisted his explosive passion. She wanted, she *wanted*…

CHAPTER FOUR

SOMEONE KNOCKED ON the door and Jaul froze, literally *froze* as if someone had hit an alarm bell. He pushed her back from him, dark eyes glittering tiger gold and a ferocious frown on his lean, darkly handsome face.

'I'm sorry,' he said flatly. 'That was a mistake.'

Chrissie was unable to pull herself together quite so quickly and as he released her she pivoted away from him towards the windows. As she raised trembling hands to press to her suddenly clammy cheeks, she was sick with self-loathing and shock and only dimly aware that someone was speaking to Jaul in his own language at the door. Feeling shaky, she sat down on a horrendous carved wooden sofa without even a cushion to soften its hard, unyielding seat.

A *mistake*? How demeaning to be told that! Only a kiss, only a stupid kiss, she was reasoning with herself in a daze of shame and denial. But how could she have let that happen, particularly when she had visited him to discuss the infinitely more important reality of the twins' very existence? It was as though something had momentarily stolen her wits, overpowering all memory and rationality in the same moment. Well, what was done was done and *he* had been equally guilty of inappropriate behaviour, she reminded herself in consolation. Of course, she had once been accustomed to Jaul's distinctly carnal can't-keep-my-hands-off-you nature, had indeed at one stage gloried in her apparent power to attract him, innocently assuming that it meant more than it did. It seemed in that line though he hadn't changed a bit.

Jaul was receiving a lengthy message from his PA. He was taken aback to be invited to a legal meeting the following morning between the legal firm chosen by Bandar and the lawyers who would apparently be arriving to represent Chrissie's interests. After her attitude to the divorce issue the night before he was disconcerted but less surprised by her unexpected visit. Had she already thought better of her behaviour? Evidently she could muster a crack divorce team virtually overnight. Perhaps she had also mulled over the financial advantages of giving him the divorce he wanted, he reasoned sardonically. When had money come to mean so much to her?

It was a question he had asked himself repeatedly two years earlier when she had accepted his father's pay-off to turn her back on their relationship and walk away. How had he missed out on that devious, greedy streak in her make-up? At the time he would have described her as the least mercenary woman he had ever met. Had she cunningly concealed her avaricious side from him in an effort to impress him? When they had been together she had gone to great lengths to prove that his wealth meant little to her. And if he was honest, he *had* been impressed because by that stage he had become bored with women who valued him for what he was worth rather than for the man he was.

Yet the woman he had valued beyond all others had proved to be the greediest of all. That was a lowering truth he hated to recall for it exposed his poor judgement when he was at the mercy of his libido. A reminder he evidently needed, he conceded darkly, acknowledging without much surprise that one look at Chrissie's beautiful face and slender but shapely proportions could still arouse him.

Chrissie was finally wondering how on earth she could broach the subject of Jaul being a father and increasingly it was sinking in for her that it would come as an enormous shock to him. Her fingers dug into the clutch bag Lizzie had pressed on her and in a sudden movement she bent her pale head and snapped it open to withdraw the birth certificates. Those documents were self-explanatory and there was really no need at all for her to start stumbling into an awkward announcement.

Chrissie extended the certificates. 'I'm sure you're wondering why I came here.' *Not to kiss you and dream about ripping off your clothes again,* she completed inwardly while her face burned with mortification. 'I had to see you because I thought you should see *these* first...'

Another frown drawing together his fine ebony brows, Jaul grasped the documents with an unhidden air of incomprehension. She hadn't mentioned the kiss and he was grateful for that, well aware of Chrissie's ability to throw a three-act drama over what he viewed as trivia. Time had shot them both back briefly into the past and that was all. Nothing more need be said, he was thinking while he grasped the fact that for some peculiar reason his estranged wife had given him a pair of birth certificates.

'What are these?' Jaul scanned the name of the mother and went cold. 'You have children?'

'And so do you,' Chrissie advised thinly. 'You got me pregnant, Jaul.'

Jaul stilled and stopped breathing. *Pregnant?* The word screamed at him. It was not possible in his mind to credit it at that first moment, but now his quick and clever brain was checking dates, making calculations, recognising that whether he liked it or not it was a possibility. A possibility he didn't want to think about though. He had children, a boy and a girl. The concept was so shattering that he literally could not think for several tense seconds. The woman he was planning to divorce was the *mother* of his children. Inwardly he reeled from that revelation, instantly grasping how that devastating truth would change everything. *Everything!*

But why was he only learning about something as incredibly important as the news that he was a father over a year *after* the event of their birth? Jaul was not accustomed to receiving the kind of shock that rocked his world on its axis. Momentarily he closed his eyes before opening them to stare at Chrissie…beautiful, deceptive Chrissie, who had hit him with an own goal of mammoth proportions.

'If this is true…and I assume that it is,' Jaul framed with the greatest difficulty he had ever had in controlling both his temper and his tone, 'why am I only being told about the existence of my son and daughter *now*?'

Of all the reactions he might have had and she had envisaged while the taxi ferried her across London, that particular one had not featured. It was a Eureka moment for Chrissie and she didn't need to leap out of a bath to be galvanised into instantaneous rage and jump to her feet. 'Is that all you've got to say to me?' she shouted at him full force.

Innumerable generations of royal ice stiffened Jaul's spine, for no male had been more minutely trained from childhood than he had been to deal with a sudden crisis without any show of unseemly emotion or ill-judged vocal exclamations. 'What were you expecting me to say?' he enquired.

The door burst open and all four of his bodyguards rushed in to stare at Chrissie in disbelief. As collected as ever, indeed as if such interruptions were part of his normal life, Jaul sent them into retreat with the instruction that on no account was he to be disturbed again. He knew what had happened: his highly anxious protection squad had heard her shout when *nobody* shouted at him and had feared that some sort of a dangerous incident was developing. But they were nervous and on edge, having never been abroad before and London was a very scary place as far as they were concerned.

Turquoise eyes glittering with rage, Chrissie knotted her fingers into fists. 'Well, maybe I expected something a little more human and you asked me a very, *very* stupid question!'

Jaul gritted his strong white teeth. 'Stupid how?'

'You asked me why you're only finding out about Tarif and Soraya now and I want to ask you…is that a joke?'

'No. It was not a joke,' Jaul responded with perfect diction, studying her with assessing dark eyes. 'Why would I joke about it? Try to calm down and think about what you're saying. This is a very serious matter.'

And that was the moment when Chrissie lost even the slight hold she still retained on her temper. The father of her children was poised there like a granite pillar and acting as coolly and politely as though they were discussing the weather. It was too much, too great an insult after that offensive question to be borne in silence. *How dared he ask her to calm down?* How dared he talk down to her when he had just about wrecked her life and abandoned her to sink or swim?

'You complete bastard,' she breathed in a raw undertone, barely able to get the harsh syllables past her parted lips. '*Why* weren't you told? You *deserted* me—'

'I did not—'

'You went back to Marwan and you never returned to me—that's desertion. You didn't answer your phone. You didn't call, email, write, even text…I never heard another word from you!' Chrissie slashed back at him shakily, bitter wounding memories surfacing inside her head to power her on. 'You left me no way of contacting you. Of course I appreciate now that that was deliberate because you *knew* before you left that you weren't coming back—'

'That is untrue—'

'Shut up!' Chrissie practically screamed at him, her sense of injustice and furious hurt too great to be silenced now that she finally had Jaul in front of her. 'Don't lie to me! At least be honest…what could you possibly have to lose now?'

His lean, devastatingly handsome features clenched hard. 'I have never lied to you—'

'Well, the "love you for ever" bit was certainly a lie! Telling me that the Oxford apartment was *our home* when your father could throw me out of it at a moment's notice was a lie! And according to him even our *marriage* was a lie!' she reminded him, half an octave higher, and it did not help her mood when Jaul visibly winced. In punishment, she snatched up a sugar bowl and flung it at him, sugar cubes flying like tiny missiles as the china bowl shattered on the edge of a small table.

Jaul was right in the middle of the three-act drama he had hoped to avoid. Urging calm wasn't working, listening quietly wasn't working either. But then all that had ever worked with Chrissie when she was angry was dragging her off to bed until they were both thoroughly satisfied. That was a totally inappropriate thought, he admitted, struggling to concentrate on what mattered most: the children. But how could children he had never heard of until this day or even seen seem real to him?

'Thanks to your father's little "mistake", Jaul, my children are listed as illegitimate and without a father!' Chrissie ranted, almost running out of breath but quickly powering up for the next. 'Now my family may not be from a culturally conservative place as sensitive as Marwan but my father didn't speak to me for over six months once he realised that I was pregnant and unmarried because he was ashamed and embarrassed—'

If possible Jaul froze to an even greater extent.

Having been convinced by King Lut that she was *not* a married woman, Chrissie had not had the power to put Jaul's name on the birth certificates as to do so he would have had to accompany her to the register of births to register their birth or have made a statutory declaration that he was the twins' father. Chrissie had also been afraid to mention a marriage that she had already been told was illegal, fearful that in some way she might have accidentally broken the law by going through with such a ceremony. She had also been very much afraid of the risk of attracting embarrassing publicity should the royal status of her children's father ever become public knowledge. Anonymity and silence all round had seemed the safest option after her fruitless visits to the Marwani Embassy.

'In fact if it hadn't been for my sister and her husband, I would've been in even more serious trouble than I already was. So don't you *dare* ask me why you weren't told that you were a father when you were such a very lousy husband or non-husband or whatever you were!' Chrissie slung tempestuously.

'Is that it?' he enquired, dark eyes glittering bright as a starry night. 'Are you finished hurling abuse?'

'That was not abuse…that was what happened!' Chrissie raved back at him, undaunted. 'Do you know what your problem is?'

Jaul knew he was about to find out.

'People don't stand up to you, don't expect you to account for the wrong you do because you're this super rich, powerful guy who's spoilt. I hate you. I absolutely *hate* you!' Chrissie shouted at him, punctuating the assurance with the milk jug that had accompanied the sugar bowl. 'You're a horrible, seducing, selfish, womanising rat!'

'I think you should go home and lie down for a while. I'll phone you later when you've calmed down a little,' Jaul murmured without any expression at all and it just made her want to scream until she was carried off and locked away as the madwoman the Marwani Embassy staff had once treated her as.

Chrissie was rigid with fury: Jaul had no idea what hell she had gone through, probably even less interest, and she very much doubted that he had absorbed what she had told him.

Pregnant, Jaul was still thinking in a daze, trying and failing to imagine Chrissie's slender figure swollen with his children, Chrissie going through the pregnancy alone while rejected in disgrace by *her* father as a single parent. For the very first time he was glad she had had the money his father had given her, even relieved by the idea because she would have needed financial support. Children, he thought again, unable to imagine them, a baby boy and a baby girl, the first twins in the royal family since his grandfather and great-uncle's birth. Dimly, he realised that he was in such deep shock that he was in an abnormal state of disorientation and detachment, completely divorced from his usual cool, rational mind.

'Just you try lying down for a while when you have two babies of only fourteen months old to look after!' Chrissie hurled as a last-ditch put-down, stalking out of the door. She ignored the fact that his bunch of bodyguards were pacing the hall like worried parents having heard the noise of shouting and breaking crockery. They rushed past her to check that their precious charge, the King, was unharmed. King indeed, she thought incredulously, for that Jaul had become a king had just never seemed real to Chrissie.

A servant rushed to open the front door to her, visibly eager to see her off the premises. If they mentioned her name at the Marwani Embassy they would all be able to get together and talk about what a raving nut job she was, the crazy Englishwoman who wept and shouted and begged. Well, that wasn't her any more because she had soon got over loving Jaul. When a man ditched you as cruelly as Jaul had ditched her, there was no coming back from such an experience. Nothing had ever hurt so much... She flung a disgusted glance back at all the shining windows of that weird mansion and if she had had a brick in her hand she would have thrown that as well.

Jaul was frozen in the doorway, only marginally conscious of his large staff now grouped in the hall to study him in consternation, desperate to know what had caused such a fracas in his deeply traditional household.

And what Jaul did next would very much have stunned Chrissie.

'Miss Whitaker is my wife...my Queen,' he announced with quiet dignity in his own language, ignoring entirely the utter shock spreading across every face turned towards him.

Chrissie went back to her sister's home and cried again, tears dripping down her face as Tarif looked up at her with his father's eyes and smiled.

Lizzie hovered, understandably unsure of what to say. 'It can't have gone that badly,' she insisted. 'Did he insist there would have to be DNA tests and stuff like that to prove the twins are his?'

'No, nothing like that. I shouted at him and threw things at him while he stood there like a stone statue,' Chrissie recounted bitterly. 'There was no satisfaction to be had out of it at all. I wanted to kill him.'

Lizzie had paled. 'I'm sure relations between you will settle down eventually. Right now, Jaul's probably in shock—'

'What's he got to be in shock about?' her sibling asked thinly.

'Discovering that he's a father—'

'I hate him. I'm going to go out tonight and have

fun with Sofia and Maurizia,' Chrissie swore, springing upright and dashing the tears from her eyes. 'Jaul
stole all that away from me!'

Lizzie knew that was true but she deemed it wiser
to say nothing. Chrissie had had a very hard time while
she was carrying the twins because it had not been an
easy pregnancy and all the pastimes of youth had been
lost to her. Her little sister had had to grow up too soon
and face heartbreak and betrayal at a time when all
women were very vulnerable but that she had done so
without a single whine of self-pity and had gone on to
establish a career in teaching had made Lizzie feel incredibly proud.

It would have been a challenge to know which of the
parties was the most surprised when Jaul showed up at
Lizzie and Cesare's home that evening.

Lizzie hovered and hurriedly called her husband,
feeling that Cesare would be politer and more diplomatic than she could be when forced to deal with the
detestable man who had married her sister and let her
down so badly.

'I would like to see Chrissie…' Jaul announced without a shade of discomfiture.

'Unfortunately that's not possible,' Cesare declared
smooth as butter. 'She's out—'

'Out?' Jaul repeated in apparent surprise.

'Clubbing,' Lizzie supplied with pleasure.

'Then I would like to see the twins,' Jaul advanced
grimly and Lizzie enjoyed a first-hand experience of
the stone-statue image Chrissie had employed.

Cesare sighed. 'I'm afraid that's not possible either. I

couldn't let you see the children without their mother's permission—'

Jaul's gaze flamed bright gold. 'They are *my* children—'

'But it doesn't say so on their birth certificates, does it?' Lizzie cut in with unashamed satisfaction. 'You'll have to come back tomorrow when Chrissie is here—'

'Where has she gone...*clubbing*?' Jaul asked with distaste.

And to Lizzie's annoyance, Cesare gave Jaul information that she would have withheld.

'Why on earth did you tell him?' she demanded when Jaul had driven off again in his glossy limousine adorned with official Marwani flags.

Cesare shot her a sudden unreadable look that disconcerted her. 'He's Chrissie's husband.'

'But she *hates* him!'

'It's not our place to interfere. Making an enemy of him isn't likely to help anyone and least of all their children, *cara mia*,' he reasoned.

Escorted into the plush VIP area of the exclusive club, Jaul was restless. His bodyguards had perked up though, he noted with a sudden amusement that pierced his exasperated mood. His protection team was overjoyed to be in what his father would have described as a 'Western den of iniquity'. He stood on the balcony overlooking the dance floor packed with scantily clad girls below but his thoughts were far removed from the sight.

Chrissie's family disliked and distrusted him and in the wake of the chaos his father had created that was hardly surprising, Jaul conceded grudgingly. Even so, such a poor reception struck at his pride and his sense of honour for in twenty-eight years of life he had never once shirked his responsibilities. With the exception of Chrissie, he acknowledged bitterly, running through all the reasons why that had happened. He cursed his own pride and vanity for not finding some way to make enquiries of his own and check out what his father had told him.

Yet such misgivings about his only parent would never have occurred to Jaul before. Jaul had been very close to his father and positively coddled. A man who had virtually panicked whenever his only child succumbed to common childhood illnesses was not a man to inspire distrust. Jaul tucked the memories away hastily, working through the bitter bite of his lingering grief for the older man while feeling disloyal about the vague doubts that Chrissie's condemnations had stirred up.

Instead Jaul found himself wondering how often Chrissie came to such clubs. He told himself that in the circumstances that was none of his business. Unhappily, traits stronger than reason and a bred-in-the-bone possessiveness for what was *his* quarrelled with that rational conviction. He was hoping that she had more clothes on than women normally wore in such places. He was also already questioning the wisdom of having followed her to such a venue. He had acted on an angry impulse, an urge that rarely led to a satisfactory conclusion. And in the same second that he was about to leave the club he saw her, a bright figure in a short fuchsia-pink dress accompanied by two other young women. She was laughing, smiling, clearly not in turmoil, he noted, gritting his teeth at the sight. He wondered why he was agonising when she, so patently, was not.

Blessing her foresight in their exchange of numbers,

he texted her, watched from above as she literally froze, full pouty pink mouth down-curving, shoulders tensing. Annoyance licked through Jaul's long, lean frame at the clear message that his presence was as welcome in the club to her as a marauding gorilla's. He summoned the waiter to order champagne and snacks.

Rage crackled through Chrissie when she read the text.

Please join me in the VIP section

Her one night out on the town in months and Jaul had to ruin it by reminding her that she was not as free as the other young women around her. Suddenly she wished she had a man in tow, rather than being with Cesare's sisters, who were simply excited to death to be invited to the VIP section. But no, whether she liked it or not she was Jaul's wife and the mother of his children and telling him to get lost wouldn't work because Jaul was relentless about getting his own way.

Once she had believed that Jaul was incredibly solid and trustworthy and honourable. She had virtually worshipped the ground he walked on and remembering that now made her feel nauseous. But then, to be fair, the night their relationship had at last changed into something more at university, Jaul had played a blinder, she recalled numbly.

She had finally started dating someone while still suppressing her attraction to Jaul with all her might. Adrian had been blond, blue-eyed and sporty and as different from Jaul as day was from night. She had gone out with Adrian several times, enjoying casual dates in cinemas and cafés and telling him no when he got too pushy about sex. Back then she'd had a complex about sex and hadn't known or much cared whether she would ever get over it because it had stemmed from something sordid that had frightened her when she was still a child. And she had never told anyone, not even Lizzie, about that sleazy secret.

Adrian and his mates had taken her to a party in a big house and at some stage of the evening her memory had shut down. She suspected Adrian had put something in her soft drink and it had been Jaul who had found her slumped by Adrian's side and clearly out of it. He had stepped in to rescue her because he had known that, like him, she didn't touch alcohol. Jaul had punched Adrian when he'd tried to object and had carried her out of the party. She had no recollection of the rest of the night, only of waking up the next morning to find herself safe in Jaul's apartment. For the first time she had seen another side to Jaul. He hadn't taken advantage of her. He had stepped in to look after her when she'd needed help, had protected her from what could have been a very nasty scenario, making her suddenly painfully aware that he was miles more mature and decent than many of the young men she met. All her prejudices against him had crumbled that same day.

'I would never hurt you,' he had murmured.

But that had proved the biggest lie of all. She was so angry with him, *still* so angry with him, she acknowledged ruefully, but what was the point of all that aggression so long after the event? Their marriage was dead and gone—that was the end result. Let it all go, put it away, she urged herself wryly, let him have his divorce and move on to a better, happier future. Their lawyers would be meeting tomorrow: the divorce would soon be rushed through for Jaul's benefit.

Chrissie sank into the designated comfortable seat right in front of Jaul and wondered why his bodyguards were bowing in her direction as if she were a real somebody. She looked amongst them for two familiar faces, but the men who had once protected Jaul in his university days were not there. Turning back to Jaul, she noticed that he was casually dressed, had actually got in wearing jeans and an open-necked white shirt, proving the point that entry to such exclusive clubs depended more on *who* you were than what you wore. The white of his shirt against his golden skin tone was eye-catching and a deeply unsettling tingle quivered through her slender body when she connected with his brilliant dark golden eyes surrounded by lashes longer and more luxuriant than her own. He *was* gorgeous, no point denying that, she allowed, her keen gaze tracking the lean, strong lines of his masculine features while she tried not to wonder who he was planning to marry *next*...

Chrissie wasn't stupid. After all, that was obviously why Jaul was in London in the first place talking about needing a divorce and fast. While he was planning to marry wife number two, he had discovered he was *still* married to wife number one. How very inconvenient, she thought bitchily while Sofia and Maurizia stared goggle-eyed at Jaul and sat down at a table across the way to happily tuck into the champagne and snacks laid out for them.

'I hope my arrival has not disrupted your evening,' Jaul remarked stiffly, striving not to react to his ringside-seat view of her long, perfect legs crossed, little feet he had kissed shod in glittery pink high heels.

With difficulty he dragged his attention up to linger on the lovely face he knew so well, willing back the almost instantaneous surge of blood to his groin with an actual prayer for self-control.

'Of course not,' Chrissie lied, angling her pale head back, shimmering hair swishing across her shoulders like silk as she strove to be gracious for the sake of peace. 'I assume you wanted to see me about something?'

Jaul confided that he had gone to her brother-in-law's home in the hope of seeing the twins.

Chrissie was disconcerted. 'You want to see Tarif and Soraya?'

Jaul elevated a fine ebony brow. 'And that surprises you?'

Chrissie reddened in sudden severe mortification. She had told him he was a father and *obviously* he was curious. To have assumed that he would simply accept that news and walk away again had been sheer folly, she conceded ruefully. 'I could bring them on a visit tomorrow morning,' she suggested, prepared to show willing in the civilised stakes. 'Before the lawyers kick in—'

'The lawyers?' Jaul repeated as if he didn't know what she was talking about.

'The divorce meeting,' Chrissie leant forward and whispered, endeavouring to be tactful in the presence of the bodyguards who, it seemed, had not taken their eyes off either her or Jaul since the moment she'd sat down.

Jaul recognised the restrictions of the meeting place he had chosen and cursed his inability to speak freely. He expelled his breath on a slow hiss. At least she was speaking to him again, at least she wasn't shouting, he reasoned grimly.

'Cesare's legal team will soon get it all sorted out,'

Chrissie told him on an upbeat note intended to offer comfort. 'He says they've dealt with much more complex stuff than this.'

Jaul's veiled dark gaze glittered and dropped down to the bareness of her left hand. 'What did you do with the rings I gave you?' he asked softly.

'They're in Cesare's safe. I was keeping them for Soraya,' Chrissie responded, wanting to let him know that she had not retained them for any sentimental reason.

'They have Arabic names—'

'A nod to their heritage,' Chrissie cut in carelessly.

'My grandfather was called Tarif—'

'It's pure coincidence,' Chrissie declared deflatingly, lying through her teeth because she *had* named her son after his grandfather, reasoning that her baby had the right to use a name from the royal family tree. 'I never would have dreamt of naming them after anyone in your family.'

In receipt of that snub, Jaul wanted to punch the wall and shout, but he mastered the surge of anger with a silent, strong self-discipline honed by long months in a hospital bed and even longer months of painfully slow rehabilitation. She hated him; his wife *hated* him. He could sense the animosity still bubbling away below her newly calm surface, could see the sharp evasiveness in her beautiful eyes.

He had brought this hellish situation down on himself, he decided harshly. Two years ago he had still been immature and impatient and reckless. He had taken what he'd wanted without hesitation and without thought of the risk he could be running…

CHAPTER FIVE

'THEY LOOK CUTE as buttons,' Lizzie said fondly, studying the twins garbed in their smartest outfits. 'Jaul will fall in love with them at first sight.'

Chrissie wrinkled her nose. 'I hope not because he's not likely to see much of them when we live in different countries. I also hope he's not always going to be asking me to put them on planes to go and see him.'

Her sister breathed in deep. 'Chrissie...I know it will be difficult but you should *want* him to be interested in his son and daughter, no matter how awkward it is for you. A father in their lives would be a plus, not a minus.'

Duly admonished for her honesty, Chrissie flushed and climbed into the limousine that Jaul had insisted on sending to collect them. She was thoroughly disconcerted to see that he had actually sent his bodyguards as well. She knew Lizzie had spoken sensible words but the prospect of sharing the twins with Jaul daunted her. He was the man she had once loved beyond bearing and the idea of her children being looked after by his next wife in Marwan chilled her. But that was the way the world was now with families and step-families and ideally everyone being relaxed about once bitter relationships that were in the past, she reminded herself irritably. Other people coped and she would have to learn to cope as well. Even so, she couldn't help thinking that it would have been easier altogether if Jaul had never come to London and had never had to be told that he was a father.

The front doors stood wide open on the massive house for their arrival. As she clutched first Tarif below one arm and then struggled to hoist Soraya, a woman in a nanny uniform came running out and offered to help.

'I'm Jane,' she announced. 'Your husband sent me out to assist.'

Chrissie was unimpressed that Jaul was too proud and exalted to come and help her with his own hands but she allowed the woman to lift Soraya. They walked into the hall and on into the ugly drawing room where the nanny deposited Soraya on a new fluffy rug covered with brand-new toys and asked if there was anything Chrissie needed for the twins.

'No, thanks. I have everything I need with me.' Chrissie settled her sizeable baby bag down on one of the wooden sofas and wondered where the heck Jaul was.

But when she looked up from settling Tarif down on the rug Jaul was in the doorway, garbed in black designer jeans and a dark red T-shirt and looking very much like some elite male supermodel from his stunning cheekbones all the way down to his sleek, beautifully built body. The thought shook her and her cheeks went pink, heat trickling through private places, reminding her of intimacies that were no longer part of her life.

'I'm sorry. I was taking a call.' Jaul moved to the edge of the rug and just halted there to stare at the twins with blatant curiosity. 'I don't know anything about babies, which is why I brought the nanny in to prepare for their visit.'

'You must've met some babies?'

'No. There are none in the family...well, there *is* no family, only me,' he reminded her, for he had no siblings and neither had his father and so there were no other family branches to join with his.

'Tarif and Soraya are your family now,' Chrissie heard herself point out and then wondered why she had said that, but there was something strangely touching about his confession of complete ignorance. 'Just get down on your knees and they'll come to you.'

'They can walk?' Jaul was entranced when Tarif made a beeline for him and crawled up onto his lap with a fearless expectation of being welcomed there.

'No, they're only crawling.' Soraya saw her brother receiving attention and headed in the same direction. 'They're starting to occasionally pull themselves upright...Tarif more than Soraya.'

Jaul smoothed Tarif's black hair back from his brow. His hand wasn't quite steady. *His* children! He still could not credit the evidence of his eyes. 'For that night they were conceived...I thank you,' he breathed huskily.

Chrissie glanced across at him and her face flamed as though he had lit a fire inside her. They had run out of condoms and Jaul had wanted to send one of his staff out to buy more and she had been furiously embarrassed by the idea, angry that he would not go on such an errand for himself. So, they had taken the risk and the twins were the result. His expression of gratitude now, however, shook her by its very unexpectedness.

Slowly, Jaul began to relax. The twins responded to his demonstrations of various toys with smiles and laughter and gurgles and they put everything in their mouths. 'They're wonderful,' he told her quietly.

'Yes…I think so too,' Chrissie said with a grin. 'Most parents think their kids are wonderful.'

It felt like a time out of time for Chrissie, for the presence of the children muted her hostility to Jaul and her tension had ebbed. 'They need a nap now,' she announced, scrambling upright intending to leave, a slender figure in jeans and a purple tee.

Jaul hit a button on the wall. 'There are cots upstairs ready for them. Jane will come.'

Chrissie stiffened. 'But I was about to go back home…'

'We have to talk. We might as well do so while our children sleep,' Jaul retorted smoothly as if it was no big deal.

Chrissie didn't want to talk to him though. She thought it was much better to let the lawyers handle everything and keep the dissolution of their sadly short little marriage unemotional and impersonal. On the other hand, she didn't want to be unreasonable and wondered if he was really hoping to see more of the twins after their nap. She climbed the stairs behind Jane, each of them cradling a twin.

An entire nursery had been assembled for the babies' use and she wasn't surprised—even a few short weeks living with Jaul had taught her that with sufficient money almost anything could be achieved overnight. Once Tarif and Soraya were settled she walked slowly downstairs again.

Jaul was in the drawing room and a fresh tray of coffee awaited them. Chrissie shot a rueful glance at it. 'You're a brave man,' she commented, thinking of the sugar bowl and jug she had hurled on her previous visit.

'You couldn't hit a wall at six paces,' he teased, a

slow grin curling his strong, sensual mouth and chasing the gravity away entirely, giving her an unsettling glimpse of the slightly younger, lighter-hearted Jaul she had married.

'Aren't we being civilised?' Chrissie remarked in turn while she poured the coffee and offered him a cake like the perfect hostess.

'Perhaps you should put the cup down now,' Jaul advised, poised straight and tall by the window. 'Because I don't want a divorce.'

Her turquoise eyes flew wide and her coffee cup rattled against the saucer she held. 'I beg your pardon?'

Jaul breathed in very slow and deep, broad chest expanding below the T-shirt. 'If the children are to take their proper place in the royal family I cannot give you a divorce now,' he explained tautly. 'I *can* get away with producing a wife and children like rabbits out of a hat and people will understand because my father's prejudice against Western women was well-known. But for the sake of the family and my country I cannot throw in an immediate divorce—'

Without the smallest warning, Chrissie felt ready to scream with vexation because it seemed to her that they were programmed to be at odds with each other. She had lain awake the night before remembering how she had foolishly threatened to make getting a divorce difficult for Jaul and she had seen no sense in taking such a stance. Surely it was wiser for her to agree to a quick divorce and move on with her life? Why the heck would she want to prolong that process and leave herself neither married nor single purely for the sake of causing Jaul some temporary aggravation? In the end she had decided that a quick divorce would be best for both of them, particularly if she was going to have to share the twins with Jaul.

'I'm sorry,' Chrissie now said flatly. 'But I *do* want a divorce and I can have one whether you like it or not. I'm afraid I don't owe you or your country anything—'

Jaul shifted a graceful hand in a silencing motion. 'Perhaps I phrased this in the wrong way. I'm asking you to give our marriage another try—'

Chrissie set down her cup with a jolt and stood up. 'No,' she said, refusing to even think about that suggestion. 'Too much of my life has been screwed up by you and I want my independence back—'

'Even if it's at the cost of your children?'

'That's not a fair question. I have done everything possible to be a good mother—'

'Tarif is the heir to my throne. I *must* take him home with me,' Jaul murmured very quietly. 'I do not want to part him from you or his sister but it is my duty to raise my heir—'

Chrissie's knees wobbled and every ounce of colour had leached from her drawn cheeks. He was talking about taking Tarif back to Marwan as if that were already a done deal. Did that mean he had already established that he had that right? Her stomach dive-bombed and her throat convulsed. 'I can't believe I'm hearing this. You're asking me to give our marriage another go because you want the kids, not me—'

'Don't be stupid,' Jaul urged with sardonic bite. 'I wanted you back the moment I laid eyes on you again. You're like my "fatal attraction" in life and I very much suspect that that works both ways.'

'And what's that supposed to mean?' Chrissie demanded tempestuously, breasts heaving below her top.

Lustrous dark eyes flickered pure gold. 'You want me too,' Jaul framed silkily. 'You want me so much you're eaten up with it and I'm the same—'

'That's the biggest piece of nonsense I've ever heard!' Chrissie proclaimed furiously.

'You need me to prove it?' Jaul launched back at her, dark eyes blazing threat.

'You couldn't prove it because it isn't true!' Chrissie argued. 'I've moved on way past you...'

'In what way?' Jaul demanded.

Her temper was jumping up and down inside her like a screaming child because she had suffered so much because of him and that he should show up again and start laying down the law about *his* wants, *his* needs was too much for her to bear.

'I've been with other men,' she lied with deliberation, knowing how possessive he was, how jealous, how all-consuming his passion could be...and knowing just how to hurt.

'I expected that,' Jaul framed in a harsh undertone. 'You didn't need to spell it out—'

But Chrissie had watched him pale below his vibrant skin and it made her feel like a total bitch, especially when she was lying, but it seemed so important to her right then to drive a wedge between them, to prove that she was completely free of him and what they had once shared. 'So, you see, I don't want you the way I once did.'

Burning bright golden eyes trailed over her from the crown of her head right down to her curling toes and she felt her body react the way it always did around Jaul. Her breasts swelled in a bra that suddenly felt too tight, her nipples pinching taut while lower down she felt hot and moist.

'And you are one hundred per cent certain of that, are you?' Jaul seethed as he stalked closer. '*So* certain you won't even give me a chance?'

Chrissie snatched in a ragged breath. The atmosphere was smouldering like a combustible substance and the tension was suffocating because she recognised that Jaul was on the edge of his hot temper, which when lost was considerably more dangerous than her own. 'Yes, I'm certain,' she told him stubbornly.

'You're a liar,' Jaul told her harshly. 'You're lying to me—you're even lying to yourself! We've been down this route before—'

'I don't know what you're talking about—'

'Oh, yes, you do, *habibti*,' Jaul contradicted. 'I'm talking about the months you made me wait for you—'

'I didn't *ask* you to wait—'

'You turned your back on the attraction between us. You refused to acknowledge it.'

'Well, I didn't think you were *my* kind of person and…oh, yes, didn't I turn out to be right about that?' Chrissie boxed back without hesitation.

'Stop it,' Jaul grated, locking both arms round her to haul her up against him.

'No, you get your hands off me…*right now*!' Chrissie snapped back angrily. 'We're getting a divorce and you're not allowed to touch me!'

'You're still my wife.'

'But you don't get to touch!' she warned a split second before his beautiful mouth, warm and wet and rawly sexual, came crashing down on hers in an electrifying collision. His tongue pressed in deep.

For a split second she imagined she saw a shower of sparks because the taste of Jaul's mouth on hers was as wildly exhilarating as hitching a ride on a rocket ship. Her legs went numb and her body hummed like an engine cranking up after a long time switched off, pulses like static tightening her nipples and warming her pelvis. It happened that fast, that her reaction was so strong it almost blew her away. Her hands slid up his arms, holding him to her, every skin cell in her body alight in a blaze.

She had told herself that it wouldn't be like that if she touched him again. She had told herself that the response she recalled was the result of infatuation, exaggerated by an imagination reluctant to let go of the sparkly romance that had turned into car-crash viewing. But she had lied, not knowingly, but out of ignorance and wishful hopes because the discovery that Jaul could still deliver a kiss that could set her on fire was downright terrifying.

Struggling to catch her breath, she looked up at him, into eyes dark and glittery as a starry night, and for a split second of madness she wanted to drown there and turn time back in its tracks. Instead, she rested her cheek against a broad shoulder, breathing in the musky, clean scent of him like a hopeless addict. He smelled so good, he smelled so *right* that it frightened her. She quivered, insanely aware of every line of his long, lean body against hers and the terrible wanting rising inside her like a drug haze she couldn't possibly fight and win against. 'Jaul?'

Long brown fingers cupped her cheekbones. 'Give me your mouth again,' he husked.

No, that wasn't going to solve anything and she knew it, but still she tilted her head back like a programmed doll and he kissed her again, longer and deeper, harder and stronger and her senses went spinning off into a fantasy land of rediscovery. It had been so long, far too long since she had even had a kiss and what could be said about a kiss? she scorned inwardly. A kiss was no big deal even with an estranged husband and he was so good at kissing, so wickedly erotic he should have been bottled and sold like precious oil. He lifted her up against him with that easy strength of his that had once thrilled her to the marrow. He hitched her legs round his waist, nuzzled his mouth against her throat where she was, oh, so sensitive, oh, so responsive, and suddenly her whole body was vibrating like a tuning fork, greedily reaching for every sensation and drinking it in.

Her eyes were tightly closed as if what she didn't see didn't have to be accounted for. This wasn't her doing this and letting Jaul carry her upstairs. This wasn't what she wanted but, oh, dear heaven, how much she wanted *him*! That mad, frenzied wanting was throbbing and pounding through her as unstoppable as a runaway train. She buried her face in his shoulder in despair at her own weakness.

'I can't do this…I *can't*,' she whispered feverishly.

In an awkward movement, Jaul nudged her head up and found her mouth again, briefly, devastatingly. 'Yes, you can, because in your heart you know I will never hurt you again.'

'It's not that simple—'

'It is as simple as you will allow it to be,' he growled, his breath fanning her cheek.

But nothing was ever that simple with Jaul, her brain reminded her. Sometimes he was too clever, too devious for her, while she was a straight-down-the-line open and honest person. He pushed a door open and then he kissed her again and carnal heat engulfed her in an irresistible tide, washing away every thought.

She was lying on something soft and yielding and above her Jaul was virtually ripping off his T-shirt, smooth brown pectoral muscles rippling down washboard abs before her eyes. And seeing that beautiful body again was too much temptation all at once because her hands rose of their own volition and smoothed up over that torso from the vee rising out of the loosened waistband of his jeans to the narrow waist and up over the lethal strength etched into the sleek lines of his hard, muscular chest. The heat of him burned her palms and a clutch of longing pulled in her belly. Desire was like an old familiar stranger, controlling her, silencing her, heightening the craving to a dangerous level. She couldn't have him, she *shouldn't* have him, but the hunger was intolerable and more than she could withstand.

He came down to her again, hot and half naked, peeling off her top and then her bra, filling his hands with the pouting mounds of her breasts, fingers grazing her tightly beaded nipples and tugging them before he put his mouth there with hungry urgency. Her back arched, arrows of flaming need slivering through her quivering length to the heart of her. Sweet sensation tugged at her with every suck of his lips, every lash of his tongue, and then he kissed her again and her fingers knotted in his black hair. Tiny little sounds broke in her convulsing throat as he tugged off her panties and traced the swollen flesh between her thighs. A single finger pierced her and she cried out, already so hot, so ready she was wet and oversensitive.

'Don't wait,' she heard herself mumble, wanting, *needing*, strung on a high of anticipation.

But Jaul never had been a male prone to following instructions in bed and he teased her first, toying with the tiny button of her desire so that she gasped and her hips jerked and her legs flailed and what remained of her control was ruthlessly wrenched from her. He shimmied down the bed and used his mouth and his tongue on her most tender flesh. From that point, she no longer knew what she was doing, was positively enslaved by the wanton hunger beating like an angry drum inside her, pushing her responses higher and higher until her whole body convulsed on a bitingly fierce climax, wave after wave of almost forgotten intense pleasure pounding through her weakened length.

'That's one,' Jaul husked with his unforgettable confidence, dark eyes shimmering gold pools of hunger as what remained of his clothing went sailing across the room. He tore the corner from a small foil pack with his teeth and came down to her, lean brown powerful body arching over hers with balletic grace and all the hard, driving promise of extravagant pleasure she had learned to expect from him.

I'm not doing this, I'm not really *doing this,* she reasoned crazily with herself, still intoxicated by the physical gratification she had denied herself for too long. The long, slow, torturous glide of him into her damp sheath was irresistible, stretching sensitive tissue before sinking deep in a deliriously energising thrust. She strained up to him and she couldn't help it because excitement was powering her and he was moving, hard and fast, sending ripples of deliciously dark erotic sensation travelling through her lower limbs. His rhythm was the blinding white heat of passion and she was lost and defenceless against the erotic moves of his lithe, strong body, caught up in the moment and reaching desperately for the highest peak with every sobbing, gasping breath. And then the scorching, blinding heat splintered into ecstasy as potent as an explosive charge and she cried out as the voluptuous, spellbinding pleasure expanded and flooded her with sweet sensation in the aftermath.

Afterwards, Chrissie wasn't even quite sure where she was because Jaul was still holding her close and that felt both familiar and strange and she didn't know how to react to it. Instead she lay there like a stick of rock, barely breathing, under attack from a roaring grip of discomfiture. On the very edge of the divorce that she had told him she wanted she had slept with him again. Humiliation engulfed her and powered her into pulling free and rolling over in silence to the other side of the bed.

Powered by no similar onslaught of self-consciousness and regret, Jaul got the message and sprang out of bed. 'We start again,' he pronounced with decision as he stretched, his long brown back rippling with muscle in the sunlight.

And somehow the very fact that it was still daylight and that her innocent children were napping somewhere in the huge house made Chrissie feel even more guilty and conflicted than ever. In that turmoil of uneasy emotion she almost didn't notice the scarring on Jaul's back as he strode towards what she assumed to be the bathroom. Striated silvery lines marked his spine and she frowned, momentarily sidestepping her other anxieties to say abruptly, 'How did you get the scars on your back?'

'In an accident…car,' Jaul told her flatly.

As he stood there, naked and brown and gorgeous, his perfect profile turned towards her, she wondered if he had always had the scars and she simply hadn't noticed them. How observant had she been of his back view? she asked herself wryly, dismissing her momentary concern to let the other feelings of confusion and self-loathing engulf her again.

'I still want the divorce,' Chrissie told him stonily.

His strong jawline clenched. 'We'll discuss it after I have a shower.'

'OK.' Like someone desperate to pull clean linen over a mistake, Chrissie was eager for him to get dressed and leave her free to do the same.

'There's another shower off the room next door,' Jaul remarked tautly. 'I'll use it.'

'Your bodyguards aren't standing outside the door, are they?' Chrissie checked.

'They'll be downstairs.' Jaul sent her a perceptive appraisal from grave dark eyes. 'It is not their business to monitor or discuss my private life and they know it well.'

Chrissie was scarlet to her hairline, could feel her very cheeks throbbing with unwelcome heat. 'I'll use the other shower,' she said quietly.

'We are married. There is nothing to be embarrassed about,' Jaul murmured soothingly.

He strode into the bathroom releasing Chrissie from paralysis and she fled from the bed, snatching up clothes, pulling them on any old way before creeping from the room and literally tiptoeing into the bathroom next door to make use of the facilities. But washing didn't noticeably make her feel any better. She had insisted that she wanted a divorce and then fallen into bed with him again and now he thought he had her exactly where he wanted her. Was that so surprising?

Chrissie would not have put it past Jaul to have deliberately set out to get her horizontal. He was no slowcoach with women, no fool when it came to what mattered. His passion was irresistible but he would know perfectly well that she would feel tormented by what had just happened between them and he probably felt quite self-satisfied because he had proved *his* point: she *did* still want him and crave him in the most basic of ways.

That meant more to Jaul than it meant to her though. When she had first met Jaul he had been a sexual predator, programmed to take advantage of willing women even though he had not behaved that way with her. In fact, although they had hit astonishing highs in the lesser intimacy stakes, Jaul had *married* her before he actually had full sex with her, making her appreciate even back then that in some ways Jaul was much more anchored in his own culture than she had ever properly appreciated. It had also made her wonder in low moments after he had disappeared if she had won Jaul purely by saying no for so long and thereby acquiring all the glorious lustre of a challenge and a worthwhile trophy. Was that the simple explanation of why the heir to a Gulf throne had chosen to deem an ordinary Yorkshire girl special enough to marry? But then had he ever planned on it being a permanent marriage?

But that past was long gone and she was over it, Chrissie reminded herself as she got dressed again. Just not as over him as she had thought she was, a little inner voice reminded her deflatingly. Jaul would think he had won now, would assume she would become his wife again. It probably was just that basic for him, his belief that if she had sex with him again it meant he had her back.

And whose fault was it that he would now be thinking that? Chrissie boiled with regret inside herself. Pure naked lust had overwhelmed her. It was a fallacy to believe that only men could react like that, she ruminated unhappily, a nonsense to assume that a woman couldn't feel the same way. She had never been with anyone other than Jaul but she had learned a lot about that side of her nature even in the short time they had actually lived together and knew that she was a passionate woman. And the only reason she hadn't slept with anyone else since Jaul was that she had yet to meet any male who had the same highly charged sexual effect on her that he did.

Jaul towelled himself dry after a shower with a reflective look on his lean, strong face while he tried to work out whether he had made the right or wrong move with Chrissie. She was so stubborn, so unforgiving. Did she have genuine cause to feel that way?

He refused to believe that his late father had lied to him, so what point was there in making enquiries at the embassy? Such an investigation into King Lut's behaviour would be downright disloyal and it would be sure to spawn unpleasant rumours and damaging gossip. His features sombre at that prospect, Jaul cursed below his breath. He had a wife. He had two children. He might have spent two years in ignorance of those facts but the reality was that now he had to live with his wife and his children in the present and not in the past, harking back to old disruptive issues that only roused bitterness and aggression in both of them.

She had taken the money and run. Did he continue to hate her for that even when he now knew that she had been pregnant and in dire need of financial help? She was younger than he was, less mature and all of a sudden he hadn't been there for her. A woman of greater selfishness might have had a termination rather than raise two children she had not planned to conceive. Whether he liked it or not, fate had ensured that he had let her down by not being there for her when he had been needed.

And on a much lighter note, he ruminated abstractedly, shapely mouth sultry with recollection, the sex was amazing. But where once it had been the icing on the cake, now it was the only glue likely to give them a future as a couple. Wasn't that why he had swept her off to bed? That laced with unashamed desire, of course.

Why was he even thinking like this? In the past, Chrissie had often made him think about stuff that generally struck him as not quite masculine and when they were first married he had resented that truth. He was not a knight on a white charger like some character out of the medieval romances she had once adored. He had never pretended to be perfect but he had always known that she wanted him to be that knight. Chrissie the realist was deeply intertwined with Chrissie the romantic.

And now he was about to be the bad guy again, he acknowledged grimly. He had no choice. He had not had a choice from the moment he'd learned of his son's existence.

Chrissie was brushing her hair when she heard the guest-room door open and she stiffened, leaving down the brush and walking to the bathroom door. Jaul was in jeans and a bright turquoise tee that clung to his impressive chest and if she felt lacerated by what had occurred, he looked infuriatingly energised, she reflected wretchedly.

'I thought we should talk in here,' Jaul confided.

Less risk of being overheard by his staff, she translated. So, what was he about to tell her that she might want to shout and scream about?

'I still want the divorce,' she repeated doggedly. 'What happened just happened but it doesn't change my mind about anything.'

Burnished golden eyes shaded by luxuriant black lashes surveyed her without perceptible surprise. 'We have a link we could still build on—'

'I don't think so,' she argued, waving a pale, slender hand in a dismissive gesture. 'Been there, done that. I could never trust you again and let's face it…you wanted a divorce as well until you found out about Tarif. I appreciate that Tarif's birth changes things for you but it doesn't change them for me.'

'And that's your final word on this subject?' Jaul pressed with sudden severity.

Chrissie lifted her chin, refusing to let mortification take over. She had made a mistake but that didn't mean she had to live with it and build her entire future around it. 'Yes, I'm sorry, but it is…'

'Then perhaps you should look at *this*…' Jaul slid a folded document out of his back pocket and held it out to her. 'I didn't want to be forced to make use of it. I had hoped to avoid it because coercing you is something I would've preferred not to do. But this particular document would have been produced by my lawyers had any divorce meeting taken place,' he explained flatly. 'However, I have cancelled that meeting.'

'What on earth is it?' Chrissie whispered anxiously.

'It's the pre-nuptial contract you signed before we got married,' Jaul informed her levelly. 'I don't think you read it properly.'

The vaguest of memories stirring, Chrissie wrenched open the sheet of paper and saw the clause marked with a helpful red asterisk in the margin. Her heart in her mouth, she read the clause relating to the custody of any children born of their marriage in which she had agreed that any child they had would live in Marwan with Jaul.

Her mouth ran dry because she vaguely remembered reading that more than two years previously and cheerfully dismissing the concept from her mind because it had not seemed remotely relevant to her at the time. After all, they had not been planning to start a family immediately and the prospect of babies and the problems of custody should their marriage run aground had seemed as remote as the Andes to her back then. They had been madly in love, at least *she* had been in love and, trusting and naive soul that she was, it had not occurred to her that some day in the not too distant future her blithe acceptance of that clause might come back to haunt her...

CHAPTER SIX

HE HAD TRIED to play nice, Jaul reflected grimly, but nice hadn't panned out too well with Chrissie, who was suspicious of his every move and had ensured that they were now down to the brutal bare bones of legal agreements and custody. Possibly he wasn't very good at playing nice, he acknowledged in exasperation, having much more experience of playing nasty. The King's word was the last word to be heard in serious disputes in Marwan and there was always an aggrieved party, convinced of unjust treatment and favouritism. He had learned that, regardless of negotiation and compromise, someone would always be dissatisfied with his decision.

Like a drowning woman forced to review the most important moments of her life, Chrissie was pale as death as she stared down at that clause in the pre-nuptial contract. Her heart was sinking down to the very soles of her feet. She could not see how she could possibly combat an agreement that she had voluntarily signed.

Jaul breathed in slow and deep, muscles rippling below the T-shirt, wide shoulders taut. 'At some future date, should you remain *convinced* that you want a divorce—'

Her turquoise eyes flared back to life like the unholy blue hot streak flickering inside a flame. 'You'd better believe that I won't change my mind!' she traded furiously.

'Then you will be entitled to your own household in Marwan in which to raise the twins. I'm afraid that is the best I can offer you should you want your freedom back,' Jaul imparted grittily, white teeth flashing bright against golden skin.

'But…for the moment, a separate household for the three of us is out of the question?' Chrissie prompted dangerously.

'I'm afraid so. At least this way, however, you retain shared custody of our children,' Jaul pointed out.

'They've never been *our* children, they've always been *mine*!' Chrissie vented painfully, biting back a flood of recrimination.

'Only because I didn't know I was a father,' Jaul parried.

'And what you refer to as "this way" means that you expect me to pretend that we still have a real marriage?' she interpreted jaggedly as she stalked to the door and spun back again. 'How could you do this to me after deserting me for two whole years? Don't you have any moral decency?'

'It is not that simple for me. In an effort to secure our children's status and acceptance by my people, I'm prepared to pretend I'm part of a happy couple. That's part of my duty of loyalty and care towards them and their needs,' Jaul framed in a raw undertone. 'They will take their place in the royal family as the prince and princess they are and that *is* my responsibility *and* yours.'

Yanking open the guest-room door, Chrissie was reckoning that she could have done without the parental slap on the wrist. He scarcely needed to remind her of the maternal obligations that had consumed her youthful freedom throughout the time they had lived apart. It was so unfair, she thought bitterly, that Jaul could have walked out on her, abandoning *his* responsibilities and then walk back into her life only when it suited him to demand that she observe a duty of care that he had royally ignored.

'Will you agree to it?' Jaul asked, striding after her impetuous exit to follow her down the corridors that led to the giant upper landing.

Adrenaline on a high, her steps faltered while common sense and survival instincts took over. The twins had become a weapon and if she wanted to keep her children she had no other option but to take up residence in Marwan.

On one level she recognised the position he was in, on another she hated him for making it her responsibility as well. It was one thing to own up to a two-year-old marriage and two young children and shock the Marwani population but it would be another thing entirely to stage that shock along with a headline-grabbing divorce in the UK while they fought a bitter custody battle over their children. Because, no matter how damning that agreement she had signed would prove to be when aired in a courtroom, Chrissie knew she would still fight for her children regardless. But such a fight would undoubtedly damage everyone involved.

Did she really want to land the stress of a custody battle on Cesare and Lizzie as well? Hadn't she already caused them as much grief as a wayward teenager with her exam agonies, touchy pride, carefully kept secrets and unplanned pregnancy? Did they really deserve to have to deal with more on her behalf? Shouldn't she be handling her own problems and standing on her own feet? Wasn't that really what adulthood was all about?

'Chrissie…?' Jaul prompted, falling still. 'I need an answer.'

'I'll do it because I don't appear to have the choice of doing what I want,' Chrissie shot back at him tightly. 'But I won't forgive you for it.'

Brilliant dark eyes veiled, his beautiful mouth compressing. 'You've never forgiven me for anything I did wrong.'

Chrissie refused to believe that was true. She must have forgiven him at some stage for something. She was not a hard, unforgiving person, was she? Her first impressions of Jaul returned to haunt her and, along with it, her long-held refusal to consider the fact that she might have misjudged him. Very faint colour warmed her cheeks.

She recalled that she had never forgiven her mother for what the older woman had put her through and frowned. Francesca had died before her younger daughter reached the age of confrontation and the older woman had taken her guilty secrets to the grave with her. Chrissie swallowed hard, struggling to shake off the dirty, shamed feeling that always engulfed her when she thought of Francesca. She was older now, wiser and less judgemental, she reasoned tautly. Her mother had not been a strong person and she had been very much abused in some of her relationships with men. Her second husband, the very last man in her life, had been the worst of all, taking advantage of Francesca's weakness and dependency on him to propel her into an unsavoury lifestyle. Some day she might tell Lizzie the truth about their mother, but certainly she could never ever imagine sharing that sordid story with Jaul.

'I think this is an incredibly weird and ugly house,' Chrissie remarked curtly on the way down the massive staircase, which reminded her of something out of an ancient Hammer Horror movie. It only lacked zombies sidling out of the mummy cases in the hall to totally freak her out.

'Blame my grandmother. She furnished this place.'

'The Englishwoman who walked out on your grandfather?' That was the bare bones of what Chrissie knew about her British predecessor in the Marwani royal family. 'Tell me about her.'

'Why?'

'Fellow feeling…aren't I sort of following in her footsteps?' Chrissie quipped, eager to talk about something, *anything* other than the agreement she had just given and what had occurred in the tumbled sheets upstairs. That extraordinary passion had left her aching in intimate places and even walking wasn't quite comfortable. Jaul had been so…wild and forceful…and she had revelled in that display of primal passion, but now she was being forced to pay the piper and put her whole life back in Jaul's hands. She should never have let herself down like that, she thought painfully. He was running rings round her now.

'I hope not. She deserted her son,' Jaul proffered censoriously. 'She met my grandfather Tarif on a safari in Africa. She was a socialite from an eccentric but aristocratic English family…Lady Sophie Gregory. Tarif fell deeply in love with her but he was simply a walk on the wild side for her…a novelty. A couple of months of life in backward Marwan where there were no ex-pats for company was too much for my grandmother. She stayed only long enough to give birth to my father and walked out only weeks afterwards.'

Chrissie knew when she was listening to a biased story. 'This is what *your* father told you?'

'Yes. I met her once though when I was a teenager. I was in Paris on an officer training course and she was at a party I was invited to,' Jaul told her grudgingly. 'She came right up to me and said, "I understand you're my grandson. Are you as stiff-necked and stubborn as your father?"'

'So, your grandmother *did* try to see her child again,' Chrissie worked out wryly from that greeting. 'In other words she wasn't quite as indifferent a mother as she was painted to you. Most probably your grandfather wouldn't *allow* your grandmother to see her son again because she walked out on their marriage. Have you ever thought of that angle?'

Jaul *hadn't* and his jawline clenched like granite because that particular family story had long been an incontestable legend set in stone and he couldn't credit that Chrissie had already come up with a likelihood that had never once occurred to him. 'There were grounds for his bitterness.'

'Such as?' Chrissie was receiving a twist of satisfaction from needling Jaul even if it was only about old family history. Why? He was wrecking her life again. He *owned* her, just as he owned their son and daughter. There was no leeway for misunderstanding in that clause in the contract, no wriggle room for a screamingly naive girl who had been so in love she hadn't foreseen a future where she might have children and end up alone and abandoned. She knew she would never forgive herself for being that stupid and that short-sighted about so very important an issue as the right to keep and raise her own babies and live where she chose.

'Lady Sophie's desertion made Tarif a laughing stock. In those days saving face was everything for a ruler but there was nothing he could do to hide the fact that *she* had left him.'

'And no doubt he never forgave her for that and kept her from her son as punishment while brainwashing that same child into a hatred and distrust of Western women,' Chrissie filled in with spirit, her disgust palpable. 'Don't forget I met your father and I was left in no doubt that he saw a woman like me as a curse on his family name. Knowing how he felt, why on earth *did* you marry me? No, scratch that, don't answer me. I *know* why you married me.'

Fine ebony brows pleating, Jaul was recalling their final argument in Oxford. She had wanted him to take her out to Marwan with him, had protested the secrecy he had insisted on and had implied that his attitude bore a closer resemblance to shame than secrecy. But that was untrue. He had known that without preparation and forewarning his father would react badly and he had flown home intending to break the news of his marriage in person. Sadly, he now knew that he should have made the announcement much sooner and had he done so he was convinced that everything that followed would have happened very differently.

'You don't know why I married you because you never have known what I was thinking,' Jaul boxed back cool as ice water. 'In reality, I was trying to protect you but, unhappily for both of us, I went about it the wrong way.'

A lift door whirred back in the hall and the nanny, accompanied by a young woman in Marwani dress, appeared, each bearing a beaming drowsy twin back to their mother.

'I'll leave now.'

'I want you to stay,' Jaul decreed.

'Listen.' Chrissie rested a hand daringly on a muscular brown forearm as she stretched up to him to whisper, 'For now, I'm staying with my family. I'll do what I have to do only when you leave for Marwan. When is that happening?'

'I have to return within twenty-four hours. I have already released the photos taken at our wedding at the embassy to the press at home.'

Chrissie lost colour. Only one wretched day of freedom left? Only *one* day more to be with her family and savour her independence and liberty to do as she liked. 'So you expect me to…what?'

'Close down your life here in the short term. Your family will naturally be welcome to visit and stay with us whenever they like.'

'Then it's about time you met my father,' Chrissie pronounced abruptly, a rueful expression in her eyes for she doubted that Jaul would enjoy the experience. Her dad was chock-full of prejudices, against foreigners, rich people and royalty to name only a few, and Brian Whitaker was not diplomatic about hiding the fact. Jaul deserved that meeting as she had not deserved hers with his late father, Lut. 'He's coming down to London tonight to visit us.'

On the way back to her sister's with the twins, Chrissie was recalling the day she had met King Lut, remembering the clammy break of sweat on her skin when she had finally grasped the alarming truth that the angry older man, dressed exactly as though he had stepped off a desert film set, was actually her father-in-law. He had not even spoken to her in English. Throughout another older man had stood anchored to his side translating his every furious gesture and bitten-out word and yet Jaul had once told her that his parent spoke fluent English. Possibly the King's temper had prevented him from finding the right words in her language, the horrible, hateful words that had never left her once he had assured her that their very marriage had been completely unlawful…

'It was *not* a proper marriage. It was never intended to be more than a casual affair and Jaul wants to be left in peace. It is *over* between you now that he's back in Marwan. He does not want you living here in his English home, nor does he want to hear from you again. Please do not embarrass him further by visiting our embassy. My son plans to marry a decent woman from his own culture and who will marry him if you cause a scandal?'

There had been a lot more along the same lines, Chrissie recalled unhappily, every word aimed at ensuring that she accepted just how unimportant she was and how unfit she was to be Jaul's wife. She had been a sexual fling, nothing more, an intruder in his apartment, an embarrassing visitor creating scenes at the embassy, in short a woman pitifully clinging to a man who no longer wanted her. Her pride had been crushed and her heart broken because she had loved Jaul with all her heart.

And now it seemed that her life had turned full circle, she reflected as the limo whisked her back to her sister's home. She knew that Cesare and Lizzie would support her if she chose to fight Jaul for the children but she could not help recalling that even Cesare had urged her to be cautious in her dealings with Jaul, because Jaul had more power and influence than the average non-resident father. In other words even her powerful and extremely shrewd brother-in-law had been doubtful of her chances of winning such a custody battle.

And there were *two* menacing sides to her dilemma, she acknowledged wretchedly. If she fought Jaul it would turn bitter and nasty and then what would happen if she ultimately lost the custody battle? How much would Jaul allow her to see of her children in the hostile aftermath of such a conflict? She shivered, clammy and cold inside as she pondered that very realistic question. Hadn't she already had the warning of learning what had happened to Jaul's British grandmother, Lady Sophie? From what she could establish that poor woman had never got to see her child again, at least not until he was an adult and too locked into his prejudices and hostility to listen to the other side of the story. Chrissie reckoned that if she wasn't careful she might fall victim to the same heartbreak and lose her children altogether.

Her other concern was the sheer selfishness of plunging Cesare and Lizzie into that same conflict with her. Lizzie was pregnant again and the very last thing she needed was added pressure and anxiety. A court case would be nerve-racking and would attract the sort of publicity that her sister and brother-in-law abhorred, for in spite of their wealth they led quiet, private lives. However, if Chrissie plunged into a divorce and custody battle with Jaul, the press were sure to pick up on it because an Arab king's secret marriage to an English-woman would be all too newsworthy to ignore. No, she couldn't possibly risk exposing her family or her children to that kind of intrusive publicity. They all deserved better from her, she conceded heavily. After all, she had chosen to marry Jaul and the consequences were hers to deal with. Why should anyone else pay the price?

CHAPTER SEVEN

CHRISSIE SAT ON Jaul's private jet during the flight to Marwan like a small grave statue, slender body straight-backed and rigid, hands circumspectly folded on her lap, eyes veiled.

Jaul compressed his sensual lips and grimly returned his attention to his laptop. What had he expected? A relaxed and happy travelling companion? It was wiser to concentrate on the positives: Chrissie was on board with his children and, even better, was considerably wearing the sort of outfit for her first public appearance that would impress his people. The simple blue shift dress enhanced the slender grace of her figure. In the sunlight coming through the porthole behind her, she looked incredibly beautiful with her hair gleaming like a liquid fall of bright reflective silver. That same exacting light accentuated her almost transparent porcelain skin and the lush perfection of her soft pink lips.

All too fast and predictably, Jaul recalled the silky brush of her hair across his thigh and the hot, erotic grip of her mouth. Long brown fingers braced on the table edge in front of him as arousal coursed through him with the force of a volcanic flow of lava, leaving him hot and hard and throbbing with need. Gritting his teeth, he concentrated instead on thinking about how she would react to the special request he had to make of her. He compressed his wide, sensual mouth, resolving to approach the topic with tact.

Chrissie's stillness cloaked her inner turmoil. She wanted to scream and shout with angry frustration. Jaul had, quite literally, hunted her down and trapped her like prey. Two years too late she was taking up the role of being his wife and the mother of his children, a role that she would once, most ironically, have eagerly embraced. A trickle of perspiration beaded her short upper lip as she recalled the incredible crush of paparazzi fighting to photograph the Marwani royal party at the airport and the sheer wall of security men it had taken to hold them back. It had not occurred to her that their marriage would so quickly incite that amount of attention. Jaul had taken it in his stride but Chrissie had been unnerved by that level of public exposure.

But then, in truth, the past twenty-four hours had been equally unsettling. Cesare and Lizzie had reacted to her announcement that she was returning to Marwan with Jaul with far less surprise than Chrissie had naively expected. Her sister and brother-in-law had assumed that Jaul and Chrissie were making an effort to rebuild their marriage for the sake of their two young children.

'And if it doesn't work out, at least you know you tried and you can come home again,' Lizzie had proclaimed in her innocence of the fact that 'coming home' was an option that Chrissie had legally surrendered two years earlier. To come home, she would have to be willing to leave her children behind her and that was not an option she could ever imagine choosing.

That same day, Chrissie had boxed up her possessions for storage and had put her apartment in the hands of a rental agency. For what had remained of her meagre twenty-four hours of freedom, she had gone shopping with her sister for a more suitable wardrobe of formal clothing. In the evening her father had arrived in London for a visit and Jaul had joined them for dinner. Jaul had dealt calmly with her father's often barbed comments and he had laughed when Chrissie had remarked on his discretion before his departure.

'When it comes to temperament, your father is a walk in the park. My father lost his head in rage at least once a week. There was no reasoning with him and he would often say offensive things. Of course, he was very much indulged growing up and because he saw himself as an all-powerful ruler he never studied to control his temper,' he had confided, startling her with his candour. 'It was a good learning experience for me.'

That glimpse into Jaul's background had sharply disconcerted Chrissie because to her it had sounded less like a learning experience and rather more like living with a tyrant. Recalling the raging man she had once briefly met, Chrissie had made no comment as she suppressed an inner shiver while contemplating the possibility that, with such an intolerant and inflexible parent, Jaul's childhood could not possibly have been as secure and privileged as she had always assumed.

Before boarding the flight, Chrissie had gone to a beauty salon to have her hair trimmed and her nails painted, small measures to enable her to present herself as the well-groomed royal wife people would be expecting to see by Jaul's side. *Royal?* That very word made her roll her eyes. The only royal thing about her was that she had allowed Jaul to *royally* shaft her in every sense of the word, she thought with rebellious bitterness.

She had agreed to return to a husband who had once abandoned her and who had yet to explain himself on that score. How on earth had she allowed him to get away with that? How had she let that huge question get buried beneath her terror of losing custody of the twins? And what the heck was Jaul *still* hiding from her?

He was probably only trying to hide the unlovely truth from her, Chrissie reasoned with scorn. But she wasn't stupid and she could work out the most likely scenario for herself. Obviously Jaul had *never* loved her; all he had ever felt for her was lust, a lust honed to a fine sharp edge by the length of time he'd had to wait to get her into bed. Had he realised soon after their marriage that he had made a dreadful mistake and that she was not at all what he wanted in a wife?

Had he then confessed all to his father? Why else would Jaul have never returned from Marwan? Was he now ashamed of having once treated her so cruelly? Of the fact that he had dumped her without even having the guts to tell her he was done with her? Of the fact he had had his father pay her off as though she were some sort of slutty gold-digger? Was that why Jaul had still to explain his own behaviour?

From below her lashes, Chrissie studied her husband with simmering intensity. Whether she liked it or not, dressed in a charcoal-grey suit stamped with the flawless cut and fit of handmade designer elegance, Jaul looked absolutely gorgeous. One look at him with his strong jawline already shadowed by faint black stubble and his guarded dark eyes pinned to her below the heavy black fringe of his lashes and her pulses hammered. She had a sudden devastating image of his lithe, sleek body sinking down over hers and, even in the mood she was in, her breathing constricted and her heart pounded like crazy. Jolted by that response, her chest tightened in a stress reaction even as she felt her nipples prickle and swell below her clothing.

In Jaul's magnetic presence those reactions came as naturally as breathing to her. Her carefully constructed barrier of scorn was already being burned off by the pool of heat spreading like liquid honey at the heart of her. It was desire, the very same lust she had mentally slated Jaul for, and it was a terrifyingly strong hunger, she acknowledged grudgingly, and unfortunately not a stimulus that died down at her bidding. If she didn't watch out and stay on her guard, he would hook her in again like a stupid fish.

But why on earth did she feel so cringe-makingly needy? She had lived perfectly well without sex until Jaul came back into her life and now it was as though he had lit a fire inside her that she couldn't put out. That burning hunger unsettled her and flung her back in time to the days when just being near Jaul had swept her up to an adrenaline-charged high where desire and emotion combined in an intoxicating rush. And no way was she planning to let herself sink back to that level, she swore inwardly.

By the time the jet was circling and getting ready to land, Chrissie's tension was on a high. She was apprehensive about the new life ahead of her in Marwan. Naturally she was. A different culture, a language she didn't speak and suddenly she was royal, an actual queen? Of course she was nervous about the mistakes she would undoubtedly make.

Furthermore in her head where it mattered she still saw herself as a Yorkshire farmer's daughter, born in poverty and raised by a troubled mother. She had made it to university and trained as a teacher but it had never once crossed her mind that one day she would be the wife of a king. Even when she had married Jaul she had failed to look ahead to that future because it had seemed so far away and unreal. She had not been aware at the time that, although seemingly in the best of health and looking much younger than his years, King Lut had already been in his seventies. The older man had suffered a massive heart attack and had died without the smallest warning.

'I should tell you that within Marwan the news of our marriage has been received very positively,' Jaul informed her soothingly as the jet engines whined into a turn. 'The palace has been flooded with congratulations, bouquets and gifts for our children.'

Chrissie was pleasantly surprised. 'But surely your people think it's very odd that it took until now for you to admit that you are married?'

'My father's prejudices against Western women and his rages were legendary and people have proved to be remarkably understanding of my reticence,' Jaul confided wryly.

Jane, their new nanny, joined them with the stewardess, the twins clad in white broderie anglaise playsuits for their first public airing. Silence fell as everyone buckled up. Chrissie breathed in slow and deep and resolved to make the best of her new future. A future from which she excluded all thought of Jaul. She didn't have to stay married to him for ever, she reminded herself doggedly. Once they were able to separate, she wouldn't even need to live below the same roof with him, she reflected, studying his bold bronzed profile and wondering why that particular thought was signally failing to lift her spirits.

When it was time to disembark, Jaul lifted Tarif out of Jane's arms. 'I want to show him off.'

'But you wouldn't let anyone photograph the twins in London,' Chrissie remarked in surprise.

'That was London. This is Marwan. Our people have the right to see this little boy in the flesh first,' he decreed without hesitation. 'He is my heir and one day he will be King.'

They disembarked and the line of people waiting to greet them outside began to move closer. Jaul's bodyguards fanned round them lest a crush develop. Somewhere a military brass band was playing and Chrissie was disconcerted to see television cameras set up below the bright blue sky. The heat was intense and it was much hotter than Chrissie had innocently expected it to be. The advance party of VIPs engaged Jaul in conversation and a smiling older woman approached Chrissie, bobbed a curtsy and told her in excellent English that Soraya was adorable. Cameras were clicking and flashing all around them and Chrissie found it stressful to keep on talking and smiling as though nothing were happening. Painfully slowly the royal party and the interested crowd surrounding them made their way into the airport building, which was mercifully air-conditioned.

That coolness was welcome to Chrissie while even more photos were being taken of them indoors. Being the centre of so much attention with the twins was a shock to her system but she was enjoyably surprised by the mood of genuine friendliness at their arrival and the number of people who spoke her own language. When Tarif began to get restive in his arms, Jaul recognised that it was time to move on and within minutes they were ensconced in a limousine, travelling down a wide boulevard. Her eyes widened when she registered the crowds of waving well-wishers. Jaul was evidently a popular ruler. Gripped by curiosity, she gazed out at streets lined with the sort of ultra-modern buildings that might have featured in any city, although the occasional glimpses of elaborate minarets and men in robes added a touch of exotica to the urban landscape.

'What's the palace like?' she asked in the rushing silence.

'It's old-fashioned,' Jaul warned her. 'Everything's as old as Queen Victoria aside of the bathrooms, kitchens and IT connections. It's been generations since the palace had a queen to take an interest in it.'

'I'd forgotten that.'

'You can change anything you like. I'm pretty much indifferent to my surroundings…unless it's completely weird and uncomfortable like the mansion in London,' he conceded wryly.

The limo had left the city streets behind and rocky plains of sand bounded the desert highway. Dusk was falling. Away in the distance Chrissie could see the looming heights of giant rolling sand dunes coloured every tawny shade from ochre to orange by the setting sun. Giant gates dissecting very high turreted walls appeared a hundred yards ahead and Chrissie sat forward with a look of bemusement. 'Is that the palace? My goodness, it's the size of a city and it looks like a Crusader castle!'

'The front part of the original fortress *was* built by the Crusaders before we threw them out,' Jaul volunteered with amusement. 'For hundreds of years as fashion changed every generation added new buildings. Even I haven't been in all of them. The family was once much larger and in those days my ancestors lived with a vast retinue of servants and soldiers, who all had to be housed.'

The guards patrolling the walls were waving their guns and roaring a welcome as the limo purred through the automatic gates.

'So, who's in charge of everything here at the palace?' Chrissie asked curiously as their vehicle passed through glorious landscaped gardens before gliding to a stately halt in front of the ancient main building with its huge domed entrance porch.

'Bandar, my principal aide, is the nominal head because he is in charge of domestic finance but my cousin, Zaliha, actively runs the royal household. Her sister is married to Bandar, who lives here on site with most of my personal staff.'

A smiling finely built brunette with sloe-dark eyes appeared in the doorway and performed a respectful dip of acknowledgement. She introduced herself as Zaliha in perfect English, tendered her good wishes and begged to hold Soraya all in the space of one breath. The welcome cool of air-conditioning engulfing her overheated skin, Chrissie walked into an amazing circular hallway with walls studded with mother of pearl. 'Shells…seashells,' she remarked in disconcertion. 'It's beautiful.'

'There's quite a bit that isn't quite so lovely,' the brunette warned her ruefully.

'Don't give my wife the wrong impression,' Jaul urged lightly.

'You speak incredibly good English,' Chrissie told her companion.

'My father was on the embassy staff in London and I went to school there,' Zaliha told her.

'Oh, my word…' Chrissie was staring into the cluttered rooms they were passing, rooms bulging at the seams with antique furniture, some of which appeared to be centuries old. 'It's worse than Victorian,' she told Jaul helplessly. 'It's more like…*medieval*.'

'And ripe for renovation,' Zaliha told her cheerfully.

'We will go straight to our rooms now,' Jaul countered before the brunette could involve Chrissie in such a discussion and he curved lean fingers round Chrissie's elbow.

'Yes, sir.' Zaliha bobbed another curtsy and went straight about her business.

'I was planning to explore a little,' Chrissie protested in a perturbed undertone as Jaul urged her round a corner and up a stone staircase.

'Later, perhaps. Right now I have something important to discuss with you,' he proffered with unexpected gravity. 'This wing of the palace is entirely ours and private,' Jaul announced as they reached the second floor.

As he opened the door into a clearly newly furnished and decorated nursery, their nanny stepped forward and grinned with pleasure at her surroundings. Two young women hurried towards them to offer their assistance with the twins.

'You and Jane will have to beat off helpers with a stick in the palace. It has been too many years since there were royal children below this roof,' Jaul commented, entwining Chrissie's fingers in his to guide her further down the wide corridor. She was relieved to see that contemporary furnishings featured in the large rooms she passed. Time might have stopped dead downstairs in what she deemed to be public rooms, but in Jaul's part of the palace time had mercifully moved on.

He swung open a door into an elegant reception room furnished in fresh shades of smoky blue and cream and stood back for her to precede him. She slid past him, taut with curiosity while the scent of him flared her nostrils, clean warm male laced with an evocative hint of the spicy cologne that was so uniquely him it made her tummy flip like a silly schoolgirl. Her cheeks burnished with colour at the reflection, Chrissie moved away from him as he doffed his jacket and loosened his tie.

'You said we had something to discuss,' she prompted with determined cool.

'My advisers have asked us to consider staging a traditional Marwani wedding to allow our people to celebrate our marriage with us,' Jaul informed her, knocking Chrissie wildly off balance with that suggestion. 'There would be a public holiday declared. The ceremony itself would be private…as is our way…but we would release photos of the occasion—'

'You're asking me to marry you *a-again*?' Chrissie stammered in shock.

'Yes. I suppose that is what I'm asking.' Lustrous dark eyes flaring gold and then veiling below black curling lashes, Jaul levelled his gaze on her.

Her frown deepened. 'You want us to remarry even though we've agreed only to stay together until you feel a divorce would be acceptable to your people?'

His stunning bone structure tightened, brilliant eyes

narrowing. 'I don't want a divorce. I haven't wanted a divorce from the moment I learned that we had two children.'

Shaken by his proposition, Chrissie sank down onto a sofa before steeling herself to say rather woodenly, 'I don't care about what you want. I only care about what you *agreed*. And you *agreed* that I could have a divorce if I wanted one.'

'But our children need both of us. I grew up without a mother—she died the day I was born. Children need mothers *and* fathers. I want this to be a *real* marriage and not a pretence,' he countered without apology.

Chrissie sprang out of her seat, revitalised by that admission. 'So, you *lied* to me in London. You just said what you had to say to persuade me to return to Marwan with you but clearly you never had any intention of giving me a divorce.'

Jaul stood his ground, wide shoulders rigid, lean, powerful body tense as he watched her pace. 'I did not lie. I merely hoped that you would eventually change your mind about wanting a divorce. Hoping is not a lie, nor is it a sin,' he assured her drily.

A bitter little laugh erupted from Chrissie at that exercise in semantics. 'But you're way too good at fooling me, Jaul. You did it two years ago when I first married you and I trusted you then and we both know how that turned out. Doesn't it occur to you that I could never want to stay with a husband I can't trust? And that going through a second wedding ceremony would only make a mockery of my feelings of betrayal?' she demanded emotively, struggling to rein back her agitated emotions. 'After all, you *still* haven't explained why you left me two years ago and never got in touch again...'

Jaul was frowning and he lifted an expressive hand to silence her. '*Chrissie*, listen to—'

'No.' Her luminous turquoise eyes were bright with challenge and she lifted her chin, daring Jaul to deny her the explanation she deserved. 'No more evasions between us, no more unanswered questions,' she spelt out tautly. 'You have nothing left to lose and you can finally be honest. Two years ago in spite of all your claims of love and for ever, you broke up with me, you dumped me… It is what it is.'

'But that isn't what happened…' In a gesture of growing frustration as the tension rose, Jaul raked long brown fingers through his luxuriant black hair. 'And what is the point of discussing this so long after the event? I want a fresh start in the present—'

'What happened back then is still *very* important to me,' Chrissie stressed, determined not to back down. 'I think you realised that our marriage was a mistake and you couldn't face telling me that to my face—'

'No, that wasn't what happened,' Jaul broke in with sudden biting harshness. 'When I left you in Oxford I had *every* intention of coming back to you. My father had asked for my help and I couldn't refuse it. A civil war had broken out in Dheya, the country on our eastern boundary, and thousands of refugees were pouring over the border. The camps were in chaos and I was needed to co-ordinate the humanitarian effort—'

'For goodness' sake, you didn't even tell me that much two years ago!' Chrissie complained, her resentment unconcealed. 'Did you think that I was too much of an airhead to understand that that was your duty?'

'No, I didn't want you asking me how long I'd be away because when I flew out I really had no idea,'

Jaul admitted with wry honesty. 'I travelled down to the border in a convoy filled with medical personnel and soldiers. A missile fired by one of the factions fighting in Dheya went astray and crossed the border into Marwan. Our convoy suffered a direct hit...'

Chrissie was so utterly shaken by that explanation that she collapsed back down onto the sofa , her legs weak and her heart suddenly thumping very hard inside her chest. 'Are you telling me that you got...hurt?'

'I was the lucky one.' Jaul grimaced. 'I survived while everyone with me was killed. I was thrown clear of the wreckage but I suffered serious head and spinal injuries and I was in a coma for months.'

In the early days of his vanishing act, Chrissie had feared that Jaul had met with an accident, only to discount that as virtual wishful thinking when time had worn on and there had still been no word from him. Nausea now shimmied sickly through her stomach and she felt almost light-headed at the shock of what he had just told her.

'But nobody told me anything. Nobody even contacted me. Why did nobody tell me what had happened to you?' she asked weakly, struggling to comprehend such an inexcusable omission.

'Very few people knew. My father put a news blackout on my condition. He was afraid that my injuries would provoke a popular backlash against Dheya and the refugees. In reality what happened to me was a horrible accident and not an uncommon event on the edge of a war zone,' he pointed out with a sardonic twist of his lips. 'I was still in a coma when my father came to see you in Oxford—'

'You were hurt, you *needed* me...and yet your father

didn't tell me!' Chrissie registered with rising incredulity and anger. 'Obviously he didn't want me to know what had happened to you but I was your wife! I had every right to be with you.'

'Don't forget that my father didn't accept that we were legally married. I had only informed him of our marriage the night before my trip to the camps and he was very angry with both of us.'

'But you were still in a coma when he came to see me,' she reminded him, her eyes darkening with disgust when she considered that aspect. 'Your father actually took advantage of the fact that you were unconscious. How low can a man sink?'

Lean dark, startlingly handsome features grim, his dark eyes sparking gold at that challenge, Jaul breathed curtly, 'He was trying to protect me, but I do not and never will *condone* his interference.'

'Oh, that's good to know!' Chrissie countered with biting sarcasm. 'He kept your wife away from you when you needed her—very protective, I don't think!'

Jaul was tempted to remind her that his father had offered her money to walk away from their relationship and forget she had ever known him and that after that meeting with his father she had agreed to do exactly that. But now that he knew that she had been pregnant and had given birth to his children, he saw the past in a very different light. She would very much have needed that money to survive as a single parent and he could no longer condemn the choice she had made.

'So, you were in a coma,' Chrissie recounted stiffly, mastering her raging rancour over his father's behaviour with the greatest of difficulty because she knew that insulting the older man would only cloud and confuse more important issues. 'When did you come out of it?'

'Only after three months when they had almost given up hope. I didn't remember you at first. I didn't remember much of anything,' Jaul admitted heavily. 'I'd had a serious head injury and I was in a very confused state of mind with only fragments of memory all jumbled up inside my head. My memories returned slowly. My father told me that he had seen you and given you the money. He also reiterated his belief that our marriage was invalid and informed me that you would not be coming to visit me.'

Chrissie had turned pale as white paper because rage was storming through her in an almost uncontrollable surge. Had she known that Jaul was in hospital, *nothing* would have kept her from his side! But while he had lain in that hospital bed, his father had manipulated the situation and played on her ignorance of the accident to destroy a marriage he had abhorred. How could even the most loving son deem that a 'protective' act? King Lut's interference had been wicked, indefensible and cruelly selfish. The effort of restraining the hot temper and hostility mounting inside her made Chrissie feel sick.

'I hate your father for what he did to us!' she snapped back at Jaul in a small, tight explosion of raw emotion that could not be suppressed. 'He intentionally wrecked our marriage and yet you *still* can't find the words to condemn him. There you were…*needing* me and he made sure that I was put out of the picture. How can you forgive that?'

Jaul swung impatiently away from her, his fierce loyalty to his late father strained by her candour. 'I must be honest with you. At that point in my recovery I didn't want to see you either. I did initially intend to visit you when I was stronger but by the time I was fit to see you so much time had passed that it seemed like a pointless exercise,' he divulged, tight-mouthed with restraint.

Inwardly Chrissie reeled as though he had struck her because that admission, that very dismissive terminology, was a body blow beyond her comprehension. 'I don't understand how you can say that it would have been pointless. How much time passed after the accident before you were fit to travel?' she demanded, folding her arms defensively as if she could hold in the emotions still churning inside her. His self-command, his granite-hard hold on control maddened her.

'It took well over a year for me even to get back on my feet again.' His lean dark features were taut and pale with the strain of being forced to recall that traumatic period of his life. 'My spine was damaged. It took further surgery and weeks of recovery before my doctors were able to estimate whether or not I could hope to walk again.'

In point of fact at a time when his whole world seemed to have fallen apart and he was confined to a hospital bed unable to move and requiring help for every little thing, Jaul had felt quite ridiculously unsurprised by the announcement that his new bride had run out on him as well. In truth he had been seriously depressed back then and traumatised by survivor's guilt because military friends and bodyguards he had known since childhood had died instantaneously in the same accident.

In addition to his deeply troubled state of mind and his belief that his father had bought Chrissie's loyalty off, he had been painfully aware that he and Chrissie had parted on very bad terms in Oxford. She'd been angry with him for leaving her behind. In so many ways back then Chrissie had been an idealistic dreamer and, while he had loved those traits so very different from his own, he had also seen them as a potential weakness should life ever become tough. What could be tougher for a youthful bride than a husband suddenly sentenced to a wheelchair? Ultimately, his conviction that their marriage was invalid as his father had asserted had played the biggest role in his lack of action. After all, if Chrissie wasn't even his wife what possible claim could he have on her?

'But surely by that stage you must've had access to a phone and to visitors and you could have contacted me yourself?' Chrissie pressed accusingly.

Jaul's broad shoulders went rigid, his jawline squaring at an aggressive slant. 'I was in a wheelchair...what would I have said to you? I will be frank—I did not want to approach you as a disabled man. You had accepted a five-million-pound settlement from my father and I assumed that money was all you had ever really wanted from me.'

Chrissie was outraged that Jaul had believed that she had taken his father's money and run. Without a doubt he had found that easier than confronting her with his disability and the risk that he might not regain the use of his legs. Jaul, the original action man and macho to the core, was very physical in his tastes. Deprived of his freedom of movement, forced to accept such bodily weakness and restriction, how must he have felt? But Chrissie suppressed that more empathetic thought and tried to concentrate purely on facts. Jaul, she realised with a sinking heart, had put his wretched pride first when he'd chosen not to approach her in a wheelchair and that truth hurt her more than anything else.

'But I didn't actually accept the money,' she whispered almost absently, so deep was her sense of rejection that he had found it impossible to reach out to her even when he was injured.

'You did.'

'No, I didn't. Your father left a bank draft for a ludicrous five million pounds on the table but I never cashed it.'

'But you said you had plenty of money when I first saw you again and naturally I *assumed*—'

'Only I wasn't referring to your father's bank draft,' Chrissie cut in ruefully. 'Cesare bought the Greek island which my sister and I had inherited from our mother. My share of the purchase price was very generous. I bought my apartment with some of it and put the rest into trust until my twenty-fifth birthday next year. That's what I meant about having plenty of money. I didn't touch a penny of your father's cash. I left that bank draft lying on the table.'

Jaul was transfixed by that claim. His keen gaze lowered, ebony brows drawing together in a frown. Five million pounds had impressed even him as an enormous sum to offer as a bribe to a young woman from an impoverished background. People lied, cheated and killed for far less money than Chrissie had been given. That was the main reason why he had never questioned his father's story but now he was determined to check out her story for himself. Could it be true that she had not claimed that money?

'When did my father's visit take place?' Jaul asked abruptly.

'About two months after you left and he was in a rage when I met him. You once told me he spoke English but he didn't use any within my hearing. His companion had to translate everything he said.'

'He had someone with him…aside of his body-guards?' Jaul shot the question at her in frowning surprise. 'Describe him.'

'Small, sixtyish, goatee beard and spectacles.'

Jaul fell very still as soon as he realised that there *was* a living witness to his father's meeting with his wife. 'My father's adviser, Yusuf,' he identified without hesitation, reflecting that Yusuf would be receiving a visit from him in the near future. Chrissie's allegations demanded and deserved closer scrutiny. If she hadn't taken the money, what had happened to it and why hadn't he been told? Keeping him unaware of the fact that his wife hadn't used the bank draft had ensured that he would misjudge her. It wasn't a thought that Jaul wanted to have but he knew that his father *must've* been informed that that bank draft had not been cashed.

Slowly, Chrissie settled down onto the sofa again, letting the fierce tension leach out of her spine. Her brain felt dazed as though she had gone ten punishing rounds with a boxer. Shock at what she had learned from Jaul was still passing through her in waves. Her bitterness and antagonism had been wrenched from her while she'd listened to the true story of what had separated them two years earlier. Jaul had *not* ditched her. Jaul had *not* voluntarily or cruelly chosen to desert her. In fact he had planned to return to her and, had fate not intervened with that accident and the lies his father had told to both of them, Jaul would almost certainly have returned to her.

For a split second she allowed herself to think of how that might have been and she swallowed painfully, struggling to imagine how she would've felt if Jaul had come back to her and if he had been with her when she'd discovered that she was pregnant. She realised that she was picturing an entirely different and infinitely happier world and fierce regret filled her, backed by a terrible anguished sense of loss because she was beginning to suspect that Jaul had been as miserable as she was when they were first separated. How *could* his father have believed he had the right to inflict such suffering on them both?

Hot, burning tears lashed the backs of Chrissie's eyes in an unsettling surge. She blinked rapidly, intense mortification threatening to engulf her because she only ever cried in the strictest privacy, a discipline learned the hard way after her life had fallen apart following Jaul's vanishing act two years earlier. She snatched in a deep, audible breath and Jaul swung away from the window, suppressing his uneasy thoughts at the prospect of confronting Yusuf, his late father's staunchest supporter.

Yusuf would not necessarily be discreet in the aftermath of such a discussion. It was a stark moment of choice for Jaul because he had to choose between his marriage and his respect for his father's memory. But he knew that that respect was not an excuse to avoid discovering an unpalatable truth. Yet if Chrissie *was* telling the truth, it would be an appalling truth that he would never be able to live with, he reflected grimly before swiftly suppressing that unproductive thought.

As he had been raised to do, he would do what he knew to be his duty and act with honour, regardless of what he found out.

'Where's the cloakroom?' Chrissie asked thickly, dragging his attention back to her.

When he saw the sheen in her turquoise eyes and the dampness on her cheeks, he tensed and took a sudden step forward.

'The first door at the top of the stairs but the bedroom en suites are closer,' Jaul volunteered, winged ebony brows pleating. 'You're upset...you're crying...'

Chrissie flew upright as though she were a puppet whose strings had been jerked without warning. 'Of course I'm not crying!' she protested huskily. 'It's stupid, it's just all this stuff about the past...it's confusing me.'

'I'm sorry,' Jaul breathed in a ragged undertone as he closed his arms round her slight, trembling figure to hold her still. 'I knew that telling you about the accident would rake it all up again, which was why I was so reluctant—'

'But I *had* to know the truth,' Chrissie told him, lifting her chin, an action that did nothing to hide the wet lustre of her eyes.

A tiny muscle pulled taut at the corner of his unsmiling mouth, his beautiful eyes flaring brilliant gold as he scored his knuckles lightly down the side of her face in a soothing gesture. 'I hurt you.'

Chrissie looked up at him and marvelled at how stunning he was even with his blue-black hair a little messy and his strong jawline stubbled. His black lashes were luxuriant above eyes of stormy gold. Wicked anticipation slid through her to create the kind of sudden tension that made her suck in her breath. As she connected with his burnished gaze a pulse was hammering like crazy above her collarbone. She wanted him to touch her so badly that her fingernails bit into her palms as her hands fisted. He was all lean muscle and potent strength as he eased her closer and her body thrummed, her blood racing like liquid lava through her veins. His warm, demanding mouth swooped down on hers and hot, blistering pleasure shot through her with the force of a lightning bolt.

Jaul lifted her up into his arms and carried her into the bedroom next door. As he settled her down on the bed her fingers feathered through his hair and instinctively closed into the silky black strands to hold him to her. 'Kiss me,' she told him, desperately needing to think of something…*anything* other than the reality that Jaul had almost died two years earlier. Had he died she would never have seen him again, never had the chance to hold him close and never had the joy of seeing him proudly hold his son in his arms.

CHAPTER EIGHT

JAUL KISSED MUCH as he made love, melding both passion and sleek proficiency into a devastating sensual assault.

Chrissie had been in emotional turmoil before he'd touched her and once that physical connection was made, she couldn't break it and she wrapped her arms round his neck, needing that security. Feverish kiss built on feverish kiss, stoking the fire flaming at the heart of her only to increase the ache there.

'If you let me have you now, I'll never let you go.' Jaul growled out that husky threat, staring down at her with compelling intensity. 'I can't fight the hunger you arouse in me.'

Chrissie gazed up at him and felt extraordinarily light-hearted for the first time since Jaul had come back into her life. He had not chosen to leave her: events had chosen for him. He had not condoned his father's interference and if he had been guilty of misjudging her on the question of that money, she needed to remember how newly married they had been and how vulnerable such ties could be in any untried relationship. Did she now punish him for his father's sins? Did she hold him to blame for having wanted to love and trust his only surviving parent? Although both Chrissie's parents had hurt her and held views contrary to her own, she had still loved them. She, more than anyone, should understand how basic and strong ran the need to love and trust a parent, she reasoned painfully. With a fingertip, she traced the fullness of his sensual lower lip and gloried in the stormy gold of his gaze, rejoicing in his innate passion.

'You don't have to fight it any more,' she told him softly.

'We're not going to rush this, *habibti*,' Jaul decreed, peeling off his shirt and depriving her of her breath in the same moment.

'Rush...' she urged, dry-mouthed, as he stripped with no more self-consciousness than a child. But then he didn't have a vain bone in his beautiful body, had absolutely no appreciation of the fact that he was a masculine work of art, a very aroused work of art, she recognised, her face warming as she momentarily stopped staring to kick off her shoes and run down the side zip on her dress. Jaul was all sleek, lean muscle, honed by exercise, lines indented across his six-pack, the vee at his hips rising out of the waistband of his boxers and dissected by the silky furrow of black hair that trailed down to the jutting hardness at his crotch.

'I rushed the last time...you walked out on me afterwards,' he reminded her wryly.

'But not because you were anything less than...er... perfect,' Chrissie framed in a rush of candour. 'But because I was all mixed up and I felt even worse after you presented me with that insane pre-nuptial contract I'd signed—'

'That's in the past...leave it there,' Jaul urged. 'We're making a new start.'

A new start. Disconcertingly, Chrissie found herself savouring that declaration. He didn't want the divorce. He wanted them to stay married and raise the children together. There was nothing wrong with that as an aspiration, was there? How could she fault him for that? If she let go of the past, could she too move forward into a more promising future? Why shouldn't she try? Why shouldn't she give their marriage another chance? What did she have to lose?

'A new start...?' she repeated unevenly.

'We're together again with our children. What could be more natural?' Jaul positively purred as he strolled towards the bed like a glossy prowling panther.

It did feel so natural to be with Jaul again, Chrissie acknowledged, studying his lean, extravagantly good-looking features while arrows of piercing heat surged through her in an intoxicating wave that left her boneless. No matter what he believed about her character, Jaul still wanted her, but then he had always wanted her and that was, at the very least, a foundation for the future.

Jaul feasted his eyes on her. 'Come here. We only have one more problem to solve. You're wearing far too many clothes,' he husked, sinking down on the bed and leaning closer to lift the hem of her dress and flip it deftly up over her head.

Chrissie emerged from the folds of the garment with luminous turquoise eyes, wide and bright against her flushed complexion. He unclasped her bra and tossed it aside. 'I want to look at you.'

Her breathing rupturing in her throat, Chrissie fought an instinctive urge to cover herself and her colour heightened as she leant back against the pillows.

Jaul curved reverent hands over the pouting swell of her breasts. 'Pure perfection,' he murmured thickly.

He tugged at the pale pink straining buds and then, emitting a groan of surrender, he lowered his head and hungrily enveloped them in his mouth. It felt so good to Chrissie that she gasped and clutched at his luxuriant black hair. Her whole body was coming alive and singing and the blaze he was awakening at the heart of her was burning fever bright, her lower limbs moving restively, her thighs pressing together on the hollow ache he had roused. At that moment, she had never wanted anything more than she wanted his touch and she shifted her hips, edgy and needy, before her hands began to explore him, reacquainting herself with the corrugated flatness of his abdomen before stroking down to the long, thick prominence of his erection. He was smooth as silk, hard as steel.

'Stop. I'm too excited,' Jaul warned her raggedly. 'I want to come inside you.'

'Rush,' she told him again with greater urgency, twitching her hips upwards again while grazing her fingertips teasingly over the crown of his manhood.

'You don't tell me what to do in bed,' Jaul husked.

With a lightness of heart she hadn't experienced in a very long time, Chrissie laughed out loud. 'Lie back for me for just five minutes…and I promise you, you'll do whatever I want,' she whispered provocatively.

'Not tonight.'

His hand skimmed down over her tummy and between her slender thighs. A fingertip traced the wet, silky entrance to her body and her hips jackknifed, hunger rising so swiftly and powerfully that she almost cried out.

Jaul shifted down the bed and found her damp, heated core with his tongue and this time she did cry out, her breathing fractured, her throat convulsing as the incredible pleasure blasted her into another reality where blissful ripples of sensation engulfed her, locking out absolutely everything else. Her head twisted back and forth on the pillow, perspiration breaking on her skin, her nipples peaking as his fingers delved deep into her and his talented tongue tormented her into ecstasy. The climax hit her like a speeding train, snatching her up and throwing her high.

'That was…amazing,' Chrissie mumbled weakly, the words slurring as he lifted her up and flipped her over to settle her down on her knees.

'I aim to please, *habibti*.'

Having positioned her on the bed to his satisfaction, Jaul drove into her tight, wet channel and the sensation of being stretched to the utmost was so irresistibly seductive that a strangled sob of encouragement escaped Chrissie. She was out of control and revelling in the awareness. A frenzy of need gripped her as he surged and ebbed inside her sensitive sheath. With every plunging entrance, her heart slammed against her ribcage and her excitement climbed another notch. He ground his body into hers and then ratcheted up the tempo with long, smooth, deep thrusts until she was literally sobbing out loud with tormented pleasure. Her spine arching, she pushed back against him, guided by an impatient frantic need she could not withstand. As that reached a peak, she went careening over the crest into an orgasm that flooded her with joy, satisfaction and warmth and listened to Jaul groan out loud in completion.

'Now *that* was truly worthy of the word *amazing*,' Jaul rasped as he turned her back over and dragged her back into the hot, damp embrace of his lean, powerful body.

He had both arms anchored round her, imprisoning her as though at any moment she might make a break for freedom. But Chrissie was exactly where she wanted to be. Strong emotions were still churning round inside her. Jaul had said that hoping was not a sin and here she was caught up in hoping too, she acknowledged ruefully. For the first time she understood herself: she still loved Jaul and in admitting that she was shedding the heavy burden of past memories and disillusionment to focus on the new start he had promised.

'So…er…you mentioned another wedding,' she reminded him gently.

'If you think you could bear it,' Jaul murmured cautiously, tensing as she buried her head below his chin, wondering whether she was driven by affection or avoidance.

'I think I could, particularly if it was more like the dream wedding I never got,' she confided softly.

'The dream wedding?' he prompted blankly.

'Because you didn't want us to attract too much attention I wore a plain black dress at the embassy do,' she reminded him. 'This time around I'd like a proper wedding gown…and, oh, yes, I want my sister to come over for it.'

'That could all be arranged. Western wedding gowns are very popular here.'

'Seriously?' Chrissie looked up at him with surprised turquoise eyes.

The sudden charismatic grin Chrissie had almost

forgotten flashed across his lean dark features. 'Seriously…but it will have to be a rush job. My advisers are hoping we can stage this the day after tomorrow—'

'The day after tomorrow?' she yelped in disbelief, pulling free of him to scramble out of bed naked. 'I need to phone Lizzie and warn her!'

Pleasantly surprised at the ease with which she had given her agreement, Jaul rose at a more leisurely pace. He laughed as he listened to Chrissie chattering to her sister on the phone line in the next room and even paused for thirty seconds to appreciate the picture his wife made standing there stark naked, her slender, graceful figure gleaming porcelain pale and pink in the sunlit room. Concerned that one of the staff might enter without offering sufficient warning, he fetched a towelling robe from the bathroom and held it out while Chrissie dug her arms into it with a lingering smile in her eyes that held his attention like a magnet. He strode back into the bedroom and dug his mobile phone out of his jacket to call Yusuf.

But his father's former aide was unavailable. Yusuf's manservant informed Jaul that his employer was in the USA visiting his daughter and that it would be two weeks before he was home again. Jaul grimaced, knowing it would be inappropriate to try and tackle such a controversial subject with Yusuf over the phone. He had no choice but to await the older man's return. And while he waited, more and more questions and inconsistencies would pile up in the back of his mind. Even worse, he acknowledged with sudden grim awareness, if Chrissie proved to be telling the truth without exaggeration on all counts, *he* would suddenly be the guilty party, who had virtually destroyed her life, and how could he ever live with that conclusion?

Chrissie put the phone down and breathed in deep, astonished to recognise that she had been gabbling to her sister like an overexcited teenager. As she asked herself what had come over her, she lodged by the window, which was bounded by a stone balcony and a glorious view of the trees flourishing in the garden below. Was she a total idiot? she was suddenly demanding of herself. She was still in love with Jaul and she wanted to give their marriage the best possible chance to thrive that she could...*but*.

And it was a very large 'but'; she had to be realistic and stop behaving like a dizzy adolescent. She needed to view their situation as it was and not wrap it up in fancy trappings, for the surest way to a failed marriage would be setting out with too high expectations only to be rewarded with a slow, steady process of disenchantment.

Jaul wasn't in love with her. Sexual chemistry wasn't love even though the powerful attraction that had first drawn them together was still red hot. Other facts spoke too loud to be ignored, however, she reflected unhappily. Jaul had come to London to see her in the first place because he'd wanted a divorce and he had only changed his mind about that *after* he'd realised that he was a father.

He only wanted to stay married to Chrissie now because she was the mother of his children and Tarif was the heir to his throne. Love and affection had nothing to do with that decision. Jaul was prepared to behave as a husband and father, not only to meet the conservative expectations of his people, but also to provide the twins with a stable and respectable home background. It was a praiseworthy motivation but it did not mean that Jaul was *happy* about embracing Chrissie as his wife and queen or that he would willingly have selected her for that role now.

After all, what choice had Jaul had? His passionate temperament was uniquely misleading. He was a wildly passionate male but, at heart, he was ruled by cool intellect and practicality. The marriage he had chosen to put behind him and dismiss had come back to haunt him in the worst way and now he was trapped with a wife he couldn't divorce without shocking and disappointing his people. Fate could well be forcing him to make the best of a bad situation. Her skin turned clammy while she pondered that humiliating theory but she knew that it would be stupid to ignore that wounding analysis of their marriage and even stupider to assume that sharing Jaul's bed meant anything more to him than the casual and convenient slaking of sexual need. Sobered by those reflections, Chrissie tightened the sash on the oversized robe and went back into the bedroom, relieved to appreciate that there were two en suites attached to it. Just at that moment she needed her own space and peace in which to rebuild her poise. Home truths, she thought reluctantly, were necessary to keep her feet on the ground but, my goodness, they could *hurt…*

CHAPTER NINE

WITH LIZZIE BY her side, Chrissie crossed the entrance hall of the British Embassy in Marwan City with her pale head held high, her hair swept up and ornamented only with a short veil and her perilously high sparkly shoes tap-tapping on the tiles.

Her dress was such a neat fit that she could barely breathe in it but she felt like ten million dollars in the exquisite dress with its shimmering embroidered fabric glistening even in the dulled light. She was a stock size...*just*, and Zaliha had discovered that several exclusive designers were willing to fly in a selection of dresses and accessories for a queen's approval. The gown hugged her arms and her upper body, nipping in at the waist before flaring out with the fluidity of the most expensive silk.

'You look spectacular,' her sister whispered with fierce pride. 'And I'm so pleased that Jaul is making such an effort to give your marriage a firmer footing in the present.'

If anything, Chrissie's smile dimmed as she had not allowed it to dim during the lengthy photographic session that had preceded her departure from the royal palace. Lizzie had not recognised that Chrissie was ful-

filling a more public than private role in agreeing to the
renewing of her wedding vows. Chrissie, conversely,
was hugely aware that a visible wedding was very much
what the people of Marwan wanted to see and rejoice
in. The first half of the day would celebrate her British
identity with the blessing at the embassy followed by
a formal wedding breakfast back at the palace. But afternoon would find Chrissie being prepared for a traditional Marwani wedding, which would be staged at the
palace at dusk and followed by a big party.

Jaul broke off his conversation with his brother-in-
law, Cesare, to focus on his bride's entrance with dark
eyes that swiftly turned to scorching gold. She was
so beautiful in that gloriously feminine gown. For the
first time he appreciated what the hole-and-corner wedding he had insisted on in London two years earlier
had cost her. That had been no dream day for a starry-
eyed bride, he conceded remorsefully. He had wanted
to present his father with a fait accompli but marrying
Chrissie in the bright spotlight of paparazzi publicity
would only have made his father more bitter and hostile.
In the end, though, his attempt not to rebel too publicly
against his father's edicts had only exacerbated the situation and had ensured that their marriage remained a
dangerous secret.

As the embassy chaplain approached her, Chrissie could barely drag her eyes from Jaul's strikingly
handsome dark features. His lean, powerful physique
sheathed in a light grey morning suit, Jaul was drop-
dead gorgeous, but Chrissie had been even more taken
with him when she had seen him wearing jeans at dawn
to get down on the floor of the nursery and play with
Tarif and Soraya before he began his working day. The

twins chattered with excitement when their father appeared now, associating his frequent visits with the kind of fun rough-and-tumble games they adored. Watching Jaul play with their children warmed the cold spot deep inside Chrissie, which repeatedly sought to warn her that if she wasn't careful she would get her heart broken again.

Jaul reached for her hand as the chaplain began to speak and Chrissie suppressed the treacherous swell of her insecurity. For a few seconds indeed, she was lost in the memory of their wedding day two years previously and of the joyful sense of security she had experienced as that ring went on her finger, a security that had proved to be sadly short-lived. Her rings were back where they belonged now because she had reclaimed them from Cesare's safe.

Chrissie smiled, reminding herself that they were making a fresh start at being together and that, so far, Jaul was doing absolutely everything right. She didn't *need* his love and devotion, she told herself impatiently. She would focus her energies on becoming the very best mother and Queen she could be, not on chasing soap-bubble dreams of romance. He had been her first love, for goodness' sake, and they had only been students. That time couldn't be reclaimed or relived and, anyway, would she even *want* to go back there? Back to the silly rows they had once had, rows redolent of their immaturity and inability to compromise?

One thing she did appreciate was that Jaul had changed. She wondered if what he had endured in the wake of the accident had made that change in him because he was considerably more tolerant and less domineering than she remembered him being.

More cameras flashed as Jaul escorted her out of the function room. In the limousine on the way back to the palace, he flashed her a charismatic smile and lifted a lean brown hand to acknowledge the crowds lining the side of the road. 'One down, only one more to go. We will feel very much married by the end of this day.'

Her turquoise eyes brightened with amusement. 'Yes...'

'Tonight we'll be travelling into the desert for a few days. I have to meet with the tribal sheikhs and it's the perfect opportunity to introduce you to their families. While we are becoming an increasingly urban society, there is not a family in the country that does not have a connection by birth or marriage to one of the tribes. Their support is influential,' he told her quietly. 'Zaliha will travel with us as an interpreter for your benefit.'

'Of course. I'll have to get lessons in Arabic.'

'It wouldn't be of much use to you in the desert. The tribes speak an ancient dialect,' Jaul told her ruefully and reached for her hand, disconcerting her. 'I really do appreciate your can-do attitude to all of this.'

'I'll do whatever I have to do to be a good queen,' Chrissie assured him, lifting her chin. 'I'm not planning to embarrass you or the children either now or in the future.'

His luxuriant black lashes lowered over a brightly assessing gleam of gold. 'A commendable goal but I have a rather more personal outlook.'

Chrissie tugged her fingers free lightly. 'Have you really?' she dared before she could bite back that cynical challenge. 'I doubt very much that you see our marriage in personal terms. How could you? The ceremonies today are the ultimate publicity blitz calculated to please your subjects.'

'What we appear to feel in public can continue in private. It doesn't have to be fake,' Jaul countered smoothly.

'Let's keep it simple, Jaul. We'll both do our best in our respective roles and see how it goes,' she suggested lightly.

'As you wish.' Jaul wondered what had happened to the outspoken and passionate young woman he had married. That Chrissie would never have settled for such prosaic goals. No, indeed she would have demanded his love and attention and shouted loudly if she failed to receive her due. Was the change in her the result of his apparent desertion and the struggles of single parenthood? Ultimately was he to blame? The thought appalled him.

Back at the palace a European-style meal was served. Tarif and Soraya joined the table in their high chairs and ate at speed before demanding the freedom of the floor, whereupon they made complete nuisances of themselves crawling below the table and tugging at shoelaces and trouser legs. Highly amused, Jaul hauled Tarif out from below the tablecloth and returned him to his nanny. Soraya was curled up sleepily on her mother's lap, forcing Chrissie to dip into her dessert with one hand. Zaliha gave her a nod when it was time for her to go off and prepare for her second wedding. Passing Soraya to the nursemaid hovering expectantly behind her chair and closely followed by Lizzie, Chrissie left the table.

Zaliha introduced Chrissie to the crowd of older women waiting in the bedroom suite, which had been set aside for the wedding preparations. Every tribe had put forward a representative to help dress the Queen. Chrissie removed her wedding gown and entered the bathroom, an old-fashioned one with a giant, sunken tiled tub that had evidently escaped Jaul's improvements. The water in the tub was awash with rose petals and some highly fragrant herbal concoction. A basin was brought to help in the washing of her hair.

'It must be done five times,' Zaliha explained in an undertone. 'Nobody knows why but it has always been done this way.'

Lizzie grinned and parked herself down on the chair provided for her. 'I'm going to enjoy every minute of watching this process,' she forecast cheerfully. 'It's so wonderfully exotic.'

Chrissie bathed and lay back while her hair was soaked in scented oil and rinsed over and over again. She emerged from the bath swathed in a big towel and climbed straight onto a massage table, where she was expertly kneaded and moisturised while at the same time an artist drew swirling, elaborate henna patterns on the backs of her hands and on her feet. The painstaking care with which every strand of her hair and every inch of her skin were anointed with some special preparation was amazingly relaxing and at one stage she dozed off for a little while, only wakening when she was forced to do so by the woman trilling in the bedroom.

'They chant for your good luck and fertility,' Zaliha explained. 'You're already a step ahead there with twins...'

While her hair was dried into a shining white-blonde sheet of silk falling down her back, make-up was applied. Zaliha passed her a turquoise silk beaded top and matching long skirt while ethnic turquoise and silver jewellery was tumbled out from a big casket onto the dressing table and picked through. A headdress of beaten silver coins was attached to her brow.

'You look like a Viking warrior princess,' Lizzie whispered teasingly. 'Jaul will love it.'

The whole regalia felt like fancy dress to Chrissie but she wore it with pride, knowing that the outfit she wore and the respect she was clearly demonstrating for Marwani traditions would please many people. Marwan was a rapidly changing society, keen to move forward into the modern technological world but afraid of losing its culture in the process. Professional photographs were taken with great care in the room next door and then she was led downstairs for the ceremony.

Jaul had been enjoying much more relaxed preparations, which consisted merely of a shower, a change of clothing and prayers with the imam before he joined the retinue of VIPs and personal staff awaiting him.

Jaul saw Chrissie the minute he entered the room. In Marwani costume, she was the very image of a perfect porcelain doll but a breathtakingly beautiful one. His body reacted more like an adolescent boy's than an adult's. Instantly he turned his head away again, blocking her out, willing back his vanquished control with the grim awareness that no woman had ever affected him the way she did. But then she was the only woman he had ever loved and nothing had ever hurt as much as the loss of her. He had closed off those emotions inside him, never to revisit them. Hadn't that been the healthy response to that much pain?

'Your wife is even more lovely in person than she is in photos, Your Majesty,' the elderly sheikh by his side remarked, shooting him out of introspection into looking at Chrissie again. 'You are a very fortunate man.'

Was it good fortune to have had her and lost her again? To have been forced to blackmail her with their children to win her back again? As his conscience bit into him Jaul thought not. He had put his children's needs first, he reminded himself doggedly, ensuring that, unlike him who had lost his mother at birth, Tarif and Soraya would grow up with their mother loving and supporting them. But what if ultimately what he offered was not enough to keep Chrissie with him? A hollow expanded inside his chest at the prospect of losing her again. The answer was simple, he acknowledged grittily. He had to make very, very sure that Chrissie *wanted* to stay with him.

Chrissie's gaze flashed round the room before arrowing back to identify Jaul. It was the first time she had seen him clad in traditional clothing. A gold-edged black cloak flowing back over his broad shoulders, Jaul wore beige linen with a pristine white buttoned undershirt, the pale colour amplifying his bronzed skin. A headdress bound with gold cord covered his black hair and mysteriously contrived to enhance the flawless cut of his spectacular bone structure, highlighting the spiky ebony lashes rimming his lustrous dark eyes and the clean, sculpted beauty of his wide, sensual lips. He looked both exotic and sleekly, darkly beautiful. She sucked in a steadying breath.

'Jaul's a bit like Cesare. It doesn't matter what you dress him in,' Lizzie whispered teasingly in her ear. 'He will always look hot.'

The wedding ceremony was formal and brief. Their hands were ritually bound together and then released again. The more light-hearted aspect of their renewal of their vows at the British Embassy was replaced by a tone of gravity as prayers were chanted. A little intimidated by the solemnity of the occasion, Chrissie turned back to face Jaul, needing reassurance. He cupped her elbow, very much aware that their every move was still under scrutiny and that any public demonstration of intimacy would be unacceptable.

'All done,' he said quietly as if she were a child who had survived having a plaster ripped off a grazed knee.

Night had fallen while they were indoors. In the palace's largest courtyard, braziers burned and colourful lights illuminated the palm trees and shrubs against the darkness. Jaul guided Chrissie to one of a pair of gilded thrones set centrally while all around them staff hurried back and forth with trays of lightly steaming food.

'I will serve you,' Jaul declared, waving away the servant eager to wait on them with a determined hand and approaching a laden table to lift a plate.

He was deep in thought. The wedding staged here in the home of his ancestors had touched him deeply. Chrissie was his wife and it was his duty to protect her, a duty he had failed in when he had first married her. While the accident had not been his fault and he could not have avoided it, he knew he had let her down. A man who took on the responsibility of a wife should always make provision for his wife's safety and security in the event of a tragedy, he reasoned guiltily. He had been young and irresponsible and thoughtless and she had paid the price for his arrogance. But he would ensure that she had no further cause to regret their marriage.

Chrissie was painfully aware of their guests watching as Jaul served her with food.

'In seeing to your needs before his own, the King shows you great honour,' Zaliha explained as a maid served them with glasses of juice.

The music began. Dancers put on an exhibition of acrobatic athleticism. Poetry was recited. Good wishes were tendered. A comedian performed a skit but, even with Jaul's translation, Chrissie didn't get the jokes. Cameras gleamed and whirred in the bright lights, quietly recording everything. As the night air grew chillier and gooseflesh prickled below the sleeves of Chrissie's light top, Jaul raised her up and dropped his cloak round her slim shoulders. 'It is time for us to leave.'

A convoy of four-wheel-drive vehicles awaited them outside. Chrissie climbed into the lead vehicle and watched as Jaul's bodyguards divided to fill the vehicles behind. Her brow indented. 'What happened to your old bodyguards?'

And she knew the instant she saw the pallor leach away his natural colour and his haunted eyes met hers that she need not have asked. 'The accident?' she whispered in distress, involuntarily recalling Hakim, the tall, thin, serious one and his younger brother, Altair, who had always had a smile on his face.

Jaul nodded in silent acknowledgement and regret.

Chrissie reached for his hand and squeezed it. 'I'm so sorry,' she said frankly, painfully aware that Jaul had grown up with the two brothers.

The convoy rocked noisily along a rough track into the desert. Chrissie almost tumbled off the seat several times until Jaul secured her with a protective arm. 'Have we far to go?' she asked, certain her teeth were going to rattle right out of her head with the jolts and bumps.

'We are almost there. We pitched the camp closer than usual to the palace.'

Jaul stepped out into the dense shadow cast by a huge tent while lights flared both outside it and within it. 'We will have every comfort here,' he assured her, helping her out. 'The twins will join us tomorrow. It would not have made sense to disrupt their sleep.'

The tent was in no shape or form what she had expected. For a start it was much more spacious than she had foreseen and partitioned off into different sections. The seating area was in the front portion and clearly for entertaining. The walls were hung with bead and wool work while the floor was covered with an exquisite rug and fur and silk throws and elaborate soft cushions provided an opulent accent to the seating. 'Wow...this is not camping as I imagined it.'

'We're not camping. Are you hungry?' Jaul enquired, thrusting open a door hidden by a hanging.

'No, I'm absolutely stuffed,' Chrissie admitted, following him into a bedroom even more magnificently decorated than the entertainment area. 'No stinting on comforts here...'

'But we will have to share a bathroom,' Jaul confided, casting open another concealed door to let her see the facilities. 'We will be as comfortable here as we would be at the palace. For generations my forebears have visited the desert in spring and late summer to meet with the tribal elders.'

Glancing in a mirror, Chrissie removed the coin headdress because, like the rest of the handmade antique jewellery she wore, it was very heavy. Stilling behind her in silence, Jaul undid the clasp of the necklace she wore without being asked and she caught it as it slid down and settled it on the mirror tray before pushing back her hair to detach the earrings.

'Which outfit did you prefer?' she suddenly asked him. 'The wedding gown or *this*…?'

'You looked fantastic in the white gown, like a model on a catwalk. But my heart *raced* when I saw you in this…' He smoothed long brown fingers over a slender shoulder. 'The colour reflects the shade of your eyes and your glorious curves are only hinted at, which I liked,' he confided huskily. 'Perhaps I am more like my ancestors than I ever dreamt and a hundred years ago I would have veiled you from all eyes but my own…'

Warmth flared in her cheeks. She had expected him to tell her that he preferred her in the wedding gown and he had surprised her with an honesty that she found extraordinarily sexy. 'Veiled?' she teased.

'Your beauty could blind a man,' Jaul husked, trailing his warm mouth across the pale skin of her shoulder and drawing her back against him. 'You blinded me the first moment I saw you but it was the wrong time in the wrong place and in the wrong company.'

'Yes,' she acknowledged, breasts swelling from the proximity of his hands and a very basic need to be touched as her breath feathered in her throat.

Yet his allusion to the discomfiture of their first meeting surprised her, for nothing could have been more awkward than encountering him fresh from bedding her friend and flatmate the night before. Even though her friend had swiftly moved on to another man and indeed moved in with him, that unhappy connection had ensured Chrissie resisted Jaul's advances.

His lips caressed her throat as he drew her down on the bed and as a shiver of almost painful sexual awareness travelled through her she blinked as he lifted her hand, splayed her fingers and smoothly threaded a ring onto her wedding finger.

'What's this?' she gasped, scanning the band of incredibly glittery gems now set next to her wedding ring. *'Pink?'*

'Pink diamonds. A gift as flawless as you. My wedding gift.'

'I never even thought of giving you a gift!' she exclaimed with a groan of frustration.

'But you gave me Tarif and Soraya, whose worth is beyond price,' Jaul declared without hesitation. 'I can never thank you enough for our children.'

Her eyes shone luminous in the lamplight because she realised he was sincere. Her fingers shifted on the sheet beneath her hand and she frowned, glancing down to see that the bed had been sprinkled with silky pink rose petals. 'Are these supposed to be a fertility aid or something?' she asked suspiciously.

'Roses have always been revered in our climate. The Marwan press has already christened you "*Our* English Rose".'

Chrissie laughed and rolled her eyes.

'It is true. You are very beautiful.'

Encountering the lustrous glint of gold in Jaul's dark deep-set eyes, Chrissie flushed because a tiny ball of heat was suddenly igniting deep down inside her. The wild potency of his compelling sexuality made her mouth run dry and her heart pound. It had always been like that: one look from Jaul ensnared her.

Long fingers curving to her cheekbone, he melded his mouth with hot, fierce pleasure to the lush softness of hers. As he licked along the sealed seam of her lips, it was like a lightning strike with electricity snaking through every fibre of Chrissie's body. Something clenched low in her pelvis, an ache stirring wanton warmth and dampness between her thighs.

'Jaul…' she whispered shakily between reddened lips.

'Very beautiful…and finally mine,' Jaul growled, peeling off his headdress and hauling her onto his lap to embark on the tiny pearl buttons running down the back of her top.

'Very much married anyway,' she mumbled, her body taking fire at the mere thought of his touch. 'That's married three times over now. There'll be no denying that.'

'I will never deny you again, *habibti*,' Jaul muttered raggedly, closing his hands round the firm swell of her unbound breasts, his fingers tugging at the straining tips before he rolled her back onto the bed. With deft ease, he tugged off her skirt and underwear and knelt down to slip off her shoes.

Chrissie watched him strip and leave everything in a messy heap. His untidiness, the result of never ever having to clear up after himself, had once infuriated her, but now it struck a familiar note that gave her lips a wry curve. His lithe, lean bronzed body was fully, unashamedly aroused. His eyes burned gold with potent hunger below languorously lowered black lashes. 'I want you so much…'

Chrissie lay across the bed feeling as wondrously seductive as Cleopatra, for the first time ever unconcerned by her nakedness. The intensity of Jaul's desire had always enthralled her. She was not perfect, she *knew* she was not perfect but Jaul had always vehemently disagreed. There had never been anyone else for her purely because only Jaul made her burn with earthy longing and only Jaul could look at her as though she were a goddess come to earth in human flesh. He slid down beside her, his stunning eyes all hot intensity as he claimed her mouth again with devouring hunger. She shifted fluidly under him, her thighs sliding apart, her legs curving up round his hips to bring the most needy part of her into line with his arousal.

'You're trying to hurry me again,' Jaul censured. 'This is a special night.'

'Every night with you is special,' Chrissie broke in, tilting up to him, inviting him into her with every weapon in her feminine armoury.

He pulled back from her briefly to reach for a condom and returned to stroke the heated damp flesh between her thighs, teasing her in ways that made her writhe and jerk with a readiness she couldn't conceal. When he finally thrust into her, she expelled her breath in a joyous hiss of sensual shock and pleasure and flung her head back. *'Yes!'* she gasped.

Jaul withdrew and glided into her again and her inner muscles clenched tight around him. With his every carnal thrust, excitement leapt higher, perspiration beading on her skin as her heart hammered. He pushed her back against the pillows, lifting her legs over his shoulders to gain better access to her willing body.

'You're a total minx, you scramble my wits,' he told her raggedly, his control breaking as she lifted her hips to deepen his penetration and his pace quickening to a more forceful rhythm.

And then there was nothing but the passion and the wild, crazy excitement he induced until she felt

as though she were about to fly clean out of her skin.
Molten heat consumed her as he pounded into her with
fierce hunger and when the finish came it was spectacular for both of them and a blaze of ecstasy that was
overwhelming.

Chrissie lay with her cheek pressed up against Jaul's
shoulder. 'I have to learn to trust you again,' she mused,
speaking her thoughts out loud because all barriers
were down. 'I know—intellectually speaking—that
you didn't *choose* to desert me but I've always had a
hard time trusting men.'

Jaul smoothed her tossed hair. 'Why?'

'Mum lived with a lot of loser men while I was growing up,' she told him ruefully. 'Either they were drunks
or gamblers or they stole her money or beat her up.'

Jaul was shocked, belatedly registering that Chrissie had always been cagey about her background and
only now was he understanding why. 'That does explain
some things about you. You were always so suspicious
of me, always expecting the worst.'

'Mum married her last partner and he was the worst
of all...' she admitted heavily.

'In what way?' Jaul prompted.

'It's sordid,' she mumbled, abruptly pulling away
from him.

Jaul hauled her back into his arms without hesitation. 'There should be nothing you can't tell me. Your
mother's mistakes are not your mistakes and I will not
judge you by them.'

Chrissie swivelled round in the circle of his arms.
'Before Mum died, my stepfather was making her work
as a prostitute,' she framed sickly. 'Men would come to
the house during the day. Lizzie doesn't know about it

because she was at secondary and she had a job after school but I was only seven and home at lunchtime. Once I went upstairs to the bathroom and I saw Mum in bed with a man and there was a huge row.'

Jaul tipped up her face, seeing the distance and defensiveness etched in her turquoise eyes. 'What happened?'

'My stepfather hit me. I was much older before I understood what was going on. After that I was locked in my room every day after school… I was very scared of my stepfather.'

'I am so very sorry you had to go through that,' Jaul breathed in a raw, driven undertone, wishing he could look up the stepfather and kill him for terrorising the sensitive, innocent child Chrissie had once been. 'But it is not your disgrace to bear.'

'It's never felt like that, though,' Chrissie confided, willing to meet his beautiful eyes again, anxiously in search of any sign of revulsion in his gaze and relieved to see only concern etched there. 'Now tell me something you're ashamed of…' she invited to distract him from asking further questions.

Not checking out his father's story about her once he was fit to do so.

But Jaul didn't want to rake up that divisive past and instead presented her with another less than stellar moment. 'I lost my virginity with a very high-class hooker in Dubai,' he told her grimly. 'Believe me, I was of an age where it was past time I found out what sex was like.'

'Why was that?' she asked curiously.

'The first real freedom I had ever had was when I went to university in the UK,' Jaul confided with a grimace. 'I had no experience whatsoever of normal life.'

Chrissie rested her head down on his shoulder and studied him with drowsy turquoise eyes of sympathy while thinking of how badly she had misunderstood him when she'd first met him and assumed he was the quintessential Arab playboy. In truth he had spent his youthful years of supposed irresponsibility in boarding school and the army with even his free time mapped out by his controlling father. If he had gone a little wild when he'd first slipped that leash, she was sure only a saint could blame him for it.

It dismayed her to appreciate how little they had actually known about each other when they had first married, but it soothed her that she understood him better now and could accept that in possession of his faculties and the true facts he would never have abandoned her.

Bandar greeted Jaul over his morning coffee by the fire the following morning.

His aide gave him a list of the day's events and passed on urgent messages before pausing to extend an envelope. 'This arrived in the diplomatic bag yesterday. It's from Yusuf and apparently it's personal and confidential.' Bandar raised his brows at that surprising label being applied to any item sent by as aloof a personality as his former boss.

Jaul stiffened and lost colour before grasping the envelope. As soon as he was alone, he tore it open. Somewhere in the depths of the tent he could hear Chrissie singing tunelessly in the shower but, for once, he failed to smile. He was reading what his father's former adviser had to say and in the short note of fervent apology one sentence stood out clearer than any other.

Bearing in mind my actions two years ago, it would have been an offence for me to enter the same room as your queen and offer my best wishes on the occasion of your wedding.

And there it was in a handful of words: what Jaul had most feared. It was confirmation of everything Chrissie had told him because it was obvious that Yusuf had felt too ashamed of his treatment of Chrissie in the past to attend their wedding. That confirmation struck Jaul like a body blow. His stomach lurched and he sprang to his feet, too unsettled to sit still. Evidently, everything Chrissie had told him was the truth. She *had* been thrown out of his Oxford apartment and humiliated. She *had* gone to the Marwani Embassy in London to enquire about her missing husband, only for those visits to be mocked and hushed up. She had *not* accepted money from his father.

Jaul had nourished a secret hope that Chrissie could be exaggerating her experiences after his disappearance, that perhaps what she had endured was not quite as traumatic as she had made it sound, but Yusuf's reaction to Chrissie's reappearance in Jaul's life as his queen was uniquely revealing. Jaul still wanted to hear the details of Yusuf's dealings with his wife on King Lut's behalf but he would wait until the older man returned to Marwan to receive them. After all, he already knew the most crucial facts, he reminded himself heavily. His wife had told him how she had suffered and he had doubted her every word, had literally prayed that her lively imagination had encouraged her to embellish her story. And wasn't this his due reward for his lack of faith in his wife and his all-consuming loyalty to his father's memory? What had happened to his loyalty to the woman he had married?

Self-evidently, his father had lied to him shamelessly over and over again. Lut clearly hadn't cared what he'd had to say or do to destroy his son's marriage. Jaul was appalled that the man he had respected and cared for could have gone to such brutally selfish lengths to deprive his son of the woman he loved.

As the sun began to climb higher in the sky, driving off the early morning chill, Jaul paced the sand, oblivious to the anxious watch of his guards. He could not escape certain devastating conclusions: he had virtually wrecked Chrissie's life and, worst of all, he had not just done it once, he had done it *twice*. The first time he had married her and left her pregnant and without support and the second time he had blackmailed her into moving to Marwan and giving their marriage a second chance. How did any man come back from such grievous mistakes? What right did he have to try and hold onto a woman he knew he didn't deserve?

While being angry and hostile at the outset, Chrissie had come round sufficiently to offer him a measure of forgiveness and understanding. But she didn't owe him either, did she? He had done nothing to earn her forgiveness. An honourable man would let her go free, Jaul reckoned, perspiration dampening his lean dark features in the heat of the sun. An honourable man would instantly own up to his mistakes and give her the freedom to make a choice about whether she wanted to stay or go…

It was the most humiliating moment to discover that he was evidently *not* an honourable man, for the prospect of facing life without Chrissie and the twins by his side was not one that Jaul could bring himself to even contemplate.

He had screwed up, he had screwed up so badly, he reasoned fiercely, that he could only do better in the future. But the shame of his misjudgement felt like a giant rock lodged in his chest. He watched Chrissie curl up on a seat in the shade while fruit and rolls were brought to her for breakfast. Her shining hair was loose round her lovely face and she wore not a scrap of make-up, her slender body fetchingly clad in khaki capris and a plain white tee. She was his wife…but for how much longer? Stress locked tight every muscle in his lithe, powerful body.

CHAPTER TEN

'WHAT HAPPENED TO that horse you idolised?' Jaul asked lazily.

'Hero's in a sanctuary close to the farm where I used to live with Dad,' Chrissie told him as they rode back to the oasis encampment with the sun slowly rising to chase the coolness from the sky. Her eyes were wide and bright, appreciative of the surprising and colourful beauty of the barren landscape at dawn. 'I'm afraid I haven't seen him in months. While I was working and looking after the twins, it was just impossible to get up there for a visit but maybe next time we're in London I could make a special trip to see him.'

'Why's your horse in a sanctuary?' Jaul pressed with obvious incomprehension.

'Because, Mr Spoilt-Rotten-Rich, when my father had to vacate the farm tenancy I no longer had any-where to house Hero and no money to pay for his up-keep either. Then, luckily for me, we sold the island to Cesare and I gave the sanctuary an endowment to give Hero a home for life,' Chrissie explained without heat as she gently stroked the neck of the beautiful Arabian mare she was riding. 'He's safe, well-looked-after and happy. It was the best I could do for him.'

Their time in the desert was almost over, Chrissie reflected, for they were travelling back to the palace as soon as they returned to the camp. The palace stables were packed with wonderful horse flesh and Jaul had had his stallion and her gorgeous high-stepping mare brought out for their use. Every day they had gone riding at dawn and at dusk when the desert heat was at its coolest. She had adored those quiet times with Jaul and the knowledge that their mutual love of horses and fresh-air activity was something they could share. But although Jaul had been endlessly attentive and reassuring she could not escape the suspicion that something was amiss with him.

While Jaul had endured long meetings with the tribal sheikhs, who had arrived every morning to speak with him and stayed throughout the day, Chrissie had spent the time with their wives and families. She enjoyed meeting people and learning about their lives and with Zaliha to translate she had held story-telling sessions with the children and all formality had been abandoned while she entertained them. Jaul had called those sessions an 'unqualified success' and had complimented her on her easy manner with his people. He had even asked her to consider working with the professionals on a nursery education development programme for Marwan, pointing out this was her area of expertise. His request had filled her with pride and pleasure, yet in spite of his praise and satisfaction she remained convinced that there was something wrong between them.

There was a distance, a reserve in Jaul that had not been there before, and he had not made love to her since their wedding night. Of course, he had been forced to sit up late with his visitors, she acknowledged ruefully.

He had come to bed in the early hours and had still risen at the crack of dawn as he always did. But since that first night, he hadn't touched her at all, indeed had suddenly become very restrained in his behaviour in a way that was totally unfamiliar and confusing to Chrissie because Jaul was such a naturally physical person. Last night, for instance, she had shifted over to his side of the bed and he had lain there as rigid as an icicle being threatened by the heat of a fire. Chrissie had intended to make encouraging moves herself but the polite goodnight he had murmured had made her pull back from that idea.

Maybe, she thought anxiously, now that she was available all the time, as it were, she didn't have quite the same appeal. Or more probably, common sense suggested gently, he was simply exhausted by early starts, late nights and the need for constant courteous diplomacy while he worked with the different factions involved in the talks that were lasting, on average, eighteen hours a day. The very last thing she should be doing with Jaul, she told herself urgently, was allowing her imagination or her insecurities to conjure up seeming problems in what was probably perfectly ordinary behaviour. Their marriage was working, wasn't it? She thought it was working but the renewed closeness she had fancied she saw during their second wedding night seemed to have evaporated again.

When they arrived back at the palace, Bandar greeted them in the entrance porch to speak urgently to Jaul. Jaul pokered up and a flush mantled his exotic cheekbones, his response to his aide clipped and cool in tone.

'What's happened?' Chrissie asked worriedly.

A tiny muscle pulled tight at the corner of Jaul's unsmiling mouth. 'My grandmother has arrived in Marwan and has asked to see me. She's staying at an hotel in the city.'

'My goodness, she must be quite an age now,' Chrissie remarked.

'I understand that she is travelling with her daughter, Rose. Obviously at some stage she remarried...my grandfather did not,' Jaul could not resist reminding her.

'I suppose, taking into account how he and your father felt about her, it would be an awkward and uncomfortable meeting for you *but*—'

Jaul froze and fell still.' I have no intention of agreeing to a meeting with the ladies. I have instructed Bandar to send my apologies and an appropriate gift.'

Chrissie closed a dismayed hand over his arm and tugged him into one of the many cluttered reception rooms off the ground-floor hall of the palace. 'You *can't* mean that?'

Jaul frowned down at her, his stunning bone structure rigid. 'Please try to understand, Chrissie. I have never heard any good of Lady Sophie, only that she is a terrible troublemaker and I have quite enough to deal with at the moment without encouraging that sort of personality into my life.'

Chrissie was disconcerted by the force and strength of his comprehensive rejection of his grandmother and his aunt and had to resist an urge to risk changing the subject by asking him what else he was struggling to deal with that was so onerous that he could not spare an elderly woman a fifteen-minute hearing even when she had come so far to see him.

'You have to change your mind about this, Jaul.'

'Although I have every respect for your opinion, I

will stand firm on this,' Jaul grated, temper licking along the edges of his roughened voice. 'This is not your business.'

'Lady Sophie is the twins' great-grandmother and that makes her my business as well.'

Jaul shot her an impatient glittering golden glance and compressed his wide, shapely mouth as he took an impatient step closer to the door. 'I refuse to discuss this any further. I have told you how I feel *and* why.'

'I'll go and see her in your stead.'

Jaul swung back lightning fast from the exit he had been making. 'No, you will not. I forbid it.'

'You forbid it?' Chrissie repeated in an almost whispered undertone, wondering when and where her husband had developed the belief that he had the right to forbid her from doing anything.

'Yes, I do,' Jaul repeated grittily and he strode off.

Forbid away, my love, Chrissie thought ruefully, *I'm afraid it won't get you anywhere because it is no longer the sixteenth century when wives blindly obeyed husbandly dictates.* As far as she was concerned, good manners alone demanded that Jaul meet with the two women when they had flown out to Marwan purely on his behalf. On the other hand she could quite understand his attitude when both his grandfather and his father had made his grandmother out to be such a horrible person. Before she could lose her nerve, however, she was determined to do what she believed was right and she asked Zaliha to track down Bandar and discover which hotel Jaul's grandmother was staying in.

A couple of hours later, a well-dressed middle-aged woman introduced herself as Rose to Chrissie at the door of the hotel suite and thanked her warmly for coming in Jaul's place. 'As I said when you phoned, my mother is becoming increasingly frail and your willingness to meet her lifted her spirits.'

'But I don't know if I can do anything to break the family stalemate,' Chrissie warned the older woman ruefully.

'When my mother read about your marriage to Jaul in the newspaper, there was no stopping her,' Rose confided. 'She was convinced that her grandson's marriage to a British woman would make a difference to her grandson's attitude.'

A tiny old lady with a fluff of white hair and faded blue eyes sat in a high-backed armchair with a cane clasped between her gnarled hands. 'I'm Sophie, your husband's grandmother,' she said simply.

Chrissie stretched out her hand. 'I'm Chrissie.'

'How much have you been told about me?'

'The barest facts,' Chrissie admitted. 'Perhaps I should share my experience with Jaul's family with you.'

Tea was served while Chrissie confided her own story, feeling that it was better to be honest and admit the difficulties she had had with Sophie's late son, Lut.

At the end of Chrissie's account, Sophie sighed. 'It's a sad thing to accept that even had I got to know my son as an adult I don't think I would've liked him. Your husband's grandfather Tarif twisted Lut against me. There was never any hope of my son listening to my side of the story. Indeed Lut accused me of being a liar but I am *not* a liar. I married Tarif when I was nineteen.'

'You were only a teenager?' Chrissie gasped, suddenly comprehending the outlandish décor of the London mansion. It had been furnished by a teenager working with an unlimited budget.

The old lady smiled. 'Yes, but I considered myself to be very mature. What teenager does not? My family was very much against the marriage but I was head over heels in love and Tarif seemed so westernised and liberal. He swore that I would be his only wife and I believed that I had nothing else to worry about. Unfortunately, excellent English and European dress aren't a sufficient guide to a man's character.'

Chrissie simply listened.

'I was already pregnant by the time we returned from our honeymoon to Marwan.' Lady Sophie paused, her thoughts clearly back in the distant past. 'That's when everything changed. My husband suddenly became unavailable and we no longer shared a bedroom...'

'Had you had an argument?'

'No. I found out that my husband had a harem full of concubines.'

Chrissie's eyes flew wide in shock. *'Concubines?'*

'Tarif saw no reason why he should give up the lifestyle of his ancestors,' the old lady told her quietly. 'He could not understand why I could not accept his having other women because I was his wife and his queen and soon to deliver the royal heir. He considered my status the greatest honour and believed I should be content with it.'

'Good grief,' Chrissie mumbled with stricken sympathy, barely able to imagine the distress that nineteen-year-old girl must have endured when she found herself living alone and unsupported in such a situation. 'What did you do?'

'I begged him to give his other women up and he refused. He was a very stubborn man. For months we shared the same wing of the palace while living as strangers. I gave birth to Lut. Afterwards, Tarif urged me to accept him as he was. He argued that it was enough of a sacrifice that he had promised not to take another wife.' Jaul's grandmother pursed her lips. 'Naturally I said no. A few weeks later my father died very suddenly and I flew home for the funeral. Tarif refused to let me take Lut with me. While I was away he phoned me and told me not to return to Marwan unless I had changed my mind about what I was willing to live with.'

'Obviously you never had a choice,' Chrissie commented quietly. 'That was cruel.'

'When I wouldn't give way and return to Marwan on his terms, Tarif refused to let me see my son. I didn't see Lut again until he was in his twenties and although he let me tell him my story, he wouldn't accept it. Lut was an enormous prude. The very word *concubine* set him off in a rage and he harangued me, accusing me of telling foul lies to besmirch his father's memory.'

Chrissie sighed. 'I'll discuss this with Jaul. He's not remotely like his father.'

'Are you absolutely sure of that?' Lady Sophie prompted with a worried look on her face. 'I can tell you that in terms of looks, Jaul is the living image of his grandfather and such sensitive issues as concubines are not discussed here where the King is omnipotent.'

Chrissie thanked her hostess for the tea before she departed with her thoughts in turmoil. She was convinced by the old lady's story, she acknowledged uneasily. But how did she know for sure that there were no longer concubines in the vastness of the royal palace complex? Was it even possible that she herself should need to fear such a situation? Could Jaul have honed his superb talents in the bedroom with nameless women in some hidden, never-discussed harem? Could it even provide an explanation for his marked lack of interest in making love to his wife? Or was she being insane in nourishing such a fantastic suspicion?

The question that she was determined not to ask Jaul grew and grew on the drive back to the palace. How likely was it that Jaul kept concubines like his not so very westernised grandfather? In this day and age not very likely, her rational mind assured her as she mounted the stairs to their private wing and went straight to see the twins.

Thirty minutes later, she glanced up to see Jaul lodged in the doorway, stunning eyes dark as coal and steady in the taut lines of his lean, darkly handsome face as he studied her.

'You know where I've been.' Chrissie sighed as she scrambled upright to follow Jaul into the room next door.

'You went against my wishes. Naturally I am annoyed,' Jaul spelled out flatly, his perfect white teeth grinding together with the strain of suppressing his temper as he stared down at her.

Of course he didn't want his wife connecting with a bitter old woman he had heard described as a fantasist! Of course he didn't want his grandmother trying to poison Chrissie with her undying hatred of his family! Chrissie already had all too many reasons to think badly of him. Furthermore, with his long-awaited meeting with Yusuf due to take place that very afternoon, Jaul was ready to confront the last of the devils that had haunted him since his receipt of Yusuf's note of apology, but quite understandably on edge at the prospect. Only when he was convinced that he knew *everything* could he talk honestly to Chrissie. There would be no more secrets between them, no unanswered questions or doubts. His wife deserved that from him at the very least.

'I visited Sophie because I hoped that in some way… goodness knows how…I might be able to heal the family rift,' Chrissie told him ruefully.

'A compassionate thought,' Jaul conceded grittily. 'What did she tell you about my family?'

Chrissie breathed in deep, mustering her courage. 'That your grandfather had concubines while he was married to her.'

Jaul looked at her in wonderment. 'She told you… *that*? *Seriously*?'

Chagrined by his patent disbelief, Chrissie murmured quietly, 'And I believed her.'

Jaul threw back his broad shoulders, his anger as instant and shattering as a sudden clap of thunder on a hot, humid day. 'That's a most offensive untruth…an outrageous calumny!'

'Is it?' Chrissie almost whispered because the atmosphere was so explosive it was as if all the oxygen were being sucked into a void. 'Because, naturally, after being told that I have to ask you if *you*—'

'Don't you *dare* ask that of me!' Jaul roared back at her, shocking her into sudden silence. Outright fury had charged his lean, hard-muscled frame. His dark eyes were blazing like golden arrows aimed at a target.

Chrissie had lost colour. She hadn't even got the actual question voiced but he knew exactly what she had been about to ask him and he was outraged to a degree that went beyond anything she had ever seen in him before.

'You have just proved my father's contention that his mother was an appalling liar.'

'If that is true, possibly he inherited that talent from his mother,' Chrissie challenged without hesitation. 'Your father was no great fan of the truth himself.'

Jaul paled beneath his bronzed skin and his hands closed into tight fists, for he could not defend his late father and he would not lie in his defence either. His father had been an irredeemable liar and in that moment he could quite understand why Chrissie had refused to accept Lut's view of Lady Sophie and had preferred to make up her own mind.

'There have not been concubines in the palace for over a century,' Jaul informed her curtly. 'To suggest that that lifestyle was still in existence in the nineteen thirties is incredible, but if it makes you feel any happier I will check those facts with Yusuf this afternoon. In Marwan, he is still the acknowledged authority on the history of the royal family. Indeed, he wrote a much-admired book on the subject.'

'Don't place your faith in the belief that your grandmother is lying,' Chrissie urged ruefully, thinking that very occasionally her husband could be startlingly naive. 'The book was probably a whitewash sanctioned and proofread by your father, Jaul. I bet there's not a disrespectful, critical word in it.'

As the exact same thought had already occurred to Jaul, he swallowed hard, black lashes lowering over his lustrous golden eyes. 'You are undoubtedly right but Yusuf will tell me the truth on all counts,' he declared with assurance. 'But nothing can ever eradicate the effect of my wife actually asking me if I too have kept concubines.'

Chrissie flushed a slow, painful pink. 'I didn't ask—'

'But you were dying to ask,' Jaul cut in drily. 'Do you trust me so little still? Do you really believe that my people would accept a man leading a dissolute life on their throne? My country wants to be seen as modern and forward-thinking and our women have an increasingly strong voice in society. I must be seen to practise what I preach in public *and* in private...'

What Jaul said was common sense and Chrissie was mortified that for a few overwrought minutes after leaving his grandmother's presence she had entertained such fantastic suspicions. Even more crucially she had not missed the flash of pain in his eyes that she could even think to ask him such a question. He was furious too but thankfully not in the same way as his late father. He didn't suffer from uncontrollable rages and watched his tongue when he lost his temper but the downside of those positives was that he would be pretty much silent until he had mulled everything over in depth.

'I'm sorry!' Chrissie said loudly and abruptly as he began to turn away. 'It was stupid...but just for a moment I felt I had to know for sure,' she endeavoured to explain, struck to the heart by his condemnation but not sure she could blame him for it.

'If you appreciated how prim and proper my father was you would never have felt that need,' Jaul asserted with a wry curve of his sensual mouth. 'He waged a war against immorality in every form inside and outside the palace. He was a repressive ruler. One of my first acts was to repeal the law restricting music and dancing in public places. If it makes you feel any happier about things, I will ask Yusuf to fill me in on what he knows about my father's dealings with my grandmother.'

As Jaul left the room with the giving of that concession, Chrissie slumped down on a sofa. Maybe she shouldn't have interfered by visiting Lady Sophie, she reasoned heavily. She had waded in blindly, seeing herself as doing something good and helpful but in actuality she had hurt and offended Jaul. His self-control in the face of the provocation she had offered could only embarrass her because she had controlled neither her imagination nor her tongue. In the circumstances Jaul had been very understanding and that shamed her the most. He was never going to love a woman stupid enough to ask him if he kept concubines, was he?

Jaul spent a couple of hours talking to his father's former aide. Yusuf left, relieved to have cleared his conscience of the secrets he had kept throughout his working career. Jaul, however, was in a far less happy frame of mind. In point of fact, he was stunned, furious and bitter and as soon as the keys he had requested were brought to him he strode through the huge palace complex and down a flight of stairs in a far corner. A servant wrestled with the giant key and then Jaul waved his guards back and entered the building alone.

The sheer size of the place shook Jaul even more. He prowled through empty rooms and courtyards, studied fountains and bathing places. Everything was in very good condition and he marvelled that his father's mania for historic conservation had triumphed over the older man's desire to rewrite the past and bury the family's murkier secrets. Rage was his overriding response to what he had learned from Yusuf until the point when he focused on the great bed placed on a dais. Slowly his dark, angry eyes widened as he finally registered the tenor of the murals swirling across the walls round the bed.

Utterly disconcerted, he froze, imagining his strait-laced father's reaction to such artistic licence and something infinitely more surprising bubbled up inside Jaul without warning. Gales of incredulous laughter convulsed his lean, powerful frame and when he had recovered from his inappropriate amusement he lounged back breathless against the edge of the bed. His brilliant eyes flared to the purest gold when he pictured how Chrissie would react to the paintings.

A note was delivered to Chrissie minutes after she had emerged from a long relaxing bath. Instantly recognising Jaul's copperplate black print, she tore it open.

You are cordially invited to spend a night in the harem with your husband.

A surprised giggle fell from her lips while a warm sense of relief swelled inside her. Jaul had recovered sufficiently from his annoyance with her to make a joke. It was a joke, of course it was, and Jaul had always had a terrific sense of humour. She leafed through drawers and selected her fanciest lingerie with hot cheeks before choosing a perfectly circumspect plain blue tailored dress, which gave not the smallest hint of what she wore underneath. A night in the harem? What did that entail? Her entire skin surface heated up and she smiled dreamily, knowing exactly what she was hoping that note meant while being wryly amused by her own secret conviction that there was something different about Jaul in recent days. Didn't that note prove how mistaken she had been?

One of Jaul's guards was waiting to take her to her husband and they trudged a long way down endless corridors and down stone flights of stairs before they reached their destination. A big, ugly, ironclad door faced them. Opening it for her, the guard stood back and Chrissie entered, wondering why the man was trying not to smile. But that question was quickly answered because a spectacular scene confronted her two steps beyond the door.

Candles were burning everywhere she looked, glowing in the dark to cast leaping shadows across the soaring domed ceiling and elaborate mosaic-tiled walls and ensuring that the water droplets cascading from the fountains sparkled like diamonds. It was beautiful, incredibly beautiful, and Chrissie knew instinctively that Jaul had done it for her. Her bright eyes stung painfully and she had to blink when the man himself appeared from behind a pillar about thirty feet from her. In contrast to their highly exotic surroundings Jaul sported faded jeans and a partially unbuttoned white shirt, the pale fabric accentuating his bronzed skin and the blackness of his unruly hair. For a split second she felt as though time itself had slipped for this was Jaul as she remembered him as a student, shorn of every atom of his forbidding reserve.

'Where on earth are we?' Chrissie asked.

'In the heart of the al-Zahid family's shadiest secret,' Jaul proffered wryly. 'The harem that even I didn't know still existed until this evening. Of course, I knew there would have been one at some stage but, taking into account my father's delicate sensibilities, I assumed it was long gone.'

Chrissie gazed past him at the giant bed. 'That looks like a bed people would throw an orgy on,' she said before she could think better of it. 'Not that I know anything about…er…orgies—'

'Look at the walls,' Jaul invited.

In the flickering shadows she saw the murals and the naked male and female figures engaged in flagrant sexual play and a hot flush lit her cheeks. 'My goodness…'

'I'm amazed that my father didn't have this place razed to the ground, but he idolised my grandfather.' Jaul sighed. 'How he retained that respectful attitude when confronted with the reality that Tarif was a man with licentious habits, I cannot begin to imagine.'

'Nor can I,' she whispered, beginning to understand why he had brought her to the harem. He had found out the truth and immediately acted with the open-minded candour she had always loved him for. When Jaul was in the wrong he never tried to cover it up or excuse himself.

'I've phoned Sophie's daughter, Rose, and apologised through her for taking so long to make an approach to my grandmother.'

'You phoned Rose…*already*?' Chrissie exclaimed.

'There were concubines here well into the last century. My grandmother *wasn't* lying,' Jaul confirmed with a sardonic twist of his lips. 'But I only learned the truth this afternoon from Yusuf. He knows all the family secrets and learning about how cruelly my grandmother was treated was only the first of several shocks I received after I questioned him.'

A frown dividing her brows, Chrissie made an instinctive move forward and rested her hand soothingly on his forearm, feeling the muscles that were pulled whipcord tight with fierce tension. 'I'm sorry, Jaul.'

As if he found her touch unbearable, Jaul shifted back a defensive step. 'For what are you sorry? That I was too much of a fool to appreciate that my father would say or do anything to *wreck* my marriage?' he framed with unleashed bitterness. 'Chrissie, I would've trusted him with my life! He was a difficult man and very controlling but in many of the ways that mattered he *was* a good father.'

Discomfited by his rejection of her sympathy, Chrissie stiffened. 'And you loved him, *of course* you did. I loved my mother when I was a child even though I had a pretty miserable childhood. Parents don't have to be perfect to be loved. But I still don't understand why your father stayed so dead set against his own mother and me when he knew your grandfather was the one at fault.'

'My father chose the easy way out. He was never going to admit the embarrassing truth. If he laid the blame of cultural differences at his mother's door, he could continue to idolise his father and believe that he was right to protect me from all Western influences.' Jaul's brilliant dark eyes veiled. 'Apparently he was afraid that I may have inherited Tarif's fatal weakness for women. I was finally able to understand why I had to rebel against him to gain the right to study in the UK.'

Chrissie was listening closely. 'You had to…*rebel*? You never told me that before.'

'I was ashamed of it. I was raised to believe that a decent son always respects a parent's greater maturity and wisdom,' Jaul admitted grudgingly. 'After the experience of a military boarding school followed by army life, I longed for the freedom to make my own choices.'

'Of course you did,' she whispered feelingly, newly aware of what a domineering old tyrant his late father had been. 'And I respect you more for having taken a stand and it's hardly surprising that you went a little wild when you first started university. I never appreciated how restricted your life had been before you came to the UK.'

Jaul studied her lovely face fixedly, the turquoise eyes soft with compassion. He was shaken that she was still trying to comfort him when he didn't deserve comfort because he had let her down worst of all. 'But that period of going wild almost cost me you,' he pointed out. 'It gave you the wrong impression.'

Tears stung her eyes and she blinked them back in desperation as she sat down on the flat tiled edge of a fountain. 'There was no way I was going to resist you for ever…the attraction was too strong.'

'I have never wanted any woman as much as I wanted you,' Jaul admitted in a raw undertone and he bent over the tray stationed on a table by a pillar to fill a glass and extend it to her. 'I have never loved any woman but you…'

At that statement, her hand shook a little as she accepted the glass, hastily sipping the cool sweetness of fruit juice. He had never loved anyone else, she was thinking, that surely had to be a point in her favour.

His lean, darkly handsome features were grim and taut with tension. In a restive, uncertain gesture he raked long, elegant fingers through his luxuriant hair, tousling it. 'I loved you yet I let you down. You were alone and pregnant and I wasn't with you. I accepted my father's lies.'

Chrissie's heart was thumping very hard. 'Jaul—what's brought all this on tonight?'

'Yusuf was with my father when he visited you in Oxford. His conscience was uneasy and he was eager to clear it,' Jaul recounted flatly. 'I was appalled when Yusuf described what happened that day. It shames me that my father could have treated my wife in such a way and that I was unable to prevent it from happening.'

The backs of her eyes were gritty with tears because she was remembering what had been one of the worst days of her life. Confronted by King Lut, she had felt alone and helpless, not to mention devastated by her father-in-law's complete rejection of her as his son's wife. 'You were in hospital,' she reminded him shakily. 'There was nothing you could have done.'

'Yusuf told me the truth.' Jaul was ashen below his dark skin, his brilliant eyes tortured as he gazed at her. 'But let us be honest here—Yusuf told me truths which I should've accepted when *you* spoke them.'

'Yes,' Chrissie cut in to confirm without hesitation. 'I have never lied to you…' A split second of silence fell before she coloured and added, 'Well, only once and I'll sort that out later.'

'I swallowed my father's lies about you and in my bitterness and hurt I learned to distrust my every memory of you. When I came back to find you last month, I should have *listened* more, thought deeper.'

'Naturally you trusted your father's word when he told you that I'd taken the money and run.'

'How was it natural?' His tone derisive in emphasis, Jaul set down her glass with a definite crack. Dark eyes flaming gold, he studied her, nostrils flaring, beautiful stubborn mouth tight at the corners with strain. 'You were my life. You were my wife. My first loyalty should always have been to you. Will you please stop trying to make excuses for my failure to support you when you *most* needed me?' he demanded hoarsely. 'I let you down in every way possible—'

'Your father did this to us. He separated us, lied to us both and hurt us both,' Chrissie responded shakily. 'Put the blame where it belongs, Jaul. You were in a coma and then you had surgery and were struggling to recuperate. You weren't in any condition to fight my corner or yours. When your father lied to you then, you were very vulnerable—'

'I'm trying to say sorry, trying to grovel but you won't let me,' Jaul muttered unevenly, his eyes suspiciously bright.

'I don't want you grovelling. I don't want your guilt—'

'This is not guilt, this is...*shame*,' he labelled roughly. 'You are my wife and I let you down and I don't want to lose you. There's nothing I won't do or say to keep you as my wife!'

Recognising his increasingly emotional frame of mind, Chrissie almost smiled. 'Oh, I think I worked that out straight after that pre-nuptial agreement was stuffed beneath my nose when I looked as though I might be ready to walk away from you,' she confided.

'It was an empty threat,' Jaul confessed grittily. 'A pre-nup has no standing as yet in a British court of law. In addition you signed it without the benefit of independent legal advice and you were very young at the time. I knew that the pre-nup wasn't worth the paper it was written on.'

It was Chrissie's turn to be taken aback. As she had listened her eyes had widened and her soft mouth had hardened. 'I should've called your bluff. But maybe I didn't fight more because I didn't want to. Has that occurred to you?'

His lush black lashes swept up and down over his frowning eyes. 'But why would you have behaved that way?'

Chrissie stiffened, reluctant to give him the words of love that were as effective as chains in binding her to both him and the twins. He knew the truth now about his father, her pride and her sense of justice finally satisfied. He knew what she had endured and he knew that she had not accepted a financial settlement in lieu of their supposedly invalid marriage. Keen to change the subject of why she was being so tolerant of his stubborn misjudgements, she said with forced lightness of tone, 'Who on earth lit all these candles?'

'Zaliha supplied the candles and the snacks. I lit them. The fountains have been kept in good working order and only had to be switched on. I couldn't allow any other female staff in here because they would have been very much shocked by the murals.'

Chrissie scanned the hundreds of candles and hid a smile, touched by the effort he had made on her behalf. 'The murals may be shocking but this place is beautiful all lit up like this.'

The beginnings of the smile that had relaxed her full pink mouth filled Jaul with a craving for the softness of her, the warmth and the strength that ran like a core of inner steel through her seemingly fragile body. He had never appreciated how strong she truly was until he'd learnt what she had had to withstand at his father's hands. His lean brown hands snapped into fists, anger stirring afresh because he had been incapable of protecting her. The guilt, which he was struggling to master, felt insurmountable.

'I should've contacted you as soon as I was mobile again,' he stated with savage regret, the hard, sculpted planes of his darkly handsome face stark with strain in the flickering light. 'But I couldn't face seeing you again knowing that I had lost you... It is hard for me to admit that but it is, at least, the truth of my feelings back then. Seeing you again, being in your presence when you were no longer mine, would have hurt too much.'

'It still mattered that much to you?' Chrissie pressed in surprise.

Jaul shot her an incredulous look. 'I loved you. I loved you with all my heart! But I lost faith in you while I lay alone in hospital.'

Pained regret slivered through Chrissie. She was furious that his father had subjected him to that ordeal of believing that she no longer cared about him. *I loved you with all my heart.* It hurt Chrissie to hear that. 'I would've been there with you if I'd known—'

'I know that now...that's what killing me!' he bit out, swinging defensively away from her, broad shoulders bunched with tension below his thin shirt.

'But it's pointless wasting all this energy on a past that's gone, done and dusted,' she declared, tilting her chin. 'We have to move on from it—'

'How can I do that when my father's lies cost us so much?' Jaul framed emotively, turning back to her. 'Once you were mine, completely, utterly mine and it is my dream that some day you will feel like that again. But, sensible and fair as I have tried to be, I still find myself thinking wholly unjust thoughts about the fact that—' His hands fisted again and he turned away again. 'No, I won't say it…such jealousy and possessiveness are wrong!'

Chrissie was frowning. 'What the heck are you talking about?' she prompted uncertainly.

'It is a topic better not discussed. What has happened has happened and we will not allow it to spoil what we do have,' Jaul declared, still restively pacing the tiled floor.

Jealousy? *Possessiveness*? Abruptly she grasped his meaning and she reddened, cheeks heating fierily. 'Are you talking about the fact that I said I was with other men while we were apart?'

His lustrous gaze narrowed. 'It's not something we need to discuss,' he told her hastily. 'You believed you were single and quite naturally…'

'Well, maybe it would've been natural but I didn't sleep with anyone else,' Chrissie told him in a rush. 'I said I did but it was a lie. I don't know how you thought I could have found the time for another man when I was pregnant most of the first year you were gone and saddled with two newborns and working the second year.'

Jaul was studying her with fixed attention. 'You… *lied*?' he queried in disbelief. 'About such an important issue?'

Chrissie winced. 'It was a weapon and I used it. It's the one and only lie I have told you. Obviously I assumed that *you*—'

Jaul stalked closer and gripped her forearms to hold

her still. '*No*. No concubines, no girlfriends, no one-night stands. Nothing...zilch.'

Her eyes opened very wide in surprise. 'But...er, why?'

'When I finally got out of that wheelchair I decided that since I had got myself in such a mess with you it would be safer to avoid another liaison and instead get married.'

The tension in Chrissie's slight shoulders relaxed and then reached full strength again because, while she was relieved he had not had any other women and his clear gaze convinced her that the once bitten, twice shy adage had worked a blinder on him, she still wanted to know who he had planned to marry. 'So, who was picked to replace me?'

Jaul flushed. 'I didn't have anyone picked but I knew my people were waiting for me to do the picking.' He brushed a gentle finger beneath her down-curved chin to raise it. 'In truth, Chrissie, I have never cared for any woman the way I care for you. I don't deserve you but you have always owned my heart—from the first moment to the last moment. I was depressed for a long time after I believed I had lost you and I was afraid of ever feeling for another woman what I felt for you.'

She lifted her hands to frame his proud cheekbones with tender fingers, emotion bright in her eyes as she gazed up into the scorching heat of his. 'And I'm afraid that I'm always going to love you,' she told him rue-fully. 'When you first came back I honestly did think I hated you but I never did get over losing you either.'

'Chrissie—'

'Shush,' she hushed him tenderly. 'Nobody else compared, nobody else can make me *feel* what you do and I do believe that you love me too.'

'I do. I love you very deeply, *habibti*.' Jaul planted a kiss against her caressing fingers, his black lashes low over golden eyes shimmering with a happiness Chrissie could not mistake. 'The day I threatened you with the pre-nup was the day I understood that I still loved you because I have never done anything so dishonest in my whole life. And I wasn't even ashamed. There was literally nothing I wouldn't do to get a second chance with you and our children.'

Chrissie wrapped her arms round his neck. 'Ruthlessness in pursuit of the right goal is acceptable.'

All her tension evaporated while he held her close and heat of a different ilk warmed at her feminine core.

'But…who is to say…what the right goal is?' Jaul quipped, running down the zip on her dress to ease it off her shoulders.

As the dress dropped to her feet, exposing the frilly silky lingerie he loved to see her in, he made a sound of appreciation low in his throat and carried her over to the orgy-sized bed to settle her down on the white linen sheet.

'My only goal,' he proffered softly, 'is to keep you as my wife and the mother of my children for ever and make you so happy that you eventually forget our separation.'

Chrissie plucked at his collar. 'I think that's a terrific motivation,' she told him sassily, her bright eyes dancing as he ripped off his shirt with more haste than cool. 'Particularly since you've been so very separate from me in bed this past week…and I haven't been at all happy.'

Jaul dealt her a troubled glance. 'I burned for you but once I received Yusuf's note...'

'What note?'

Jaul explained the note. 'And in the same moment I read it I knew I had got everything wrong with you. I couldn't afford to take anything for granted.'

His wife ran worshipping fingers idly along the rippling muscles of his abdomen. 'I thought you'd lost interest.'

'You must be joking!' Jaul exclaimed, rolling her back to come down over her, his taut lower body hard with an arousal she could feel. 'I always want you. I just knew I didn't deserve you.'

Chrissie ran an appreciative hand down over a lean, powerful thigh. 'Love makes people more forgiving and I love you an awful lot.'

His kiss was hot, hungry and wildly exciting and her heart pounded and her pulses raced. Happiness was spinning and dancing inside her like a sudden burst of golden sunshine.

'And I love you,' he confessed with a flashing grin that tugged at her heart because the twins so strongly resembled him. 'I love you more than I ever thought I could love anyone and I always will.'

Three years after that incredibly romantic reconciliation in the former harem, Chrissie watched the twins squabble over a ride-on plastic car they were playing with in a shaded courtyard. At four years old, Tarif and Soraya were lively and opinionated and in need of firm handling from both their parents. Rising, Chrissie uttered a sharp word to break up the quarrel, threatening to remove the car entirely if the children refused to share it peaceably. It was interesting to sit back down again and watch her children negotiate a compromise.

Lizzie phoned while Chrissie was savouring peppermint tea served with tiny cakes. Smoothing the barely visible bump that thickened her figure, she thought how grateful she was that her morning sickness had not lasted into her second trimester. Indeed her second pregnancy was progressing much more smoothly than her first and she put that down to the lack of stress in her current life. She chatted at length to her sister, who was due to arrive with her family and their father for a visit at the end of the week. Her family were regular visitors and distance had not driven a wedge between the sisters.

When their nanny reclaimed the twins for an early evening meal, Chrissie wandered down to the stables to visit Hero. Two years earlier, her elderly pony had arrived to take up residence in the ritziest stall in the royal block. Their reunion had been a wonderful surprise for Chrissie and she had been overwhelmed that Jaul, incredibly busy as he was, had taken the time and trouble to ensure that Hero could live out what remained of his days near his mistress in Marwan.

Having become heavily involved in the development of the nursery education programme, Chrissie had found her first year in Marwan had raced past her. Jaul's people were friendly and supportive and although she sometimes attended formal occasions with Jaul, rubbing shoulders with diplomats, foreign dignitaries and businessmen, for much of the time she was simply Jaul's wife. Family life and time to spend with the children were immensely important to both of them.

Having visited Hero, Chrissie headed back to their

private wing to shower and change. Every year they celebrated that night the barriers between them had finally dropped and they spent the night in the harem. That was where they had rediscovered their love and happiness and it was a wonderful way of remembering how they had started out and keeping faith with the promises they had exchanged.

Dusk was falling when Jaul began lighting candles and a meal was being set out below the pillars. The murals were covered by discreet curtains, ensuring that no staff member could be shocked or offended by those depictions of earthly lust and love. Jaul liked to think that love must have featured in some of the relationships that had taken place in the harem but he could not begin to imagine how his grandfather Tarif had chosen shallow physical relationships over the far deeper and more lasting bonds he could have formed with the wife who had loved him.

Jaul frowned as he thought of his grandmother, regretting that their time together had been so short. Lady Sophie had died peacefully in her sleep the year before. Prior to that, Jaul had made frequent visits to the old lady's home in London, keen to make up as best he could for the decades his late father had spent ignoring his mother's very existence.

The iron ring on the huge outer door was smartly rapped and rapped a second time when he was only halfway down the room to answer it. Jaul grinned, well acquainted with his wife's impatience.

'I haven't quite finished the candles,' he warned her.

'I'm here to help.' Chrissie looked up into his stunning dark golden eyes and could have sworn that her knees wobbled.

'No, you're pregnant. You're not allowed to do anything but put your feet up.' Jaul ushered her over to an armchair furnished with a footstool.

'Anything?' Chrissie teased as she kicked off her shoes and sat down.

'Conserve your energy for what's really important.' Glancing wickedly at the bed awaiting them with his eyes alight with amusement, Jaul knelt down beside her to reach for her hand and slide a platinum ring adorned with a glowing sapphire onto her middle finger. 'Thank you for another wonderful year.'

Chrissie studied her latest gift in consternation. 'We agreed that you weren't going to buy me any more jewellery.'

'I didn't agree. I simply chose silence over argument.'

'Sometimes you can be so devious.' Chrissie lifted a hand to brush an errant lock of blue-black hair off his brow.

'And you love it,' Jaul told her with assurance, planting a kiss on the delicate skin of her inner wrist while tracing tender fingertips over the slight swell of her pregnant tummy. 'You wear everything you feel on the surface but I hide it...except when I'm with you. I love you, *habibti*.'

'I know.' And Chrissie gloried in that sense of security, standing up to enable him to band his arms around her and claim her mouth with the hunger that neither of them ever tried to hide or suppress.

'I'm so excited about the baby,' he confided. 'I missed so much with the twins. This time around I will treasure every moment with you.'

'I bet you embarrass me by fainting or something,' Chrissie forecast, surveying him with loving intensity as the dancing light and shadow of the candles played over his lean, strong face.

But Jaul won that bet. He was fully conscious for the birth of his second son, Prince Hafiz, a healthy seven-pound baby with his mother's astonishingly blue eyes. There was a hint of his English grandfather in his bone structure. His elder brother gave him a teddy and Soraya gave him a picture she had drawn. In the first official photographs, with Hafiz's parents holding him safe in their arms, happiness and contentment radiated from the entire royal family.

* * * * *

MARRIAGE: TO CLAIM HIS TWINS

PENNY JORDAN

PROLOGUE

ALEXANDER KONSTANTINAKOS, powerful, formidable, billionaire head of an internationally renowned container shipping line originally founded by his late grandfather, stood in the middle of the elegantly luxurious drawing room of his home on the Greek Ionian island of Theopolis, his gaze riveted on the faces of the twin boys in the photograph he was holding.

Two black-haired, olive-skinned and dark-eyed identical faces looked back at him, their mother kneeling down beside them. The three of them were shabbily dressed in cheap-looking clothes.

Tall, dark-haired, with the features of two thousand years of alpha-male warriors and victors sculpted into the bones of his handsome face the same way that their determination was sculpted into his psyche, he stood in the now silent room, the accusation his sister had just made was still echoing through his head.

'They have to be your sons,' she had accused Nikos, their younger brother. 'They have our family features stamped on them, and you were at university in Manchester.'

Alexander—Sander to his family—didn't need to keep gazing at the photograph Elena had taken with her mobile phone on her way through Manchester Airport after visiting her husband's family to confirm her statement, or to memorise the boys' faces. They were already carved into his memory for all time.

'I don't know anything about them,' his younger brother Nikos denied, breaking the silence. 'They aren't mine, Sander, I promise you. Please believe me.'

'Of course they're yours,' Elena corrected their younger brother. 'Just look at those faces. Nikos is lying, Sander. Those children are of our blood.'

Sander looked at his younger sister and brother, on the verge of quarrelling just as they had always done as children. There were only two years between them, but he had been born five years before Elena and seven before Nikos, and after their grandfather's death as the only adult family member left in their lives he had naturally taken on the responsibility of acting as a father figure to them. That had often meant arbitrating between them when they argued.

This time, though, it wasn't arbitration that was called for.

Sander looked at the photograph again and then announced curtly, 'Of our blood, but not of Nikos's making. Nikos is speaking the truth. The children are not his.'

Elena stared at him.

'How can you know that?'

Sander turned towards the windows and looked beyond them to where the horizon met the deep blue of the Aegean Sea. Outwardly he might appear calm, but inside his chest his heart was thudding with fury. Inside his head images were forming, memories he had thought well buried surfacing.

'I know it because they are mine,' he answered his sister, watching as her eyes widened with the shock of his disclosure.

She wasn't the only one who was shocked, Sander acknowledged. He had been shocked himself when he had looked at her phone and immediately recognised the young woman kneeling beside the two young boys who so undeniably bore the stamp of their fathering—*his* fathering. Oddly, she looked if anything younger now than she had the night he had met her in a Manchester club favoured by young footballers, and thus the haunt of the girls who chased after them. He had been taken there by a business acquaintance, who had left him to his own devices having picked up a girl himself, urging Sander to do the same.

Sander's mouth hardened. He had buried the memory of that night as deeply as he could. A one-night stand with an alcohol-fuelled girl dressed in overly tight and incredibly revealing clothes, wearing too much make-up, who had made such a deliberate play for him. At one point she had actually caught hold of his hand, as though about to drag him to bed with her. It wasn't something any real man with any pride or self-respect could ever be proud of—not even when there were the kind of extenuating circumstances there had been that night. She had been one of a clutch of such girls, openly seeking the favours of the well-paid young footballers who favoured the place. Greedy, amoral young women, whose one desire was to find themselves a rich lover or better still a rich husband. The club, he had been told, was well known for attracting such young women.

He had had sex with her out of anger and resentment—against her for pushing him, and against his grandfather for trying to control his life. He'd been refusing to allow him a greater say in the running of the business which, in his stubborn determination not to move with the times, he had been slowly destroying. And against his parents—his father for dying, even though that had been over a decade ago, leaving him without his support, and his mother, who had married his father out of duty whilst continuing to love another man. All those things, all that anger had welled up inside him, and the result was now here in front of him.

His sons.

His.

A feeling like nothing he had ever experienced before seized hold of him. A feeling that, until it had struck him, he would have flatly denied he would ever experience. He was a modern man—a man of logic, not emotion, and certainly not the kind of emotion he was feeling right now. Gut wrenching, instinctive, tearing at him—an emotion born of a cultural inheritance that said that a man's children, especially his sons, belonged under his roof.

Those boys were his. Their place was here with him, not in England. Here they could learn what it meant to be his sons, a Konstantinakos of Theopolis, could grow into their heritage. He could father them and guide them as his sense of responsibility demanded that he should. How much damage had they already suffered through the woman who had borne them?

He had given them life without knowing it, but now that he did know he would stop at nothing to bring them home to Theopolis, where they belonged.

CHAPTER ONE

CURSING as she heard the doorbell ring, Ruby remained where she was, on her hands and knees, hoping that whoever it was would give up and go away, leaving her in peace to get on with her cleaning. However, the bell rang again, this time almost imperiously. Someone was pressing hard on the bell.

Cursing again under her breath, Ruby backed out of the downstairs cloakroom, feeling hot and sticky, and not in any mood to have her busy blitz on cleaning whilst her twin sons were at school interrupted. She got to her feet, pushing her soft blonde curls off her face as she did so, before marching towards the front door of the house she shared with two older sisters and her own twin sons. She yanked it open.

'Look, I'm—' Her sentence went unfinished, her voice suspended by shock as she stared at the man standing on the doorstep.

Shock, disbelief, fear, anger, panic, and a sharp spear of something else that she didn't recognise exploded inside her like a fireball, with such powerful intensity that her body was drained of so much energy that she was left feeling shaky and weak, trembling inwardly beneath the onslaught of emotions.

Of course he *would* be dressed immaculately, in a dark business suit worn over a crisp blue shirt, whilst she was wearing her old jeans and a baggy tee shirt. Not that it really mattered how she looked. After all, she had no reason to want to impress him—had she? And she certainly had no reason to want him to think of her as a desirable woman, groomed and dressed for his approval. She had to clench her stomach muscles against the shudder of revulsion that threatened to betray her. The face that had haunted her dreams and then her nightmares hadn't changed—or aged. If anything he looked even more devastatingly handsome and virile than she had remembered, the dark gold gaze that had mesmerised her so effectively every bit as compelling now as it had been then. Or was it because she was a woman now and not the girl she had been that she was so immediately and shockingly aware of what a very sexual man he was? Ruby didn't know, and she didn't *want* to know.

The disbelief that had frozen her into silence had turned like snow in the sun to a dangerous slush of fear and horror inside her head—and her heart? *No!* Whatever effect he had once had on her heart, Sander Konstantinakos had no power to touch it now.

But still the small betraying word, 'You,' slid from the fullness of the naturally warm-coloured lips that had caused her parents to name her Ruby, causing a look of mixed contempt and arrogance to flash from the intense gold of Sander's eyes. Eyes the colour of the king of the jungle—as befitted a man who was in effect the ruler of the Mediterranean island that was his home.

Instinctively Ruby started to close the door on him, wanting to shut out not just Sander himself but everything he represented, but he was too quick for her, taking hold of the door and forcing it open so that he could step into the hall—and then close the door behind him, enclosing them both in the small domestic space, with its smell of cleaning fluid. Strong as it was, it still wasn't strong enough to protect her from the scent of *him*. A rash of prickly sensation raised the hairs at the back of her neck and then ran down her spine. This was ridiculous. Sander meant nothing to her now, just as she had meant nothing to him that night... But she mustn't think about that. She must concentrate instead on what she was now, not what she had been then, and she must remember the promise she had made to the twins when they had been born—she would put the past behind her.

What she had never expected was that that past would seek her out, and now it had...

'What are you doing here?' she demanded, determined to wrest control of the situation from Sander. 'What do you want?'

His mouth might be aesthetically perfect, with that well-cut top lip balancing the promise of sensuality with his fuller bottom lip, but there was nothing sensual about the tight-lipped look he was giving her, and his words were as sharply cold as the air outside the Manchester hotel in which he had abandoned her that winter morning.

'I think you know the answer to that,' he said, his English as fluent and as accentless as she remembered. 'What I want, what I have come for and what I mean to have, are my sons.'

'*Your* sons?' Fiercely proud of her twin sons, and equally fiercely maternally protective of them, there was nothing he could have said which would have been more guaranteed to arouse Ruby's anger than his verbal claim on them. Angry colour burned in the smooth perfection of Ruby's normally calm face, and her blue-green eyes were fiery with the fierce passion of her emotions.

It was over six years since this man had taken her, used her and then abandoned her as casually as though she was a…a nothing. A cheap, impulsively bought garment which in the light of day he had discarded for its cheapness. Oh, yes, she knew that she had only herself to blame for what had happened to her that fatal night. *She* had been the one to flirt with him, even if that flirtation had been alcohol-induced, and no matter how she tried to excuse her behaviour it still shamed her. But not its result—not her beautiful, adorable, much loved sons. They could never shame her, and from the moment they had been born she had been determined to be a mother of whom they could be proud—a mother with whom they could feel secure, and a mother who, no matter how much she regretted the manner in which they had been conceived, would not for one minute even want to go back in time and avoid their conception. Her sons were her life. *Her* sons.

'My sons—' she began, only to be interrupted.

'*My* sons, you mean—since in my country it is the father who has the right to claim his children, not the mother.'

'My sons were not fathered by you,' Ruby continued firmly and of course untruthfully.

'Liar,' Sander countered, reaching inside his jacket to produce a photograph which he held up in front of her.

The blood left Ruby's face. The photograph had been taken at Manchester Airport, when they had all gone to see her middle sister off on her recent flight to Italy, and the resemblance of the twins to the man who had fathered them was cruelly and undeniably revealed. The two boys were cast perfectly in their father's image, right down to the unintentionally arrogant masculine air they could adopt at times, as though deep down somewhere in their genes there was an awareness of the man who had fathered them.

Watching the colour come and go in Ruby's face, Sander allowed himself to give her a triumphant look. Of *course* the boys were his. He had known it the first second he had looked at the image on his sister's mobile phone. Their mirror image resemblance to him had sent a jolt of emotion through him unlike anything he had previously experienced.

It hadn't taken the private agency he had contacted very long to trace Ruby—although Sander had frowned over comments in the report he had received from them that implied that Ruby was a devoted mother who dedicated herself to raising her sons and was unlikely to give them up willingly. But Sander had decided that Ruby's very devotion to his sons might be the best tool he could use to ensure that she gave them up to him.

'My sons' place is with me, on the island that is their home and which ultimately will be their inheritance. Under our laws they belong to me.'

'Belong? They are children, not possessions, and no court in this country would let you take them from me.'

She was beginning to panic, but she was determined not to let him see it.

'You think not? You are living in a house that belongs to your sister, on which she has a mortgage she can no longer afford to repay, you have no money of your own, no job. No training—nothing! I, on the other hand, can provide my sons with everything that you cannot—a home, a good education, a future.'

Although she was shaken by the knowledge of how thoroughly he had done his homework, had had her investigated, Ruby was still determined to hold her ground and not allow him to overwhelm her.

'Maybe so. But can you provide them with love and the knowledge that they are truly loved and wanted? Of course you can't—because you don't love them. How can you? You don't know them.'

There—let him answer *that*! But even as she made her defiant stand Ruby's heart was warning her that Sander had raised an issue that she could not ignore and would ultimately have to face. Honesty compelled her to admit it.

'I do know that one day they will want to know who fathered them and what their family history is,' she said.

It was hard for her to make that admission—just as it had been hard for her to answer the questions the boys had already asked, saying that they did have a daddy but he lived in a different country. Those words had reminded her of what she was denying her sons because of the circumstances in which she had conceived them. One day, though, their questions would be those of teenagers, not little boys, and far more searching, far more knowing.

Ruby looked away from Sander, instinctively wanting to hide her inner fears from him. The problem of telling the boys how she had come to have them lay across her heart and her conscience in an ever present heavy weight. At the moment they simply accepted that, like many of the other children they were at school with, they did not have a daddy living with them. But one day they would start to ask more questions, and she had hoped desperately that she would not have to tell them the truth until they were old enough to accept it without judging her. Now Sander had stirred up all the anxieties she had tried to put to one side. More than anything else she wanted to be a good mother, to give her boys the gift of a secure childhood filled with love; she wanted them to grow up knowing they were loved, confident and happy, without the burden of having to worry about adult relationships. For that reason she was determined never, ever to begin a relationship with anyone. A changing parade of 'uncles' and 'stepfathers' wasn't what she wanted for her boys.

But now Sander, with his demands and his questions, was forcing her to think about the future and her sons' reactions to the reality of their conception. The fact that they did not have a father who loved them.

Anger and panic swirled through her.

'Why are you doing this?' she demanded. 'The boys mean nothing to you. They are five years old, and you didn't even know that they existed until now.'

'That is true. But as for them meaning nothing to me—you are wrong. They are of my blood, and that alone means that I have a responsibility to ensure that they are brought up within their family.'

He wasn't going to tell her about that atavistic surge of emotion and connection he had felt the minute he had seen the twins' photograph. Sander still didn't really understand it himself. He only knew that it had brought him here, and that it would keep him here until she handed over to him his sons.

'It can't have been easy for you financially, bringing them up.'

Sander was offering her sympathy? Ruby was immediately suspicious. She longed to tell him that what *hadn't* been easy for her was discovering at seventeen that she was pregnant by a man who had slept with her and then left her, but somehow she managed to resist doing so.

Sander gestured round the hall.

'Even if your sister is able to keep up the mortgage payments on this house, have you thought about what would happen if either of your sisters wanted to marry and move out? At the moment you are financially dependent on their goodwill. As a caring mother, naturally you will want your sons to have the best possible education and a comfortable life. I can provide them with both, and provide you with the money to live your own life. It can't be much fun for you, tied to two small children all the time.'

She had been right to be suspicious, Ruby recognised, as the full meaning of Sander's offer hit her. Did he really expect her to *sell* her sons to him? Didn't he realise how obscene his offer was? Or did he simply not care?

His determination made her cautious in her response, her instincts warning her to be careful about any innocent admission she might make as to the financial hardship they were all currently going through, in case Sander tried to use that information against her at a later date. So, instead of reacting with the anger she felt, she said instead, 'The twins are only five. Now that they're at school I'm planning to continue my education. As for me having fun—the boys provide me with all the fun I want or need.'

'You'll forgive me if I say that I find that hard to believe, given the circumstances under which we met,' was Sander's smooth and cruel response.

'That was six years ago, and in circumstances that—' Ruby broke off. Why should she explain herself to him? The people closest to her—her sisters—knew and understood what had driven her to the reckless behaviour that had resulted in the twins' conception, and their love and support for her had never wavered. She owed Sander nothing after all—much less the revelation of her teenage vulnerabilities. 'That was then,' she corrected herself, adding firmly, 'This is now.'

The knowing look Sander was giving her made Ruby want to protest—*You're wrong. I'm not what you think. That wasn't the real me that night.* But common sense and pride made her hold back the words.

'I'm prepared to be very generous to you financially in return for you handing the twins over to me,' Sander continued. 'Very generous indeed. You're still young.'

In fact he had been surprised to discover that the night they had met she had been only seventeen. Dressed and made-up as she had been, he had assumed that she was much older. Sander frowned. He hadn't enjoyed the sharp spike of distaste he had experienced against himself at knowing he had taken such a young girl to bed. Had he known her age he would have... What? Given her a stern talking to and sent her home in a cab? Had he been in control of himself that night he would not have gone to bed with her at all, no matter what her age, but the unpalatable truth was that he had *not* been in control of himself. He had been in the grip of anger and a sense of frustration he had never experienced either before or since that night—a firestorm of savage, bitter emotion that had driven him into behaviour that, if he was honest, still irked his pride and sense of self. Other men might exhibit such behaviour, but he had always thought of himself as above that kind of thing. He had been wrong, and now the evidence of that behaviour was confronting him in the shape of the sons he had fathered. Sander believed he had a duty to ensure that they did not suffer because of that behaviour. That was what had brought him here.

And there was no way he was going to leave until he had got what he had come for.

And just that?

Ruby shook her head.

'Buy my children, you mean?'

Sander could hear the hostility in Ruby's voice as well as see it in her eyes.

'Because that *is* what you're talking about,' Ruby accused him, adding fiercely, 'And if I'd had any thought of allowing you into their lives, what you've just said would make me change my mind. There's nothing you could offer me that would make me want to risk my sons' emotional future by allowing *you* to have any kind of contact with them.'

Her words were having more of an effect on him than Sander liked to admit. A man of pride and power, used to commanding not just the obedience but also the respect and the admiration of others, he was stung by Ruby's criticism of him. He wasn't used to being refused anything by anyone—much less by a woman he remembered as an over-made-up and under-dressed little tart who had come on to him openly and obviously. Not that there was anything of that girl about her now, dressed in faded jeans and a loose top, her face free of make-up and her hair left to curl naturally of its own accord. The girl he remembered had smelled of cheap scent; the woman in front of him smelled of cleaning product. He would have to change his approach if he was to overcome her objections, Sander recognised.

Quickly changing tack, he challenged her. 'Nothing

I could offer *you*, maybe, but what about what I can offer my sons? You speak of their emotions. Have you thought, I wonder, how they are going to feel when they grow up to realise what you have denied them in refusing to let them know their father?'

'That's not fair,' Ruby objected angrily, knowing that Sander had found her most vulnerable spot where the twins were concerned.

'What is not fair, surely, is you denying my sons the opportunity to know their father and the culture that is their birthright?'

'As your bastards?' The horrible word tasted bitter, but it had to be said. 'Forced to stand in second place to your legitimate children, and no doubt be resented by your wife?'

'I have no other children, nor any wife.'

Why was her heart hammering so heavily, thudding into her chest wall? It didn't matter to her whether or not Sander was married, did it?

'I warn you now, Ruby, that I intend to have my sons with me. Whatever it takes to achieve that and by whatever means.'

Ruby's mouth went dry. Stories she had read about children being kidnapped by a parent and stolen away out of the country flooded into her mind. Sander was a very rich and a very powerful man. She had discovered that in the early days after she had met him, when she had stupidly imagined that he would come back to her and had avidly read everything she could about him, wanting to learn everything she could—until the reality of the situation had forced her to accept that the fantasy she had created of Sander marrying her and looking after her was just that: a fantasy created by her need to find someone to replace the parents she had lost and keep her safe.

It was true that Sander could give the boys far more than she could materially, and the unwelcome thought slid into her mind that there could come a day when, as Sander had cruelly predicted, the twins might actually resent her and blame her for preventing them from bene-fitting from their father's wealth and, more importantly, from knowing him. Boys needed a strong male figure in their lives they could relate to. Everyone knew that. Secretly she had been worrying about the lack of any male influence in their lives. But if at times she had been tempted to pray for a solution to that problem she had cer-tainly not envisaged that solution coming in the form of the boys' natural father. A kindly, grandfather-type figure for them was as much as she had hoped for, because after their birth she had decided that she would never take the risk of getting involved with a man who might turn out to be only a temporary presence in her sons' lives. She would rather remain celibate than risk that.

The truth, in her opinion, was that children thrived best with two parents in a stable relationship—a mother and a father, both committed to their wellbeing.

A mother and a father. More than most, she knew the damage that could be done when that stability wasn't there.

A sense of standing on the edge of a precipice filled

her—an awareness that the decision she made now would affect her sons for the rest of their lives. Shakily she admitted to herself that she wished her sisters were there to help her, but they weren't. They had their own lives, and ultimately the boys were *her* responsibility, their happiness resting in *her* hands. Sander was determined to have them. He had said so. He was a wealthy, powerful and charismatic man who would have no difficulty whatsoever in persuading others that the boys should be with him. But she was their mother. She couldn't let him take them from her—for their sakes even more than her own. Sander didn't love them; he merely wanted them. She doubted he was capable of understanding what love was. Yes, he would provide well for them materially, but children needed far more than that, and her sons needed *her*. She had raised them from birth; they needed her even more than she needed them.

If she couldn't stop Sander from claiming his sons, then she owed it to them to make sure that she remained with them. Sander wouldn't want that, of course. He despised and disliked her.

Her heart started to thud uncomfortably heavily and far too fast as it fought against the solution proposed by her brain, but now that the thought was there it couldn't be ignored. Sander had said there was nothing he would not do to have his sons living with him. Well, maybe she should put his claim to the test, because she knew that there was no sacrifice she herself would not make for their sakes—no sacrifice at all. The challenge she intended to put to him was a huge risk for her to take, but for the boys' sake she was prepared to take it. It was, after all, a challenge she was bound to win—because Sander would never accept the terms with which she was about to confront him. She was sure of that. She let out her pent up breath.

'You say the boys' place is with you?'

'It is.'

'They are five years old and I am their mother.' Ruby took a deep breath, hoping that her voice wouldn't shake with the nervousness she was fighting to suppress and thus betray her. 'If you really care about their wellbeing as much as you claim then you must know that they are too young to be separated from me.'

She had a point, Sander was forced to admit, even though he didn't like doing so.

'You need to be very sure about why you want the twins, Sander.' Ruby pressed home her point. 'And that your desire to have them isn't merely a rich man's whim. Because the only way I will allow them to be with you is if I am there with them—as their mother and your wife.'

CHAPTER TWO

THERE—she had said it. Thrown down the gauntlet, so to speak, and given him her challenge.

In the silence that followed Ruby could literally hear her own heart beating as she held her breath, waiting for Sander to refuse her demand—because she knew that he *would* refuse it, and having refused it he must surely be forced to step back and accept that the boys' place was with her.

Trying not to give in to the shakiness invading her body, Ruby could hardly believe that she had actually had the courage to say what she had. She could tell from Sander's expression that her demand had shocked him, although he was quick to mask his reaction.

Marriage, Sander thought quickly, mentally assessing his options. He wanted his sons. There was no doubt in his mind about that, nor any doubt that they were his. Marriage to their mother would give him certain rights over them, but it would also give Ruby certain rights over his wealth. That, of course, was exactly what she wanted. Marriage to him followed by an equally speedy

divorce and a very generous financial divorce settlement. He could read her mind so easily. Even so, she
had caught him off-guard—although he told himself
cynically that he should perhaps have been prepared for
her demand. He was, after all, a very wealthy man.

'I applaud your sharp-witted business acumen,' he
told Ruby drily, in a neutral voice that gave away nothing of the fury he was really feeling. 'You rejected my
initial offer of a generous payment under the guise of
being a devoted mother, when in reality you were
already planning to play for higher stakes.'

'That's not true,' Ruby denied hotly, astonished by
his interpretation of her demand. 'Your money means
nothing to me, Sander—nothing at all,' she told him
truthfully, adding for good measure, 'And neither do
you. For me, the fact that you choose to think of my
offer in terms of money simply underlines all the reasons why I am not prepared to allow my sons anywhere
near you unless I am there.'

'That is how *you* feel, but what about how *they* might
feel?' Sander pressed her. 'A good mother would never
behave so selfishly. She would put her children's interests first.'

How speedily Sander had turned the tables on her,
Ruby recognised. What had begun as a challenge to
him she had been confident would make him back down
had now turned into a double-edged sword which right
now he was wielding very skilfully against her, cutting
what she had thought was secure ground away from
under her feet.

'They need their mother—' she started.

'They are *my* sons,' Sander interrupted her angrily. 'And I mean to have them. If I have to marry you to facilitate that, then so be it. But make no mistake, Ruby. I intend to have my sons.'

His response stunned her. She had been expecting him to refuse, to back down, to go away and leave them alone—anything rather than marry her. Sander had called her bluff and left her defenceless.

Now Ruby could see a reality she hadn't seen before. Sander really did want the boys and he meant to have them. He was rich and powerful, well able to provide materially for his sons. What chance would she have of keeping them if he pursued her through the courts? At best all she could hope for was shared custody, with the boys passed to and fro between them, torn between two homes, and that was the last thing she wanted for them. *Why* had Sander had to discover that he had fathered them? Hadn't life been cruel enough to her as it was?

Marriage to him, which she had not in any kind of way wanted, had now devastatingly turned into the protection she was forced to recognise she might need if she was to continue to have the permanent place in her sons' lives that she had previously taken for granted.

Marriage to Sander wouldn't just provide her sons with a father, she recognised now through growing panic, it would also protect her rights as a mother. As long as they were married the twins would have both parents there for them.

Both parents. Ruby swallowed painfully. Wasn't it

true that she had spent many sleepless nights worrying about the future and the effect not having a father figure might have on her sons?

A father figure, but not their real father. She had *never* imagined them having Sander in their lives—not after those first agonising weeks of being forced to accept that she meant nothing to him.

She wasn't going to give up, though. She would fight with every bit of her strength for her sons.

Holding her head up she told him fiercely, 'Very well, then. The choice is yours, Sander. If you genuinely want the boys because they are your sons, and because you want to get to know them and be part of their lives, then you will accept that separating them from me will inflict huge emotional damage on them. You will understand, as I do, no matter how much that understanding galls you, that children need the security of having two parents they know are there for them—will always be there for them. You will be prepared to make the same sacrifice that I am prepared to make to provide them with the security that comes from having two parents committed to them and to each other through marriage.'

'Sacrifice?' Sander demanded. 'I am a billionaire. I don't think there are many women who would consider marriage to me a *sacrifice*.'

Did he really believe that? If so, it just showed how right she was to want to ensure that her sons grew up knowing there were far more important things in life than money.

'You are very cynical,' she told him. 'There are any

number of women who would be appalled by what you have just said—women who put love before money, women like me who put their children first, women who would run from a man like you. I don't want your money, and I am quite willing to sign a document saying so.'

'Oh, you will be doing that. Make no mistake about it,' Sander assured her ruthlessly. Did she really expect him to fall for her lies and her faked lack of interest in his money? 'There is no way I will abandon my sons to the care of a mother who could very soon be without a roof over her head—a mother who would have to rely on charity in order to feed and clothe them—a mother who dressed like a tart and offered herself to a man she didn't know.'

Ruby flinched as though he had physically hit her, but she still managed to ask quickly, 'Were *you* any better? Or does the fact that you are a man and I'm a woman somehow mean that my behaviour was worse than yours? I was a seventeen-year-old-girl; you were an adult male.'

A seventeen-year-old girl. Angered by the reminder, Sander reacted against it. 'You certainly weren't dressed like a schoolgirl—or an innocent. And you were the one who propositioned me, not the other way round.'

And now he was going to be forced to marry her. Sander didn't want to marry anyone—much less a woman like her.

What he had seen in his parents' marriage, the bitterness and resentment between them, had made him

vow never to marry himself. That vow had been the
cause of acrimony and dissent between him and his
grandfather, a despot who believed he had the right to
barter his own flesh and blood in marriage as though
they were just another part of his fleet of tankers.

Refusing Ruby's proposal would give her an advantage. She could and would undoubtedly attempt to use
his refusal against him were there to be a court case
between them over the twins. But her obstinacy and her
attempt to get the better of him had hardened Sander's
determination to claim his sons—even if it now meant
using underhand methods to do so. Once they were on
his island, its laws would ensure that he, as their father,
had the right to keep them.

The familiar sound of a car drawing up outside and
doors opening had Ruby ignoring Sander to hurry to the
door. She suddenly realised what time it was, and that
the twins were being dropped off by the neighbour with
whom she shared school run duties. Opening the door,
she hurried down the drive to thank her neighbour and
help the twins out of the car, gathering up school bags
and lunchboxes as she did, clucking over the fact that
neither boy had fastened his coat despite the fact that it
was still only March and cold.

Identical in every way, except for the tiny mole behind
Freddie's right ear, the boys stood and stared at the expensive car parked on the drive, and then looked at Ruby.

'Whose car is that?' Freddie asked, round-eyed.

Ruby couldn't answer him. Why hadn't she realised
the time and got rid of Sander before the twins came

home from school? Now they were bound to ask questions—questions she wasn't going to be able to answer honestly—and she hated the thought of lying to them.

Freddie was still waiting for her to answer. Forcing a reassuring smile, she told him, 'It's just…someone's. Come on, let's get inside before the two of you catch cold with your coats unfastened like that.'

'I'm hungry. Can we have toast with peanut butter?' Harry asked her hopefully.

Peanut butter was his current favourite.

'We'll see,' was Ruby's answer as she pushed then gently into the hall in front of her. 'Upstairs now, boys,' she told them both, trying to remain as calm as she could even as they stood and stared in silence at Sander, who now seemed to be taking up a good deal of space in the hallway.

He was tall, well over six foot, and in other circumstances it would have made her smile to see the way Harry tipped his head right back to look up at him. Freddie, though, suddenly very much the man of the family as the elder of the two. He moved closer to her, as if instinctively seeking to protect her, and some silent communication between the two of them caused his twin to fall back to her other side to do the same.

Unwanted emotional tears stung Ruby's eyes. Her darling boys. They didn't deserve any of this, and it was *her* fault that things were as they were. Before she could stop herself she dropped down on one knee, putting an arm around each twin, holding them to her. Freddie was the more sensitive of the two, although he tried to conceal it, and he turned into her immediately, burying his face in her neck and holding her tightly, whilst Harry looked briefly towards Sander—wanting to go to him? Ruby wondered wretchedly—before copying his brother.

Sander couldn't move. The second he had seen the two boys he had known that there was nothing he would not do for them—including tearing out his own heart and offering it to them on a plate. The sheer force of his love for them was like a tidal wave, a tsunami that swept everything else aside. They were his—of his family, of his blood, of his body. They were his. And yet, watching them, he recognised immediately how they felt about their mother. He had seen the protective stance they had taken up and his heart filled with pride to see that instinctive maleness in them.

An old memory stirred within him: strong sunlight striking down on his bare head, the raised angry voices of his parents above him. He too had turned to his mother, as his sons had turned to theirs, but there had been no loving maternal arms to hold him. Instead his mother had spun round, heading for her car, slamming the door after she'd climbed into it, leaving him behind, tyres spinning on the gravel, sending up a shower of small stones. He had turned then to his father, but he too had turned away from him and walked back to the house. His parents had been too caught up in their own lives and their resentment of one another to have time for him.

Sander looked down at his sons—and at their mother.

They were all their sons had. He thought again of his own parents, and realised on another surge of emotion that there was nothing he would not do to give his sons what he had never had.

'Marriage it is, then. But I warn you now it will be a marriage that will last for life. That is the measure of my commitment to them,' he told her, looking at the boys.

If she hadn't been holding the twins Ruby thought she might well have fallen down in shock—shock and dismay. She searched Sander's face for some sign that he didn't really mean what he was saying, but all she could see was a quiet, implacable determination.

The twins were turning in her arms to look at Sander again. Any moment now they would start asking questions.

'Upstairs, you two,' she repeated, taking off their navy duffel coats. 'Change out of your uniforms and then wash your hands.'

They made a dash past Sander, deliberately ignoring him, before climbing the stairs together—a pair of sturdy, healthy male children, with lean little-boy bodies and their father's features beneath identical mops of dark curls.

'There will be two conditions,' Sander continued coldly. 'The first is that you will sign a prenuptial agreement. Our marriage will be for the benefit of our sons, not the benefit of your bank account.'

Appalled and hurt by this fresh evidence of how little he thought of her, Ruby swallowed her pride—she was doing this for her boys, after all—and demanded through gritted teeth, 'And the second condition?'

'Your confirmation and proof that you are taking the birth control pill. I've seen the evidence of how little care you have for such matters. I have no wish for another child to be conceived as carelessly as the twins were.'

Now Ruby was too outraged to conceal her feelings.

'There is no question of that happening. The last thing I want is to have to share your bed again.'

She dared to claim *that*, after the way she had already behaved?

Her outburst lashed Sander's pride into a savage need to punish her.

'But you *will* share it, and you will beg me to satisfy that hunger in you I have already witnessed. Your desire for sexual satisfaction has been honed in the arms of far too many men for you to be able to control it now.'

'No! That's not true.'

Ruby could feel her face burning. She didn't need reminding about the wanton way in which she had not only given herself to him but actively encouraged him to take her. Her memories of that night were burned into her conscience for ever. Not one of her senses would ever forget the role they had played in her self-humiliation—the way her voice had sobbed and risen on an increasing note of aching longing that had resulted in a cry of abandoned pleasure that still echoed in her ears, the greedy need of her hands to touch and know his body, the hunger of her lips to caress his flesh and taste his kisses, the increased arousal the scent of his skin had brought her. Each and all of them had added to a wild torrent of sexual longing that had taken her to the edge of her universe and then beyond it, to a place of such spectacular loss of self that she never wanted to go there again.

Shaking herself free of the memories threatening to deluge her, Ruby returned staunchly, 'That was different…a mistake.' Her hands curled into her palms in bitter self-defence as she saw the cynical look he was giving her. 'And it's one that I never want to repeat. There's no way I'd ever want to share your bed again.'

Her denial unleashed Sander's anger. She was lying, he was sure of it, and he would prove it to her. He wasn't a vain man, but he knew that women found him attractive, and Ruby had certainly done everything she could that night to make it plain to him that she wanted him. Normally he would never have even considered bedding her—he liked to do his own hunting—but her persistence had been like a piece of grit in his shoe, wearing down his resistance and helping to fuel the anger already burning inside him. *That* was why he had lost control. Because of his grandfather. Not because of Ruby herself, or because the aroused little cries she had made against his skin had proved so irresistible that he had lost sight of everything but his need to possess her. He could still remember the way she had cried out when he had finally thrust into her, as though what she was experiencing was completely new to her. She had clung to him, sobbing her pleasure into his skin as she trembled and shuddered against him.

Why was he thinking of that now?

The savagery of his fury, inflamed by both her demand for marriage and her denial of his accusation, deafened him to the note of raw pain in her voice. Before he could stop himself he had taken hold of her and was possessing her mouth in a kiss of scorching, pride-fuelled fury.

Too shocked to struggle against his possession, by the time she realised what was happening it was too late. Ruby's own anger surged in defiance, passionate enough to overwhelm her self-control and battle with the full heat of Sander's desire to punish her. Desire for him was the last thing she had expected to feel, but, shockingly, the hard possession of Sander's mouth on her own turned a key in a lock she had thought so damaged by what he had already made her endure that it could never be turned again. Turned it with frightening ease.

This shouldn't be happening. It could not be happening. But, shamefully, it was.

Her panic fought with the desire that burned through her and lost, overcome as swiftly as though molten lava was pouring through her, obliterating everything that stood in its path. Her lips parted beneath the driving pressure of Sander's probing tongue, an agonised whimper of longing drawn from her throat. She could feel the passion in Sander's kiss, and the hard arousal of his body, but instead of acting as a warning that knowledge only served to further enflame her own desire, quickening the pulse already beating within her own sex.

Somewhere within the torrent of anger motivating him Sander could hear an inner voice warning him that this was how it had been before—this same furious, aching, agonised need and arousal that was possessing him now. It should have been impossible for him to want her. It should always have been impossible. And yet, like some mythical, dark malformed creature, supposedly entombed and shut away for ever, his desire had found the superhuman strength to break the bonds imprisoning it. His tongue possessed the eager willingness of the softness of her mouth and his body was already hard, anticipating the corresponding willingness of the most intimate part of her if he didn't stop soon…

Ruby shuddered with mindless sensual delight as Sander's tongue began to thrust potently and rhythmically against her own. Beneath her clothes her nipples swelled and hardened, their ache spreading swiftly through her. Sander's hand cupped her breast, causing her to moan deep in her throat.

She was all female sensual heat, all eager willingness, her very responsiveness designed to trap, Sander recognised. If he didn't stop now he wouldn't be able to stop himself from taking her where they stood, from dragging the clothes from her body in his need to feel her bare skin against his touch, from sinking himself deep within her and feeling her body close round him, possessing him as he possessed her, both of them driven by the mindless, incessant ache that he was surely cursed to feel for her every time he touched her.

He found the buttons on her shirt, swiftly unfastening them. The feel of his hands on her body drew Ruby back into the past. Then he had undressed her expertly and swiftly, in between sensually erotic kisses that had melted away her ability to think or reason, leaving her aching for more, just as he was doing now. His left hand lifted her hair so that he could taste the warm sweetness of that place just where her neck joined her shoulder.

Ruby felt the warmth of his breath against her bare skin. Flames were erupting inside her—the eager flames of denied longing leaping upwards, consuming her resistance. Mindless shudders of hot pleasure rippled through her. Her shirt was open, her breasts exposed to Sander's gaze.

He shouldn't be doing this, Sander warned himself. He shouldn't be giving in to the demands of his pride. But that was *all* he was doing. The heat running through his veins was only caused by angry pride, nothing else.

Her breasts were as perfect as he remembered, the dark rose nipples flaring into deep aureoles that contrasted with the paleness of her skin. He watched as they lifted and fell with the increased speed of her breathing, lifting his hand to cup one, knowing already that it would fit his hand as perfectly as though it was made to be held by him. Beneath the stroke of his thumb-pad her nipple hardened. Sander closed his eyes, remembering how in that long-ago hotel bedroom it had seemed as though her nipple was pushing itself against his touch, demanding the caress of first his thumb and forefinger, then his lips and tongue. Her response had been wild and immediate, swelling and hardening his own body.

He didn't want her, not really, but his pride was now demanding her punishment, the destruction of her claim that she didn't want him.

Ruby could feel herself being dragged back to the past. A small cry of protest gave away her torment.

Abruptly Sander thrust her away from him, brought back to reality by the sound.

They stood watching one another, fighting to control the urgency of their breathing, the urgency of their need. Exposed, raw, and in Ruby's eyes ugly, it was almost a tangible force between them.

They both felt the strength of it and its danger. Ruby could see that knowledge in Sander's eyes, just as she knew he must see it reflected in her own.

The weight of her shame ached through her.

Ruby's face was drained of colour, her eyes huge with shock in her small face.

Sander was just as shocked by the intensity of the desire that had come out of nowhere to threaten his self-control—but he was better at hiding it than Ruby, and he was in no mood to find any pity for her. He was still battling with the unwanted knowledge of just how much he had wanted her.

'You will take the contraceptive pill,' he told her coldly. His heart started to pound heavily in recognition of what his words meant and invited, and the ache in his body surged against his self-control, but somehow he forced himself to ignore the demands of his own desire, to continue. 'I will not accept any consequences of you not doing so.'

Never had she felt so weak, Ruby thought shakily—and not just physically weak, but emotionally and mentally weak as well. In the space of a few short minutes the protective cover she had woven around herself had been ripped from her, exposing her to the full horror of a weakness she had thought controlled and contained. It should be impossible for her to want Sander, to be aroused by him. Should be.

Reaction to what had happened was setting in. She felt physically sick, dazed, unable to function properly, torn apart by the conflicting nature of her physical desire and her burning sense of shame and disbelief that she should feel that desire… Wild thoughts jostled through her head. Perhaps she should not merely ask her doctor for a prescription for the birth control pill but for an anti-Sander pill as well—something that would destroy her desire for him? She needed a pill for that? Surely the way he had spoken to her, the way he had treated her, should be enough to ensure that she loathed the thought of him touching her? Surely her pride and the humiliation he had heaped on her should be strong enough to protect her?

She couldn't marry him. Not now. Panic filled her.

'I've changed my mind,' she told him quickly. 'About…about us getting married.'

Sander frowned. His immediate response to her statement was a fierce surge of determination to prevent her from changing her mind. For the sake of his sons. Nothing else. And certainly not because of the ache that was still pounding through him.

'So the future of our sons is not as important to you as you claimed after all?' he challenged her.

She was trapped, Ruby acknowledged, trapped in a prison of her own making. All she could do was cling to the fragile hope that somehow she would find the strength to deny the desire he could arouse in her so easily.

'Of course it is,' she protested.

'Then we shall be married, and you will accept my terms and conditions.'

'And if I refuse?'

'Then I will move heaven and earth and the stars between them to take my sons from you.'

He meant what he was saying, Ruby could tell. She had no choice other than to bow her head in acceptance of his demands.

He had defeated her, Sander knew, but the taste of his triumph did not have the sweetness he had expected.

'The demands placed on me by my business mean that the sooner the arrangements are completed the better. I shall arrange for the necessary paperwork to be carried out with regard to the prenuptial agreement I shall require you to sign and for our marriage. You must—'

A sudden bang from upstairs, followed by a sharp cry of pain, had them both turning towards the stairs.

Anxious for the safety of her sons, Ruby rushed past Sander, hurrying up the stairs to the boys' room, unaware that Sander was right behind her as she pushed open the door to find Harry on the floor sobbing whilst Freddie stood clutching one of their toy cars.

'Freddie pushed me,' Harry told her.

'No, I didn't. He was trying to take my car.'

'Let me have a look,' Ruby instructed Harry, quickly checking to make sure that no real damage had been done before sitting back on her heels and turning to look at Freddie. But instead of coming to her for comfort Freddie was standing in front of Sander, who had obviously followed her into the room, looking up at him as though seeking his support, and Sander had his hand on Freddie's arm, as though protecting him.

The raw intensity of her emotions gripped her by the throat—grief for all that the twins had missed in not having a father, guilt because she was the cause of that, pain because she loved them so much but her love alone could not give them the tools they would need to grow into well balanced men, and fear for her own self-respect.

His hand resting protectively on the shoulder of his son, Sander looked grimly at Ruby. His sons needed him in their lives, and nothing—least of all a woman like Ruby— was going to prevent him from being there for them.

Oblivious to the atmosphere between the two grown-ups Freddie repeated, 'It's *my* car.'

'No, it's not. It's mine,' Harry argued.

Their argument pulled Ruby's attention back to them. They were devoted to one another, but every now and again they would argue like this over a toy, as though each of them was trying to seek authority over the other. It was a boy thing, other mothers had assured her, but Ruby hated to see them fall out.

'I've got a suggestion to make.' Sander's voice was calm, and yet authoritative in a way that immediately had both boys looking at him. 'If you both promise not to argue over this car again then I will buy you a new toy each, so you won't have to share.'

Ruby sucked in an outraged breath, her maternal instincts overwhelming the vulnerability she felt towards Sander as a woman. What he was doing was outright bribery. Since she didn't have the money to give the boys one each of things she had impressed on them the need to share and share alike, and now, with a handful of words, Sander had appealed to their natural acquisitive instincts with his offer.

She could see from the eager look in both pairs of dark gold eyes that her rules about sharing had been forgotten even before Harry challenged Sander excitedly, 'When...when can we have them?'

Harry was on his feet now, rushing over to join his twin and lean confidently against Sander's other leg whilst he looked up excitedly at him, his words tumbling over themselves as he told Sander, 'I want a car like the one outside...'

'So do I,' Freddie agreed, determined not to be outdone and to assert his elder brother status.

'I'm taking both of you and your mother to London.'

This was news to Ruby, but she wasn't given the chance to say anything because Sander was already continuing.

'There's a big toyshop there where we can look for your cars—but only if you promise me not to quarrel over your toys in future.'

Two dark heads nodded enthusiastically in assent, and two identical watermelon grins split her sons' faces as they gazed up worshipfully at Sander.

Ruby struggled to contain her feelings. Seeing her sons with Sander, watching the way they reacted to him, had brought home to her more effectively than a thousand arguments could ever have done just what they were missing without him—not financially, but emotionally.

Was it her imagination, or was she right in thinking that already they seemed to be standing taller, speaking more confidently, even displaying a body language they had automatically copied from their father? A small pang of sadness filled her. They weren't babies any longer, *her* babies, wholly dependent on her for everything; they were growing up, and their reaction to Sander proved what she had already known—they needed a male role model in their lives. Helplessly she submitted to the power of the wave of maternal love that surged through her, but her head lifted proudly as she returned Sander's silently challenging look.

Automatically Ruby reached out to stroke the tousled dark curls exactly at the moment that Sander did the same. Their hands touched. Immediately Ruby recoiled from the contact, unable to stop the swift rush of knowledge that slid into her head. Once Sander's hands had touched her far more intimately than they were doing now, taking her and possessing her with a potent mix of knowledge and male arousal, and something else which in her ignorance and innocence she had told herself was passionate desire for her and her alone, but which of course had been nothing of the sort.

That reality had left her emotions badly bruised. His was the only sexual male touch she had ever known. Memories she had thought sealed away for ever were trying to surface. Memories aroused by that kiss Sander had forced on her earlier. Ruby shuddered in mute loathing of her own weakness, but it was too late. The mental images her memories were painting would not be denied—images of Sander's hands on her body, the sound of his breathing against her ear and then later her skin. But, no, she must not think of those things. Instead she must be strong. She must resist and deny his ability to arouse her. She was not that young girl any more, she was a woman, a mother, and her sons' needs must come before her own.

CHAPTER THREE

RUBY'S head was pounding with a tension headache, and her stomach cramped—familiar reactions to stress, which she knew could well result in her ending up with something close to a full-scale migraine attack. But this wasn't the time for her to be ill, or indeed to show any weakness—even if she had hardly slept since and had woken this morning feeling nauseous.

The twins were dressed in the new jumpers and jeans her sisters had bought them for Christmas, and wearing the new trainers she had spent her preciously saved money on after she had seen the frowning look Sander had given their old ones when he had called to discuss everything—'everything' being all the arrangements he had made, not just for their stay in London but for their marriage as well, before the four of them would leave for the island that would be their home. They were too excited to sit down, insisting instead on standing in front of the window so that they could see Sander arrive to pick them all up for their visit to London.

Would she have made a different decision if her

sisters had been at home? Ruby didn't see how she could have done. They had been wonderful to her, insisting that they would support her financially so that she could stay at home with the boys, but Ruby had become increasingly aware not just of the financial pressure they were under, but also the fact that one day surely her sisters would fall in love. When they did she didn't want to feel she and the twins were standing in their way because they felt duty-bound to go on supporting them.

No, she had made the right decision. For the twins, who were both wildly excited about the coming trip to London and who had happily accepted her careful announcement to them that she was going to marry Sander, and for her sisters, who had given her and the twins so much love and support.

The twins had reacted to the news that she and Sander were going to be married with excitement and delight, and Freddie had informed her hopefully, 'Luke Simpson has a daddy. He takes him to watch football, and to McDonalds, and he bought him a new bicycle.'

The reality was that everything seemed to be working in Sander's favour. She couldn't even use the excuse of saying that she couldn't take the boys out of school to refuse to go to London, since they were now on holiday for Easter.

When they went back to school it would be to the small English speaking school on the island where, Sander had informed her, those islanders who wished their children to grow up speaking English could send them.

The conversation she and Sander had had about the

twins' future had been more of a question and answer
session, with her asking the questions and Sander sup-
plying the answers. All she knew about their future life
was that Sander preferred to live and work on the island
his family had ruled for several centuries, although the
container shipping business he had built up into a world-
wide concern also had offices and staff at all the world's
major commercial ports, including Felixstowe in
England. Sander had also told her that his second in
command was his younger brother, who had trained in
IT and was based in Athens.

When it came to the boys' future education, Sander
had told her that he was completely against them going
to boarding school—much to her own relief. He had
said that when the time came they would spend term
time in England as a family, returning to the island when
the boys were out of school.

In addition to the younger brother, Sander had informed her, he also had a sister—the same sister Ruby
had learned had taken the photograph of the twins that
had alerted Sander to their existence. Like his brother,
she too lived in Athens with her husband.

'So it will just be the two of us and the boys, then?'
she had pressed warily.

'That is the norm, isn't it?' he had countered. 'The
nuclear family, comprising a father, a mother and
their children.'

Stupidly, perhaps, she hadn't thought as far as how they
would live, but the way her thoughts had recoiled from
the reality of their new life together had shown her how

apprehensive she was. Because she feared him, or because she feared wanting him? Her face burned even now, remembering her inability to answer that inner question.

It had been far easier to deal with the practicalities of what lay ahead rather than allow herself to be overwhelmed by the complex emotional issues it raised.

Now, waiting for Sander to collect them, with letters for her sisters explaining what she was doing and why written and waiting for them on their return to the UK—the situation wasn't something she felt she wanted to discuss with them over the phone—Ruby could feel the pain in her temple increasing, whilst her stomach churned with anxiety. Everything would have been so very different if only she hadn't give in to that shameful physical desire Sander had somehow managed to arouse in her. In her handbag were the birth control pills Sander had demanded that she take. She had been tempted to defy him, to insist that she could rely on her own willpower to ensure that there was no further sexual intimacy between them. But she was still horrified by the memory of what had happened between them in her hallway, still struggling to take in the fact that it had happened. The speed of it, the intensity of it, had been like a fire erupting out of nowhere to blaze so fiercely that it was beyond control. It had left her feeling vulnerable and unable to trust herself.

There must not be another child, Sander had told her. And wasn't the truth that she herself did not *want* to create another new life with a man who had no respect for her, no feelings of kindness towards her, and certainly no love for her? Love? Hadn't she grown out of the dangerous self-deceit of dressing up naked lust in the fantasy illusion of 'love'? Clothing it in the kind of foolish dreams that belonged to naive adolescents? Before Sander had kissed her she would have sworn and believed that there was nothing he could do to her, no intimacy he could enforce on her, that would arouse her own desire. But the searing heat of the kiss he had subjected her to had burned away her defences.

She hated having to admit to herself that she couldn't rely on her own pride and self-control, but the only thing she could cling to was the knowledge that Sander had been as close to losing *his* control as she had been of losing hers. Of all the cruel tricks that nature could play on two human beings, surely that must be the worst? To create within them a desire for one another that could burn away every shred of protection, leaving them exposed to a need that neither of them wanted. If she could have ripped her own desire out of her body she would have done. It was an alien, unwanted presence, an enemy within her that she must find a way to destroy.

'He's here!'

Freddie's excited announcement cut through her introspection. Both boys were racing to the door and pulling it open, jumping up and down with eager delight when the car door opened and Sander stepped out.

He might be dressed casually, in a black polo shirt, beige chinos and a dark tan leather jacket, but Sander still had that unmistakable air about him that said he was a man other men looked up to and women wanted to be close to, Ruby was forced to admit unwillingly. It wasn't just that he was good-looking—many men were that. No, Sander had something else—something that was a mixture of an aura of power blended with raw male sexuality. She had sensed it as a naive teenager and been drawn to him because of it, and even now, when she was old enough and wise enough to know better, she still felt the pull of his sexual magnetism, its threat to suck her into treacherous waters.

A shiver that was almost a mocking caress stroked over her, making her hug her arms around her body to conceal the sudden unwanted peaking of her nipples. Not because of Sander, she assured herself. No, it was the cold from the open door that was causing her body's sensitive reactions.

Sander's brooding gaze swept over Ruby and rested momentarily on her breasts. Like a leashed cougar, the desire inside him surged against its restraint, leaping and clawing against its imprisonment, the force of its power straining the muscles he had locked against it.

These last couple of weeks he had spent more hours than he wanted to count wrestling with the ache for her that burned in his groin—possessed by it, driven by it, and half maddened by it in equal parts.

No woman had ever been allowed to control him through his desire for her, and for the space of a handful of seconds he was torn—tempted to listen to the inner voice that was warning him to walk away from her, from the desire that had erupted out of nowhere when he had kissed her. A desire like that couldn't be controlled, it could only be appeased. Like some ancient mythical god it demanded sacrifice and self-immolation on its altar.

And then he saw the twins running towards him, and any thought of protecting himself vanished, overwhelmed by the surge of love that flooded him. He hunkered down and held out his arms to them.

Watching the small scene, Ruby felt her throat threaten to close up on a huge lump of emotion. A father with his sons, holding them, protecting them, loving them. There was nothing she would not risk to give her sons that, she acknowledged fiercely.

Holding his sons, Sander knew that there was nothing more important to him than they were—no matter how much he mistrusted their mother.

'Mummy says that we can call you Daddy if we want to.'

That was Freddie, Sander recognised. He had always thought of himself as someone who could control and conceal his emotions, but right now they were definitely threatening to overwhelm him.

'And do you want to?' he asked them, his hold tightening.

'Luke at school has a daddy. He bought him a new bicycle.'

He was being tested, Sander recognised, unable to stop himself from looking towards Ruby.

'Apparently Luke's father also takes him to football

matches and to McDonalds.' She managed to answer Sander's unspoken question.

Sander looked at the twins.

'The bicycles are a maybe—once we've found bikes that are the right size for you—and the football is a definite yes. As for McDonalds—well, I think we should leave it to your mother to decide about that.'

Ruby was torn between relief and resentment. Anyone would think he'd been dealing with the twins from birth. He couldn't have given them a better answer if she had scripted it herself.

'Are you ready?' Sander asked Ruby, in the cold, distant voice he always used when he spoke to her.

Ruby looked down at the jeans and loose-fitting sweater she was wearing, the jeans tucked into the boots her sister had given her for Christmas. No doubt Sander was more used to the company of stunning-looking women dressed in designer clothes and jewels—women who had probably spent hours primping and preening themselves to impress him. A small forlorn ache came from nowhere to pierce her heart. Pretty clothes, never mind designer clothes, were a luxury she simply couldn't afford, and they would have been impractical for her life even if she could.

'Yes, we're ready. Boys, go and get your duffel coats,' she instructed, turning back into the hall to get the case she had packed, and almost being knocked over by the twins as they rushed by.

It was Sander's fingers closing round her arm that saved her from stumbling, but the shock of the physical contact with him froze her into immobility, making her feel far more in danger of losing her balance than the twins' dash past her had done.

Her arm felt thin and frail, in direct contrast to the sturdiness of the twins' limbs, he thought. And her face was pinched, as though she didn't always get enough to eat. A question hovered inside his head...an awareness of deprivation that he pushed away from himself.

Although he was standing behind her she could still smell the scent of his cologne, and feel the warmth coming off his body. Inside her head an image formed of the way he had kissed her such a short time ago. Panic and fear clawed at her stomach, adding to her existing tension. She saw Sander's gaze drop to her mouth and her whole body began to tremble.

It would be so easy to give in to the desire clawing at him—so easy to take her as quickly and wantonly as the way she was offering herself to him. His body wanted that. It wanted the heat of her eager muscles wrapped greedily round it, riding his deepening thrusts. It wanted the swift, savage release her body promised.

It might, but did he really want the kind of cheap, tawdry thrill a woman like her peddled—had been peddling the night they had met?

Ruby's small anguished moan as she pulled free of him brought him back to reality.

'Is this your only case?' he demanded, looking away from her to the shabby case on the hall floor.

Ruby nodded her head, and Sander's mouth twisted with contempt. Of course she would want to underline her poverty to him. Marriage to him was her access to a brand new bank account, filled with money. No doubt she was already planning her first spending spree. He remembered how much delight his mother had always taken in spending his father's money, buying herself couture clothes and expensive jewellery. As a child he'd thought her so beautiful, too dazzled by her glamorous exterior to recognise the corruption that it concealed.

Sander was tempted to ignore the hint Ruby was plainly intending to give him and let her travel to the island with the single shabby case, but that would mean punishing his sons as well as her, he suspected—and besides, he had no wish to make his marriage the subject of speculation and gossip, which it would be if Ruby didn't have a wardrobe commensurate with his own wealth and position.

'Our marriage will take place this Friday,' he told her. 'On Saturday we fly to the island. You've done as I instructed with regard to the birth control pill, I trust?'

'Yes,' Ruby confirmed.

'Can you prove it?'

Ruby was outraged that he should doubt her, but scorched pride had her fumbling angrily with the clasp of her handbag, both her hands shaking with the force of her emotions as she delved into her bag and produced the foil-backed pack of pills, quite plainly showing the empty spaces from the pills she had already taken.

If she had hoped to shame Sander into an apology she soon recognised that one would not be forthcoming. A curt nod of his head was the only response he seemed willing to give her before he continued cynically,

'And, having fulfilled your obligation, you now expect me to fulfil what you no doubt consider to be mine, I expect? To furnish you with the wherewithal to replace your single suitcase with a full set of new ones and clothes with which to fill them.'

The open cynicism in his voice burned Ruby's already scorched pride like salt poured into an open wound. 'Your only obligation to me is to be a good father to the twins.'

'No,' he corrected her coldly, 'that is my obligation to them.' He didn't like her response. It wasn't the one he had expected. It didn't match the profile he had mentally drawn up for her. Somehow she had managed to stray from the script he had written. The one in which she revealed herself to be an unworthy mother, leaving him holding the high ground and the moral right to continue to despise her. 'There is no need to be self-sacrificing.' Her resistance to the role he had cast for her made him feel all the more determined to prove himself right. 'As my wife, naturally you must present an appropriate appearance—although I must caution you against buying clothes of the type you were wearing the night you propositioned me. It is the role of my wife you will be playing in future. Not the role of a whore.'

Ruby had no words to refute his contemptuous insult, but she wasn't going to accept his charity. 'We already have plenty of clothes. We don't need any more,' she insisted vehemently.

She was daring to try to reject what he knew to be the truth about her. She must be taught a lesson that would ensure that she did not do so again. She *would* wear clothes bought with his money, so that they would both know just what she was. He might be forced to marry her in order to be able to lay legal claim to his sons, but he wasn't going to let her forget that she belonged to that group of women all too willing to sell their bodies to any man rich enough to provide them with the lifestyle of designer clothes and easy money they craved.

'Plenty of clothes?' he taunted her. 'In one case? When there are three of you? My sons and my wife will be dressed in a manner appropriate to their station in life, and not—'

'Not what?' Ruby challenged him.

'Do you *really* need me to answer that question?' was his silkily derisory response.

The shabby case was in the boot of a very expensive and luxurious-looking car, the twins were safely strapped into their seats, her decision had already been made— and yet now that it came to it Ruby wavered on the front doorstep, looking back into the house.

'Where's your coat?'

Sander's question distracted her.

'I don't need one,' she fibbed. The truth was that she didn't have a proper winter coat, but she wasn't going to tell Sander that—not after what he'd already said. He was waiting, holding the car door open for her. Shivering in the easterly March wind, Ruby locked the front door. Her head pounding painfully, she got into the car. Its interior smelled of expensive leather, very different from the smell inside the taxi that had transported them back to Sander's hotel that fateful night…

Her mouth went dry.

The twins were both engrossed in the TVs installed in the back of the front seats. Sander was concentrating on his driving. Now wasn't the time to think about that night, she told herself. But it was too late. The memories were already storming her defences and flooding over them.

Her parents' death in an accident had been a terrible shock, followed by her sister's decision to sell their family home. Ruby hadn't realised then that their parents had died heavily in debt. Her oldest sister had tried to protect her by not telling her, and so she had assumed that her decision to sell the house was motivated by the decision to set up her own interior design business in Cheshire. Angry with her sister, she had deliberately chosen to befriend a girl new to the area, knowing that her sister disapproved of the freedom Tracy's parents allowed her, and of Tracy herself. Although she was only eighteen months older than Ruby, Tracy had been far more worldly, dressing in tight-fitting clothes in the latest and skimpiest fashions, her hair dyed blonde and her face heavily made-up.

Secretly, although she hadn't been prepared to admit it—especially not to her older sister—Ruby had been shocked by some of the disclosures Tracy had made about the things she had done. Tracy's goal in life was to get a footballer boyfriend. She had heard that young footballers in Manchester patronised a certain club in the city, and had asked Ruby to go there with her.

Alarmed by Tracy's disclosures, Ruby hadn't really wanted to go. But when she had tried to say so, telling Tracy that she doubted her sister would give her permission, Tracy had mocked her and accused her of being a baby who needed her sister's permission for everything she did. Of course Ruby had denied that she was any such thing, whereupon Tracy had challenged her to prove it by daring her to go with her.

She had been just seventeen, and a very naive seventeen at that, with her whole world turned upside down by events over which she'd had no control. But no matter how often both her sisters had reassured her since then that her rebellion had been completely natural, understandable, and that she was not to blame for what had happened, Ruby knew that deep down inside she would always feel guilty.

Before they'd left for Manchester Tracy had promised Ruby a 'makeover' and poured them both a glass of vodka and orange juice. It had gone straight to Ruby's head as she had never drunk alcohol. The drink had left her feeling so light-headed that she hadn't protested or objected when Tracy had insisted that Ruby change into one of her own short skirts and a tight-fitting top, before making up Ruby's face in a similar style to her own, with dark eyeliner, heavy thick mascara loaded on her eyelashes and lots of deep pink lipgloss.

The girl staring back at Ruby from the mirror, with her tousled hair and her pink pout had been so unrecognisable as herself that under the effect of the vodka and orange Ruby had only been able to stare at her reflection in dizzy astonishment.

She might only have been seventeen, but she had known even before she had watched Tracy sweet talking the bouncer into letting them into the club that neither her parents nor her sisters would have approved of her being there, but by then she had been too afraid of Tracy's mockery and contempt to tell her that she had changed her mind and wanted to go home.

She'd watched other girls going in—older girls than her, dressed up to the nines in tiny little tops and skirts that revealed dark sunbed tans—and she'd known instinctively and immediately that she would feel out of place.

Inside, the club had been hot and stuffy, packed with girls with the same goal in mind as Tracy.

Several young men had come up to them as they'd stood close to the bar. Tracy had refused Ruby's suggestion that they sit down at a tucked-away table with a derisory, 'Don't be daft—no one will see us if we do that.' But Tracy had shaken her head, ignoring the boys and telling Ruby, 'They're nothing. Just ordinary lads out on the pull.'

She'd bought them both drinks—cocktails which had seemed innocuous when Ruby sipped thirstily at hers, because of the heat in the club, but which had quickly made her feel even more dizzy and disorientated than the vodka and orange juice had done.

The club had been packed and noisy, and Ruby's head had begun to ache. She had felt alien and alone, with the alcohol heightening her emotions: bringing home to her the reality of her parents' death, bringing to a head all the despair and misery she had been feeling.

Tracy had started talking to a young man, deliberately excluding Ruby from their conversation and keeping her back to her.

Suddenly and achingly Ruby had longed for the security of the home life she had lost—of knowing that there was someone in her life to take care of her and protect her, someone who loved her, instead of getting cross with her like her elder sister did. And that had been when she had looked across the bar and seen Sander.

Something about him had set him apart from the other men in the bar. For a start he'd been far more smartly dressed, in a suit, with his dark hair groomed, and an air of command and power and certainty had emanated from him that Ruby's insecure senses immediately recognised and were drawn to… In her alcohol-induced state, Sander had looked like an island of security and safety in a sea of confusion and misery. She hadn't been able to take her eyes off him, and when he had looked back at her, her mouth had gone so dry with the anticipation of speaking to him that she had had to wet her lips with the tip of her tongue. The way that Sander's gaze had followed that movement, showing her that he was singling her out from all the other girls in the bar, had reinforced Ruby's cocktail-produced belief that there was a link between them—that he was drawing her to him, that they were meant to meet, and that somehow once she was close to him she would be safe, and he would save her from her own fears and protect her just as her parents had done.

She had no memory of actually going to him, only of reaching him, feeling like a swimmer who had crested turbulent waves to reach the security of a calm sea where she could float safely. When she had smiled up at Sander she had felt as though she already knew him. But of course she hadn't. She hadn't known anything, Ruby reflected bitterly now, as she dragged her thoughts away from the past and massaged her throbbing temple as Sander drove onto the motorway slip road and the car picked up speed.

CHAPTER FOUR

SANDER had booked them into the Carlton Towers Hotel, just off Sloane Street. They had an enormous suite of three bedrooms, each with its own bathroom, and a good-sized sitting room as well.

Ruby had felt dreadfully out of place as they'd walked through the downstairs lobby, compared with the elegantly groomed women surrounded by expensive-looking shopping bags who were having afternoon tea in the lounge. But she had soon forgotten them once they had been shown into their suite and she had realised that Sander would be staying in the suite with them.

Her heart was beating far too fast, her whole body suddenly charged and sensitised, so that she was far too aware of Sander. His presence in the room, even though there were several feet between them and he was fully dressed, somehow had the same effect on her body as though he was standing close to her and touching her. The sound of his voice made her think she could almost feel the warmth of his breath on her skin. Her body was starting to react even to her thoughts, tiny darts of sensation heightening her awareness of him.

He raised his hand, gesturing towards the bedrooms as he told her, 'I've asked for one of the rooms to be made up with twin beds for the boys.'

Inside her head she could feel that hand cupping her breast. Beneath her clothes her breasts swelled and ached whilst she tried desperately to stifle her body's arousal. Why was this happening to her? She'd lived happily without sex for nearly six years. Why was her body reacting like this now?

It was just reacting to memory, that was all. Her desire for Sander, like that memory, belonged to the past and had no place in the present. Ruby tried to convince herself, but she knew that it wasn't true. The fact that he could arouse her to intense desire for him was something she didn't want to think about. Her stomach was churning, adding to the feeling of nausea already being produced by her headache. She had actually been sick when they had stopped for a break at a motorway service station, and had had to purchase a travel pack of toothbrush and toothpaste to refresh her mouth. Now all she really wanted to do was lie down in a dark room, but of course that was impossible.

'You and I will occupy the other two rooms, of course,' Sander was saying. 'I expect that you will wish to have the room closest to the boys?'

'I could have shared a room with them,' was Ruby's response. Because sharing with the boys would surely prevent any more of those unwanted memories from surfacing? 'There was no need for you to book three rooms.'

'If I had only booked two the hotel would have assumed you would be sharing my bed, not sleeping with the twins,' was Sander's response.

Immediately another image flashed through her head: two naked bodies entwined on a large bed, the man's hands holding and caressing the woman, whilst her head was thrown back in wild ecstasy. Sander's hands and her head. Heat filled her body. Her own mental images were making her panic. What she was experiencing was probably caused by the same kind of thing that caused the victims of dreadful trauma to have flashbacks they couldn't control, she told herself. They meant nothing other than that Sander's unexpected and unwanted reappearance in her life was causing her to remember the event that had had such a dramatic effect on her life.

To her relief the twins, who had been inspecting the suite, came rushing into the sitting room. Harry ran over to her to inform her, 'Guess what? There's a TV in our bedroom, and—'

'A TV which will remain switched off whilst you are in bed,' Ruby told him firmly, relieved to be able to return to the familiar role of motherhood. 'You know the rules.' She was very strict about limiting the boys' television viewing, preferring them to make their own entertainment.

Sander's comment about the rooms had penetrated her mind and was still lodged there—a small, unnerving time bomb of a comment that was having an effect on her that was out of all proportion to its reality. The sound of Sander saying 'my bed' had made her heart jerk around inside her chest as though it was on a string—and why? She had no desire to share that bed with him; he meant nothing to her now. It was merely the result of only ever having had one sexual partner and being sexually inexperienced. It had left her reacting to a man saying the words 'my bed' as though she were a teenager, blushing at every mention of anything remotely connected to sex, Ruby derided herself.

'I thought we'd use the rest of the afternoon to get the boys kitted out with the clothes they'll need for the island. We can walk to Harrods from here, or get a cab if you wish.'

The last thing Ruby felt like doing was shopping, but she was determined not to show any weakness. Sander would only accuse of being a bad mother if she did.

Hopefully she might see a chemist, where she could get something for her headache. It had been so long since she had last had one of these debilitating attacks that she didn't have anything she could take for it. Determinedly trying to ignore her continuing feeling of nausea, she nodded her head, and then winced as the pain increased.

'The boys will need summer clothes,' Sander told her. 'Even in March the temperature on the island can be as high as twenty-two degrees centigrade, and it rises to well over thirty in the summer.'

Two hours later Ruby was battling between angry frustration at the way in which Sander had overruled all her attempts to minimise the amount of money he was spending by choosing the cheapest items she could find and a mother's natural pride in her sons, who had drawn smiles of approval from the assistants with their appearance in their new clothes: smart, boyish separates from the summer ranges that had just come in, and in which Ruby had to admit they looked adorable.

As a reward for their good behaviour Sander had insisted on taking them to the toy department, where he'd bought them both complicated-looking state-of-the-art boys' toys that had them both speechless with delight.

The whole time they had been shopping with the boys Ruby had been conscious of the admiring looks Sander had attracted from other women—women who no doubt would have been only too delighted to be marrying him in two days' time, Ruby acknowledged, and her heart gave a flurry of tense beats in response to her thoughts.

'I've got some business matters to attend to this evening,' Sander told her as they made a detour on the way back to the hotel to allow the boys to walk in Hyde Park—a suggestion from Sander which Ruby had welcomed, hoping that the fresh air would ease the pounding in her head.

After acknowledging Sander's comment Ruby focused on keeping an eye on the twins, who were walking ahead of them.

Sander continued. 'But first I've arranged for a jeweller to come to the hotel with a selection of wedding and engagement rings. I've also made an appointment for you tomorrow morning at the spa and hair salon in Harvey Nichols, and then afterwards a personal shopper will help you choose your own new wardrobe. I thought I'd take the boys to the Natural History Museum whilst you're doing that, to keep them occupied.'

Ruby stopped walking and turned to look at him, her eyes blazing with temper.

'I don't need a spa appointment, or a new hairstyle, or a new wardrobe, thank you very much. And I certainly don't want an engagement ring.'

She was lying, of course. Or did she think she could get more out of him by pretending she didn't want anything?

Oblivious to Sander's thoughts, Ruby continued, 'And if my present appearance isn't good enough for you, then too bad. Because it's good enough for me.'

Quickly hurrying after the twins, Ruby tried to ignore how unwell she was feeling. Even though she couldn't see him she knew that Sander had caught up with her and was standing behind her. Her body could feel him there, but stubbornly she refused to turn round.

'You have two choices,' Sander informed her coolly. 'Either you accept the arrangements I have made for you, or you will accept the clothes I shall instruct the store to select on your behalf. There is no option for you, as my wife, to dress as you are doing now. You are so eager to display your body to male eyes that you aren't even wearing a coat—all the better for them to assess what is on offer, no doubt.'

'That's a disgusting thing to say, and totally untrue. You must *know* the reason I'm not wearing a coat is—'

Abruptly Ruby stopped speaking realising that she had allowed her anger to betray her into making an admission she had no wish to make.

'Yes?' Sander probed.

'Is that I forgot to bring one with me,' Ruby told him lamely. The truth was that she had not been able to afford to buy herself one—not with the twins constantly outgrowing their clothes. But she wasn't going to expose herself to more humiliation by admitting that to Sander.

How could he be marrying a woman like this one? Sander wondered savagely. It would have suited his purposes far more if the report he had received from the agents he had hired to find Ruby had included something to suggest that she was a neglectful mother, thus giving him real grounds for legally removing them from their mother. The report, though, had done nothing of the sort—had actually dared to claim that Ruby was a good mother, the kind of mother whose absence from their lives would damage his sons. That was a risk he was not prepared to take.

Ignoring Ruby's defiant statement, Sander went on, 'The boys are approaching an age where they will be aware of appearance and other people's opinions. They are going to have to deal with settling into a different environment, and I'm sure that the last thing you want to do is make it harder for them. I have a duty to the Konstantinakos position as the ruling and thus most important family on the island. That duty involves a certain amount of entertaining. It will be expected that as my wife you take part in that. Additionally, my sister, her friends, and the wives of those of my executives who live in Athens are very fashion-conscious. They would be quick to sense that our marriage is not all it should be were you to make a point of dressing as you do now. And that could impact on our sons.'

Our sons. Ruby felt as though her heart had been squeezed by a giant hand. She was very tempted to resort to the immature tactic of pointing out that since he hadn't even been aware of the twins' existence until recently he was hardly in a position to take a stance on delivering advice to her on what might or might not affect them—but what was the point? He had won— again, she was forced to acknowledge. Because now she would be very conscious of the fact that she was being judged by her appearance, and that if she was found wanting it would reflect on the twins. Acceptance by their peers was very important to children. Ruby knew that even at the boys' young age children hated being 'different' or being embarrassed. For their sake she would have to accept Sander's charity, even though her pride hated the idea.

She hated feeling so helpless and dependent on others. She loved her sisters, and was infinitely grateful to them for all that they had done for her and the boys, but it was hard sometimes always having to depend on others, never being able to claim the pride and self-respect that came from being financially self-supporting. She had hoped that once the boys were properly settled at school she might be able to earn a degree that ultimately would allow her to find work, but now she was going to be even more dependent on the financial generosity of someone else than she was already. But it wasn't her pride that was important, Ruby reminded herself. It was her sons' emotional happiness. They hadn't asked to be born. And she hadn't asked for Sander's opinion on her appearance—or his money. She was twenty-three, and it was ridiculous of her to feel so helpless and humiliated that she was close to defeated tears.

To conceal her emotions she leaned down towards the boys, to warn them not to run too far ahead of them, watching as they nodded their heads.

It was when she straightened up that it happened. Perhaps she moved too quickly. Ruby didn't know, but one minute she was straightening up and the next she felt so dizzy from the pain in her head that she lost her balance. She would have fallen if Sander hadn't reacted so quickly, reaching out to grab hold of her so that she fell against his body rather than tumbling to the ground.

Immediately she was transported back to the past. The circumstances might be very different, but then too she had stumbled, and Sander had rescued her. Then, though, the cause of her fall had been the unfamiliar height of the borrowed shoes Tracy had insisted she should wear, and the effect of too many cocktails. The result was very much the same. Now, just as then, she could feel the steady thud of Sander's heart against her body, whilst her own raced and bounced, the frantic speed of its beat making her feel breathless and far too weak to try to struggle against the arms holding her. Then too his proximity had filled her senses with the

scent of his skin, the alien maleness of hard muscle
beneath warm flesh, the power of that maleness, both
physically and emotionally, and most of all her own
need to simply be held by him. Then she had been
thrilled to be in his arms, but now… Panic curled through
her. That was not how she was supposed to feel, and it
certainly wasn't what she wanted to feel. Sander was her
enemy—an enemy she was forced to share her sons with
because he was their father, an enemy who had ripped
from her the protection of her naivety with his cruel
contempt for her.

Determinedly Ruby started to push herself free, but
instead of releasing her Sander tightened his hold of her.

He'd seen that she was slender, Sander acknowledged, but it was only now that he was holding her and
could actually feel the bones beneath her flesh that he
was able to recognise how thin she was. She was shivering too, despite her claim not to need a coat. Once
again he was reminded of the report he had commissioned on her. Was it possible that in order to ensure that
her sons ate well and were not deprived of the nourish-
ment they needed she herself had been going without?
Sander had held his sons, and he knew just how solid
and strong their bodies were. The amount of energy
they possessed alone was testament to their good health.
And it was *their* good health that mattered to him, not
that of their mother, whose presence in his life as well
as theirs was something he had told himself he would
have to accept for their sakes.

Even so… He looked down into Ruby's face. Her

skin was paler than he remembered, but he had put that down to the fact that when he had first met her her face had been plastered in make-up, whilst now she wore none. Her cheekbones might be more pronounced, but her lips were still full and soft—the lips of sensual siren who knew just how to use her body to her own advantage. Sander had never been under any illusions as to why Ruby had approached him. He had heard her and her friend discussing the rich footballers they intended to target. Unable to find one, Ruby had obviously decided to target him instead.

Sander frowned, unwilling to contrast the frail vulnerability of the woman he was holding with the girl he remembered, and even more unwilling to allow himself to feel concern for her. Why should he care about her? He didn't. And yet as she struggled to pull free of him, her eyes huge in her fine boned face, a sudden gleam of March sunshine pierced the heavy grey of the late afternoon sky to reveal the perfection of her skin and stroke fingers of light through her blonde curls, Sander had sudden reluctance to let her go. In rejection of it he immediately released her.

It was the unexpected swiftness of her release after Sander's grip had seemed to be tightening on her that was causing her to feel so…confused, Ruby told herself, refusing to allow herself to use the betraying word *bereft*, which had tried to slip through her defences. Why should she feel bereft? She wanted to be free. Sander's hold had no appeal for her. She certainly hadn't spent the last six years longing to be back in his arms. Why should she, when her last memory of them had been the biting pressure of his fingers in her flesh as he thrust her away from him in a gesture of angry contempt?

It had started to rain, causing Ruby to shiver and call the boys to them. It was no good her longing for the security of home, she told herself as they headed back to the hotel in the taxi Sander had flagged down, with the twins squashed in between them so that she didn't have to come into contact with him. She must focus on the future and all that it would hold for her sons. Their happiness was far more important to her than her own, and it was obvious to her how easily they were adapting to Sander's presence in their lives. An acceptance oiled by the promise of expensive toys, Ruby thought bitterly, knowing that her sons were too young for her to be able to explain to them that a parent's love wasn't always best shown though gifts and treats, and knowing too that it would be part of her future role to ensure that they were not spoiled by their father's wealth or blinded to the reality of other people's lives and struggles.

Once they were back in their suite, in the privacy of her bathroom, Ruby tried to take two of the painkiller tablets she had bought from the chemist's she had gone into on the pretext of needing some toothpaste. But her stomach heaved at the mere thought of attempting to swallow them, nausea overwhelming her.

Still feeling sick, and weakened by her pounding headache, as soon as the twins had had something to eat she bathed them and put them to bed.

They had only been asleep a few minutes when the

jeweller Sander had summoned arrived, removing a roll of cloth from his briefcase, after Sander had introduced him to Ruby and they had all sat down.

Placing the roll on the class coffee table, he unfolded it—and Ruby had to suppress a gasp of shock when she saw the glitter of the rings inside it.

They were all beautiful, but something made Ruby recoil from them. It seemed somehow shabby and wrong to think of wearing something so precious. A ring should represent love and commitment that were equally precious and enduring instead of the hollow emptiness her marriage would be.

'You choose,' she told Sander emptily, not wanting to look at them.

Her lack of interest in the priceless gems glittering in front of her made Sander frown. His mother had loved jewellery. He could see her now, seated at her dressing table, dressed to go out for the evening, admiring the antique Cartier bangles glittering on her arms.

'Your birth paid for these,' she had told him. 'Your grandfather insisted that your father should only buy me one, so I had to remind him that I had given birth to his heir. Thank goodness you weren't a girl. Your grandfather is so mean that he would have seen to it that I got nothing if you had been. Remember when you are a man, Sander, that the more expensive the piece of jewellery you give a woman, the more willing she will be, and thus the more you can demand of her.' She had laughed then, pouting her glossy red lip-sticked lips at her own reflection and adding, 'I shouldn't really give away the secrets of my sex to you, should I?'

His beautiful, shallow, greedy mother—chosen as a bride for his father by his grandfather because of her aristocratic Greek ancestry, marrying his father because she hated her own family's poverty. When he had grown old enough to recognise the way in which his gentle academic father had been humiliated and treated with contempt by the father who had forced the marriage on him, and the wife who thought of him only as an open bank account, Sander had sworn he would never follow in his father's footsteps and allow the same thing to happen to him.

What was Ruby hoping for by pretending a lack of interest? Something more expensive? Angrily Sander looked at the rings, his hand hovering over the smallest solitaire he could see. His intention was to punish her by choosing it for her—until his attention was drawn to another ring close to it, its two perfect diamonds shimmering in the light.

Feeling too ill to care what kind of engagement ring she had, Ruby exhaled in relief when she saw Sander select one of the rings. All she wanted was for the whole distasteful charade to be over.

'We'll have this one,' Sander told the jeweller abruptly, his voice harsh with the irritation he felt against himself for his own sentimentality.

It was the jeweller who handed the ring to Ruby, not Sander. She took it unwillingly, sliding the cold metal onto her finger, her eyes widening and her heart turning over inside her chest as she looked at it properly for the first time. Two perfect diamonds nestled together on a slender band, slightly offset from one another and yet touching—twin diamonds for their twin sons. Her throat closed up, her gaze seeking Sander's despite her attempt to stop it doing so, her emotions clearly on display. But there was no answering warmth in Sander's eyes, only a cold hardness that froze her out.

'An excellent choice,' the jeweller was saying. 'Each stone weighs two carets, and they are a particularly good quality. And of course ethically mined, just as you requested,' he informed Sander.

His comment took Ruby by surprise. From what she knew of Sander she wouldn't have thought it would matter to him *how* the diamonds had been mined, but obviously it did. Meaning what? That she had mis-judged him? Meaning nothing, Ruby told herself fiercely. She didn't want to revisit her opinion of Sander, never mind re-evaluate it. Why not? Because she was afraid that if she did so, if she allowed herself to see him in a different light, then she might become even more vulnerable to him than she already was? Emotionally vulnerable as well as sexually vulnerable? No, that must not happen.

Her panic increased her existing nausea, and it was a relief when the jeweller finally left. His departure was quickly followed by Sander's, to his business meeting.

Finally she could give in to her need to go and lie down—after she had checked on the twins, of course.

CHAPTER FIVE

'YOUR hair is lovely and thick, but since it is so curly I think it would look better if we put a few different lengths into it.' Those had been the words of the salon's senior stylist when he had first come over to examine Ruby's hair. She had simply nodded her head, not really caring how he cut her hair. She was still feeling unwell, her head still aching, and she knew from experience that these headaches could last for two and even three days once they took hold, before finally lifting.

Now, though, as the stylist stepped back from the mirror and asked, 'What do you think?' Ruby was forced to admit that she was almost lost for words over the difference his skill had made to her hair, transforming it from an untidy tumble of curls into a stunningly chic style that feathered against her face and swung softly onto her shoulders—the kind of style she had seen worn by several of the women taking tea at the hotel the previous afternoon, a deceptively simple style that breathed expense and elegance.

'I...I love it,' she admitted wanly.

'It's easy to maintain and will fall back into shape after you've washed it. You're lucky to have naturally blonde hair.'

Thanking him, Ruby allowed herself to be led away. At least she had managed to eat some dry toast this morning, and keep down a couple of the painkillers which had eased her head a little, thankfully.

Her next appointment was at the beauty spa, and when she caught other women giving her a second look as she made her way there she guessed that they must be querying the elegance of her new hairstyle set against the shabbiness of her clothes and her make-up-free face.

She hated admitting it, but it *was* true that first impressions counted, and that people—especially women—judged members of their own sex by their appearance. The last thing she wanted was for the twins to be embarrassed by a mother other women looked down on. Even young children were very perceptive and quick to notice such things.

The spa and beauty salon was ahead of her. Taking a deep breath, Ruby held her head high as she walked in.

Two hours later, when she walked out again with the personal shopper who had come to collect her and help her choose a new wardrobe, Ruby couldn't help giving quick, disbelieving glances into the mirrors she passed, still unable to totally believe that the young woman looking back at her really was her. Her nails were manicured and painted a fashionable dark shade, her eyebrows were trimmed, and her make-up was applied in such a subtle and delicate way that it barely looked as though she was wearing any at all. Yet at the same time her eyes looked larger and darker, her mouth fuller and softer, and her complexion so delicately perfect that Ruby couldn't take her eyes off the glowing face looking back at her. Although she would never admit it to Sander, her makeover had been fun once she had got over her initial discomfort at being fussed over and pampered. Now she felt like a young woman rather than an anxious mother.

'I understand you want clothes suitable for living on a Greek island, rather than merely holidaying there, and that your life there will include various social and business engagements?' Without waiting for Ruby's answer the personal shopper continued. 'Fortunately we have got some of our new season stock in as well as several designers' cruise collections, so I'm sure we shall be able to find everything you need. As for your wedding dress…'

Ruby's heart leapt inside her chest. Somehow she hadn't expected Sander to specify that she needed a wedding dress.

'It's just a very quiet registry office ceremony,' she told the personal shopper.

'But her wedding day and what she wore when she married the man she loves is still something that a woman always remembers,' the other woman insisted.

The personal shopper was only thinking of the store's profit, Ruby reminded herself. There was no real reason for her to have such an emotional reaction to the words. After all, she didn't love Sander and he certainly didn't love her. What she wore was immaterial, since neither of them was likely to want to look back in future years to remember the day they married. Her thoughts had produced a hard painful lump in her throat and an unwanted ache inside her chest. Why? She was twenty-three years old and the mother of five-year-old sons. She had long ago abandoned any thoughts of romance and love and all that went with those things, dismissing them as the emotional equivalent of chocolate—sweet on the tongue for a very short time, highly addictive and dangerously habit-forming. Best avoided in favour of a sensible and sustaining emotional diet. Like the love she had for her sons and the bond she shared with her sisters. Those were emotions and commitments that would last for a lifetime, whilst from what she had seen and heard romantic love was a delusion.

The twins were fascinated by the exhibits in the Natural History Museum. They had happily held Sander's hand and pressed gratifyingly close to him for protection, calling him Daddy and showing every indication of being happy to be with him, so why did he feel so aware of Ruby's absence, somehow incomplete? It was for the boys' sake, Sander assured himself, because he was concerned that they might be missing their mother, nothing more.

Without quite knowing how it had happened, Ruby had acquired a far more extensive and expensive wardrobe than she had wanted. Every time she had protested or objected the personal shopper had overruled her—politely and pleasantly, but nonetheless determinedly—insisting that her instructions were that Ruby must have a complete wardrobe that would cover a wide variety of situations. And of course the clothes were sinfully gorgeous—beautifully cut trousers and shorts in cream linen, with a matching waistcoat lined in the same silk as the unstructured shirt that went with them, soft flowing silk dresses, silk and cotton tops, formal fitted cocktail dresses, along with more casual but still frighteningly expensive 'leisure and beach clothes', as the personal shopper had described them. There were also shoes for every occasion and each outfit, and underwear—scraps of silk and lace that Ruby had wanted to reject in favour of something far more sensible, but which somehow or other had been added to the growing rail of clothes described by the personal shopper as 'must-haves'.

Now all that was left was the wedding dress, and the personal shopper was producing with a flourish a cream dress with a matching jacket telling Ruby proudly, 'Vera Wang, from her new collection. Since the dress is short and beautifully tailored it is ideal for a registry office wedding, and of course you could wear it afterwards as a cocktail dress. It was actually ordered by another customer, but unfortunately when it came it was too small for her. I'm sure that it will fit you, and the way the fabric is pleated will suit your body shape.'

What she meant was that the waterfall of pleated

ruching that was a feature of the cream silk-satin dress would disguise how thin she was, Ruby suspected.

The dress was beautiful, elegant and feminine, and exactly the kind of dress that a woman would remember wearing on her wedding day—which was exactly why she didn't want to wear it. But the dresser was waiting expectantly.

It fitted her perfectly. Cut by a master hand, it shaped her body in a way that made her waist appear far narrower surely than it actually was, whilst somehow adding a feminine curvaceousness to her shape that made Ruby think she was looking at someone else in the mirror and not herself: the someone else she might have been if things had been different. If Sander had loved her?

Shakily Ruby shook her head and started to take the dress off, desperate to escape from the cruel reality of the image the mirror had thrown back at her. She could never be the woman she had seen in the mirror—a woman so loved by her man that she had the right to claim everything the dress offered her and promised him.

'No. I don't want it,' she told the bewildered-looking personal shopper. 'Please take it away. I'll wear something else.'

'But it was perfect on you…'

Still Ruby shook her head.

She was in the changing room getting dressed when the personal shopper reappeared, carrying a warm-looking, casually styled off-white parka.

'I nearly forgot,' she told Ruby, 'your husband-to-be said that you had left your coat at home by accident and that you needed something warm to wear whilst you are in London.'

Wordlessly Ruby took the parka from her. It was lined with soft checked wool, and well-made as well as stylish.

'It's a new designer,' the shopper told her. 'And a line that we're just trialling. She's Italian, trained by Prada.'

Ruby bent her head so that the personal shopper wouldn't see the emotion sheening her eyes. Sander might have protected her in public by pretending to believe that she had forgotten her coat, but in private he had humiliated her—because Ruby knew that he had guessed that she didn't really possess a winter coat, and that she had been shivering with cold yesterday when they had walked in the park.

Walking back to the hotel wrapped in her new parka, Ruby reflected miserably that beneath the new hairstyle and the pretty make-up she was still exactly what she had been beforehand—they couldn't change her, could not take away the burden of the guilt she still carried because of what she had once been. Expensive clothes were only a pretence—just like her marriage to Sander would be.

For her. Yes, but not for the twins. They must never know how she felt. The last thing she wanted was for them to grow up feeling that she had sacrificed herself for them. They must believe that she was happy.

She had intended to go straight to the suite, but the assessing look a woman in the lobby gave her, before smiling slightly to herself, as though she was satisfied that Ruby couldn't compete with her, stung her pride enough to have her changing her mind and heading for the lounge instead.

A well-trained waitress showed her to a small table right at the front of the lounge. Ruby would have preferred to have hidden herself away in a dark corner, her brief surge of defiance having retreated leaving her feeling self-conscious and very alone. She wasn't used to being on her own. Normally when she went out she had the twins with her, or one of her sisters.

When the waitress came to take her order Ruby asked for tea. She hadn't eaten anything all day but she wasn't hungry. She was too on edge for that.

The lounge was filling up. Several very smart-looking women were coming in, followed by a group of businessmen in suits, one of whom gave her such a deliberate look followed by a warm smile that Ruby felt her face beginning to burn.

She was just about to pour herself a cup of tea when she saw the twins hurrying towards her followed by Sander. His hair, like the twins', was damp, as though he had just stepped out of the shower. Her heart lurched into her ribs. Her hand had started to tremble so badly that she had to put down the teapot. The twins were clamouring to tell her about their day, but even though she tried desperately to focus on them her gaze remained riveted to Sander, who had now stopped walking and was looking at her.

It wasn't her changed appearance that had brought him to an abrupt halt, though.

In Sander's eyes the new hairstyle and pretty make-up were merely window-dressing that highlighted what he already knew and what had been confirmed to him when Ruby had opened the door of her home to him a few days earlier—namely that the delicacy of her features possessed a rare beauty.

No, what had caused him to stop dead almost in mid-stride was the sense of male pride the sight of the trio in front of him brought. His sons and their mother. Not just his sons, but the *three* of them. They went together, belonged together—belonged to him? Sander shook his head, trying to dispel his atavistic and unfamiliar reactions with regard to Ruby, both angered by them and wanting to reject them. They were so astonishingly the opposite of what he wanted to feel. What was happening to him?

Her transformation passed him by other than the fact that he noticed the way she was wearing her hair revealed the slender column of her throat and that her face had a bit more colour in it.

Ruby, already self-conscious about the changes to her appearance, held her breath, waiting for Sander to make some comment. After all the sight of her had brought him to a halt. But when he reached the table he simply frowned and demanded to know why she hadn't ordered something to eat.

'Because all I wanted was a cup of tea,' she answered him. Didn't he like her new haircut? Was that why he was looking so grim? Well, she certainly wasn't going to ask him if he approved of the change. She turned to the boys, asking them, 'Did you like the Natural History Museum?'

'Yes,' Harry confirmed. 'And then Daddy took us swimming.'

Swimming? Ruby directed a concerned look at Sander.

'There's a pool here in the hotel,' he explained. 'Since the boys will be living on an island, I wanted to make sure that they can swim.'

'Daddy bought us new swimming trunks,' Freddie told her.

'There should be two adults with them when they go in a pool,' Ruby couldn't stop herself from saying. 'A child can drown in seconds and—'

'There was a lifeguard on duty.' Sander stopped her. 'They're both naturals in the water, but that will be in their genes. My brother swam for Greece as a junior.'

'Mummy's hair is different,' Harry suddenly announced.

Self-consciousness crawled along her spine. Now surely Sander must say something about her transformation, give at least some hint of approval since he was the one who had orchestrated her makeover, but instead he merely stated almost indifferently, 'I hope you got everything you are going to need, as there won't be time for any more shopping. As I said, I've arranged for us to fly to the island the day after the marriage ceremony.'

Ruby nodded her head. It was silly of her to feel disappointed because Sander hadn't said anything about her new look. Silly or dangerous? His approval or lack of it shouldn't mean anything to her at all.

The boys would be hungry, and she was tired. She was their mother, though, and it was far more important that she focused on her maternal responsibilities rather than worrying about Sander's approval or lack of it.

'I'll take the boys up to the suite and organise a meal for them,' she told Sander.

'Good idea. I've got some ends to tie up with the Embassy,' he said brusquely, with a brief nod of his head.

'What about dinner?' Ruby's mouth had gone dry, and the silence that greeted her question made her feel she had committed as much of a *faux pas* as if she'd asked him to go to bed with her.

Feeling hot and angry with herself for inadvertently giving Sander the impression that she wanted to have dinner with him, she swallowed against the dry feeling in her mouth.

Why had Ruby's simple question brought back that atavistic feeling he had had earlier? Sander asked himself angrily. For a moment he let himself imagine the two of them having dinner together. The two of them? Surely he meant the four of them—for it was because of the twins and only because of them that he had decided to allow her back into his life. Sander knew better than to allow himself to be tricked by female emotions, be they maternal or sexual. As he had good cause to know, those emotions could be summoned out of nowhere and disappear back there just as quickly.

'I've already arranged to have dinner with an old friend,' he lied. 'I don't know what time I'll be back.'

An old friend, Sander had said. Did that mean he was having dinner with another woman? A lover, perhaps?

Ruby wondered later, after the boys had eaten their tea and she had forced herself to eat something with them. She knew so little about Sander's life and the people in it. A feeling of panic began to grow inside her.

'Mummy, come and look at our island,' Freddie was demanding, standing in front of a laptop that he was trying to open.

'No, Freddie, you mustn't touch that,' Ruby protested,

'It's all right, Mummy,' Harry assured her adopting a heartbreakingly familiar pose of male confidence. 'Daddy said that we could look.'

Freddie had got the laptop lid up—like all children, the twins were very at home with modern technology— and before Ruby could say anything the screen was filled with the image of an almost crescent shaped island, with what looked like a range of rugged mountains running the full length of its spine.

In the early days, after she had first met him, Ruby had tried to find out as much as she could about Sander, still refusing to believe then that all she had been to him was a one-night stand.

She had learned that the island, whose closest neighbour was Cyprus, had been invaded and conquered many times, and that in Sander's veins ran the ruling blood of conquering Moors from the time of the Crusades—even though now the island population considered itself to be Greek. She had also learned that Sander's family had ruled the island for many centuries, and that his grandfather, the current patriarch, had built

up a shipping business in the wake of the Second World
War which had brought new wealth and employment to
the island. However, once she had been forced to recognise that she meant nothing to Sander she had stopped
seeking out information about him.

'Bath time,' she told her sons firmly.

Their new clothes and her own had been delivered
whilst they had been downstairs, along with some very
smart new cases, and once the twins were in bed she
intended to spend her evening packing in readiness for
their flight to the island.

Only once the boys were bathed and in bed Ruby was
drawn back to the computer, with its tantalising image
of the island.

Almost without realising what she was doing she
clicked on the small red dot that represented its capital.
Several thumbnail images immediately appeared. Ruby
clicked on the first of them to enlarge it, and revealed a
dazzlingly white fortress, perched high on a cliff above
an impossibly blue green sea, its Moorish-looking
towers reaching up into a deep blue sky. Another thumbnail enlarged to show what she assumed was the front
of the same building, looking more classically Greek in
design and dominating a formal square. The royal blue
of the traditionally dressed guards' jackets worn over
brilliantly white skirts made a striking image.

The other images revealed a hauntingly beautiful
landscape of sandy bays backed by cliffs, small fishing
harbours, and white-capped mountains covered in wild
flowers. These were contrasted by a modern cargo dock

complex, and small towns of bright white buildings and dark shadowed alleyways. It was impossible not to be captivated by the images of the island, Ruby admitted, but at the same time viewing them had brought home to her how different and even alien the island was to everything she and the twins knew. Was she doing the right thing? She knew nothing of Sander's family, or his way of life, and once on the island she would be totally at his mercy. But if she hadn't agreed to go with them he would have tried to take the twins from her, she was sure. This way at least she would be with them.

A fierce tide of maternal love surged through her. The twins meant everything to her. Their emotional security both now and in the future was what would bring her happiness, and was far more important to her than anything else—especially the unwanted and humiliating desire that Sander was somehow able to arouse in her. Her mouth had gone dry again. At seventeen she might have been able to excuse herself for being vulnerable to Sander's sexual charisma, but she was not seventeen any more. Even if her single solitary memory of sexual passion was still limited to what she had experienced with Sander. He, of course, had no doubt shared his bed with an unending parade of women since he had ejected her so cruelly from both it and his life.

She looked at the computer, suddenly unable to resist the temptation to do a web search on Sander's name. It wasn't prying, not really. She had the boys to think of after all.

She wasn't sure what she had expected to find, but

her eyes widened over the discovery that Sander was now ruler of the island—a role that carried the title of King, although, according to the website, he had decided to dispense with its usage, preferring to adopt a more democratic approach to ruling the island than that exercised by his predecessors.

Apparently his parents had died when Sander was eighteen, in a flying accident. The plane they'd been in piloted by a cousin of Sander's mother. A shock as though she had inadvertently touched a live wire shot through her. They had both been orphaned at almost the same age. Like hers, Sander's parents had been killed in an accident. If she had known that when they had first met… What difference would it have made? None.

Sander was thirty-four, to her twenty-three; a man at the height of his powers. A small shiver raked her skin, like the sensual rasp of a lover's tongue against sensitised flesh. Inside her head an image immediately formed: Sander's dark tanned hand cupping her own naked breast, his tongue curling round her swollen nipple. The small shiver became a racking shudder. Quickly Ruby tried to banish the image, closing down the computer screen. She was feeling nauseous again. Shakily, she made her way to the bathroom.

CHAPTER SIX

'I NOW pronounce you man and wife.'

It was over, done. There was no going back. Ruby was shaking inwardly, but she refused to let Sander see how upset she was.

Upset? A small tremor made her body shudder inside the cream Vera Wang dress she had not wanted to wear but which the personal shopper had included amongst her purchases and which for some reason she had felt obliged to wear. It was, after all, her wedding day. A fresh tremor broke through her self-control. What was the matter with her? What had she expected? Hearts and flowers? A declaration of undying devotion? This was Sander she was marrying, Sander who had not looked at her once during the brief ceremony in the anonymous register office, who couldn't have made it plainer how little he wanted her as his wife. Well, no more than she wanted him as her husband.

Sander looked down at Ruby's left hand. The ring he had just slipped onto her marriage finger was slightly loose, despite the fact that it should have fitted. She was far too thin and seemed to be getting thinner. But why should her fragility concern him?

It didn't. Women were adept at creating fictional images in order to deceive others. To her sons Ruby was no doubt a much loved mother, a constant and secure presence in their lives. At their age that had been his own feeling about his mother. Bitterness curled through him, spreading its poisonous infection.

In the years since the deaths of his parents he had often wondered if his father had given in so readily to his mother's financial demands because secretly he had loved her, even though he'd known she'd only despised him, and she, knowing that, had used his love against him. It was a fate he had sworn would never be his own.

And yet here he was married, and to a woman he already knew he could not trust—a woman who had given herself to him with such sensuality and intimacy that even now after so many years he was unable to strip from his memory the images she had left upon it. He had been a fool to let her get close enough to him once to do that. He wasn't going to let it happen again.

Neither of them spoke in the taxi taking them back to the hotel. Ruby already knew Sander had some business matters to attend to, which thankfully meant that she would have some time to herself in which to come to terms with the commitment she had just made.

After Sander had escorted them to the suite and then left without a word to her, after kissing the boys, Ruby reminded herself that she had not only walked willingly into this marriage, she was the one who had first suggested it.

The boys were tired—worn out, Ruby suspected, by the excitement of being in London. A short sleep would do them all good, and might help to ease her cramped, nauseous stomach and aching head.

After removing her wedding dress and pulling on her old dressing gown, she put the twins to bed. Once she had assured herself that they were asleep she went into her own bathroom, fumbling in her handbag for some headache tablets and accidentally removing the strip of birth control pills instead. They reminded her that although Sander might have made her take them she must not let him make her want him. Her hands shook as she replaced them to remove the pack of painkillers. Just that simple action had started her head pounding again, but thankfully this time at least she wasn't sick.

She was so tired that after a bath to help her relax she could barely dry herself, never mind bother to put on a nightdress. Instead she simply crawled beneath the duvet on her bed, falling asleep almost immediately.

Ruby woke up reluctantly, dragged from her sleep by a sense of nagging urgency. It only took her a matter of seconds to realise what had caused it. The silence. She couldn't hear the twins. How long had she been asleep? Her heart jolted anxiously into her ribs when she looked at her watch and realised that it was over three hours since she had tucked the twins into their beds. Why were they so quiet?

Trembling with apprehension, she pushed back the bedclothes, grabbing the towel she had discarded earlier and wrapping it around herself as she ran barefoot from her own room to the twins'.

It was empty. Her heart lurched sickeningly, and then started to beat frantically fast with fear.

On shaking legs Ruby ran through the suite, opening doors, calling their names, even checking the security lock on the main door to the suite just in case they had somehow opened it. All the time the hideous reality of what might have happened was lying in wait for her inside her head.

In the dreadful silence of the suite—only a parent could know and understand how a silence that should have been filled with the sound of children's voices could feel—she sank down onto one of the sofas.

The reason the twins weren't here must be because Sander had taken them. There could be no other explanation. He must have come back whilst she was asleep and seized his opportunity. He hadn't wanted to marry her any more than she had wanted to marry him. What he had wanted was the twins. His sons. And now he had them.

Were they already on a plane to the island? *His* island, where he made the laws and where she would never be able to reach them. He had their passports after all. A legal necessity, he had said, and she had stupidly accepted that.

Shock, grief, fear and anger—she could feel them all, but over and above those feelings was concern for her sons and fury that Sander could have done something so potentially harmful to them.

She could hear a noise: the sound of the main door to the suite opening, followed by the excited babble of two familiar voices.

The twins!

She was on her feet, hardly daring to believe that she wasn't simply imagining hearing them out of her own need, and then they were there, in the room with her, running towards her and telling her excitedly, 'Daddy took us to a café for our tea, because you were asleep,' bringing the smell of cold air in with them.

Dropping onto her knees, Ruby hugged them to her not trusting herself to speak, holding the small wriggling bodies tightly. They were her life, her heart, her everything. She could hardly bear to let them go.

Sander was standing watching her, making her acutely conscious as she struggled to stand up that all that covered her nudity was the towel she had wrapped round her.

Going back to her bedroom, she discarded the towel and grabbed a clean pair of knickers before reaching for her old and worn velour dressing gown. She was too worked up and too anxious to get back to the twins as quickly as she could to care what she looked like or what Sander thought. The fact that he hadn't taken them as she had initially feared paled into insignificance compared with her realisation that he could have done so. Now that she had had a taste of what it felt like to think she had lost them, she knew more than ever that there was nothing she would not do or sacrifice to keep them with her.

Her hands trembled violently as she tied the belt on

her dressing gown. From the sitting room she could hear the sound of cartoon voices from the television, and when she went back in the boys were sitting together, watching a children's TV programme, whilst Sander was seated at the small desk with his laptop open in front of him.

Neither of them had spoken, but the tension and hostility crackling in the air between them spoke a language they could both hear and understand.

Her headache might have gone, but it had been replaced with an equally sickening sense of guilt, Ruby acknowledged, when she sat down an hour later to read to the boys, now bathed and in bed. She watched them as they fell asleep after their bedtime story. Today something had happened that she had never experienced before. She had slept so deeply that she had not heard anything when Sander returned and took her sons. How could that be? How could she have been so careless of their safety?

She didn't want to leave them. She wanted to stay here all night with them.

The bedroom door opened. Immediately Ruby stiffened, whispering, 'What do you want?'

'I've come to say goodnight to my sons.'

'They're asleep.' She got up and walked to the door, intending to go through it and then close it, excluding him, but Sander was holding it and she was the one forced to leave and then watch as he went to kiss their sleeping faces.

Turning on her heel, Ruby headed for her own room. But before she stepped inside it her self-control broke and she whirled round, telling Sander, 'You had no right to take the boys out without asking me first.'

'They are my sons. I have every right. And as for telling you—'

Telling her, not asking her. Ruby noted his correction, consumed now by the kind of anger that followed the trauma of terrible shock and fear, which was a form of relief at discovering that the unthinkable hadn't happened after all.

'You were asleep.'

'You could have woken me. You *should* have woken me. It's my right as their mother to know where they are.'

'Your *right*? What about *their* rights? What about their right to have a mother who doesn't put her own needs first? I suppose a woman who goes out at night picking up men needs to sleep during the day. And knowing you as I do, I imagine that is what *you* do.'

Sickened by what he was implying, Ruby said fiercely, '*Knowing* me? You don't know me at all. And the unpleasant little scenario you have just outlined has never and would never take place. I have never so much as gone out at night and left the twins, never mind gone out picking up men. The reason I was asleep was because I haven't been feeling well—not that I expect you to believe me. You'd much rather make up something you can insult me with than listen to the truth.'

'I've had firsthand experience of the truth of what you are.'

Ruby's face burned. 'You're basing your judgement of me on one brief meeting, when I was—'

'Too drunk to know what you were doing?'

His cynical contempt was too much for Ruby's composure. For years she had tortured and tormented herself because of what she had done. She didn't need Sander weighing in to add to that self-punishment and pain. She shook her head in angry denial.

'Foolish and naive enough to want to create a fairy story out of something and someone belonging in reality to a horror story,' she said bitterly. Too carried away by the anger bursting past her self-control, she continued, 'You need not have wasted your contempt on me, because it can't possibly match the contempt I feel for myself, for deluding myself that you were someone special.'

Ruby felt sick and dizzy. Memories of what they had once shared were rushing in, roaring over her mental barriers and springing into vivid life inside her. She had been such a fool, so willing and eager to go to him, seeking in his arms the security and safety she had lost and thinking in her naivety that she would find them by binding herself to him in the most intimate way there was.

'So much drama,' Sander taunted her, 'and all of it so unnecessary, since I know it for the deceit that it is.'

'You are the one who is deceiving yourself by believing what you do,' Ruby threw at him emotionally.

'You dare to accuse *me* of self-deception?' Sander demanded, stepping towards her as he spoke, forcing her to step back into her bedroom. She backed up so quickly that she ended up standing on the trailing belt of her dressing gown. The soft, worn fabric gave way immediately, exposing the pale curve of her breast and the darker flesh of her nipple.

Sander saw what had happened before Ruby was aware of it herself, and his voice dropped to a cynical softness as he said, 'So that's what you want, is it? Same old Ruby. Well, why not? You certainly owe me something.'

Ruby's despairing, 'No!' was lost, crushed beneath the cruel strength of his mouth as it fastened on hers, and the sound of the door slamming as he pushed it closed was a death knell on her chances of escape.

Her robe quickly gave way to the swift expertise of Sander's determined hands, sliding from Ruby's body whilst he punished her with his kiss. In the mirror Sander could see the narrow curve of her naked back. Her skin, palely luminous, reminded him of the inside of the shells washed up on the beach below his home. Against his will old memories stirred, of how beneath his touch and against it she had trembled and then shuddered, calling out to him in open pleasure, so easily aroused by even the lightest caress. A wanton who had made no attempt to conceal the passion that drove her, or her own pleasure in his satisfaction of it, crying out to him to please her.

Sander drove his tongue between her lips as fiercely as he wanted to drive out her memory. The honeyed sensuality of her mouth closed round him, inviting his tongue-tip's exploration of its sweetest hidden places. The simple plain white knickers she was wearing jarred against the raw sexuality of his own arousal. He wanted her naked and eager, stripped of the lies and deceit with which she was so keen to veil her own reality. He would make her admit to what she was, show her that he knew the true naked reality of her. His hands gripped her and held her, moving down over her body to push aside her protective covering.

Her figure was as perfect as it was possible for a woman's figure to be—or it would be if she carried a few more pounds, Sander acknowledged. From her shoulders, her torso narrowed down into a handspan waist before curving out into feminine hips and the high, rounded cheeks of her bottom. Her legs were long and slender, designed to wrap erotically and greedily around the man she chose to give her the pleasure she craved. Her breasts were full and soft, and he could remember how sensitive her nipples had been, the suckle of his mouth against them making her cry out in ecstasy.

Why was he tormenting himself with mere memories when she was here and his for the taking, her body already shivering in his hold with anticipation of the pleasure to come?

She was naked and in Sander's power. She should fight him and reject him, Ruby knew. She wanted to, but her body wanted something else. Her body wanted Sander.

Like some dark power conjured up by a master sorcerer desire swept through her, overwhelming reason and pride, igniting a need so intense that she felt as though an alien force were possessing her, dictating actions and reactions it was impossible for her to control.

It was as though in Sander's arms she became a different person—a wildly passionate, elementally sensual woman of such intensity that everything she was crystallised in the act of being taken by him and taking him in turn.

It might be her wish to fight what possessed her, but it was also her destiny to submit to it as Sander's mouth moved from its fierce possession of hers to an equally erotic exploration of her throat, lingering on the pulse there that so recklessly gave away her arousal.

It was not enough to have her naked to his gaze and his touch. He needed to have the feel of her against his own skin. She was an ache, a need, a compulsion that wouldn't allow him to rest until he had conquered her and she had submitted to his mastery of her pleasure. He wanted, needed, to hear her cry out that desire to him before he could allow himself to submit to his own desire for her. He needed her to offer up her pleasure to him before he could lose himself within her and take his own.

He was caught in a trap as old as Eve herself—caught and held in the silken web of a desire only she had the power to spin. The savagery of his anger that this should be so was only matched by the savagery of his need for the explosion of fevered sensuality now possessing them both. It was a form of madness, a fever, a possession he couldn't escape.

Scooping her up in his arms, Sander carried Ruby to the bed, watching her watch him as he placed her on it and then wrenched off his own clothes, seeing the way her eyes betrayed her reaction to the sight of him, naked and ready for her.

Her eyes dark and wide with delight, Ruby reached

out to touch the formidable thickness of Sander's erection, marvelling at the texture of his flesh beneath her fingers. Engrossed and entranced, she stroked her fingertips over the length of him, easing back the hooded cover to reveal the sensitive flesh beneath it, not the woman she knew as herself any more, but instead a Ruby who was possessed by the powerful dark force of their shared desire—a Ruby whose breath quickened and whose belly tightened in pleasurable longing.

She looked up at Sander and saw in his eyes the same need she knew was in her own. She lifted her hand from his body, and as though it had been a signal to him he pushed her back on the bed, following her down, shaping and moulding her breasts with his hands, feeding her need for the erotic pleasure she knew he could give her with the heat of his lips and his tongue on her nipples, until she arched up against him, whimpering beneath the unbearable intensity of her own pleasure.

The feel of his hand cupping her sex wasn't just something she welcomed. It was something she needed.

Her body was wet and ready for him, just as it had been before. Just for a heartbeat the mistrust that was his mother's legacy to him surfaced past Sander's desire. There must not be another unwanted conception.

'The pill—' he began,

Ruby nodded her head.

A sheen of perspiration gleamed on his tanned flesh, and the scent of his arousal was heightening her own. It was frightening, this intensity of desire, this sharpening and focusing of her senses so that only Sander filled them. It had frightened her six years ago and it still frightened her now. The need he aroused within her demanded that she gave everything of herself over to him—all that she was, every last bit of her. The verbal demand he was making now was nothing compared with that.

'Yes. I'm taking it.'

'You swear?'

'I swear…'

Sander heard the unsteady note of need trembling in her voice. She was impatient for him, but no more than he was for her. He had fought to hold back the tide of longing for her from the minute he had seen her again. It had mocked his efforts to deny it, and now it was overwhelming him, the fire burning within him consuming him. Right now, in this heartbeat of time, nothing else mattered. He was in the grip of a force so powerful that he had to submit to it.

They moved together, without the need for words, movement matching movement, a duel of shared anger and longing. Her body welcomed his, holding it, sheathing it, moving with it and against it, demanding that he move faster and deeper, driving them both to that place from which they could soar to the heavens and then fall back to earth.

It was here now—that shuddering climax of sensation, gripping her, gripping Sander, causing the spurting spill of the seeds of new life within her. Only this time there would be no new life because she was on the pill.

They lay together in the darkness, their breathing unsteady and audible in the silence.

Now—now when it was over, and his flesh was washed with the cold reality of how quickly he had given in to his need for her—Sander was forced to accept the truth. He could not control the physical desire she aroused in him. It had overwhelmed him, and it would overwhelm him again. That knowledge was a bitter blow to his pride.

Without looking at her, he told her emotionlessly, 'From now on I am the only man you will have sex with. Is that understood? I will not have my wife shaming me by offering herself to other men. And to ensure that you don't I shall make it my business to see to it that your eager appetite for sexual pleasure is kept satisfied.'

Sander knew that his words were merely a mask for the reality that he could neither bear the thought of her with another man nor control his own desire for her, no matter how much he despised himself for his weakness.

Ruby could feel her face burning with humiliation. She wanted to tell him that she didn't understand what happened to her when she was in his arms. She wanted to tell him that other men did not have the same effect on her. She wanted to tell him that he was the only man she had ever had sex with. But she knew that he wouldn't listen.

Later, alone in his own room, Sander tried to explain to himself why the minute he touched Ruby he became filled with a compulsion to possess her. His desire for her was stronger than his resolve to resist it, and he couldn't. What she made him feel and want was unique to her, loath as he was to admit that.

CHAPTER SEVEN

GIVEN Sander's wealth, Ruby had half expected that they might fly first-class to the island—but what she had not expected was that they would be travelling in the unimagined luxury of a private jet, with them the only passengers on board. But that was exactly what had happened, and now, with the boys taken by the steward to sit with the captain for a few minutes, she and Sander were alone in the cabin, with its cream leather upholstery and off-white carpets.

'The money it must cost to own and run something like this would feed hundreds of poor families,' Ruby couldn't stop herself from saying.

Her comment, and the unspoken accusation it held, made Sander frown. He had never once heard his mother express concern for 'poor families', and the fact that Ruby had done so felt like a sharp paper cut on the tender skin of his judgement of her—something small and insignificant in one sense, but in another something he could not ignore, no matter how much he might want to do so.

To his own disbelief he found himself defending his

position, telling her, 'I don't actually own it. I merely belong to a small consortium of businessmen who share and charter it when they need it. As for feeding the poor—on the island we operate a system which ensures that no one goes hungry and that every child has access to an education matched to their skills and abilities. We also have a free health service and a good pension system—the latter two schemes put in place by my father.'

Why on earth did he think he had to justify anything he did to *Ruby*?

It was dark when their flight finally put down on the island, the darkness obscuring their surroundings apart from what they could see in the blaze of the runway lights as they stepped down from the plane and into the warm velvet embrace of the Mediterranean evening. A soft breeze ruffled the boys' hair as they clung to Ruby's sides, suddenly uncertain and unsure of themselves. A golf cart type of vehicle was their transport for the short distance to the arrivals building, where Sander shook hands with the officials waiting to greet him before ushering them outside again to the limousine waiting for them. It was Sander who lifted the sleepy children into it, settling Harry on his lap and then putting his free arm around Freddie, whilst Ruby was left to sit on her own. Her arms felt empty without the twins, and she felt a maternal urge to reach for them, but she resisted it, not wanting to disturb them now that they were asleep.

The headache and subsequent nausea it had caused

her had thankfully not returned, although she still didn't feel one hundred percent.

The car moved swiftly down a straight smooth road before eventually turning off it onto a more winding road, on one side of which Ruby could see the sea glinting in the moonlight. On the other side of them was a steep wall of rock, which eventually gave way to an old fashioned fortress-like city wall, with a gateway in it through which they drove, past tall buildings and then along a narrow street which broadened out into the large formal square Ruby had seen on the internet.

'This is the main square of the city, with the Royal Palace up ahead of us,' Sander informed her.

'Is that where we'll be living?' Ruby asked apprehensively.

Sander shook his head.

'No. The palace is used only for formal occasions now, and as an administrative centre. After my grandfather died I had my own villa built just outside the city. I don't care for pomp and circumstance. My people's quality of life is what is important to me, just as it was to my father. I cannot expect to have their respect if I do not give them mine.'

Ruby looked away from him. His comments showed the kind of attitude she admired, but how could she allow herself to admire Sander? It was bad enough that he could arouse her physically without her being vulnerable to him emotionally as well.

'The city must be very old,' she said instead.

'Very,' Sander agreed.

As always when he returned to the island after an absence, he was torn in opposing directions. He loved the island and its people, but he also had the painful memories of his childhood here to contend with.

In an effort to banish them and concentrate on something else, he told Ruby, 'The Phoenicians and the Egyptians traded here, just as they did with our nearest neighbour Cyprus. Like Cyprus, we too have large deposits of copper here, and possession of the island was fought over fiercely during the Persian wars. In the end a marriage alliance between the opposing forces brought the fighting to an end. That has traditionally been the way in which territorial disputes have been settled here—' He broke off to look at her as he heard the small sound Ruby made.

Ruby shivered, unable to stop herself from saying, 'It must have been dreadful for the poor brides who were forced into marriage.'

'It is not the exclusive right of *your* sex to detest a forced marriage.'

Sander's voice was so harsh that the twins stirred against him in their sleep, focusing Ruby's attention on her sons, although she was still able to insist defensively, 'Historically a man has always had more rights within marriage than a woman.'

'The right to freedom of choice is enshrined in the human psyche of both sexes and should be respected above all other things,' Sander insisted.

Ruby looked at him in disbelief. 'How can you say that after the way you have forced me…?'

'You were the one who insisted on marriage.'

'Because I had no other choice.'

'There is always a choice.'

'Not for a mother. She will always put her children first.'

Her voice held a conviction that Sander told himself had to be false, and the cynical look he gave her said as much, causing Ruby's face to burn as she remembered how she had fallen asleep, leaving the twins unprotected.

Looking away from her, Sander thought angrily that Ruby might *think* she had deceived him by claiming her reason for insisting he married her was that she wanted to protect her sons, but he knew perfectly well that it was the fact that she believed marriage to him would give her a share in his wealth. That was what she really wanted to protect.

But she had signed a prenuptial agreement that barred her from making any claim on his money should they ever divorce, an inner voice defended her unexpectedly. She probably thought she could have the prenup set aside, Sander argued against it. Her children loved her, the inner voice pointed out. They would not exhibit the love and trust they did if she was a bad mother. He had loved *his* mother at their age, Sander pointed out. But he had hardly seen his mother or spent much time with her. She had been an exotic stranger, someone he had longed to see, and yet when he had seen her she had made him feel anxious to please her, and wary of her sudden petulant outbursts if he accidentally touched her expensive clothes. Anna, who was now in charge of the villa's household, had been more of a true mother—not just to him, but to all of them.

As Anna had been with them, Ruby was with the twins all the time. Logically he had to admit that it simply wasn't possible for anyone to carry out the pretence of being a caring parent twenty-four seven if it was just an act. A woman who loved both money and her children? Was that possible? It galled Sander that he should even be asking himself that question. What was the matter with him? He knew exactly what she was—why should he now be finding reasons to think better of her?

Sander looked away from Ruby and out into the darkness beyond the car window. The boys were soft warm weights against his body. His sons, and he loved them utterly and completely, no matter who or what their mother was. It was for their sakes that he wanted to find some good in her, for their sakes that his inner voice was trying to insist she was a good mother—for what caring father would *not* want that for his children, especially when that father knew what it was to have a mother who did not care.

Was it her imagination, or were the twins already turning more to Sander than they did to her? Miserably Ruby stared through the car window next to her. Whilst they had been talking they had left the city behind and were now travelling along another coastal road, with the sea to one side of them. But where previously there had been steep cliffs now the land rolled more gently away from the road.

It was far too late and far too selfish of her to wish that Sander had not come back into her life, Ruby admitted as the silence between them grew, filled by Sander's contempt for her and entrapping her in her own ever-present guilt. It was that guilt for having conceived the twins so carelessly and thoughtlessly that had in part brought her here, Ruby recognised. Guilt and her overwhelming desire to give her sons the same kind of happy, unshadowed, secure childhood in a family protected by two loving parents that she herself had enjoyed until her parents' death. But that security had been ripped from her. Her heart started to thud in a mixture of remembered pain and fierce hope that her sons would never experience what she had.

On his side of the luxurious leather upholstered car Sander stared out into the darkness—a darkness that for him was populated by the ghosts of his own past. In his grandfather's day the family had lived in the palace, unable to speak to either their parents or their grandfather unless those adults chose to seek them out. Yet despite maintaining his own distance from Sander and his siblings, their grandfather had somehow managed to know every detail of his grandchildren's lives, regularly sending for them so that he could list their flaws and faults and petty childhood crimes.

His sister and brother had been afraid of their grandfather, but Sander, the eldest child and ultimately the heir to his grandfather's shipping empire, had quickly learned that the best way to deal with his grandparent was to stand up to him. Sander's pride had been honed on the whetstone of his grandfather's mockery and baiting, as he'd constantly challenged Sander to prove himself to him whilst at the same time having no compunction about seeking to destroy his pride in himself to maintain his own superiority.

An English boarding school followed by university had given him a welcome respite from his grandfather's overbearing and bullying ways, but it had been after Sander had left university and started work in the family business that the real clashes between them had begun.

The continuation of the family and the business had been all that really mattered to his grandfather. His son and his grandchildren had been merely pawns to be used to further that cause. Sander had grown up hearing his grandfather discussing the various merits of young heiresses whom Sander might be wise to marry, but what he had learned from his mother, allied to his own naturally alpha personality and the time he had spent away from the island whilst he was at school and university, had made Sander determined not to allow his grandfather to bully him into marriage as he had done his father.

There had been many arguments between them on the subject, with his grandfather constantly trying to manipulate and bully Sander into meeting one or other of the young women he'd deemed suitable to be the mother of the next heir. In the end, infuriated and sickened by his grandfather's attempts at manipulation and coercion, Sander had announced to his grandfather that he was wasting his time as he never intended to marry, since he already had an heir in his brother.

His grandfather had then threatened to disinherit him, and Sander had challenged him to go ahead, telling him that he would find employment with one of their rivals. There the matter had rested for several weeks, giving Sander the impression that finally his grandfather had realised that he was not going to be controlled as his own parents had been controlled. But then, virtually on the eve of a long planned visit by Sander to the UK, to meet with some important clients in Manchester, he had discovered that his grandfather was planning to use his absence to advise the press of an impending engagement between Sander and the young widow of another ship-owner. Apart from anything else Sander knew that the young widow in question had a string of lovers and a serious drug habit, but neither of those potential draw-backs had been of any interest to his grandfather.

Of course Sander had confronted his grandfather, and both of them had been equally angry with the other. His grandfather had refused to back down, and Sander had warned him that if he went ahead with a public an-nouncement then he would refute that announcement equally publicly.

By the time he had reached Manchester Sander's anger hadn't cooled and his resolve to live his own life had actively hardened—to the extent that he had decided that on his return to Greece he was going to cut all ties with his grandfather and set up his own rival business from scratch.

And it had been in that frame of mind, filled with a dangerous mix of emotions, that he had met Ruby. He could see her now, eyeing him up from the other side of the crowded club, her blonde hair as carefully tousled as her lipglossed mouth had been deliberately pouted. The short skirt she'd worn had revealed slender legs, her tight top had been pulled in to display her tiny waist, and the soft rounded upper curves of her breasts had been openly on display. In short she had looked no different from the dozens of other eager, willing and easily available young women who came to the club specifically because it was known to be a haunt for louche young footballers and their entourages.

The only reason Sander had been in the club had been to meet a contact who knew people Sander thought might be prepared to give his proposed new venture some business. Whilst he was there Sander had received a phone call from a friend, urging him not to act against his own best interests. Immediately Sander had known that somehow his grandfather had got wind of what he was planning, and that someone had betrayed him. Fury—against his grandfather, against all those people in his life he had trusted but who had betrayed him— had overwhelmed him, exploding through his veins, pulsing against all constraints like the molten heat of a volcano building up inside him until it could not be contained any longer, the force of it erupting to spew its dangerous contents over everything in its path. And Ruby had been in the path of that fury, a readymade sacrifice to his anger, all too willing to allow him to use her for whatever purpose he chose.

All it had taken to bring her to his side had been one

cynical and deliberately lingering glance. She had leaned close to him in the crush of the club, her breath smelling of vodka and her skin of soap. He remembered how that realisation had momentarily checked him. The other girls around her had reeked of cheap scent. He had offered to buy her a drink and she had shaken her head, looking at him with such openly hungry eyes that her lack of self-respect had further inflamed his fury. He had questioned to himself why girls like her preferred to use their bodies to support themselves instead of their brains, giving themselves to men not directly for money but in the hope that they would end up as the girlfriend of a wealthy man.

Well, there had been no place in his life for a 'girlfriend', but right then there *had* been a rage, a tension inside him that he knew the use of her body in the most basic way there was would do much to alleviate. He had reached for his drink—not his first of the evening—finished it with one swallow, before turning to her and saying brusquely, 'Come on.'

A bump in the road woke the twins up, and Harry's 'Are we there yet?' dragged Sander's thoughts from the past to the present.

'Nearly,' he answered him. 'We're turning into the drive to the villa now.'

As he spoke the car swung off the road at such a sharp angle that Ruby slid along the leather seat, almost bumping her head on the side of the car. Unlike her, though, the twins were safe, protected by the arms Sander had tightened around them the minute the car had started to turn. Sander loved the twins, but he did not love her.

The pain that gripped her caught Ruby off guard. She wasn't jealous of her own sons, was she? Of course not. The last thing she wanted was Sander's arms around *her*, she told herself angrily as they drove through a pair of ornate wrought-iron gates and then down a long straight drive bordered with Cypress trees and illuminated by lights set into the ground.

At the end of the drive was a gravelled rectangle, and beyond that the villa itself, discreetly floodlit to reveal its elegant modern lines and proportions.

'Anna, who is in charge of the household, will have everything ready for you and the twins. She and Georgiou, her husband, who has driven us here, look after the villa and its gardens between them. They have their own private quarters over the garage block, which is separate from the villa itself,' Sander informed Ruby as the car crunched to a halt over the gravel.

Almost immediately the front door to the villa was opened to reveal a tall, well-built woman with dark hair streaked with grey and a serene expression.

It gave Ruby a fierce pang of emotion to see the way the twins automatically put their hands in Sander's and not her own as they walked with their father towards her. Her smile of welcome for Sander was one of love and delight, and Ruby watched in amazement as Sander returned her warm hug with obvious affection. Somehow it was not what she had expected. Anna—Ruby assumed the woman was Anna—was plainly far more to Sander than merely the person who was in charge of his household.

Now she was bending down to greet the boys, not overwhelming them by hugging them as she had Sander, Ruby noted approvingly, but instead waiting for them to go to her.

Sander gave them a little push and told them, 'This is Anna. She looked after me when I was a boy, and now she will look after you.'

Immediately Ruby's maternal hackles rose. Her sons did not need Anna or anyone else to look after them. They had her. She stepped forward herself, placing one hand on each of her son's shoulders, and then was completely disarmed when Anna smiled warmly and approvingly at her, as though welcoming what she had done rather than seeing it as either a challenge or a warning.

When Sander introduced her to Anna as his wife, it was obvious that Anna had been expecting them. What had Sander said to his family and those who knew him about the twins? How had he explained away the fact that he was suddenly producing them—and her? Ruby didn't know but she did know that Anna at least was delighted to welcome the twins as Sander's sons. It was plain she was ready to adore and spoil them, and was going to end up completely under their thumbs.

'Anna will show you round the villa and provide you and the boys with something to eat,' Sander informed Ruby.

He said something in Greek to Anna, who beamed at him and nodded her head vigorously, and then he was gone, striding across the white limestone floor of the entrance hall and disappearing through one of the dark wooden doors set into the white walls.

That feeling gripping her wasn't a sense of loss, was it? A feeling of being abandoned? A longing for Sander to return, because without him their small family was incomplete? Because without him *she* was incomplete?

As soon as the treacherous words whispered across her mind Ruby stiffened in denial of them. But they had left an echo that wasn't easily silenced, reminding her of all that she had suffered when she had first been foolish enough to think that he cared about her.

CHAPTER EIGHT

'I'LL show you your rooms first,' Anna told Ruby, 'and then perhaps you would like a cup of tea before you see the rest of the villa?'

There was something genuinely warm and kind and, well, *motherly* about Anna that had Ruby's initial wary hostility melting away as they walked together up the marble stairs, the twins in between them.

When they reached the top and saw the long wide landing stretching out ahead of them the twins looked at Ruby hopefully.

Shaking her head, she began, 'No—no running inside—' Only to have Anna smile broadly at her.

'This is their home now, they may run if you permit it,' she told her.

'Very well,' Ruby told them, relieved by Anna's understanding of the need of two young children to let off steam, and both women watched as the boys ran down the corridor.

'Looking at them is like looking at Sander when he

was a similar age, except that—' Anna stopped, her smile fading.

'Except that what?' Ruby asked her, sensitively defensive of any possible criticism being lodged against her precious sons.

As though she had guessed what Ruby was thinking, Anna patted Ruby on the arm.

'You are a good mother—anyone can see that. Your goodness and your love for them is reflected in your sons' smiles. Sander's mother was not like that. Her children were a duty she resented, and they all, especially Sander, learned young not to turn to their mother for love and comfort.'

Anna's quiet words formed an image inside Ruby's head she didn't want to see—an image of a young and vulnerable Sander, a child with sadness in his eyes, standing alone and hurt by his mother's lack of love for him.

The boys raced back to them, putting an end to any more confidences from Anna about Sander's childhood, and Ruby's sympathy for the child that Sander had been was swiftly pushed to one side when she discovered that the two of them were going to be sharing a bedroom and a bed.

Why did she feel so unnerved and apprehensive? Ruby asked herself later, after Anna had helped her put the twins to bed and she was in the kitchen, drinking the fresh cup of tea Anna had insisted on making for her. Sander had already made it plain that she must accept that their marriage would include sexual intimacy. They both already knew that she wanted him, and she had already suffered the humiliation *that* had brought her, so what was there left for her to fear?

There was emotional vulnerability, Ruby admitted. With her sexual vulnerability to Sander there was already a danger that she could become sexually dependent on him, and that was bad enough. If she also became emotionally vulnerable to him might she not then become emotionally dependent on him? Where had that thought come from? She was a million miles from feeling anything emotional for Sander, wasn't she?

Excusing herself to Anna, Ruby explained that she wanted to go up and check the twins were still sleeping as they had left them, not wanting them to wake alone in such new surroundings.

The twins' bedroom, like the one she was to share with Sander, looked out onto a courtyard and an infinity pool with the sea beyond it. But whilst Sander's bedroom had glass doors that opened out onto the patio area that surrounded the pool, the boys' room merely had a window—a safety feature for which she was extremely grateful. Glass bedroom doors, a swimming pool, and two adventurous five-year-olds were a mix that would arouse anxiety in any protective mother.

She needn't have worried about the twins. They were both sleeping soundly, their faces turned toward one another. Love for them filled her. But as she bent towards them to kiss them it wasn't their faces she could see but that of another young child, a child whose dark eyes, so like those of her sons, were shadowed with pain and angry pride. Sander's eyes. They still held that

angry pride now, as an adult, when he looked at her. And
the pain? Her question furrowed Ruby's brow. Emotional pain was not something she had previously
equated with Sander. But the circumstances a child experienced growing up affected it all its life. She believed
that wholeheartedly. If she hadn't done so then she
would not feel as strongly as she did about Sander being
a part of the twins' lives. So what had happened to
Sander's pain? Was it buried somewhere deep inside
him? A sad, sore place that could never heal? A wound
that was the cruellest wound of all to a child—the lack
of its mother's love?

Confused by her own thoughts, Ruby left her sleeping sons. She was tired and ready for bed herself. Her
heart started beating unsteadily. Tired and ready for
bed? Ready to share Sander's bed?

The villa was beautifully decorated. The guest suite
Anna had shown Ruby, and in which she would have
preferred to be sleeping, was elegantly modern, the
clean lines of its furniture softened by gauzy drapes, the
cool white and taupe of the colour scheme broken up
with touches of Mediterranean blues and greens in the
artwork adorning the walls.

From the twins' room Ruby made her way to the
room she was sharing with Sander—not because she
wanted to look again at the large bed and let her imagination taunt her with images of what they would share
there, but because she needed to unpack, Ruby told
herself firmly. Only when she opened the door to the
bedroom the cases that had been there before had

vanished, and from the *en suite* bathroom through the open door she could smell the sharp citrus scent of male soap and hear the sound of the shower.

Had Sander had her cases removed? Had he told Anna that he didn't want to share a room with her? Relief warred with a jolt of female protectiveness of her position as his wife. She liked Anna, but she didn't want the other woman to think that Sander was rejecting her. That would be humiliating. More humiliating than being forced in the silence of the night to cry out in longing to a husband who could arouse in her a hunger she could not control?

Ruby moved restlessly from one foot to the other, and then froze as the door to the *en suite* bathroom opened fully and Sander walked into the bedroom.

He had wrapped a towel round his hips. His body was still damp from his shower, and the white towel threw into relief the powerful tanned male V shape of his torso and the breadth of his shoulders, tapering down over strong muscles to his chest, to the hard flatness of his belly. The shadowing of dark hair slicked wetly against his skin emphasised a maleness that had Ruby trapped in its sensual spell. She wanted to look away from him. She wanted not to remember, not to feel, not to be so easily and completely overwhelmed by the need that just looking at him brought back to simmering heat. But she didn't have that kind of self-control. Instead of satiating her desire for him, what they had already shared seemed only to have increased her need for him.

Her own intense sensuality bewildered her. She had

lived for six years without ever once wanting to have sex, and yet now she only had to look at Sander to be consumed by this alien desire that seemed to have taken possession of her. Possession. Just thinking the word increased the heat licking at her body, tightening the pulse flickering eagerly deep inside her.

It was Ruby's fault that he wanted her, Sander told himself. It was she, with her soft mouth and her hungry gaze, with her eagerness, who was responsible for his own inability to control the savage surging of his need to possess her. It was because of her that he felt this ache, this driven, agonising urgency that unleashed within him something he barely recognised as part of himself.

Like a wild storm, a tornado threatening to suck them both up into its perilous grasp, Ruby could feel the pressure of their combined desire. Fear filled her. She didn't want this. It shamed and weakened her. Dragging her gaze from Sander's body, she started to run towards the door in blind panic. But Sander moved faster, reaching the door before her, and the impetus of her panic slammed her into his body, the impact shocking through her.

Tears of anger—against herself, against him, and against the aching desire flooding her—filled her eyes and she curled her hands into small fists and beat them impotently against his chest. Sander seized hold of her wrists.

'I don't want to feel like this,' she cried, agonized.

'But you do. You want this, and you want me,' he told her, before he took the denial from her lips with the ruthless pressure of his own.

Just the taste of her unleashed within him a hunger he couldn't control. The softness of her lips, the sound she made when he kissed her, the way her whole body shuddered against his with longing, drove him in what felt like a form of madness, a need, to a place where nothing else existed or mattered, where bringing her desire within the control of his ability to satisfy it felt as though it was what he had been born for.

Each sound she made, each shudder of pleasure her body gave, each urgent movement against his touch that begged silently for more became a goal he had to reach— a test of his maleness he had to master, so that he would always be the only man she desired, *his* pleasuring of her the only pleasure that could satisfy her. Something about the pale silkiness of her skin as he slid her clothes from it made him want to touch it over and over again. His hands already knew the shape and texture of her breasts, but that knowing only made him want to feel their soft weight even more. His lips and tongue and teeth might have aroused the swollen darkness of her nipples to previous pleasure, but now he wanted to recreate that pleasure. He wanted to slide his hand over the flatness of her belly and feel her suck it in as she fought to deny the effect of his touch and lost that fight. He wanted to part the slender thighs and feel them quiver, hear the small moan from between her lips, watch as she tried and failed to stop her thighs from opening eagerly to allow him the intimacy of her sex. He loved the way her soft, delicately shaped outer lips, so primly folded, opened to the slow stroke of his fingers, her wetness eagerly awaiting him.

A shocked cry of protest streaked with primitive longing burst from Ruby's throat as Sander gave in to the demand of his own arousal and moved down her body, to kiss the soft flesh on the inside of her thighs and then stroke the tip of his tongue the length of the female valley his skilled fingers had laid bare to his caress.

Waves of pleasure were racing through her, dragging her back to a level of sensuality where she was as out of her depth as a fledgling swimmer swept out by the tide into deep water. Each stroke of his tongue-tip against the most sensitive part of her took her deeper, until her own pleasure was swamping her, pulling her down into its embrace, until the rhythm it imposed on her was all that she knew, her response to it dictated and controlled by the lap of Sander's tongue as finally it overwhelmed her and she was drowning in it, giving herself over completely to it.

Later, filling her with his aching flesh, feeling her desire catch fire again as her body moved with his, inciting him towards his own destruction, Sander knew with razor-sharp clarity, in the seconds before he cried out in the exultation of release, that what he was doing might be trapping her in her desire for him but it was also feeding his need for her.

CHAPTER NINE

FROM the shade of the vine-covered pergola, Ruby watched the twins as they splashed in the swimming pool under Sander's watchful eye. It was just over six weeks now since they had arrived on the island, and the twins were loving their new life. They worshipped Sander. He was a good father, Ruby was forced to admit, giving them his time and attention, and most important of all his love. She glanced towards the house. Anna would be bringing their lunch out to them soon. A prickle of despair trickled down her spine as chilling as cold water.

This morning she was finally forcing herself to confront the possibility that she might be pregnant! The breakfasts she had been unable to eat in the morning, the tiredness that engulfed her every afternoon, the slight swelling of her breasts—all could have other explanations, but her missed period was now adding to the body of evidence.

Could she really be pregnant? Her heart jumped sickeningly inside her chest. There must be no more children, Sander had said. She must take the contraceptive pill. She had done, without missing a single one, but her symptoms were exactly the same as those she had experienced with the twins. Sander would be angry—furious, even—but what could he do? She was his wife, they were married, and she was having his child. A child she already knew he would not want.

Ruby could feel anxiety-induced nausea clogging her throat and causing perspiration to break out on her forehead. Was she right in thinking that Anna already suspected? Anna was an angel, wonderful with the children—almost a grandmother to them. After all, she had mothered Sander and his sister and brother. Somehow she seemed to know when Ruby was feeling tired and not very well, taking charge of the twins for her, giving her a kind pat when she fell back on the fiction that her lack of energy and nausea were the result of their move to a hot climate.

Sander was getting the twins out of the pool. Anna had arrived with their lunch. Determinedly, Ruby pushed her anxiety to one side.

Sander was used to working at home when he needed to, but since he had brought Ruby and his sons to the island he had discovered that he actually preferred to work at home. So that he could be with his sons, or so that he could be with Ruby? That was nonsense. A stupid question which he could not bring himself to answer.

Angrily he tried to concentrate on the screen in front of him. This afternoon he was finding it hard to concentrate on the e-mails he should be answering. Because he was thinking about Ruby? If he was then it was because of the conversation he had had with Anna earlier in the day, when she had commented on what a good mother Ruby was.

'A good mother and a good wife,' had been her exact words. 'You are a lucky man.'

Anna was a shrewd judge of character. She had never liked his mother, and she had protected them all from their grandfather's temper whenever she could. She had given him the only female love he had ever known. Homely, loyal Anna liked and approved of Ruby, a woman with more in common with his mother than she had with her.

Sander frowned. He might have seen the financially grasping side of Ruby that echoed the behaviour of his mother, but he had also seen her with the twins, and he was forced to admit that she *was* a loving and protective mother—a mother who gave her love willingly and generously to her sons…just as she gave herself willingly and generously to him…

Now what was he thinking? He was a fool if he started allowing himself to believe that. But did he want to believe it? No, Sander denied himself. Why should he want to believe that she gave him anything? Only a weak man or a fool allowed himself to think like that, and he was neither. But didn't the fact that he couldn't stop himself from wanting her reveal the worst kind of male weakness?

Wasn't the truth that even though he had tried to

deny it to himself he had not been able to forget her? From that first meeting the memory of her had lain in his mind like a thorn in his flesh, driven in too deeply to be easily removed, the pain activated whenever an unwary movement caused it to make its presence felt.

He had taken her and used her as a release for his pent-up fury after his argument with his grandfather, telling himself that his behaviour was justified because she herself had sought him out.

Inside his head Sander could hear his grandfather's raised voice, see the fist he had smashed down onto his desk in his rage that Sander should defy him.

Sander moved restlessly in his computer chair. It was too late now to regret allowing himself to recall that final argument with his grandfather and the events that had followed it. Far too late. Because the past was here with him, invading his present and filling it with unwanted memories, and he was back in that Manchester hotel room, watching Ruby sleep curled up against him.

His mobile had started to ring in the grey light of the dawn. She had protested in her sleep as he'd moved away from her but she hadn't woken up.

The call had been from Anna, her anxiety and shock reaching him across the miles as she told him that she had found his grandfather collapsed on the floor of his office and that he was on his way to hospital.

Sander had moved as quickly as he could, waking Ruby and telling her brusquely that he wanted her out of his bed, his room and the hotel, using her yet again as a means of expelling the mingled guilt and anger the phone call had brought him.

She had looked shocked and uncomprehending, he remembered, no doubt having hoped for rather more from him than a few brief hours in bed. Then tears had welled up in her eyes and she had tried to cling to him. Irritated that she wasn't playing by the rules, he had thrust her off, reaching into his jacket pocket for his wallet and removing several crisp fifty-pound notes from it. It had increased his irritation when she had started to play the drama queen, backing off from him, shaking her head, looking at him as though he had stamped on a kitten, not offered her a very generous payment for her services.

His terse, 'Get dressed—unless you want the hotel staff to evict you as you are,' had had the desired effect. But even so he had escorted her downstairs and out to the taxi rank outside the hotel himself, putting her into a cab and then watching to make sure that she had actually left before completing his arrangements to get home.

As it turned out his grandfather had died within minutes of reaching the hospital, from a second major heart attack.

In his office Sander had found the document his grandfather had obviously been working on before he collapsed, and had seen that it was a notice to the papers stating that Sander was on the point of announcing his engagement. His guilt had evaporated. His guilt but not his anger. And yet despite everything Sander had still mourned him. Evidence of the same weakness that was undermining him now with regard to Ruby. A leopard did not change its spots just because someone was foolish enough to want it to do so.

After his grandfather's death Sandra had renewed his vow to himself to remain single.

How fate must have been laughing at him then, knowing that the seeds of his own destiny had already been sown and had taken root.

He turned back to the computer, but it was no use. Once opened, the door to his memories of that fateful night with Ruby could not be closed.

The hotel bedroom, with its dark furniture, had been shadowed and silent, the heavy drapes deadening the sound of the traffic outside and yet somehow at the same time emphasising the unsteadiness of Ruby's breathing—small, shallow breaths that had lifted her breasts against her tight, low-cut top. The light from the standard lamp—switched on when the bed had been turned down for the night—had outlined the prominence of her nipples. When she had seen him looking at them she had lifted her hands towards her breasts, as though to protect them from his gaze. He could remember how that simple action had intensified his anger at her denial of everything she was about, infuriating him in the same way that his grandfather had. The raging argument he'd had with his grandfather earlier that day had still been fresh in his mind. The two angers had met and joined together, doubling the intensity of his fury, driving him with a ferocious and overpowering need to possess her.

He had gone to her and pulled down her hands. Her body had trembled slightly in his hold. Had he hesitated then, trying to check the raging torrent within him, or did he just want to think that he had? The image he was creating of himself was that of a man out of control, unable to halt the force of his own emotions. In another man it would have filled him with distaste. But Ruby, he remembered, had stepped closer to him, not away from him, and it had been then that he had removed her top, taking with it her bra, leaving her breasts exposed. His actions had been instinctive, born of rage rather than desire, but somehow the sight of her nakedness, her breasts so perfectly shaped, had transmuted that rage into an equally intense surge of need—to touch them and caress them, to possess the flaunting sensuality of their tip tilted temptation.

They had both drawn in a breath, as though sharing the same thoughts and the same desire, and the tension of that desire had stretched their self-control until the air around them had almost thrummed with the vibration of it. Then Ruby had made a small sound in the back of her throat, and as though it had been some kind of signal to his senses his self-control had snapped. He had reached for her, no words needed as he'd kissed her, feeling her tremble in his arms as he probed the softly closed line of her lips. She had deliberately kept them closed in order to torment him. But two could play that game, and so, instead of forcing them to give way, he had tormented them into doing so, with soft, deliberately brief kisses, until Ruby had reached for the back of his neck, her fingers curling into his hair, and whimpered with protesting need against his mouth.

Sander closed his eyes and opened them again as he recalled the surge of male triumph that had seized him then and the passion it had carried with it—a feeling he had never experienced either before Ruby or after her, surely originating from his anger against his grandfather and nothing else. Certainly not from some special effect that only Ruby could have on his senses. The very thought of that was enough to have him shifting angrily in his seat. No woman would *ever* be allowed to have that kind of power over him. Because he feared what might happen to him once he allowed himself to want a woman with that kind of intensity?

Better to return to his memories than to pursue *that* train of thought, Sander decided.

As they had kissed he had been able to feel Ruby's naked breasts pressed up against him. He had slipped his hands between their bodies, forcing her slightly away from him so that he could cup the soft weight of them. Just remembering that moment now was enough to bring back an unwanted echo of the sensation of his own desire, roaring through his body as an unstoppable force. It hadn't been enough to flick his tongue-tip against each hardened nipple and feel it quivering under its soft lash. Nothing had been enough until he had drawn the swollen flesh into his mouth, enticing its increased response with the delicate grate of his teeth.

He had heard Ruby cry out and felt her shudder. His hands had been swift to dispose of her skirt so that he could slide his hands into her unexpectedly respectable plain white knickers, to hold and knead the soft flesh of her buttocks. Swollen and stiff with the ferocity of his anger-induced arousal, he had lifted her onto the bed, plundering the softness of her plum painted mouth in between removing his own clothes, driven by the heat of his frustration against his grandfather, not caring about the girl whose body was underneath him, only knowing that within it he could find release.

Ruby had wrapped her arms round him whilst he had plundered her mouth, burying her face in his shoulder once he was naked, pretending to be too shy to look at him, never mind touch him. But he hadn't been interested in playing games. To him she had simply been a means to an end. And as for her touching him… Sander tensed his muscles against his remembered awareness of exactly what her intimate touch on him would have precipitated. His body had been in no mood to wait and in no condition to need stimulus or further arousal. That alone was something he would have claimed impossible prior to that night. No other situation had ever driven him to such a peak of erotic immediacy.

No other situation or no other woman? Grimly Sander tried to block the unwanted question. His subconscious had no business raising such an unnecessary suggestion. He didn't want to probe any further into the past. But even though he pulled the laptop back towards himself and opened his e-mails, he still couldn't concentrate on them. His mind was refusing to co-operate, returning instead to its memories. Against his will more

old images Ruby began to surface, refusing to be
ignored. He was back in that hotel bedroom in
Manchester. Sander closed his eyes and gave in.

In the dim light Ruby's body had been alabaster-
pale, her skin flawless and her body delicately female.
The lamplight had thrown a shadow from the soft
mound of flesh covered by her knickers, which he had
swiftly removed. That, he remembered, had caused him
to glance up at the tangled mass of hair surrounding her
face, surprised to discover that the colour of her hair was
natural. Somehow the fact that she was naturally blonde
didn't go with the image she had created, with her thick
make-up and tight, clinging clothes.

She had met his look and then looked away, the
colour coming and going in her face as her glance rested
on his body and then skittered away.

If her naturally blonde hair had been at odds with his
assessment of her, then her breathy voice, unsteady and
on the verge of awed apprehension, had been enough to
fill him with contempt.

'You look very big,' she had delivered, within a heartbeat of her glance skittering away from his erection.

Had she really thought him both foolish and vain
enough to be taken in by a ploy like that? If so he had
made sure that she knew that he wasn't by taunting her
deliberately, parting her legs with his hand.

'But not bigger than any of the others, I'm sure.'

She had said something—a few gasped words—but
he hadn't been listening by then. He had been too busy
exploring the wet eagerness of her sex, stroking his fin-

gertip its length until he reached the hard pulse of her clitoris, and by that stage she had begun to move against his touch and moan softly at the same time, in a rising crescendo of excitement.

He had told himself that her supposed arousal was almost bound to be partly faked but unexpectedly his body had responded to it as though it was real. It had increased his own urgency, so that he had replaced his fingers with the deliberate thrust of his sex. She had tensed then, looking up at him with widened dark eyes that had filled with fake tears when he had thrust properly into her, urged by the wanton tightness of her muscles as they clung to him, as though wanting to hold and possess him. Their resistance had incited him to drive deeper and deeper into her, just for the pleasure of feeling their velvet clasp. He had come quickly and hotly, his lack of control catching him off-guard, her body tightening around him as he pulsed into her.

Sander wrenched his thoughts back to the present. What had happened with Ruby was not an interlude in his life or an aspect of himself that reflected well on him, he was forced to admit. In fact part of the reason he had chosen to lock these memories away in the first place had been because of his sense of angry distaste. Like something rotten, they carried with them the mental equivalent of a bad odour that couldn't be ignored or masked. If he judged Ruby harshly for her part in their encounter, then he judged himself even more harshly— especially now that he knew the consequences of those few out of control seconds of raw male sensuality.

It was because he didn't like the fact that his sons had been conceived in such a way that he was experiencing the regrets he was having now, Sander told himself. He owed them a better beginning to their life than that.

What was it that was gnawing at him now? Regret because his sons had been conceived so carelessly, so uncaringly, and in anger? Or something more than that? Regret that he hadn't taken more time to—? To what? To get to know the mother of his sons better or to think of the consequences of his actions? Because deep down inside he felt guilty about the way he had treated Ruby? She had only been seventeen after all.

He hadn't known that then, Sander defended himself. He had assumed she was much older. And if he had known…?

Sander stood up and paced the floor of his office, stopping abruptly as he relived how, virtually as soon as he had released her, Ruby had gone to the bathroom. He had turned on his side, ignoring her absence, even then aware of how far his behaviour had fallen short of his own normal high standards. But even though he had wanted to blot out the reality of the situation, and Ruby herself, he had still somehow been unable to stop listening to the sound of the shower running and then ceasing, had been aware against his will of her return to the bed, her skin cold and slightly damp as she pressed up against his back, shivering slightly. He had had no need for intimacy with her any more. She had served her purpose, and he preferred sleeping alone. And yet for some reason, despite all of that, he had turned over and taken her in his arms, feeling her body stiffen and then relax as he held her.

She had fallen asleep with her head on his chest, murmuring in protest in her sleep every time he tried to ease away from her, so that he had spent the night with her cuddled up against him. And wasn't it true that somehow she had done something to him during those night hours? Impressed herself against his body and his senses so that once in a while over the years that had followed he would wake up from a deep sleep, expecting to find her there lying against him and feeling as though a part of him was missing because she wasn't?

How long had he fought off that admission, denying its existence, pretending to himself that since he had returned to the island this time his sleep had never once been disturbed by that aching absence? He moved impatiently towards the window, opening it to breathe in fresh air in an attempt to clear his head.

What had brought all this on? Surely not a simple comment from Anna that she considered Ruby to be a good mother. A good mother *and* a good wife, he reminded himself.

His mobile had started to ring. He reached for it, frowning when he saw his sister's name flash up on the screen.

'Sander, we've been back from America nearly a week now. When are you going to bring Ruby to Athens so that I can meet her?'

Elena liked to talk, and it was several minutes before Sander could end the call, having agreed that, since he was due to pay one of his regular visits to the Athens office anyway, he would take Ruby with him so that she and Elena could meet.

CHAPTER TEN

SHE had better find out for sure that she was pregnant, and if so tell Sander. She couldn't put it off much longer, Ruby warned herself. She wasn't the only one to blame after all. It took two, and she *had* taken her birth control pills.

She had also been unwell, she reminded herself, and in the anxiety and despair of everything that had been happening in London she had forgotten that that could undermine the effectiveness of the pills. Surely Sander would be able to understand that? But what if he didn't? What if he accused her of deliberately flouting his wishes? But what possible reason could she logically have for doing that? He was a successful, intelligent businessman. He would be bound to recognise that there was no logical reason for her to deliberately allow herself to become pregnant. He might be a successful, intelligent businessman, but he had also been a child whose mother had betrayed him. Would *that* have any bearing on the fact that she was pregnant? On the face of it, no—but Ruby had an instinctive feeling that it might.

She would tell him tonight, Ruby promised herself, once the boys were in bed.

Her mind made up, Ruby was just starting to relax when Sander himself appeared, striding from the house onto the patio area, quite plainly in search of her. Her heart somersaulted with guilt. Had he somehow guessed? At least if he had then her pregnancy would be out in the open and they could discuss it rationally. It was only when he told her that his sister had been on the phone, and that they would be leaving for Athens in morning and staying there for the night, that Ruby realised, cravenly, that a part of her had actually hoped that he *had* guessed, and that she would be spared the responsibility of telling him that she had once again conceived.

Since he hadn't guessed, though, it was sensible, surely, to wait until they returned from Athens to tell him? That way they would have more time to discuss the issue properly. He would be angry, she knew that, but she was clinging to the knowledge that he loved the twins, and using that knowledge to reassure herself that, angry though he would no doubt be with her, he would love this new baby as well.

'I've got a small apartment in Athens that I use when I'm there on business. We'll stay there. The twins will be safe and well looked after here, with Anna.'

'Leave them behind?' Ruby checked. 'They haven't spent a single night without me since they were born.'

Her anxious declaration couldn't possibly be fake, Sander recognised. It had been too immediate and automatic for that. He tried to imagine his own mother refusing a trip to a cosmopolitan city filled with expensive designer shops to stay with her children, and acknowledged that it would never have happened. His mother had hated living on the island, had visited it as infrequently as she could, and he himself had been sent to boarding school in England as soon as he had reached his seventh birthday.

'Elena will want to spend time with you, and I have business matters to attend to. The boys will be far happier here on the island in Anna's care than they would be in a city like Athens.'

When Ruby bit her lip, her eyes still shadowed, he continued, 'I can assure you that you can trust Anna to look after them properly. If I did not believe that myself, there would be no question of us leaving them.'

Immediately Ruby's gaze cleared.

'Oh, I know I can trust your judgement when it comes to their welfare. I know how much you love them.'

Her immediate and open admission that she accepted not only his judgement for their sons but with it his right to make such a judgement was having the most extraordinary effect on him, Sander realised. Like bright sunlight piercing a hitherto dark and impenetrable black cloud. He was bemused and dazzled by the sudden surge of pleasure her words gave him—the feeling that they were united, and that she...that she *trusted* him, Sander recognised. Ruby trusted him to make the right decision for their sons. A surge of unfamiliar emotion swamped him, and he had an alien and overpowering urge to take her in his arms and hold her tight. He took a step towards her, and then stopped as his need to protect himself cut in.

Unaware of Sander's reaction to her statement, Ruby sighed. She was being silly, she knew. The twins *would* be perfectly safe with Anna. Was it really for their sakes she wanted them with her? Or was it because she felt their presence was a form of protection and was nervous at the thought of meeting Sander's sister? Had they had a normal marriage she would have been able to admit her apprehension to Sander—but then if they were in a normal marriage she would already have told him about the new baby, and that news would have been a matter of joy and happiness for both of them.

'You will like Elena—although, as I told her often when she was a little girl, she talks all the time and sometimes forgets to let others speak.' Anna shook her head as she relayed this information to Ruby. She was helping her to pack for the trip to Athens—her offer, Ruby suspected, more because she had sensed her trepidation and wanted to reassure her than because she really felt Ruby needed help.

'She is very proud of her brothers, especially Sander, and she will be glad that he has married you when she sees how much you love him.'

Ruby dropped the pair of shoes she had been holding, glad that the act of bending down to pick them up gave her an opportunity to hide her shock. How much she loved Sander? What on earth had made Anna think and say that? She didn't love him at all.

Did she?

Of course not. After all, he hadn't exactly given her any reason to love him, had he?

Since when had love needed a reason? What reason had she needed in that Manchester club, when she had looked across the bar and felt her heart leap inside her chest, as though he himself had tugged it and her towards him?

That had been the silly, naive reaction of a girl desperate to create a fairytale hero—a saviour to rescue her from her grief, Ruby told herself, beginning to panic.

Anna was mistaken. She had to be. But when she had recovered her composure enough to look at the other woman she saw from the warm compassion in her eyes that Anna herself certainly didn't think that she was wrong.

Was it possible? *Could* she have started to love Sander without realising it? Could the aching, overwhelming physical desire for him she could not subdue be caused by love and not merely physical need? He was, after all, the father of her children, and she couldn't deny that initially when she had realised that she was pregnant a part of her had believed she had conceived because of the intensity of her emotional response to him. Because she had been naive, and frightened and alone, she had wanted to believe that the twins had been created out of love.

And this new baby—didn't it too deserve to have its mother's body accept the seed that began its life with love?

'You will like Elena,' Anna repeated, 'and she will like you.'

* * *

Ruby was clinging to those words several hours later, after their plane had touched down in Athens and they were in the arrivals hall, as an extremely stylish dark-haired young woman came hurrying towards them, her eyes covered by a pair of designer sunglasses.

'Sander. I thought I was going to be late. The traffic is horrendous—and the smog! No wonder all our precious ancient buildings are in so much danger. Andreas said to tell you that he is pretty sure he has secured the Taiwan contract—oh, and I want you both to come to dinner tonight. Nothing too formal…'

'Elena, you are like a runaway train. Stop and let me introduce you to Ruby.' Sander's tone was firm but wry, causing his sister to laugh and then turn to Ruby, catching her off-guard when she immediately enveloped her in a warm hug.

'Anna has told me what a fortunate man Sander is to have married you. I can't wait to meet the twins. Wasn't I clever, spotting them at Manchester Airport? But for me you and Sander might never have made up your quarrel and been reconciled.'

They were out of the airport now, and Sander was saying, 'You'd better let me drive, Elena. I have some expensive memories of what happens when you drive and talk at the same time.'

'Oh, you.' Elena mock pouted as she handed over her car keys, and then told Ruby, 'It wasn't really my fault. The other driver should never have been parked where he was in the first place.'

Anna was right—she was going to like Elena, Ruby

acknowledged as her sister-in-law kept up a stream of inconsequential chatter and banter whilst Sander drove them through the heavy Athens traffic.

Elena had obviously questioned Sander about their relationship, and from what she had said Ruby suspected that he had made it seem as though the twins had been conceived during an established relationship between them rather than a one-night stand. That had been kind of him. Kind and thoughtful. Protecting the twins and protecting her. The warm glow she could feel inside herself couldn't possibly be happiness, could it?

The Athens night was warm, the soft air stroking Ruby's skin as she and Sander walked from the taxi that had just dropped them off to the entrance to the exclusive modern building that housed Sander's Athens apartment. They had spent the evening with Elena and Andreas at their house on the outskirts of the city, and tomorrow morning they would be returning to the island. Of course she was looking forward to seeing the twins, but… Was she simply deceiving herself, because it was what she wanted, or had there really been a softening in Sander's attitude towards her today? A kindness and a warmth that had made her feel as though she was poised on the brink of something special and wonderful?

Sander looked at Ruby. She was wearing a pale peach silk dress patterned with a design of pale grey fans. It had shoestring straps, a fitted bodice and a gently shaped slim skirt. Its gentle draping hinted at the feminine shape of her figure without revealing too much of it, and the strappy bodice revealed the tan her skin had acquired in the weeks she had spent on the island. Tonight, watching her over dinner as she had talked and smiled and laughed with his sister and her husband, he had felt pride in her as his wife, as well as desire for her as a man. Something—Sander wasn't prepared to give it a name—had begun to change. Somehow *he* had begun to change. Because Ruby was a good mother? Because she had trusted him about the twins' care? Because tonight she had shown an intelligence, a gentleness and a sense of humour that—a little to his own surprise— he had recognised were uniquely hers, setting her apart from his mother and every other woman he had known?

Sander wasn't ready to answer those questions, but he was ready and eager to make love to his wife.

To make love to her *as* his wife. A simple enough statement, but for Sander it resonated with admissions that he would have derided as impossible the day he had married her.

As they entered the apartment building Sander reached for Ruby's hand. Neither of them said anything, but Ruby's heart leapt and then thudded into the side of her chest. The hope she had been trying desperately not to let go to her head was now soaring like a helium balloon.

On the way up to the apartment in the lift she pleaded mentally, 'Please let everything be all right. Please let things work out for…for *all* of us.' And by all she included the new life she was carrying as well.

She *was* going to tell Sander, but today whilst she had had the chance she had slipped into a chemist's shop and bought a pregnancy testing kit—just to be doubly sure. She would wait until they were back on the island to use it, and then she *would* tell Sander. Then, but not now. Because she wanted tonight to be very special. Tonight she wanted for herself. Tonight she wanted to make love with Sander, knowing that she loved him.

In the small sitting room of the apartment, Sander removed the jacket of his linen suit, dropping it onto one of the chairs. The small action tightened the fabric of his shirt against the muscles of his back, and Ruby's gaze absorbed their movement, the now familiar ache of longing softening her belly and then spreading swiftly through her. Her sudden need to breathe more deeply, to take in oxygen, lifted her breasts against the lining of her dress, causing her already aroused and sensitive nipples to react even more to the unintentional drag of the fabric. When Sander straightened up and turned round he could see their swollen outline pressing eagerly against the barrier of her dress. His own body reacted to their provocation immediately, confirming the need for her he had already known he felt.

She couldn't stand here like this, Ruby warned herself. If she did Sander was bound to think she was doing so because she wanted him and was all too likely to say so. She didn't want that. She didn't want to be accused of being a woman who could not live without sexual satisfaction. What she wanted was to be told that he couldn't resist her, that he adored her and loved her.

Quickly Ruby turned towards the door, not wanting

Sander to see her expression, but to her astonishment before she could reach it he said quietly, 'You looked beautiful tonight in that dress.'

Sander was telling her she looked beautiful?

Ruby couldn't move. She couldn't do anything other than stare at him, torn between longing and disbelief.

Sander was coming towards her, standing in front of her, lifting his hands to slide the straps of her dress off her shoulders as he told her softly, 'But you will look even more beautiful without it.'

The words were nothing, and yet at the same time they were everything. Ruby trembled from head to foot, hardly daring to breathe as Sander unzipped her dress so that it could fall to the floor and then cupped the side of her face and kissed her.

She was in Sander's arms, and he was kissing her, and she was kissing him back. Kissing him back, holding him, feeling all her doubts and fears slipping away from her like sand sucked away by the sea as her love for him claimed her.

The sensation of Sander's hands on her body, shaping it and caressing it, carried her on a surging tide of her own desire, like a tribute offered to an all powerful conqueror. His lightest touch made her body shudder softly in swiftly building paroxysms of pleasure. She had hungered to have him desire her like this, without the harsh bitterness of his anger. In the deepest hidden places of her heart Ruby recognised that, even if she had hidden that need from herself. She had hungered, ached, and denied that aching—yearned for him and forbidden that yearning. But now, here tonight in his arms, the lies she had told to protect herself were melting away, burned away by the heat of his hands on her body, leaping from nerve-ending to nerve-ending. Beneath Sander's mouth Ruby moaned in heightened pleasure when his thumb-pad rubbed over her nipple, hot, sweet and aching need pulsing beneath his touch. Her body was clamouring for him to free it, to lay it bare to his eyes, his hands, his mouth, so that he could plunder its desire, feed it and feast on it, until she could endure the ache of her own need no longer and she clung to him whilst he took her to the heights and the final explosion that would give him all that she was and all that she had to give, make her helpless under the power of his possession and her own need for it, for him.

This was how it had been that first night in Manchester, with her senses overwhelmed by the intensity of what she was experiencing. So much so, in fact, that she had scarcely noticed the loss of her virginity. She'd been so desperate for his possession and for the pleasure it had brought her.

She was his, and Sander allowed himself to glory in that primeval knowledge. His body was on fire for her, aching beyond bearing with his need for her, but he wanted to draw out their pleasure—to savour it and store the unique bouquet of it in his memory for ever. He bent and picked her up, carrying her through into the bedroom, their gazes meeting and locking in the sensually charged warmth of the dimly lit room.

'I've never forgotten you—do you know that? I've

never been able to get your memory out of my head. The way you trembled against me when I touched you, the scent of your skin, the quick, unsteady way you breathed when I did this.'

Ruby fought to suppress her breathing now, as Sander caressed the side of her neck and then stroked his fingertips the length of her naked spine.

'Yes, just like that.'

Helplessly Ruby whimpered against the lash of her own pleasure, protesting that Sander was tormenting her and she couldn't bear any more, but Sander ignored her, tracing a line of kisses along her shoulderblade. When he had done that the first time she had arched her back in open delight, helpless against the onslaught of her own desire. Sander lifted her arm and began kissing the inside of her wrist and then the inside of her elbow. He had never known that it was possible for him to feel like this, Sander acknowledged. The sensual sweetness of Ruby's response to him was crashing through all the defences he had raised against the way she was making him feel.

He kissed her mouth, probing its soft, welcoming warmth with his tongue, whilst Ruby trembled against him, her naked body arching up to his, the feel of her skin through his clothes a torment he could hardly bear.

Ruby was lost beneath the hot, intimate possession of Sander's kiss—a kiss that was sending fiery darts of arousal and need rushing through her body to turn the existing dull ache low down within it into an open pulsing need. Her breasts yearned for his touch, her nipples throbbing and swollen like fruit so ripe their readiness could hardly be contained within their skin. She wanted to feel his hands on her body, stroking, caressing, satisfying her growing need. Wanted his lips kissing and sucking the ache from her breasts and transforming it to the liquid heat of pleasure. But instead he was pulling away from her, lifting his body from hers, abandoning her when she needed him so desperately. Frantically Ruby shook her head, her protest an inarticulate soft moan as she sat up in the bed.

As though he knew how she felt, and what she feared, Sander reached for her hand and carried it to his own body, laying it flat against the hard swell of his flesh under the fabric of his suit trousers, his gaze never leaving her face as it registered her passion stoked delight in his erection, and its sensual underlining of his own desire for her.

Very slowly her fingertips traced the length and thickness of his flesh, everything she was feeling visible to him in the soft parting of her mouth, the brief flick of her tongue-tip against her lips and the excitement darkening her absorbed gaze.

Impatiently Sander started to unfasten his shirt. Distracted by his movements, Ruby looked up at him and then moved closer, kneeling on the bed in front of him as she took over the task from him. She leaned forward to kiss the flesh each unfastened button exposed, and then gave in to the impulse driving her to know more than the warmth of his skin against her lips, stroking her tongue-tip along his breastbone, breathing in the pheromone-laden scent of his body as it shuddered beneath her caress. His chest was hard-muscled, his nipples flat and dark. Lost in the heady pleasure of being so close to him, Ruby reached out and touched the hard flesh with her fingertip, and then on an impulse that came out of nowhere she bent her head and kissed the same spot, exploring it with the tip of her tongue.

Reaction ricocheted through Sander, engulfing and consuming him. He'd been unfastening his trousers whilst Ruby explored him, and now he wrenched off what was left of his clothes before taking Ruby in his arms to kiss her with the full force of his building need.

The sensation of Sander's body against her, with no barriers between them, swept away what were left of Ruby's inhibitions. Wrapping her arms around Sander's neck, she clung to him, returning his kiss with equal passion, sighing her approval when his hands cupped her breasts.

This was what his heart had been yearning for, Sander admitted. This giving and receiving, this intimacy with no barriers, this woman above all women. Ruby was everything he wanted and more, Sander acknowledged, making his own slow voyage of rediscovery over Ruby's silk-soft body.

Sander prided himself on being a skilled lover, but he had never been in this position before. He had never felt like this before. He wasn't prepared for his own reaction to the way he felt. He wasn't prepared for the way it powered his own desire to a level he had never known before, threatening his self-control, creating within him a desire to possess and pleasure every part of her, to bring her to orgasm over and over again, until he possessed her pleasure and her with it. He wanted to imprint himself on her desire so that no other man could ever unlock its sweetness. He wanted *her*, Sander acknowledged, and he fed the fast-surging appetite of his own arousal on the sound of her unsteady breathing, interspersed with sobs of pleasure, as he sucked on the hard peaks of her nipples and kneaded the soft flesh of her breasts.

Ruby arched up towards him, her hands clasped on the back of his neck to hold him against her. She had thought that Sander had already taken her to the utmost peak of sensual pleasure, but she had been wrong. Now, with the barriers between them down, she knew that what had gone before had been a mere shadow of what she was feeling now. Lightning-fast bolts of almost unbearable erotic arousal sheeted through her body with every tug of Sander's mouth on her nipples, going to ground deep inside her, feeding the hot pulse already beating there, until merely arching up against him wasn't enough to appease the savage dragging need possessing her. Instead she had to open her legs and press herself against him, her breath catching on a grateful moan of relief when Sander responded to her need with the firm pressure of his hand over her sex.

Against his hand Sander could feel the heavy pulsing beat of Ruby's need. It drove the ache within his own flesh to a maddening desire to take her quickly and hotly, making him fight for the self-control that threatened to desert him when he parted the swollen outer lips of her sex to find the wetness within them.

It was almost more than Ruby could stand to have Sander touching her so intimately, and yet at the same time nowhere nearly intimately enough. His fingertip rimmed the opening to her sex. A fresh lightning bolt shot through her. She could feel her body opening to him in eagerness and hunger, heard a sound of agonised relief bubbling in her throat when Sander slid one and then two fingers slowly inside her.

He didn't need Ruby's fingers gripping his arm or her nails digging into his flesh to tell him what she was feeling. Sander could feel her need in his own flesh and hers as the movement of her body quickened and tightened. Even before she cried out to him he was aware of her release, and the quick, fierce pleasure of her orgasm filled his own body with fierce male satisfaction, swelling his sex to a hard urgency to play its part in more of that pleasure.

But not yet—not until he was sure that he had given her all the pleasure he could.

For Ruby, the sensation of Sander's lips caressing their way down her supine body was initially one of relaxed easy sweetness—a tender caress after the white-hot heat that had gone before it. She had no intimation, no warning of the fresh urgency to come, until Sander's lips drifted across her lower belly and the ache she had thought satisfied began to pulse and swell in a new surge of need that shocked her into an attempt to deny its existence.

But Sander wouldn't let her. Her protests were ignored, and the growing pleasure of her wanton flesh was cherished with hot swirls of desire painted on her inner thighs by the stroke of his tongue—a tongue that searched out her desire even more intimately, until its movement against the hard swollen pulse of her clitoris had her abandoning her self-control once more and offering herself up to him.

This time her orgasm was short and sharp, leaving her trembling on the edge of something more. Agonised by the ache of that need, Ruby reached out to touch Sander's body, but he stopped her, shaking his head as he told her thickly, 'No. Don't. Let me do this instead.'

She could feel the glide of his body against her own, his sex hard and slick, probing the eager moistness of hers, and her muscles quickened in eager longing, matching each slow, deliberate ever deeper thrust of his body within her own.

Aaahhh—how she remembered the first time he had shown her this pleasure and revealed its mystery. The way it had taken her beyond that small sharp pain which had caught at her breath and held her motionless beneath his thrust for a handful of seconds before her arousal had made its own demands on her, her muscles softening to enfold him, just as they were doing now, then firming to caress him, her body driven by its need to have him ever deeper within her.

This was what her body had yearned and hungered for—this completeness and wholeness, beyond any other, as she clung to Sander, taking him fully within her and holding him there, welcoming and matching the growing speed of his rhythm.

He was lost, Sander recognised. His self-control, his inner self stripped away, taking from him his power to do anything other than submit to his own need as it rolled over him and picked him up with its unstoppable force.

He heard himself cry out, a male sound of mingled agony and triumph, as Ruby's fresh orgasm took them both over the edge, his body flooding hers with his own release.

Her body still racked by small aftershocks of the seismic pleasure that had erupted inside her, Ruby lay silently against Sander's chest, heard their racing heartbeats gradually slowing.

Tonight they had shared something special, something precious, Ruby thought, and her heart overflowed with love.

CHAPTER ELEVEN

THE twins' matter-of-fact response to their return to the island proved more than any amount of words how comfortable they had been in Anna's care during her absence, Ruby reflected ruefully in her bedroom, as she changed out of the clothes she had travelled home in. Sander had gone straight to his office to check his e-mails.

But getting changed wasn't all she needed to do.

Her handbag was on the bed. She opened it and removed the pregnancy testing kit she had bought in Athens. Her hands trembled slightly as she took it from its packaging, her eyes blurring with emotion as she read the instructions. Six years ago when she had done this she had been so afraid, sick with fear, dreading the result.

She was equally anxious now, but for very different reasons.

Things had changed since she had first realised that she might be pregnant again, she tried to reassure herself. When Anna had referred to her love for Sander, initially Ruby had wanted to deny it. But once that truth had been laid bare for her to see she hadn't been able to ignore it. Of *course* she loved Sander. The real shock was that she hadn't realised that for herself but had needed Anna to tell her. Now, just thinking about him filled her with aching longing and pain.

Maybe this baby would build the bridge between them, if she lowered her own pride and told him how she felt. She had begged him to give her the possession of his body—would it really be so very difficult to plead with him to accept her love? To plead with him that this child might be born into happiness and the love of both its parents? He loved the twins—surely he would love this child as well, even if he refused to accept her love for him? Telling herself that she must have faith that the love she had seen Sander give the twins would not be reserved for the twins alone, she walked towards the bathroom.

Ten minutes later Ruby was still standing in the bathroom, her gaze fixed on the telltale line. She had known, of course—impossible for her not to have done. But nothing was the same as visible confirmation. Against Sander's explicit wishes she had conceived his child. Ruby thought of the contraceptive pills she had taken so carefully and regularly every evening, in obedience to Sander's conditions for their marriage. Perhaps this baby, conceived against all the odds, was meant to be—a gift to them both that they could share together? She put her hand on her still flat body and took a deep breath. She would have to tell Sander now, and the sooner the better.

The sudden childish scream of anger she could hear from outside had her letting the test fall onto the marble surface surrounding the hand basin as she ran to the patio doors in the bedroom in automatic response to the outraged sound. Outside on the patio, as she had expected, she found the twins quarrelling over a toy. Freddie was attempting to drag it away from Harry, whilst Harry wailed in protest. Anna, alerted as Ruby had been by the noise, wasn't far behind her, and the two of them quickly defused the situation.

Once they had done so, Anna said matter-of-factly, 'You will have your hands full if it is twins again that you are carrying.'

Ruby shook her head. She wasn't really surprised that Anna had guessed. The homemade ginger biscuits that had discreetly begun to appear with her morning cup of weak tea had already hinted to her that Anna shared her own suspicions.

Sander pushed back his chair. They had only arrived at the villa an hour ago, and yet already he was conscious of an urge to seek out Ruby, and with it an awareness that he was actually missing her company—and not just in bed. Such feelings made him feel vulnerable, something that Sander instinctively resisted and resented, and yet at the same time he was opening his office door and striding down the corridor in the direction of their bedroom.

Ruby would be outside with the twins. As their father, he could legitimately get changed and go and join them. Doing so would not betray him. And if he was there as much so that he could be with Ruby as with his sons, then only he needed to know that. The conditioning of a lifetime of fearing emotional betrayal could not be overturned in the space of a few short weeks. Others close to him, like Anna and Elena, might admire Ruby and think her a good wife, but Sander told himself that he needed more proof that he could trust her.

He noted the presence of Ruby's open handbag on their bed as he made his way to the bathroom, but it was only after he had showered and changed that he noticed the discarded pregnancy test.

The first thing Ruby saw when she went back into the bedroom was Sander's suit jacket on the bed. Her heart started to hammer too heavily and far too fast, with a mixture of guilt and fear. She walked towards the bathroom, coming to an abrupt halt when she saw Sander standing beside the basin, holding the telltale test.

There was a blank look in his eyes, as though he couldn't quite believe what he was seeing. A blank look that was soon burned away by the anger she could see replacing it as he looked at her.

'You're pregnant.'

It was an accusation, not a question, and Ruby's heart sank.

'Yes,' she admitted. 'I thought I might be, but I wanted to be sure before I told you. I know what you said when we got married about me taking the pill because you didn't want another child—and I did take it,' she told him truthfully. When he didn't say anything, but simply continued to look at her she was panicked into pleading emotionally, 'Please don't look at me like that. You love the twins, and this baby, *your* baby, deserves to be loved as well.'

'*My* child? Since you have said yourself that you were on the pill, it cannot possibly be my child. We both know that. Do you really think me such a fool that I would let you pass off a brat conceived with one of the no doubt many men who happened to be enjoying your body before I found you? If so, then you are the one who is a fool. But you are not a fool, are you, Ruby? You are a venal, lying, amoral and greedy woman.'

The words exploded into the room like randomly discharged machine gun fire, meant to destroy everything it hit. Right now she might be too numb to feel anything, but Ruby knew that she had been mortally wounded.

'You obviously knew when you demanded that I marry you that you were carrying this child,' Sander accused her savagely.

He had claimed that he was not a fool, but the opposite was true. He had allowed her to tempt him out of the security of the emotional mindset he had grown up with and to believe that maybe—just maybe—he had been wrong about her. But of course he had not been. He deserved the punishment of what he was feeling now for dropping his guard, for deliberately ignoring all the safeguards he had put in place to protect himself. The bitter, angry thoughts raked Sander's pride with poison-dipped talons.

'I thought you had married me for the financial gain you believed you could get from our marriage, but I can see now that I didn't recognise the true depth of your greed and lack of morals.'

Ruby couldn't bear any more.

'I married you for the sake of our sons,' she told him fiercely. 'And this child I am carrying now is yours. Yes, I took the pill, but if you remember I wasn't well whilst we were in London. I believe that is how I came to conceive. In some circumstances a…a stomach upset and nausea can damage the pill's efficiency.'

'A very convenient excuse,' Sander sneered. 'Do you *really* expect me to believe it, knowing you as I do? You didn't marry me for the twins' sake, Ruby. You married me for my money.'

'That's not true,' Ruby denied. How could he think so badly of her? Anger joined her pain. Sander had called himself a fool, but *she* was the fool. For loving him, and for believing that she could reach out to him with that love.

'I know you,' he repeated, and hearing those words Ruby felt her self-control break.

'No, you don't know me, Sander. All you know is your own blind prejudice. When this baby is born I shall have its DNA tested, and I can promise you now that he or she will be proved to be your child and a true sibling to the twins. However, by then it will be too late for you to know it and love it as your son or daughter, Sander, because there is no way I intend to allow my children to grow up with a father who feels and speaks as you do. You love the twins, I can see that, but as they grow to be men your attitude to me, their mother, your suspicions of me, are bound to contaminate their attitude to my sex. I will *not* have my sons growing up like you—unable to recognise love, unable to value it, unable to even see it.

'Do you know what my worst sin has been? The thing I regret the most? It's loving *you*, Sander. Because in loving you, I am not being a good mother to my children. You've constantly thrown at me my behaviour the first time we met, accusing me of being some wanton who came on to you. The truth is that I was a seventeen-year-old virgin—oh, yes you may look at me like that but it's true—a naive and recklessly silly girl who, in the aftermath of losing her parents, ached so much for love to replace what she had lost that she convinced herself a man she saw across a crowded bar was her saviour, a hero, someone special who would lift her up out of the misery of her pain and loss and hold her safe in his arms. That was the true nature of my crime, Sander—idolising you and turning you into something you could never be.

'And as for all those other men you like to accuse me of being with—they never existed. Not a single one of them. Do you *really* think I would be stupid enough to trust another man after the way you treated me? Yes, I expect I deserved it for behaving so stupidly. You wanted to teach me a lesson, I expect. I'm only surprised, knowing you as I now do, that you seem unable to accept that your lesson was successful.

'There was only one reason I asked you for marriage, Sander—because I thought it would make you back off.

But then, when I realised you genuinely wanted the twins, it was as I told you at the time—because I believe very strongly that children thrive best emotionally within the security of a family unit that contains two parents who intend to stay together. I grew up in that kind of family unit, and naturally it was what I wanted for my sons.

'What you've just accused me of changes everything. I don't want you poisoning the boys' minds with your own horrible mindset. This baby *will* be their true sibling, but somehow I doubt that even DNA evidence will convince you of that. Quite simply it isn't what you want to believe. You want to believe the worst of me. Perhaps you even need to believe it. In which case I feel very sorry for you. My job as a mother is to protect all my children. The twins are two very intelligent boys. They will quickly see that you do not accept their sister or brother and they might even mimic your behaviour. I will not allow that to happen.'

Initially he had been resolutely determined to deny that there could be any truth in Ruby's angry outburst. But beneath the complex defence system his own hurt emotions had built up to protect him from the pain caused by his mother, tendrils of something 'other' had begun to unfurl. So small at first that he thought he could brush them away. But when he tried Sander discovered that they were rooted in a bedrock of inner need it stunned him to discover. When had this yearning to throw off the defensive chains that imprisoned him taken root? How could this part of him actually be willing to take Ruby's side against himself? Struggling against the opposing forces within himself, Sander fought desperately for a way forward.

This was so much worse than anything she had imagined might happen, Ruby acknowledged. She had feared that Sander would be angry, but it had never occurred to her that he would refuse to accept that the child she had conceived was his. She should hate him for that. She wished that she could. Hatred would be cleansing and almost satisfying.

She would have to leave the island, of course. But she wasn't going anywhere without the twins. They would miss Sander dreadfully, but she couldn't risk them starting to think and feel as he did. She couldn't let his bitterness infect them.

She turned to look through the still open patio doors, her vision blurred by the tears she was determined not to let him see.

'There's no point in us continuing this discussion,' she told him. 'Since it's obvious that you prefer to think the worst of me.'

Without waiting to see if he was going to make any response Ruby headed for the patio, anxious to put as much distance between them as she could before her emotions overwhelmed her and the tears burning the backs of her eyes fell.

From the bedroom Sander watched her, his thoughts still at war with themselves. Ruby had reached the top of the flight of marble steps that led down to the lower part of the garden.

Blinking fiercely to hold back her tears, Ruby stepped forward, somehow mistiming her step, so that the heel of her shoe caught on the top step, pitching her forward.

Sander saw her stumble and then fall, tumbling down the marble steps. He raced after her, taking the steps two at a time to reach her crumpled body where it lay still at the bottom of the first flight of steps.

She was conscious—just. And her two words to him as he kneeled over her were agonized. 'My baby…'

CHAPTER TWELVE

'She's coming round now. Ruby, can you hear us?'

Her clouded vision slowly cleared and the vague outlines of white-clad figures formed into two nurses and a doctor, all three of them smiling reassuringly at her. Hospital. She was in hospital? Automatically she began to panic.

'It's all right, Ruby. You had a nasty fall, but you're all right now. We've had to keep you sedated for a few days, to give your body time to rest, and we've performed some tests, so you're bound to feel woozy and confused. Just relax.'

Relax! Ruby put her hand on top of the flat white sheet pulled tightly over her body. She was attached to some kind of drip, she realised.

'My baby?' she demanded anxiously.

The nurse closest to her looked at the doctor.

She'd lost her baby. Her fall—she remembered it now—had killed her baby. The pain was all-encompassing. She had let her baby down. She hadn't protected it properly, either from her fall or from its father's rejection. She felt too numb with grief to cry.

The nurse patted her hand. The doctor smiled at her.

'Your baby is fine, Ruby.'

She looked at them both in disbelief.

'You're just telling me that, aren't you? I've lost the baby really, haven't I?'

The doctor looked back at the nurse. 'I think we should let Ruby have a look for herself.' Turning to Ruby, he told her, 'The nurse will take you for a scan, Ruby, and then you will be able to see for yourself that your baby is perfectly well. Which is more than I will be able to say for you, if you continue to upset yourself.'

An hour later Ruby was back in her hospital room, still gazing in awed delight at the image she'd been given—an image which showed quite clearly that her baby was indeed safe.

'You and your baby have both been very lucky,' the nurse told her when she came in a few minutes later to check up on her. 'You sustained a nasty head injury, and when you were taken into hospital on Theopolis they feared that a blood clot had developed. It meant they would have to terminate your pregnancy. Your husband refused to give his consent. He arranged for you to be brought here to this hospital in Athens, and for a specialist to be brought from America to treat you. Your husband said that you would never forgive him and he would never forgive himself if your pregnancy had to be terminated.'

Sander had said that? Ruby didn't know what to think.

'I dare say he will be here soon,' the nurse continued. 'Initially he insisted on staying here in the hospital with you, but Professor Smythson told him to go home and get some rest once you were in the clear.'

As though on cue the door to her room opened and Sander was standing there. Discreetly the nurse whisked herself out of the room, leaving them alone together.

'The twins…' Ruby began anxiously.

'They know that you had a fall and that you had to come to hospital to be "mended". They're missing you, of course, but Anna is doing her best to keep them occupied.'

'The nurse was just telling me that it's thanks to you I still have my baby.'

'Our baby,' Sander corrected her quietly.

Ruby didn't know what to say—or think—so her emotions did both for her. Tears slid down her face.

'Ruby, don't,' Sander begged, leaving the foot of her bed, where he had been standing, to come and take hold of her hand, now disconnected from the drip she had been on as she no longer needed it. 'When I saw you falling down those steps I knew that no matter what I'd said, or what I thought I'd believed, the truth was that I loved you. I think I knew it that last night we spent in Athens, but I told myself that letting go of my doubts about you must be a slow and measured process. It took the realisation that I might have lost you to show me the truth. I deliberately blinded myself to what was real, just as you said. I wanted and needed to believe the very worst of you, and because of that—because of my fear of loving you and my pride in that fear—you and our child almost lost your lives.'

'My fall was an accident.'

'An accident that resulted from my blind refusal to accept what you were trying to tell me. Can you forgive me?'

'I love you, Sander. You know that. What I want now is for you to forgive yourself.' Ruby looked up at him. 'And not just forgive yourself about me.' Did she dare to say what she wanted to say? If she didn't seize this opportunity to do so she would regret it, Ruby warned herself, for Sander's sake more than for her own.

'I know your mother hurt you, Sander.'

'My mother never loved any of us. We were a duty she had to bear—literally as well as figuratively. My brother and sister and myself were the price she paid for my father's wealth, and for living the life she really wanted—a life of shallow, gaudy excess, lived in luxury at someone else's expense. The only time we saw her was when she wanted my father to give her more money. There was no room in her heart for us, no desire to make room there for us.'

Ruby's heart ached with compassion for him.

'It wasn't your fault that she rejected you, Sander. The flaw was within her, not you.'

His grip on her hand tightened convulsively.

'I guess I've always been distrustful of women— probably as a result of my relationship with my mother. When I saw you in that club I saw you in my mother's image. I didn't want to look beneath the surface. I believe now that a part of me did recognise how innocent and vulnerable you really were, but I was determined to reject it. I used you as a means of expressing my anger against my grandfather. My behaviour was un-forgivable.'

'No.' Ruby shook her head. 'Under the circumstances it was predictable. Had I been the experienced party girl you thought, I suspect I would have known that some-thing more than desire was driving you. We both made mistakes, Sander, but that doesn't mean we can't forgive ourselves and put them behind us. We were both defen-sive when we got married. You because of your mother, and me because I was ashamed of the way I'd behaved with you—giving away my virginity to a man who couldn't wait to throw me out of his bed and his life once he had had what he wanted.'

'Don't…' Sander groaned remorsefully. 'I'm sorry I said what I did about this new baby, Ruby. When you fell just before you lost consciousness you whispered to me—"my baby"—and I knew then that no matter what I had said, or thought I believed, the child inside you was mine, that it was impossible for it to have been fathered by anyone else. Can we start again? Can you still love me after the way I've behaved?'

In answer to his question Ruby lifted herself up off her pillows and kissed him gently, before telling him, 'It would be impossible for me not to love you, Sander.'

It was just over a month since Ruby, fully recovered from her fall, had returned to the island, and each day her happiness grew. Or so it seemed to her. Sander had already proved to her that he was a loving father to the twins, and now, in addition to proving to her that he intended to be an equally good father to the child she was carrying, he had also dedicated himself to proving to her that he was a wonderfully loving husband.

Lying next to him in their bed, Ruby felt her heart swell with joy and love. Smiling in the darkness, she turned toward Sander, pressing a loving kiss against his chin.

'You know what will happen if you keep on doing that,' he warned her mock-seriously.

Ruby laughed. 'I thought I was the one who was unable to resist you, not the other way round,' she teased as she nestled closer to him, the soft curves of her naked body a sweet, warm temptation against his own.

'Does it feel like I'm able to resist you?' Sander asked her.

His hands were already stroking her skin; his breath was warm against her lips. Eagerly Ruby moved closer to him. It was still the same—that heart-stopping feeling of anticipation and longing that filled her when she knew he was going to kiss her.

'I love you...'

The words were breathed against her ear and then repeated against her lips, before Sander finally slowly stroked his tongue-tip against them deliberately, until Ruby couldn't wait any longer and placed her hands either side of his head. Her lips parted, a little shudder of longing rippling through her.

The sound of the accelerated speed of their breathing mingled with the movement of flesh against fabric, soft whispering sounds of sensuality and expectant desire.

As always, the sweetness of Ruby's arousal increased Sander's own desire. She showed her love for him so naturally and openly, with her desire whispered in soft words of love and longing, and encouragement and promises filling the air, breathed against his skin in an erotic litany of emotion. He could now admit that part of him had responded to that in her from the very start, and had in turn loved her for it, even if he had barricaded that knowledge away from himself.

The shape of her body was changing now, and her pregnancy was a gentle swell that he caressed gently before he kissed her growing bump.

Looking down at his dark head, Ruby stroked the smooth flesh at the nape of his neck. She knew now how much both she and this new baby meant to him.

Lying down beside her, Sander cupped her breast, allowing his lips to tease her nipple provocatively, his fingertips drifting tormentingly across her lower belly in a caress he knew she loved. Ruby closed her eyes and clung to him, riding the wave of her own desire as it swelled and pulsed inside her, smiling at the now familiar torment of building pleasure, of raw, sensual need that Sander knew exactly how to stretch out until it became almost unbearable.

Sander knew that if he placed his hand over her mound now he would be able to feel the insistent pulse it covered—just as he knew that the unsteady increase in her breathing meant that the stroke of his fingers within her would bring her almost immediately to orgasm, and that after that orgasm he would re-ignite her desire so that he could satisfy them both with the thrust of his body within hers. He could feel his self-control starting to give way.

His hand moved further down her body. The soft, scented wetness of her sex and the way she offered it to him with such sensual generosity turned his heart over inside his chest. He looked up at her as he parted the folded outer lips. A shudder ripped through her eyes, dark and wild with need. His fingertips stroked slowly through her wetness and then back again, to rub against the source of her desire, hard and swollen beneath his touch, making his own body throb in increasingly insistent demand. His lips caressed her nipple more urgently, his gaze registering the flush staining her skin and the growing intensity of the small shudders gripping her body.

'San—der...'

It was the way she said his name that did it—a soft plea of longing plaited with a tormenting thread of enticement that smashed through what was left of his self-control.

Ruby shuddered wildly beneath the sensation of Sander's mouth on her skin—her breasts, her belly, her thighs, and then finally her sex, where his tongue-tip stroked and probed and possessed until the pleasure made her gasp and then cry out.

Sander couldn't wait any longer. As it was he had to fight against himself to draw out their shared pleasure instead of giving in to the demand of his own flesh and its need to lose itself within her, holding them both on the rack of their shared longing before finally thrusting slowly into her, letting the responsive muscles of her body take him and possess him until they were riding the pleasure together to the ecstasy of shared love and release.

'I love you.'

'I love you.'

'You are my life, my world, light in my darkness, my Ruby beyond price.'

Held safe in Sander's arms, Ruby closed her eyes, knowing that when she woke in the morning and for every morning, of their lives together, she would wake up held safe and loved.

EPILOGUE

'OH, RUBY, she's beautiful.'

Smiling proudly, Ruby looked on as her sisters admired their new niece, who was now just over one month old.

It had been a wonderful surprise when Sander had told her that he had arranged for her sisters and their husbands to visit the island, and Ruby thought it the best present he could have given her—barring, of course, his love and their new daughter.

'She's the image of Sander,' Lizzie announced, with an eldest sister authority that Ruby had no desire to refute.

After all, it was true that Hebe was the image of her father and her twin brothers, and, whilst Sander had said prior to her birth that if they had a girl he would like her to look like her mother, Ruby rather thought that he didn't mind one little bit that she was a dark-haired, dark-eyed daddy's girl.

'It looks as though she can wind Sander and the boys round her little finger already.' Charlotte joined the conversation, adding ruefully, 'I'm itching to cuddle her properly, but this one—' she patted the bulge of her seven-month pregnancy ruefully '—obviously doesn't want me to. He kicked so hard when I tried.'

'Ah, so it *is* a boy, then.'

Ruby and Lizzie pounced in unison, laughing when their middle sister tried to protest and then glanced toward her husband, Raphael. He was standing with Sander, and Lizzie's husband Ilios, who was holding their two-month-old son Perry with the deftness of experienced fatherhood. The three men laughed and talked together.

'Well, yes, I think so from what I saw at the last scan!' she admitted ruefully. 'Of course I could be wrong, and the truth is that Raphael doesn't mind whether we have a boy or a girl, although personally...' She gave a small sigh and then said softly, 'I know it's silly, but I can't stop myself from imagining a little boy with Raphael's features.'

'It isn't silly at all,' Ruby immediately defended her. 'It's only natural. I love the fact that the twins and Hebe look like Sander.'

'I feel the same way about Perry,' Lizzie agreed, adding, 'That's what love does for you.'

Automatically they all turned to watch their husbands. 'It's lovely that our three babies will be so close in age—especially as the twins have one another,' Ruby added.

'Sander is so proud of the boys, Ruby. And proud of you, for the way you brought them up alone.'

'I wasn't alone,' Ruby objected, pointing out emotionally, 'They and I had both of you to support us and love us. I could never have managed without you.'

'And we would never have wanted you to—would we, Charlotte?' Lizzie told her.

'Never,' Charlotte agreed, squeezing Ruby's hand.

For a moment it was just the three of them again, sisters bonded together by the tragedy they had shared, and by their love and loyalty for one another, but then Charlotte broke the silence, enclosing them all to say softly, 'I think we must have some very special guardian angels watching over us.'

Once again they looked toward their husbands, before turning back to one another.

'We've certainly been lucky to meet and fall in love with such very special men,' Ruby said.

'And all the more special because they think *they* are the lucky ones in having met us.' Lizzie shook her head and then said ruefully, 'None of us could have imagined how things were going to turn out when I was worrying so much about having to go out to Thessalonica.'

The look she gave Ilios as she spoke said very clearly to her sisters how much she loved her husband, causing both of them to turn and look at their own husbands with similar emotion.

'There is something other than how happy we are now that we do need to discuss,' she continued, explaining when Charlotte and Ruby looked at her, 'The house. Ilios insisted on clearing the mortgage for me, because at that stage I still thought that you would both need it, and I transferred it into your joint names. Since none of us need it now, what I'd like to suggest is that we donate it to charity. I've been making a few enquiries, and there is a Cheshire-based charity that provides help for single mothers. If we deed the house to the charity then they can either use it to provide accommodation or sell it and use the money in other ways. What do you think?'

'I think it's an excellent idea.'

'I agree.'

'So that's decided, then.'

'There might be one small problem,' Ruby warned. 'Since Ilios cleared the mortgage, I rather suspect that Sander and Raphael will want to match his donation.'

Once again all three of them looked towards their husbands, exchanging smiles when the men looked back.

Three such male and strong men—strong enough to admit that they had been conquered by love and to show openly just how much that love meant to them.

'We are so very lucky,' Ruby announced, knowing that she was speaking for her sisters as well as for herself.

Sander, who had detached himself from Ilios and Raphael and was on his way towards them, overheard her, and stopped to tell her firmly, 'No, it is we who are the lucky ones. Lucky and blessed by the gods and by fate to have won the love of three such true Graces.'

PREGNANT WITH HIS ROYAL TWINS

LOUISA HEATON

This book is for anyone who suffers from anxiety. Who has to find the courage from deep within just to leave the house. It's an endless battle, but this book is for you.

xxx

CHAPTER ONE

FREYA SURREPTITIOUSLY SLIPPED the packet from her locker and into her uniform pocket, hiding it under her notepad. The lack of her period and the increasing nausea she was experiencing each morning seemed obvious signs enough, but Freya wanted proof. Scientific proof.

Night shift it might be, but to her this was morning, and walking into the staff room and smelling the strong coffee that had been put on to brew had almost made her share with everyone the ginger biscuits she had forced down for breakfast. It had taken a gargantuan effort to control her stomach, and a sheen of sweat had prickled her brow and top lip as she'd fumbled with her locker. Her fingers had almost tripped over themselves in her haste.

Heading to the ladies' loo, she told Mona she'd just be five minutes and that she'd catch up to her at the staff briefing in a moment.

'Okay, hun, see you in five.' Mona smiled and headed off, her hand clutched around a mug of that nausea-inducing coffee.

The toilets were right next door to the hub, so Freya slipped in and locked the door behind her, leaning back against it, letting out a long, slow breath of relief. She took a moment to stand there and see if her stomach settled.

There didn't seem any doubt about what was happening

to her, but she needed to do this just the same. She pulled the pregnancy test from her pocket and stared hard at it, not quite believing that she was actually going to.

She'd always *hoped* that one day she would become a mother. But the actual chances of that ever happening to her had—she believed—become very slim the day she had been scarred for life. Because who would want her now?

'Come on, Freya…you're better than this,' she whispered to herself, trying to drum up the courage to get herself through the next few minutes.

Freya loved the nightshift, working on Maternity here at Queen's Hospital. There was something extra-special about working nights. The quiet. The solitude. The intimate joy of bringing a new life into the world and being with that family as they watched their first sunrise together. A new day. A new family. Life changing. Getting *better.* New hopes. New dreams. There weren't the distractions of daytime—telephones constantly ringing, visiting families all over the place. It was secluded. Fewer busybodies.

It was the perfect hiding place for her, the hospital at night time, and those nights afforded Freya the anonymity that she craved. Lights were kept low. There were shadows to stay in, no harsh fluorescent lighting to reveal to her patients the true extent of her scarring.

It was better now than it had been. She had some smooth skin now, over her cheeks and forehead, where just two years before she'd had angry red pits and lines, her face constantly set and immovable, like a horrific Halloween mask.

Not now. Not now she'd had her many, *many* reconstructive surgeries. Thirty-three times under the skilled scalpel of her plastic surgeon.

And yet she was still hiding—even more so—in a bathroom. Her hands sweating and fidgety as she kept glancing down at the testing kit.

'Only one thing to do, really,' she told herself aloud,

shaking her head at the absolute silliness of giving herself a pep talk.

She peed on the stick and laid it on the back of the sink as she washed her hands and then took a step back. She stared at her reflection in the mirror, refusing to look down and see the result. She saw the fear in her eyes, but she also recognised something she hadn't seen for years—*hope*.

'This is what you've always wanted,' she whispered.

But wanting something and actually *achieving* it, when you believed it to be impossible, was another thing altogether. If it *were* possible then she'd finally get her childhood dream. To hold her own child in her arms and not just other people's. To have her own baby and be a mum. Even if that meant she'd have to revert back to living in sunlight. With all those other people.

Even if they didn't stare at her, or do that second glance thing, she still felt that they were looking. It was human nature to look at someone different and pretend that you weren't. And your face was the hardest thing to hide.

Still…this wasn't exactly how she'd imagined it happening. As a little girl she'd dreamt of marrying a handsome man, having his babies and being in a settled relationship.

She had no one. Even 'the guy' had been a mad, terrific impulse, when her body had been thrumming with joy about the fact that she was out amongst people, having fun, enjoying a party behind the veil of her fancy dress costume.

It had been so long since she'd last been to a social event. Too long. Years since she'd stood in a room full of people, chatting, laughing at poor jokes, being *normal*.

Mike had taken that away from her. That joy and freedom. His jealous actions had imprisoned her in a world of night and pain, surgeries and hiding. Feeling unable to show her face to the world without fearing people's reactions. A frightened child turning away as if to clutch her mother's skirts when a stranger did a double-take and tried not to look appalled or disgusted or worse.

The veil she'd worn that night had hidden everything. The high-necked Victorian steam punk outfit had hidden the scars on her neck that had not yet been tackled, and the veil had added a note of mystery.

That night people had looked at her with intrigue and with delight. They'd smiled...they'd complimented her on how *wonderful* she looked. Their words had made her giddy with happiness. She'd been normal there. Like them.

And then *he'd* been there. The guy. The pirate. He'd seemed uncomfortable. Had appeared to be waiting for enough time to pass so he could make his escape.

She knew how that felt. She'd felt a kind of companionship with him, despite their not having exchanged a word.

It had helped, of course, that he had seductively dark eyes and a wickedly tempting mouth, and she'd almost stopped herself. She'd taken a moment to register the fact that she was *attracted* to a man when the very idea of that had been anathema to her for so many years.

But not that night. The costume, the veil, had given her a sense of bravery she hadn't felt for a long time.

'I'm Freya. Pleased to meet you.'

'Jamie.'

'I saw you eyeing up the exit. Getting ready to make a break for it?'

'I've been thinking about it.'

'Please don't. Stay for a little while longer. Let me get you a drink.'

It had been crazy how emboldened she'd felt. Her entire body had been thrumming with adrenaline and serotonin, her heart pounding like a revved-up engine. She'd felt alive, happy, normal again—having a conversation with an attractive man, feeling the thrill of first attraction.

Silly. Childish, maybe, when she really ought to have known better, but it had just felt so good!

He had made her feel that way. The way he'd looked at her, his eyes sparkling with inky delight, his full lips curved in a wicked smile. He'd laughed with joy at her anecdotes, had genuinely seemed happy to stay.

She'd felt warm and wanted again. Desire had filled her the second he'd let go of the stem of his glass and let his fingers trail delicately over the back of her hand. She'd focused on that movement, watched his fingertips on her skin—her very sensitive skin. She'd looked up and met his eyes, and the most extraordinary question had left her lips.

'*Are you married?*'

'*No.*'

'*With someone?*'

'*No.*'

'*Do you want to be?*'

She'd startled herself with the sheer audacity of her question. That wasn't *her*! Freya MacFadden did not proposition strange men!

She'd pulled her hand away then, retreating into the shell she was so accustomed to being inside. But then he'd reached for her hand again. Not to stop her from running away. Not to try and possess her or control her. But just to get her to make eye contact with him.

'*I'm guessing you didn't mean to say that?*'

'*No.*'

'*Then we can both forget it. Don't worry.*'

'*I'm sorry.*'

'*Don't ever be.*'

He'd been so kind. So understanding. So she hadn't bolted and neither had he.

They'd continued to sit with each other and talk about what the other guests were wearing and why the charity they

were there to support was so important. They'd laughed and
had a good time, enjoying each other's company.

He'd offered to walk her out at the end, and she'd let him,
intending to say goodbye at the door. To fetch her coat and
leave. For ever to remain an enigmatic stranger at a party
that he would remember with fondness. Like Cinderella
leaving the ball at midnight, only without the glass slipper.

Freya let out a deep breath. She couldn't stay here in
the bathroom for too long. There was a hand-over from
the day shift.

Freya loved her daytime colleagues, and they her, but she
was happy when they went home. Because then she could
begin to craft the intimacy that the night shift brought.
Lowering the lights. Softening the voices.

It was time.

She couldn't wait any longer.

It was now or never.

She looked down.

And sucked in a breath.

'I'm pregnant.'

She looked back at her reflection, disbelieving.

'I'm *pregnant*?'

She didn't know whether to laugh hysterically or to cry,
to gasp or anything else!

She was pregnant.

There was no question as to *how* it had happened. She
remembered that night all too well. The father of her child
was quite clear in her mind. How could he *not* be? Even if
she didn't actually know *who* he was. Or where he came
from.

Their meeting that night had been quite by chance—as
sudden and exciting and as passionate as she'd imagined it
could be. Scary and exhilarating, and one of the best nights
of her life. She'd thrown caution to the wind and felt fully

alive again for just a moment. For one desperate moment she had been someone else.

She had gone to the ball knowing she would be able to hide behind her veil and costume all night. It had been very gothic-looking, high-necked, with lots of black and dark purple, layers and petticoats. And there had been a top hat, embellished with a large swathe of plum ribbon, copper cogs and whatnots, and a veil of amethyst silk covering her nose and mouth like a Bedouin bride, leaving only her eyes visible.

Her best feature. The only part of her face not scarred or damaged by the acid. She'd been lucky in that respect. Most acid attack victims were blinded.

Her dashing admirer had tried to remove her veil when he'd leant in to kiss her, but she'd stopped him.

'Don't, please. It's better this way.'

He'd smiled and used his mouth in other ways...

Now everyone at the hand-over would be waiting for her, and they'd all look at her when she went back through. The longer she left it, the worse it would be.

She put the cap on the test stick and slipped it into her pocket, then unlocked the bathroom door. Shoulders back, trying to feel relaxed, she headed off to the briefing.

Okay. I can do this. I'm an expert at pretending everything is fine.

The staff were all gathered around the hub of the unit. Whenever a new patient was admitted, or whenever family came to visit, they would walk down this one corridor that led to the hub. From there they would be directed down different corridors—to the right for postnatal and discharges, straight ahead for medical assessment and long-stay patients, to the left for labour and delivery, and beyond that, Theatre.

From the hub, they could see who was trying to buzz through the main doors to gain access to the ward, with the help of a security camera. They could also see the admissions boards, listing who was in which bed and what stage they were at.

There were usually thank-you cards there, perched on the desk, or stuck to the wall behind them, along with a tin or a box of chocolates kindly donated by a grateful family, and on the walls were some very beautiful black and white photographs of babies, taken by their very skilled photographer Addison.

Senior midwife Jules was leaning up against the hub, and she smiled when she saw Freya coming. 'Here she is! Last but not least.'

Freya sidled in amongst the group, keeping her eyes down and trying desperately to blend in. She could feel all eyes upon her and folded herself down into a chair to make herself smaller. She had kept people waiting when they just wanted to go home.

She gratefully accepted a copy of the admissions sheet that Mona passed over to her.

'It's been a busy day today, and it looks like you girls aren't going to have it easy tonight either. In the labour suite, we've got two labouring mums. In Bed One is Andrea Simpson—she's a gravida one, para zero at term plus two days, currently at three centimetres dilated and comfortable, but she had a spontaneous rupture of membranes at home. She's currently on the trace machine and will need to come off in about ten minutes. In Bed Two we have Lisa Chambers, she's a gravida three, para four. Two lots of twins and currently about to deliver her first singleton baby. She's had two previous elective Caesareans and is trying for a VBAC on this one.'

Freya nodded, scribbling notes. A VBAC was a vaginal birth after Caesarean—a 'trial of scar', as some people put it, to see if the mother could deliver vaginally.

'She's labouring fast. At six-thirty she was at six centimetres and she's currently making do on gas and air.'

Freya sat and listened to the rest of Jules's assessment. They had in total twenty-one patients: two on the labour ward, seven on Antenatal and twelve on Postnatal, five of whom were post-surgery.

And the phones would continue to ring. There would also be unexpected walk-ins, and no doubt A&E would send up one or two.

But she didn't mind. Her job was her life. Her passion. The only thing that brought her real joy. It was all she'd ever wanted to be, growing up. A midwife and a mum. And, as of ten startling minutes ago, it looked as if she was going to achieve being both of those.

Freya was excellent at her job, and she truly believed she was only so good at it because it was something she adored doing. Every new baby born was a minor miracle. Every witnessed birth a joy and a privilege. Every moment she sat and held a mother's hand through a contraction was another courageous moment.

It was a weird place, Maternity. A place where staff and patients met often for the first time, total strangers, and then just hours later Freya would know so much about a person—about their family, their hopes and dreams, their sense of humour, what their favourite foods were, what they craved, what they wanted to be, what they wanted to name their children...

She saw them at their worst, but more often at their best and bravest, and when her patients left Freya knew she would always be remembered as being a part of that family's life. Someone who had shared in their most special and cherished moments. Never to be forgotten.

It was an immense responsibility.

Jules put down her papers. 'Now, ladies, I want you to calm yourselves, but we have in our midst a new midwife!

His name's Jamie and he's hiding at the back. Give us all a wave, Jamie!'

Jamie? No. Relax. It's a common name.

Freya didn't want to turn and look. She knew how that would make the poor guy feel, having all those women turning and staring at him, eyeing him up. But she knew that it would look odd if hers was the only head that didn't turn. It would single her out. So she gave him a quick glance.

Lovely. No...wait a minute...

She whipped her head back round, her mind whirling, and pretended to scribble some more notes about what Jules had just reported on her sheet. But her pen remained still above the paper.

It's him. It's him! Oh, God, oh, God, oh...

Her trembling fingers touched her lips and her nausea returned in a torrent so powerful she thought she might be sick with nerves right there and then—all over Mona's shoes. She wanted to get up and bolt. Run as fast as she could. But it was impossible.

She frantically eyed the spaces between the rows of staff and wondered how quickly she could make a break for it at the end of the briefing.

It couldn't be possible. How *could* it be him? Her one-night stand.

'Jamie is with us for a couple of months, filling in for Sandra who's away on maternity leave, so I'd like to say welcome to the team, Jamie, it's good to have you here. For the rest of you—Jamie has been working all over the country in various midwifery posts, so he's got a lot of experience, and I hope you'll all take the time to welcome him here, to Queen's.'

Jules smiled.

'Right, then. We're all off. Have a good shift, ladies. And Jamie!'

She smiled, waved, and the majority of staff disappeared off to the locker room, to grab their things and go.

Freya, frozen to the spot, wished she could do the same.

Okay, so the simplest thing to do is to stay out of his way.

So far she'd done a sterling job of that.

Mona was showing him around, pointing out where everything was, getting him acquainted with the temperamental computer and how to admit people to the ward—that kind of thing. Freya, on the other hand, had just been given the task to introduce herself to the two labouring mothers and work on the labour ward—which she was very happy about because that gave her the opportunity to stay in her patients' rooms and not see or have to engage with *him*.

The irony of the situation was not lost on her. The first time they had met she had been brimming with temporary confidence, an urge to experience life again as a normal woman meeting a handsome guy at a party. But now she was back to reality. Hiding and skulking around corners, trying her best to avoid him. The man she'd propositioned.

And what the hell were the odds of him turning up on the very same day that she took a pregnancy test? It had to be millions to one, didn't it? Or at the very least a few hundred thousand to one?

Jules had said he'd been working in various posts around the country. Why hadn't he got a job at one of those? Why did he keep moving?

What's wrong with him?

The weight of the pregnancy test in her left pocket seemed to increase, its weight like a millstone.

She entered Andrea Simpson's room quietly.

'Hello, it's Andrea, isn't it? I'm Freya and I'm going to be your midwife tonight.'

She smiled at her new charge and then glanced over at her partner, who was putting his phone in his back pocket and standing up to say hello.

He reached over to shake her hand and she saw him do that thing with his eyes that everyone did when they noticed her face—noticed that she'd been burned, somehow, despite her corrective surgery and skin grafts. Noticed that she'd had *work done*.

His gaze flittered across her features and then there was *that* pause.

'Hi, I'm George,' he introduced himself. 'I'm just here to do what I'm told.'

Freya smiled. 'Mum's the boss in this room.'

She glanced over at the belt placement on Andrea's abdomen and checked the trace on the machine. The trace looked good. No decelerations and the occasional contraction, currently seven or eight minutes apart. Still a way to go for Andrea.

'I want you to stay on this for ten more minutes, then I'll take it off—is that all right?'

Andrea nodded, reaching for a bottle of water and taking a short drink.

'Do you have a birth plan?'

'Just to have as much pain relief as I can get.'

'Okay. And what sort of pain relief are you thinking of?'

'I want to start with gas and air, see how I go with that, and then maybe get pethidine. But I'm open to whatever you suggest at the time.'

Freya smiled. 'So am I. This is *your* birth, *your* body. I'll be guided by you as long as it's safe. Okay?'

'Yes...'

Freya could see that Andrea had questions. 'Nervous?'

Andrea giggled. 'A bit. This is all so *new*!'

Tell me about it.

Freya had seen hundreds of babies come into the world. She never tired of it. Each birth was different and special, and now she knew that if all went well and she didn't miscarry she'd be doing this herself in a few months. Lying on a bed…labouring. It was actually going to happen.

'You'll do fine.'

She laid a reassuring hand on her patient's and wondered who'd be there to hold *her* hand during labour? Her mum?

Her mind treacherously placed Jamie beside her bed and she felt goosebumps shiver down her skin.

No. It can't be him.

It can't be.

But isn't that what you always wanted? A cosy, happy family unit?

It had been. Once.

It was *her*. He'd have known those blue eyes anywhere. The eyes that had been haunting his dreams for weeks now.

He'd been invited to that charity ball after he'd attended a small event in Brighton that was meant to have been low-key. But word must have reached the ears of the hospital that the heir to the throne of Majidar, Prince Jameel Al Bakhari, was around and an invitation had got through to his people.

It had been for such a good cause he hadn't been able to refuse it. A children's burns unit. He'd seen the damage burns could cause, from a simple firework accident right through to injuries sustained in a war zone, and it was shocking for anyone. A painful, arduous road to recovery. But for it to happen to a child was doubly devastating.

So he'd attended, dressed as a pirate, complete with a large hoop earring and a curved plastic scimitar that had hung from his waist by a sash.

He'd not intended to stay for very long. He'd made them keep his presence there quiet, as he didn't enjoy people bowing and scraping around him. He hated that whole sycophantic thing that happened around members of his royal family. It was part of why he'd left Majidar. To be a normal person.

It was why he tried to live his life following his passion. And his passion was to deliver babies. Something that was not considered 'suitable' for a prince back in his own country.

But what could you do when it was your calling? Delivering babies was what he had always yearned to do, and he'd never been destined for the throne. His elder brother had been the heir and was now ruler. So surely, he'd reasoned, it was better to spend his life doing something worthwhile and selfless instead of parading around crowds of people, smiling and waving, a spare heir that no one needed?

He'd faced some considerable opposition. Mostly from his father, who'd been appalled that his second son wanted to do what he viewed as 'women's work'. His father had forbidden him ever to speak of it again and, respecting his father, he had kept that promise. Until his father had passed away. Then his brother Ilias had taken the throne, and Jamie had approached his new King and told him of his vocation.

Ilias had proudly granted his younger brother the freedom to pursue it.

So he'd gone to the ball, telling the organisers that he didn't want to draw attention to himself, and asking that they did not make any special announcement that he was there, just let him join in as any other person would.

Jamie had mingled, smiled, shaken people's hands—and found himself losing the will to live and wondering when would be a polite time to leave... And then he'd spotted *her* in a corner of the room.

Almost as tall as he, she'd been dressed from top to toe in black, accented in dark purple, with some weird cogs and a strange pair of pilot goggles attached to her hat. Her face had been covered by a Bedouin-style gauze veil that had reminded him of home.

Her honey-blonde hair had tumbled down her back, almost to her waist, and above that veil had sparkled the most gorgeous blue eyes he had ever seen. Blue like the ocean and the sky, and just as wild and free.

'I'm Freya. Pleased to meet you.'

'Jamie.'

'I saw you eyeing up the exit. Getting ready to make a break for it?'

He had been. But not any more.

So he'd stayed. And they'd talked. And laughed.

Freya had been delightful, charming and intelligent, and so easy to be with. She'd told him a story about the last time she'd attempted to flee a party. She'd been eleven years old and it had been the first time her parents hadn't stayed with her. She'd been frightened by all the noise and all the people and had scurried away when no one was looking and run home to hide in her dad's garden shed.

She'd grimaced as she'd recalled how she'd stayed there, terrified out of her wits not only about being found out, but also because there had been a massive spider in the corner, watching her. He'd laughed when she'd told him she'd almost peed her pants because her bladder had been killing her from drinking too much pop. But she hadn't been able to go home too early, or her parents would have known that she'd run away.

'No spiders here,' he'd said.

'No.'

'Nothing to be afraid of. I'll protect you.'

'Now, why would you do that? You hardly know me. I might be dangerous.'

'I think I can handle you.'

His pulse had thrummed against his skin, his temperature rising, his whole body aware. Of *her*. She hadn't removed the veil, but she'd kept on peering at him over it with devilment in her gaze, and he'd felt drawn to her excitement and bravado. She hadn't been drunk on alcohol. Her eyes had been clear, pupils not pinpointed, so no drugs. But she'd definitely been intoxicated by *something*, and he'd begun to suspect that he was feeling the same way, too.

There'd been something about her. So different from everyone else at the party. But what had it been? What had made her unique? Had it been the veil? The air of mystery? Or just those eyes? Eyes that had looked so young, but had also spoken of a wisdom beyond her years. As if she knew something that no one else did. As if she'd experienced life and the gamut of emotions that came with it. And yet that night she'd been drawn to him, and he to her. She a purple and black veiled moth and he the flame.

'Do you trust me?'

She'd smiled. *'Can any woman trust a pirate?'*

'I'm not just a pirate.'

The corners of her mouth had twitched and she'd glanced at his mouth, then back to his eyes, and he'd been hit with such a blow of lust he hadn't been able to help himself. He'd tried to look away, to take a deep breath, to regain control over his senses.

'I need to go,' she'd said.

'Let me walk you home.'

'No need. I have transport.'

'Then let me walk you to it.'

He'd offered her his arm and she'd taken it, smiling through the gauze and looking up at him, her eyes gleaming.

He'd been overcome by a bolt of desire.

But what to do about it? He considered himself a gentleman. He had principles...he'd only just met her...but there was *something*...

They'd stood there staring at each other, each of them

trying to force the words to say goodbye, but neither of them ready to leave just yet. Her eyes had glinted at him in the darkness, with a look that said she wanted more than this...

The first door they'd tried had been unlocked, and they'd found themselves inside a supply closet, filled with clean linen and pressed staff uniforms.

He'd stood in front of her, just looking at her, noticing the small flecks of green and gold in her eyes. They'd shone like jewels, and her pupils had been large and black as she'd reached for his shirt and pulled him close.

He'd lost himself in her. Completely forgotten who he was, where he was. All that had mattered had been the feel of her, the taste of her, as he'd hitched up her skirts, her million and one petticoats, slid his hands up those long, slim legs...

Freya...

Like two lost souls that had found each other, they had clutched and grasped, gasped and groaned. He'd reached to remove the veil, so that he could kiss her, so that he could seek out her lips and claim her for his very own, but she'd stopped him, stilled his hand.

'Leave it. Please.'

'But, Freya...'

'No kissing...please.'

He'd respected her wishes. That veil had made her seem like forbidden fruit. An enigma. Her hat had fallen to the floor and her long blonde locks had tumbled around her shoulders like golden waves. And the dark stockings on her ever so creamy thighs had aroused a feeling in him that he'd never quite experienced before.

They'd given each other everything.

And when they were spent they had slumped against each other and just stood there, wrapped in each other. Just breathing. Just existing. It was all that they'd needed.

A sound by the door had made them break apart and rearrange their clothing.

She'd glanced at him, guiltily. *'I must go.'*

He'd stared at her, not knowing what to say. He'd felt as if there was so much he *wanted* to say to her, but it had all got stuck in his throat and he'd remained silent. He'd wanted to tell her to stay. To come back to the hotel with him. He'd wanted to ask her if he could see her again and that had both shocked and scared him—because he *never* made commitments.

But she'd slipped from the closet, and by the time he'd adjusted his clothes and made himself presentable again she'd been gone.

He'd scanned the ballroom, looking for her fall of blonde hair, looking for those all-seeing eyes, but she'd gone.

Jamie had signalled his security people and told them to look out for her, to check the car park, but like an enigmatic spy she had simply disappeared. Disappointed, he had got into his own car and been driven home.

But now she was here.

She'd turned to look at him after Jules had asked everyone to welcome him. She was *here*. Of all the places in the world he could have looked. In this hospital. On this ward. With him. Those eyes of hers had pierced his soul once again, reawakening his dormant desire and making every cell of his body cry out for her.

But there'd been something else. Something that had rocked him. Something he hadn't noticed before. And now he understood about the veil.

Freya was scarred. Something had happened to her. To her face. She'd had work done. Skin grafts, no doubt. Painful surgeries and recovery. How many? What had happened to her? A house fire? Was that why she'd been at the charity event for the burns unit?

And he'd sensed her fear. Her shock. Had seen the horror in her eyes as she'd realised who he was. Then he'd seen her shame, because she'd noticed how he'd reacted when he saw her properly.

Angry with himself, he'd wanted to reach out, touch her, tell her that she should not be ashamed—but she'd bolted.

Jamie sensed a soul like his own. Someone who preferred the everyday to the limelight. Someone who avoided crowds and adulation. Someone who preferred to hide behind a mask.

He felt her magnetism. Her draw.

And helplessly he allowed himself to be pulled in.

'It is you, isn't it?'

Freya had quickly run to the kitchenette to make her patient's husband a cup of tea. She'd slid into the small room, breathing a sigh of relief, wondering just how the hell she was going to get through work for the next few weeks if *he* was going to be here, covering for Sandra.

She'd just been kneeling down to put the milk back in the fridge when she'd heard the door open behind her and then his voice.

Freya closed her eyes and looked down, hoping the loose tendrils of her hair would cover her face. She didn't want this. Didn't *need* this. Tonight had already been overwhelming—finding out she was pregnant—but to have him here too? To have to have *this* conversation? Now? At work?

'I'm sorry, I need to take this drink to my patient.'

She held the mug of tea in her hand, not turning to face him, but so very aware of his presence behind her in this small, suddenly claustrophobic room.

This man had made her body sing. Nerve-endings that she'd thought were dead had come alive that night and she had felt every single part of her body as he'd played her like a delicate harp. Knowing what to touch and how to touch, how to make her gasp, sigh and groan. She'd experienced things with this man that she had never felt before. He'd made her reveal a side to herself that she'd never known.

But he'd been with a woman who didn't exist in reality, and she didn't need to see his disappointment when he realised.

Just being this close to him now was doing crazy things to her insides and turning her legs to jelly. And was it hot? Her armpits were tingling with sweat.

They'd had an amazing night. And it would stay that way as long as he didn't ruin the illusion by seeing her for who she really was. He'd probably thought that she was some rare beauty, but if he saw her properly he would soon be surprised. No doubt about that.

She didn't want to have to watch it happen right in front of her. That *look*. She'd already noticed his shock when they were at the hub, and work was meant to be her happy place. He was ruining everything.

Holding the mug of tea before her, she kept her head down to pass him so she could get to the door.

He stepped back, keeping a respectful distance, which she appreciated, but as she reached for the handle he spoke again.

'It *is* you.'

Keeping her eyes downcast, she stared at the floor, not wanting to see him take in her scars, her wounds. To see that she was damaged goods. This man had *wanted* her! Wanted her so badly! And it had been wondrous—a memory she'd cherished since that night. A moment of freedom from the poor existence with which Mike had left her. And she had revelled in that.

Did she want to see him realise that the woman he had given himself to was not the one of his dreams? No. Just for once she wanted to be a good memory for someone. For them to believe her beautiful.

'I'm sorry, I have to go.'

'Look at me.'

'Jamie, please...' She glanced upwards for just a moment and painfully met his gaze, her eyes blurry with unshed tears, waiting to see him realise his mistake...

Only it didn't happen. He simply looked directly at her. Showed no shock this time. No horror.

'If only you knew how much I've wanted to see you again.'

Confused, she stared back. Felt the tears finally escape her eyes and trickle down her cheeks.

'What...?'

What was he saying? What did he mean? Why wasn't he reacting to her face like everyone else did?

'You're unforgettable—do you know that?'

She swallowed hard, looking away, down at the steaming mug. 'For all the wrong reasons.'

She got out of the kitchenette as quickly as she could. What *was* it with them and small rooms? Kitchenettes. Supply cupboards. Was Jamie set to startle her in anything less than six by six? Should she stay away from bathroom cubicles, too?

As she hurried back to her patient's room she madly wiped her eyes and sniffed a few times, to try and look presentable for Andrea and her husband.

What had just happened? How had he managed to turn her understanding of the world completely on its head?

She slipped her hand into her pocket, to reassure herself that the pregnancy test was still there. Only it wasn't. Her pocket was empty except for her notebook and pen.

She looked back to the kitchenette and saw Jamie come out, his face a mass of confused emotions as his eyes met hers.

Over the small white stick in his hand.

CHAPTER TWO

IT MUST HAVE fallen from her pocket. But when? And how?

And then she remembered crouching down to get the milk from the fridge. Something similar had happened before, due to the design of the pocket on her uniform. It was below the waist, low down. She'd lost her mobile phone once that way, hearing it clatter onto the floor. She'd not heard the test stick fall. Probably because she'd heard his voice instead. Felt his presence.

'It is you. Isn't it?'

His words had cut through everything.

Her mind had been on other things. Other concerns. She'd closed that fridge fast. Stood up quickly and made that tea, trying not to look at him, trying to get away as quickly as she could.

She was saved from going over to him and taking the test from his hands. The call light above Bed Two flashed and she went in to see how Lisa Chambers, her labouring mother there, was doing.

Lisa was pacing the room, her abdomen swollen before her, her hands pressed into her back.

'I felt the need to push with that last one, Freya.'

She handed the mug of tea over to Lisa's husband and then guided Lisa back to the bed. 'I'll need to check you before you can push.'

She didn't need Lisa pushing too early. It might cause a swelling of the cervix and make delivery more difficult.

Regaining control of her own body, she checked her patient's. 'You're right, Lisa. You're ten centimetres. You can push with the next contraction.'

Lisa got up off the bed. 'I can't lie down, though.'

'That's fine. Let your body lead you and I'll help. Just tell me when you're ready.'

Lisa beckoned to her husband to stand on the other side of the bed and take her hands. Then she squatted on the other side.

'When the contraction comes, take a big, deep breath, Lisa—chin to your chest and *push*, right into your bottom.'

Lisa nodded, waiting, then closed her eyes and sucked in that breath.

Freya quickly washed her hands, dried them and gloved up. Lisa might be five times a mother, but this was her first vaginal delivery. It might take some time and, with the best will in the world and not wanting to prolong her patient's suffering, she hoped that it would.

Because she herself needed some time before she could leave this room. Needed to think of what she would say. What she would do. How she could escape this situation she'd found herself in.

Lisa was an excellent patient, though, and obviously keen to see her fifth child. Because within forty-five minutes of her first needing to push, her son slithered into Freya's waiting hands.

She passed the baby to his sobbing mother, clamped and cut the cord, then helped Lisa into bed and wrapped a towel around her son to help keep him warm.

The baby cried—bursts of pure sound, a completely new person announcing his arrival. Freya smiled at the newly created family of seven and quietly gave Lisa the injection of syntocinon that would hasten delivery of the placenta, as per her patient's request.

It seemed to take no time at all to deliver it, check it, assess the baby's APGAR score, then Lisa's, and realise that Lisa hadn't torn at all. Her five-pound, twelve-ounce son had arrived perfectly.

There was no reason for Freya to stay at all. She prided herself on leaving her families to have some private time as soon as she could after the birth. So they could welcome and get to know their new baby on their own. But tonight she hesitated by the door.

'Congratulations, you two.'

'Thanks, Freya. I couldn't have done it without you.'

'Nonsense. You were a model patient.' She smiled, trying to pluck up the courage to go out there and face him. *That* conversation.

She could only hope and pray that he was busy with a patient of his own.

But she had no such luck.

Jamie was just walking back to the hub desk, sliding his pen into his top pocket. His dark eyes instantly met hers. Challenged her. Demanded an explanation.

She almost faltered. But she had Lisa's notes to finish writing up, and when that was done she needed to check on Andrea. She'd taken her off the trace a while ago and she'd been steadily contracting every five minutes the last time she'd seen her.

Jamie stood still as she walked past him, and she hoped he wouldn't see that her nerves were making her hands tremble and shake as she sat down at the desk.

'It's not what you think.' She glanced up at him, then away again. *Dammit*. He was just as handsome as she remembered. Even more so, this close. He was hauntingly beautiful.

Jamie sat down in the chair next to her. 'What *do* I think?'

She paused, her pen over Lisa's notes. 'It belongs to a patient.'

'A patient?'

'Yes. I must have put it in my pocket without realising and—'

'We don't do pregnancy testing here. Mona was quite clear when she showed me around that the fertility clinic is in a whole other ward next to this one.'

She tried her hardest not to look at him. Not to meet the searing gaze that she knew would instantly divine the truth. If her cheeks could have flamed red, then they would.

She looked at him, guilt filling her eyes.

He gazed at her for a moment, his face deadly serious. 'Tell me the truth. It's yours?'

Her eyes closed, almost as if the admission would cause her pain. 'Yes…' A whisper.

'Am I…?'

The words choked in his throat and she opened her eyes again in anguish. She hardly knew this man. He was a temp. A locum. A drifter. How could she tell this stranger that the baby in her womb was most definitely his? Because she didn't sleep around. She never met anyone—never gave herself the chance to.

She didn't need to get that kind of close to any man, to develop feelings for any man, because look at what had happened to her when she did. She'd suffered more than she'd ever believed it was possible for one body to suffer after getting involved with Mike. The pain she'd gone through, both emotionally and physically, had almost destroyed her.

She never wanted that again. Never wanted to risk it. Having that one night with Jamie—a stranger—had been a moment in which she'd thrown caution to the wind, feeling herself so physically attracted to the pirate she'd met at the

ball that she'd decided she would risk it. Keeping her anonymity, she would never have to deal with him afterwards.

Because why *shouldn't* she have slept with him? It was
allowed, and it had felt *so good* to let all that other stuff go.

But they'd both been stupid. Believing that one night
wouldn't have consequences. Believing that they could
walk away.

They should have known the risks.

They'd been wrong! And no one could be angrier with
her than she was with herself.

She'd once sat on a hospital bed, with a plastic compres-
sion mask over her burnt features, and promised her mother
that she would never get involved with another man ever
again. Would never cause her family anguish ever again.
Because what Mike had done—throwing that acid at her
face—hadn't just affected her. The tragedy had affected
her family and even Mike's family, who were distraught
that their son was in prison.

And all because she'd got involved with him.

And now she was pregnant. With Jamie's baby.

'Yes. You're the father.'

She saw him look down at the ground. Could almost
hear the cogs going around in his skull, almost sense his
thoughts as he tried to distance himself from her. Maybe
even planned to leave this place. Get a temporary post
somewhere else less complicated.

'Right.' A pause. 'It's very early on. Four…maybe five
weeks?'

She nodded.

'You need to start taking folic acid.'

'I know.'

'You need to look after yourself.'

She knew he was just trying to say the sensible thing,
trying to help and maybe trying to make sense of it in his
own head. This had to be a huge shock to him too. But to

Freya it sounded as if he was telling her what to do, and no man would ever tell her what to do again.

Her control was slipping. 'You don't need to tell me how to do anything. You don't own me.'

'I'm not. I'm just trying—'

'You're just trying to take over! So back off, Jamie, I don't need this in my life!'

She tried her hardest not to shout, but it was difficult. All she wanted to do was run away, but it was as if the walls were closing in and she would soon be trapped with him. A man. A stranger. Tied to him for eternity when she knew nothing about him. He could be anybody.

He sat forward in his chair. 'You're pregnant with *my child*. I don't think you realise what this means.'

She leaned forward too, anger and rage fuelling her bravado, matching his stance. 'I'm a midwife. Of course I know what it means.'

She stood, grabbing her notes and pen, deciding she would check on Andrea. She would finish her notes in there—give Jamie a chance to think about what she'd said.

He was *not* going to tell what to do.

He was going to be a father.

Of course if nothing went wrong they would have to marry. If the people of Majidar ever found out that he'd got a woman pregnant and then abandoned her to have the child alone they'd be appalled. And so would he. He wasn't just a prince, he was a man, and as such he had a responsibility to do the right thing. No child of his would grow up to be illegitimate—he just wouldn't accept it. The baby was his and he would be its father.

Honour in this country was different from honour in his. He saw it on the television every day—men getting women pregnant and then leaving them to raise the child alone. There were single parents everywhere, and that was fine for them—but not for him. Not at all. He could never knowingly sire a child and then abandon it to God only knew what kind of future.

This was *his* child. And, whether Freya liked it or not, he had a duty to it.

And to her.

But what had happened to her? What was making her so frightened and on edge? Why couldn't she look him directly in the eye? Was it her scars? Her face? Did her shame stem from that? Or was it the unexpected pregnancy?

Clearly she was in shock. All he'd tried to do was make this easier for her. Try and shoulder some of the responsibility.

Because it was his and his alone. And because of who he was it was imperative that he do the right thing.

He would need to speak to his advisor.

At just after six in the morning Andrea delivered a healthy baby girl.

Freya was reluctant to leave her patient's room and go back out there and face Jamie again, but she knew that she had to.

She could only hope that as there was less than one hour until the end of her shift he might be busy elsewhere and she would be able to get through it without having to see him.

She'd had her fill of pushy men. To be fair, she'd only been with one, but that one—Mike—had been enough for two lifetimes.

It had started innocently enough. Mike had asked her not to go out with her friends from college one evening.

'Why not?'

'I just can't bear to imagine you out on the town like that. I've seen gaggles of girls dressed to impress and off their heads on tequila shots. I know what guys think of girls

like that, and I don't want them looking at you like you're a piece of meat.'

She'd thought he was being sweet! That he cared so much about her.

He'd begged her not to go, and to make him feel better she'd cancelled. The next week, when the girls had wanted to go out again, rather than just accept the invitation straight away she'd said she needed to check with Mike first.

Slowly she had stopped having any contact with her friends. Then he'd started making comments about how her family looked down their noses at him and how family meet-ups made him uncomfortable—could they stay home?

Bit by bit he had isolated her, until her entire life had been his to control and manipulate. She'd felt as if she couldn't breathe and she'd tried to break away. He'd found her, begged her to stay, promised he would change.

Only he hadn't. If anything he had got worse—his insecurities, his paranoia.

She'd bolted one day when he was at work and run home to live with her mum again. She'd thought she was free, that her life was hers again, until that terrible day on the high street…

Freya was grateful to see that the hub looked clear and she headed over, her back aching slightly, and slumped into a chair to complete Andrea's notes. The open tin of chocolates called her name and she unwrapped one and popped a caramel barrel into her mouth.

Mmm…just what I need.

The chocolate began to soften in her mouth, and as she chewed she realised just how hungry she was. She'd not really taken a proper break whilst Andrea laboured, and suddenly she was starving—craving a full English breakfast, washed down with a mug of strong tea.

A banana was placed right in front of her. She frowned and looked up to see who had given it to her.

'Jamie...'

'Eat this. You haven't had anything all night.'

She moved the banana away from her. 'Thank you, but I have other plans.'

'So you say—but you're not the only one who gets to make decisions about yourself any more. This is my baby too and you need to eat. *Healthily*, preferably.'

He grabbed hold of the tin of sweets and moved it away from her.

Angrily, Freya grabbed the tin back. 'Keep your voice down. I don't need the whole ward hearing about it.'

'Are you going to eat the banana?'

She glanced at the fruit, lying harmlessly on the desk, and felt repulsed by it. The idea of taking a bite of it turned her stomach. She craved hot food. Preferably dripping in grease.

'Not right now.' She felt a little hypocritical. She'd often lectured pregnant women about eating well for a healthy pregnancy and here she was craving fat. And maybe another chocolate from that tin.

'So when are you going to eat?'

'When I get out of here. At home, where I can cook myself something.'

She didn't want to tell him that she didn't like to go out during the day. Didn't like to sit by herself in cafés filled with staring people.

'Where do you live?'

She looked at him incredulously. 'Why would I tell you that?'

'Because, like it or not, we're involved now and I want to look after you.'

'I don't know you!'

'You knew me enough to make a child with me.'

He stared hard at her, his eyes dark and dangerous, as if daring her to try and wriggle out of that one.

'Well, I didn't know I was doing that at the time.'

It was enough to make her remember their assignation—her back against the wall as he hoisted her legs around his waist and thrust into her, her hands frantically grasping at him. Both of them made courageous by darkness and anonymity.

No. She would not tell him her address. He might be anyone and her home was her safe space. Her haven. A place where she could relax and just *be*. It was her bolt-hole, and there was no way she was going to give him that information.

'You're not going to do this, you know.'

'Do what?'

'Go all alpha on me. Order me about.' She could hear her own voice quaking as she stood up for herself.

'I care about you.'

'No, you don't. You got me pregnant and now you think that you've got to be seen to be doing the right thing. Well, I'm giving you an out. You're off the hook—you can walk away.'

It would be easier, wouldn't it? To do it alone? Without a man? Because men were frightening. They didn't know what it felt like to be a woman. To know that half the population was bigger and physically stronger than you. That they could overpower you if they cared to try. Not to be able to walk down a street without fearing the footsteps you could hear behind you. Always having to be aware of your surroundings. Of who might be looking at you strangely. Were they just curious, or were they about to pounce?

He leaned forward and stared at her. 'I don't know what experiences previous men have given you, but let me tell you something. *I am not that kind of man.* When I do something I take full responsibility for it. And that means taking care of you and taking care of that baby.'

'But you don't have to. I can do it alone.'

'I do have to. It's my child. It has to be honourable.'

'Why does it have to be *honourable*?'

Even as she said the words she realised how childish she sounded. Why wouldn't she want her baby to be honourable? Was she cheapening it already? By saying it didn't matter if it was 'honourable'?

But this was *her* baby! She had dreamt of this for years!

He recoiled as if she'd slapped him, as if he was appalled that she could think anything else.

'Because it has to be. I won't have it any other way.'

She moved the banana. She could smell it and it was beginning to turn her stomach.

'If everything you do is "honourable", then how come you had a quickie with a stranger in a closet? Surely being *honourable* would make you at least a hotel-room-with-satin-sheets kind of man?'

'Maybe I am?' he challenged, pushing the banana back towards her. 'There is plenty that you don't know about me, Freya MacFadden.'

The use of her name made her narrow her eyes as she looked at him. God, he was beautiful. Almond-shaped eyes, dark as ink, cheekbones a model would die for, and his lips...

Oh, goodness, I remember those...

Freya cleared her throat and tried to sound as if she was in control of this conversation. 'Well, perhaps you'd care to enlighten me?'

Jamie checked around them, as if keen to make sure they were alone and no one was listening in.

'I can't tell you right now. You wouldn't believe me. Perhaps if you agreed to meet me here?'

He pulled a card from his uniform pocket and slid it across to her. It was a glossy black card with the name of a hotel in silver.

Why did he want to meet her in a hotel? What kind of

movie did Jamie think he was living in? He was deluded. This was normal life. People didn't do that. There was no way she was going to meet a total stranger in a *hotel*!

'Can't you just tell me?'

'You wouldn't believe it. Please meet me there.'

It would be a public place. Safe. But it would be in daylight. When there were other people about. Not in his room. Nowhere they could be alone. But she would have to face other people's stares.

'When?'

'Tomorrow? Before your shift? We do need to talk about this and we can't do it here.'

She could maybe put on some sunglasses and wrap a thick scarf around her neck, then no one would stare at her. She could get there before everyone else was up and milling around for breakfast. She could listen to what he had to say, give him his five minutes, then slink out quietly.

'Fine. About six? That gives us an hour before work.'

'Thank you.'

She nodded, then picked up the banana, gave it back to him and said, 'Now, take that away, please, before I throw up all over this desk.'

His mouth curled slightly at the corners. 'Tomorrow I'll bring you grapes.'

The Franklin Hotel sat atop a hill, so that as Freya drove towards it she had a sense of awe and magnificence as she approached the beautiful Georgian manor. Looking at it from a distance, she wondered how Jamie could afford to stay in such an opulent place.

I don't have to go in. I don't have to hear what he has to say.

But she knew she would. Because, no matter how terrified she felt, she knew that she owed her baby the chance to know something about its father. So she could look her child in the eye and tell him, or her, that she'd tried everything.

It looked welcoming and warm, with yellow lights gleaming out in the darkness of the early morning, the sky above a blue which was fading from inky navy to palest azure.

Parking her little hatchback next to rows of expensive cars with chauffeurs sitting in them made her feel a little uneasy. Why had Jamie asked her to meet him here? What was it that she was about to learn from him?

He was a midwife. A damned sexy one, if she was honest, with an accent to die for and eyes that looked right into her soul and grasped her by the heart. She'd never met anyone like him. The mystery was what could he tell her here that she would never have believed if he'd just told her at work?

Whether she liked it or not, whilst this baby nestled in her womb they would be tied to one another—and Jamie seemed determined to be in her life.

Adjusting her scarf and lowering her sunglasses, she strolled across the gravel driveway, her nerves jittery, her legs weak. In the hotel, gentle music playing from a piano met her ears. To her right was a reception desk, where exquisite and perfectly presented staff waited to attend to every guest's needs.

'May I help you, madam?' asked a young man in a navy suit with enough gel in his hair to sink a ship.

No, it's fine. I'm just leaving.

'I'm supposed to be meeting a Mr Jamie Baker?'

'Miss MacFadden? We've been expecting you.' He smiled, revealing perfectly white teeth. 'Please take the lift to my right and go up to the third floor.'

Take the lift? Go to the third floor? That wasn't meeting in a public space. That meant going to his room. Where there was a bed.

'Oh…um… What room number?'

'Mr Baker has the entire third floor.'

Freya blinked. What? Who went to a hotel and took up an entire floor? That was the sort of thing celebrities did with their entourages, or royalty, or…

'You wouldn't believe me if I told you.'

What was going on? It was all so confusing. He was just a guy, right? A normal guy.

Was he rich?

The night they'd met at the gala she'd known there was a member of royalty there. She'd heard the rumour but she'd never been introduced to anyone. There'd been no announcement. Everyone had hidden behind their masks and it had been exciting. You could talk to *anyone* and not know it!

Including royalty.

Have sex in a closet with them, if you so chose…

Freya swallowed hard, trying to control her rapidly weakening legs as she hesitantly went over to the lifts and pressed the button.

I could still go. I could run. Just get the hell out of here!

She stood there, fidgeting with the tassels on her scarf, as she waited for the lift to come down to the ground floor.

I owe it to our baby.

Was Jamie a member of some royal family? How could that be?

She thought about turning tail and running—changing her mind and hiding somewhere. Her parents' beach house on Hayling Island, perhaps. It was the place she went when she needed to hide and think. She'd gone there when she'd first been released from hospital, months after the acid attack, and she'd had to wear that damned orthotic burns mask every day, marking her out as different.

She'd felt like a leper. As if there was a bright neon arrow over her head screaming that here was someone *not normal*.

The house on Hayling Island would soon be filling up with summer rentals, but hopefully no one was there right now. Jamie wouldn't know where to find her. It would be good for her to take a break while the morning sickness was in full swing.

The lift pinged, signalling its arrival, and the doors slid open. On the back wall of the lift was an ornate mirror and she gazed at her reflection, wondering what the woman in the mirror should do. Run like hell? It was like staring into a prison.

All ye who enter here...

But Freya had seen more than enough women arrive on her ward to give birth alone, without a father involved, and she had felt sorry for all those children who would grow up without an interested father.

Jamie *wanted* to be involved. He'd said he would not shirk his responsibility. All she'd ever wanted was to be loved and to have a baby—something she'd thought would never happen after her acid attack—and here she was, pregnant and with a guy who said he wanted to be involved. She owed him a chance, the opportunity to show her what he could provide for their child.

With hesitation Freya stepped into the lift and pressed the button for the third floor, eyeing the reception area with longing as the lift doors closed her in.

As the lift ascended she gripped the strap of her bag as if it was a lifeline. An anchor to real life. The sensation that her world was about to change for ever was drowning her in anticipation, and she wished she'd eaten more of those ginger biscuits before coming, because her stomach felt as if it was about to explode.

The lift stopped rising. *Ping!* The doors slid open to reveal two men in dark suits.

Her stomach flipped and she looked from one to the other.

Guards? Why does Jamie need guards?

They were wearing those earpieces that secret service men had on television. They asked her to put her bag through a scanner, and then she had to walk through a metal detector shaped like a doorway before they escorted her down the corridor towards a pair of ornate doors.

What on earth have I got myself into?

Silently she followed, feeling like a little girl between giants. Were they wearing guns beneath their jackets? Her mouth went dry at the thought of it and she gripped her bag tighter, as if that small item would somehow protect her from what was to come.

At ornate double doors the men stopped and grabbed a handle each, stepping back to open the doors wide.

Freya sucked in a steadying breath as her eyes hungrily took in the details of the room. A four-poster bed set with golden drapes in an opulent room adorned with fine art and floor-to-ceiling windows. Gilt-edged tables, fresh flowers in vases that were almost as tall as she was. And standing in the middle, in a long white tunic and trousers, was Jamie. As if he'd been waiting for her.

She stared at him, not sure what to do. Or say.

Now she could understand why he hadn't just told her all this.

'You're right,' she said, clearing her throat and looking straight at him. 'I would never have believed you.'

Jamie poured her some tea, adding two cubes of sugar to the drink. He frowned slightly when he saw how her hands were shaking when she went to take it from him, then set it down on the table instead and took her hands in his to calm them.

'It's all right, Freya.'

'Is it?' She looked at him askance. 'Who *are* you, Jamie?'

'My name is Jameel Al Bakhari and I am heir to the

throne of Majidar. My older brother Ilias is King, ruling with his wife Queen Jasmeen, but they have been unable to sire any children so I am next in line. I also have a younger sister, Zahra, who has just married.'

It all sounded as if it was from a film. 'Heir to the throne…?'

'Yes.'

'Royalty?'

'Yes.'

It was a struggle to process. 'But…but you work as a midwife.'

'Yes.'

'Why? Why do that, when you're a…a prince?'

He smiled. 'I did not ask to be born a prince. Ruling a kingdom and waving at crowds from a distance is not what I felt I was meant to do. I want to *know* people. Help them personally. When my father sat upon the throne he took us with him to a hospital, where he was opening a new neo-natal unit. I was very young—maybe eight or nine. We toured the labour ward, saw the new state-of-the-art the-atre and the incubators that held tiny newborns. I was fas-cinated by the babies, and when we returned to the palace an idea took hold. The more I thought about it, the more I realised I wanted to deliver babies. To hold the miracle of life in my own two hands and experience the joy of bring-ing a new life into the world.'

Freya nodded. 'But why be a midwife? You could have been a doctor. An obstetrician. A surgeon!'

'I could. But those paths didn't interest me. I wanted to deliver the babies. An obstetrician gets called in only if there's a problem. A surgeon just takes care of Caesareans. I wanted to be there through the whole labour—to monitor progress, develop that close relationship a midwife creates with each patient. My mother spoke fondly of all her mid-wives. I would beg her to tell me, over and over again, the stories of our births—mine, my brother's and my sister's. Even after all those years she could remember every detail, and it was the midwives of whom she spoke the most highly. I wanted to be that person. To have that impact on people's lives. To be remembered in such a way. Selfish, perhaps, but true.'

'I don't think it's selfish.'

He inclined his head in thanks. 'I asked my father if I could study towards midwifery. Focus on the sciences so that midwifery could be my calling. But he would not allow it. He said it was not appropriate for a prince of my standing to attend to such work usually reserved for women.'

Freya couldn't imagine what she might have felt if her mother had forbidden her from becoming a midwife. 'What happened?'

'I had to put my wishes to one side until my father died and my brother Ilias took the throne. I assumed then, like they did, that they would soon overwhelm the palace with little babies and that I would no longer be next in line to sit upon the throne and rule. So I begged Ilias to let me come to England to follow my education and have the life that I wanted. Ilias is much more modern in his thinking and he agreed that I should have the life of my own choosing.'

'You said your brother doesn't have any children?'

'No. Ilias and Jasmeen have never been blessed. Therefore I am still next in line to sit on the throne—something I have no desire to do, but must endure when the time comes. And it *will* come. Eventually. My brother, as considerate as he is, has begun asking me when I will return. He tells me that I must be seen to be upholding some of my royal duties, so that when my time comes the people will know me better and accept my succession.'

'So you have to go back?'

'Not immediately. Ilias is still young—just a few years older than me—but his health is not the best.'

Freya looked down at her tea. The nausea and shock had subsided somewhat now, and she felt more comfortable about taking a sip. 'So what you're trying to say, in a roundabout way, is that I'm carrying the heir to your throne?'

Jamie inhaled a deep breath as he looked at her. She seemed tiny suddenly. He hadn't wanted to scare her, or overwhelm her, but he'd known if he'd tried to explain this on the hospital ward she would never have believed it. She needed to see it. Experience this.

'Yes.'

His acknowledgement was too much. Too overwhelming. She suddenly felt as if she was being suffocated as her mind whirled with all the possibilities that would entail. She got up and began to pace. Walking back and forth, back and forth as she thought hard about how she could get out of this situation.

A royal baby? Heir to a throne? It would mean her life changing. Never to be hers again. All her choices taken from her. All her control gone and given over to someone else.

'Tradition dictates that if everything remains well we should marry before the child is born.'

What? Marriage? No, no, no, no...

She shook her head frantically. 'I'm sorry, but no. I can't. I can't do that, Jamie. I *won't*!'

He stood up too, and reached for her arm, but she swiped his hand away.

'Marrying you would make me...what? A princess? A *queen*? I can't be that! Stared at... With people judging me on a global scale... Why do you think I do night shifts? I love my little world. I'm happy there. I'm accepted. Do you think I want *any* of what you're offering?'

'But, Freya, we need to—'

It was all spiralling away. Her control—everything. Disappearing into a black hole that was vast and powerful. It couldn't happen. She wouldn't let it! She had the right to say no!

She didn't know this man. Even though she'd been intimate with him, conceived a child with him, worked with him. She didn't know him.

Didn't know how he would react if she backed away...

Would he be like Mike? Refuse to let her go?

I need to get away.

Her hand reached into her bag and grasped her mobile phone. She pulled it out and activated the phone keypad, pressed the numbers nine-nine-nine and hesitated. Ready to press 'Call' if anything went wrong.

'No, Jamie. *We* don't need to do anything. *You* don't need to do anything. You can forget about me—you can walk away and pretend that I never existed. You can go back to your kingdom, when the time arrives, and marry a proper princess—someone beautiful, someone the people will expect.'

'You *are* beautiful.'

She laughed at his response. 'You're just saying that. Do you really think you would have asked a girl like me to marry you if I wasn't pregnant? With *this* face? I don't think so.'

He stood in front of her. 'Your face doesn't matter. You are a strong, beautiful woman.'

'Of course it matters. It's what people see! It's what they judge you on. I know this better than anyone. I appreciate that you're trying to say and do the right thing, but it's not the right thing for Majidar. It's not the right thing for *me*. Your people don't need me by the side of their King. A one-night stand who got pregnant? A commoner from another country? *No.* I absolve you of all responsibility. Send me money each month, if that will make you feel better about it, but please, Jamie, I beg of you, walk away. It will be better for you if you just let me go.'

She was trying to sound reasonable. Trying to sound calm and steady so that he would remain so, too. Her thumb hovered over the 'Call' button. He hadn't seen the number she had keyed in and she appreciated that he was keeping his distance physically. But she would press it if she had to.

'I cannot. I *will* not.'

Freya sighed, her eyes filling with sorrow. 'I can't be who you need me to be. I can't live that sort of life. That's not who I am.'

'Neither am I. But it is my destiny. And now, because of the child, it is also yours.'

Freya closed her eyes as if she were in pain, and then she opened them again, looking at him with tears in her eyes, as if she were sorry to be causing such distress. Sorry to have to deny him.

She was afraid to say the next words, but knew she had to, so that he was clear on where she stood. 'No, Jamie. Never.'

And then she backed away. She yanked open the large doors to his suite and hurried down the corridor, expecting at any moment that the guards would drag her back, her finger still hovering over the button on her phone.

But the guards simply followed her at a respectful distance.

The lift was waiting for her and she got in and punched the button for the ground floor. Only when the doors slid closed and she was safe inside did she clear the numbers and slip her phone back into her bag.

It had taken every ounce of her strength to refuse him. To say no and walk away, not knowing how he might react. The likelihood of him being like Mike was slim, but then she'd thought Mike was okay, too. And look at what had happened there.

As she ran across Reception and out into the cool morning air she hoped this meant it was all over. That he would not bother her again.

She had given him her answer.

He would do much better if he were to accept it.

CHAPTER THREE

SHE TRIED TO stay away from Jamie at work. She sensed he was giving her space, and she appreciated that, but she could tell by the way he looked at her from across the room that as far as *he* was concerned this was far from over.

There was no way she could accept his terms. *Marry* him? Become a princess, or whatever she would be? Have her child schooled to become a king or queen themselves? Living a life of privilege, no doubt, but one that would be like a prison. Never to pop to the shops when she wanted, go for a walk when she liked, without fearing that some-one might get too close to the royal person...

It was ridiculous.

Her child wouldn't live like that. She wanted a normal life for her baby—a normal education, real friends, a real life and choices. She wanted to sit on the South Downs and have a picnic with her child. Fly a kite and take a dog for a walk. She wanted to walk barefoot on the beach and jump waves with him or her, laugh out loud and eat ice cream and fish and chips.

Normality.

It was the only thing she craved for her child. For her-self. To live a normal life. Not the life that she had had since the attack, hiding from people and crowds. Not the childhood that Jamie had had, raised behind the walls of a palace. Something else. The childhood she'd had when she'd been growing up. When her face had been unspoilt by sulphuric acid—when her future had looked bright and the whole world had been a possibility.

Mike had limited her. Told her what she should wear, what she should eat, who she could talk to. And when he hadn't been able to control her, hadn't been able to keep her, he had tried to make sure that no one else would want her.

Saying no to Jamie had taken every ounce of bravery she had. But she wouldn't allow another man to control her, and Jamie's request demanded something of her that she couldn't give. Basically, it seemed to her that he wanted her whole life—her dedication, her child—to be given to him and his country. A country she had never even heard of just one week ago.

Jamie had a duty to his throne, but she didn't. Nor did their child. And she refused to tie either of them down to it.

A person's skin is made up of proteins. Protein makes up the structure of cells and the enzymes within them. Acid, when it comes into contact with protein, changes its innate structure and causes it to break down immediately upon contact. It's excruciating, the pain—difficult to relieve. The strongest medications often have no effect...

Freya sat in the hospital staffroom, waiting for her shift to start. Her mind was torturing her with the memory of that day so long ago, when her world had been turned upside down.

She'd tried to hold up her hands to protect her face, but it had been too late, and then suddenly—instantly—the terrifying scorching of her skin had begun.

She'd thought those screams were from other people, but they'd been her own. Freya had collapsed onto the pavement, her eyes squeezed tightly shut, afraid to open them in case she couldn't see, screaming at people to help her.

Some guy had tried pouring water over her face to dilute the acid, but it had simply run down her neck and begun burning her there, too.

It had seemed an age before the paramedics had arrived. Before the morphine had hit her veins, before they'd tried to irrigate her skin and whisked her to hospital.

Despite the burning she'd begun to feel cold. Shock, they said. Apparently, burns could cause hypothermia. Who knew?

It was a day she would never forget. And all because a man had refused to let her go.

She'd told Jamie no. She'd turned down his marriage proposal, refused to let him take her and the baby back to his country. How would he react now?

As if her worries had summoned him, Jamie entered the staffroom. His gaze met hers, briefly, and then he looked away.

What did that mean? Was he upset? Angry? Was he the type to seek revenge?

So far he seemed reasonable. Normal. A little sad, maybe, but nothing like Mike. But for how long? What about when he got called back to his country and the time came for him to leave? Would he put pressure on her then? Would he try to blackmail her? Threaten her?

She didn't want to tar him with the same brush as Mike, but her history with men so far had not been good. She couldn't read him yet. Didn't understand him. Perhaps if she remained polite and respectful he would remain that way too? Perhaps if she got to know him a little more she might understand him better?

But she was afraid to do that.

Getting to know him meant spending time with him...

Caroline Müller was well into her labour—contracting every two minutes, alternating between taking amusing selfies with her husband Stefan when she was between contractions, and breathing and retreating into herself when she was having pain, going all Zen, peaceful and in control.

It was a marvel to behold.

Freya was happy she could distract herself at work—the place where she could absorb herself in her patient's labour and just for a few hours forget about her own life.

'How are you doing, Caroline? Still coping?'

Caroline had requested no pain relief. She wanted to try and give birth naturally to her first child. Freya wanted to support her in that, but also to let her know that she could change her mind whenever she needed to.

'I'm good, I think.' Her patient nodded, as if she were reassuring herself that she could do this. 'Do you think I'm doing okay?'

Freya smiled. 'You're coping wonderfully. Eight centimetres dilated and still no pain relief! You're a marvel.'

Freya was very keen on honouring a woman's choice. Of all the things in the world a woman could do, going through labour and childbirth was an extremely personal thing. No one else could do it for her. She was on her own. Pulling on the resources and reserves that only she had within her own body.

It was an eye-opening and eye-watering experience. No one could know how they would cope with those levels of pain. And if a mother wanted to give birth without pain relief or with every medication going then Freya would support her either way. Childbirth wasn't a competition, and the mother alone was the one who must decide her course of treatment. It was important to empower a woman with the knowledge that any choice over her body was her own.

Caroline blew out a breath and nodded. 'Thanks. Did you know Stefan's mother wanted to be here at the birth?'

Freya looked at Stefan. 'I didn't.'

'I told her she wasn't welcome—which didn't go down

very well. I didn't want my own mother here, so there was no way I was having my in-laws loitering around my nether regions.'

Freya and Stefan smiled at each other.

'My mother can be quite controlling,' he said. 'This is her first grandchild and we've had to be quite firm with her about not booking things in advance.'

'What sort of things?'

'Enrolling him or her in a private nursery, hiring a nanny, booking her personal swimming instructor to give our newborn swimming lessons, *and* pre-book a German teacher so that our child will grow up to be bilingual. German is my mother's natural tongue,' he explained, smiling with amusement.

'Wow!' Freya mused. 'She sounds wonderfully keen to provide your little one with the very best.'

'She has to be reined in or she doesn't know when to stop!' Caroline said, and grimaced as another contraction began to build.

She closed her eyes, relaxed her brow and began to breathe steadily in through her nose and then slowly and smoothly out through her mouth. She stood to one side of the bed, leaning on the mattress, swaying her hips from side to side as the contraction intensified.

'That's it, Caroline, you're doing really well. Keep breathing.'

Freya rubbed the small of her patient's back, wondering how royal families raised their babies.

Weren't they all surrounded by nannies? Whisked off to nurseries and only brought to their parents to hold when they were clean and fed and presentable?

Actually, she had no idea how royals looked after a new baby. Nor did she have any idea about a desert kingdom's culture.

But what she *did* know was that she didn't want her

child to be taken away from her. This was *her* baby and she wanted to raise it. With Jamie's help, if he wanted, but she would have the final say in everything.

There would be no taking the baby away to a nursery at night time. She wanted to deal with midnight feeds and nappy explosions. She wanted to soothe her baby when it started to teethe. She wanted to be the one who took her child to the doctor for vaccinations and check-ups, to comfort it when it cried because some stranger had poked at it with a needle or a stethoscope.

Was it too much to ask? This might be Jamie's baby too, and he might come from a royal line of kings, but it was also *her* baby and she *wasn't* royal. She was normal—girl-next-door. And she wanted her child to have a normal life.

Caroline began to groan out loud—thick guttural noises coming from deep within her. 'Oh, I think I want to push!'

'Try not to. Not just yet. I need to check you again... make sure you're fully dilated.'

She was. With a wide smile she informed Caroline that with the next contraction she could start pushing, and that hopefully, within the next hour, they would have their longed-for baby.

'Will I really?' Caroline began to cry. Happy tears springing from her eyes as she reached for her husband's hand, clutching it tightly.

He squeezed back. 'We will.'

Caroline wanted to remain standing between contractions, and then lowered herself into a crouch beside by the bed each time she pushed. She pushed long and hard, her face reddening, sweat pouring down with her efforts, until after about forty minutes she began to crown.

'You're nearly there now!' Freya watched intently and quietly as Caroline gave birth to the baby's head. It had thick black hair and Caroline reached down to touch.

'My baby!' she cried.

'One final push, Caroline! You can do this!'

Freya supported the baby with her gloved hands as it was delivered, and then passed the crying baby over to its mother, who lifted her up from between her legs to cradle her against her chest.

'Oh, my God! It's a girl! We have a little girl, Stefan!'

Freya clamped the cord and Stefan cut it, and then she helped guide the new mum onto the bed, so she could rest whilst Freya took care of all the little things that needed doing. The syntocinon. Checking to see if mum needed stitches. For any sign of haemorrhage.

She draped a couple of towels around the baby to help keep it warm as Caroline placed her daughter against her skin beneath her hospital gown. Then Freya checked the placenta to make sure it was complete and healthy.

After she'd written the pertinent times and details into her patient's file, she took the baby to weigh it and check its APGAR score—the scale against which all newborn babies were measured to ensure they were coping with life outside of the womb.

Handing the baby back for more skin-to-skin, she asked if Caroline and Stefan had chosen a name yet?

'Hannah Rose.'

'That's beautiful,' she said.

'Thank you. Thank you for everything, Freya—we really mean it. We couldn't have done it without you.'

She smiled her thanks. 'I couldn't have done it, without you! I'll leave you on your own for a little while. Press the buzzer if you need me, but I'll be back to take you down to the postnatal ward.'

She left the new parents to it—Stefan already taking pictures with his phone—and quietly closed the door behind her. Then, carrying her patient's notes, she headed over to the desk and sat down.

Freya was hungry...thirsty. She hadn't had anything for

hours, having stayed with her patient for most of the night, popping out only once to use the toilet because her bladder had threatened to explode if she didn't.

Mona came out of the small kitchenette, carrying a tray filled with mugs of tea. 'Ah! Perfect timing. Want one?'

'Ooh, yes, please!' Freya grabbed a hot mug and gratefully took a sip. 'My patient just delivered a baby girl—Hannah Rose. Isn't that a beautiful name?'

'Gorgeous! How did she get through it?'

'Not a single scrap of pain medication!' Freya stated proudly.

'Good for her! I have no pain threshold whatsoever. I practically needed an epidural for a tiny blister I got on my heel. What about you?' Then Mona's face darkened as she realised what she'd said. 'Sorry...'

But Freya wasn't offended. Mona was her closest friend here, and she knew she hadn't meant anything nasty by it.

Freya thought back to her days spent in hospital after the acid attack. The pain she'd been in. The pain she'd had to live through for months as her face recovered. The nightmares. The flashbacks. The searing, agonising torture of debridement. She'd had enough pain for one lifetime.

She smiled. 'I want everything they can give me.'

Jamie had been watching her carefully over the last few weeks. As much as he could, anyway. Clearly she was trying to avoid being with him. He kept catching her noticing him arrive in the staffroom or at the reception desk and suddenly getting that *I'm busy* look before she got up to go and do something.

He was finding it terribly frustrating when all he wanted to do was talk to her. Find out how she was. Whether she was feeling okay. She had to be due for the first scan of the baby any day now, but she'd made no mention of it to him and he didn't want to miss it. Nor did he like this distance she was creating between them, as if she didn't want him involved, because that was not how he planned to have his first child. Being cast aside as if he was just a sperm donor.

Having a baby was one of the most wonderful things a woman could do. To become a parent one of the most rewarding privileges. He really hoped that Freya would thaw towards him, but he could understand why she hadn't yet.

Mona had told him what had happened to her years ago. Some possessive ex had thrown acid in her face. The very idea of that made him feel sick. It caused a rage to build in him towards a man he knew was already in prison.

Mona hadn't said much else, clearly reluctant to gossip about her friend, but he'd had to ask. He'd spent so many nights wondering why she was keeping him at such a distance. Why she seemed so edgy and uncomfortable. Why she kept looking at him as if he was some firework that might go off at any minute. It had made him wonder what had happened to her. And now he knew.

Freya MacFadden was having a strange effect on him. She was so petite, so dainty, and he loved seeing her walk in with her long blonde hair hanging loose down her back, watching her scoop it up, twist it and pin it into place each shift. It was an action so casually done, without looking in a mirror, and she always managed a tousled look which, with those big blue eyes of hers, was a winning combination.

The scars didn't bother him at all. Not like that. What bothered him about them was that someone had done that to her. Intentionally. That she had suffered, and that her life had been changed for evermore. He'd visited clinics that cared for women attacked like this, and he'd never seen such suffering before or since. It was a memory that haunted him, but he'd learnt something from those women—that they had tremendous courage. That they bore a bravery within them that he could never hope to emulate.

Freya was the same.

He was worried that she didn't seem to be letting him in, but he understood why and knew that he would have to bide his time if she were to trust him.

He leaned against her locker, straightening when he heard her coming down the corridor, chatting to Mona. He hoped to end this stalemate between them—to get them talking again. Ask her how she was…if she needed anything.

He saw her notice him. Watched as she debated whether to avoid using her locker after all. But then she seemed to overcome that hesitation and came over to him.

'Excuse me, I need to get inside.'

He stepped back, giving her space. 'Could we talk for a moment?'

She looked up at him hesitantly. 'About what?'

'About us.'

'There is no "us".' She glanced over at their colleagues, afraid of being overheard. But no one appeared to be listening.

She shoved her bag into her locker and hung up her coat. Then she did the hair thing that he loved and clipped her ID badge to her uniform.

'Can you tell me if you're feeling okay? If there's anything I can do?'

'I'm feeling fine. A bit sick, but eating often seems to help.'

He could see in her face that she was still closed off from him. Unwilling to share. He understood that, and he was willing to wait.

'Well, if there's anything I can do for you then please let me know.'

She nodded and bit her lip.

'Can I get you a tea? A coffee?'

She glanced over at their friends by the kettle and the sink. 'No, but thank you.'

'Have you told anyone?'

Her eyes darkened. 'No. Not yet. Have you?'

He shook his head. 'No.'

'Right. What will happen when you do?'

He imagined the reaction of his family. They would be insistent upon marriage. They would be insistent about him coming home and building his life as a father and future King of Majidar.

'They'll be delighted.'

Her eyes narrowed, as if she were trying to assess him for the truth. *'Right.'*

'Oh, I brought you these.' From behind his back he drew out a brown paper bag filled with grapes. 'As promised.'

A small smile *almost* broke out across her face, but she checked it and instead frowned. 'I'm not sick.'

'No, I know.'

'You don't have to do this...' she whispered.

He nodded and whispered back, 'I do. So if you need anything—*anything*—I hope you will ask me.'

And he left her at her locker to go and grab himself a drink.

Little inroads...small kindnesses. That was what she needed. He needed to build her trust. He needed to show her that he could be relied upon to look out for her and keep her safe. She needed to see that he was everything that the man who'd attacked her was not. That he believed in kindness and respect and love. That he believed in honour and duty and that he would shirk neither.

Baby steps.

The next shift they had together Freya nodded her head towards him, as if to say *good morning*. The one after that she actually said hello.

Jamie gave her more space and time.

One night shift she came in and straight away headed

for the staff toilet, emerging fifteen minutes later looking a little green. He presented her with ginger tea—something that his mother had sworn by. Another time when she looked queasy and was meant to check on a patient in Postnatal, he offered to answer the call bell instead.

Where he could, he took the time to try and lighten her load. To make it easier for her whilst she was going through this difficult time.

Their colleagues had begun to suspect that something was up, and Mona had been the one to ask Freya during a night shift.

'Are you *pregnant*?'

Clearly Freya had realised it was pointless to try and deny it. Not when the signs were so obvious and she was surrounded by people who specialised in pregnancy and babies.

The team had been delighted! Hugging her and congratulating her.

'Who's the father?'

Freya had baulked at answering, but she had looked at him, as if to give him permission to answer.

He'd stepped forward. 'I am.'

Well, that had sent the gossip mill into high speed!

He had seen that Freya wasn't overly happy about being the centre of attention, but she'd seemed to cope with it—probably because these were her friends and people she trusted.

After that everyone had tried their best to help Freya out whilst the morning sickness was so devastating. She really was suffering, poor thing.

'Are you guys, like, together?' Mona had asked him.

Jamie had longed to say *Not yet*, but had felt that would be pushing too far, before Freya was ready. This was not a world in which two people could be forced into marriage. It was not something that had been arranged since they were children. It was not a unification of two countries solidifying a pact by marrying off a prince and princess.

This was real life. Freya was a commoner. A woman from the west. She had different expectations from life and a whole lot of baggage that she needed to sift through before she realised he was a good guy.

'Your first scan should be soon,' he said as he brought her another cup of ginger tea one day.

'It is.'

'I was wondering…only if you feel right about it…if I might come with you?'

She looked at him carefully, almost as if she were appraising him. She'd been giving him this look a lot just lately.

'Okay.'

His heart almost burst with joy. *Okay?*

'Sure. It's your baby too.'

'Thank you, Freya!'

He almost imploded with excitement, but managed to contain himself. Strong emotions, sudden reactions, were not the kind of thing that would make Freya feel safe. She needed to see that he was stable, even if his insides were fizzing with glee and he wanted to jump about and yell for all the world to hear.

They sat together, waiting for the ultrasound technician to call Freya's name.

She felt uncomfortable. Not just because she'd had to drink a huge amount of water beforehand, and hold it in, but also because she was back in what she considered the 'normal' world. Daylight hours. Where there were too many people about. People who, she noticed, kept glancing at her, trying to work out what was different about her. Noticing her face…

Part of her wanted to stare back at them. Challenge them

with a single raised eyebrow as if to ask, *What are you looking at?* But she wasn't brave enough or rude enough.

Freya had been raised to show respect to people. To be polite and to treat others the way she wished to be treated herself. She couldn't do that to strangers. They didn't deserve it. They were just being curious. It was human nature to take a second look at something that didn't quite fit.

She wondered how many of them were wondering how on earth she could be sitting there with this gorgeous man next to her.

Jamie clearly had no idea of his allure. Ink-dark hair, midnight eyes that penetrated the soul, and a bearing that screamed royalty—due, no doubt, to a childhood that had consisted of years of being told to sit up straight, shoulders back. Not to slouch. To meet people's eyes. Assess the situation. Listen. Look commanding.

She felt tiny next to him. Inconsequential. He was so tall, proud and strong, and she was small, scarred and nauseous.

How much of her feeling sick was due to the pregnancy, though? Her stress levels were high. She dreaded to think what her blood pressure was. But she had to admit she wouldn't have got through these last few weeks of her first trimester without Jamie's help.

He had been instrumental in getting her through it, and she'd quickly come to realise that she had begun to rely on him being close. Always there with a hot, steaming mug of ginger tea, or some peppermints, or one of the strawberry milkshakes which she had begun craving. Whatever she'd needed—a rest, a moment to herself, someone to take care of her patients whilst she clutched the toilet bowl—he'd provided it. Her friends, too, yes. But Jamie had been the most considerate and for that she was grateful.

And scared.

He was getting under her skin. She was beginning to like him. Once she'd come on shift and, when she'd realised that he wasn't rostered on with her, a huge sense of disappointment and loss had hit her like a brick.

How had that happened?

She never wanted to rely on a man again.

And yet here she was. Not only was she tied to this man but he was also a prince, he had a duty, and she was refusing to accept that. She knew she must somehow be tearing him in two. He had a duty to his country. To his people.

I'm hurting him and yet he doesn't complain.

They didn't look right together—no wonder people were staring. She was just a girl. A scarred, damaged girl. And he… Well, Jamie was something else entirely, and he deserved a beautiful princess to stand by his side and make pretty babies with him.

'Freya MacFadden?'

She straightened, rising to her feet. Behind her, she felt Jamie stand and follow her into the darkened room.

They went through the preliminaries with the technician. Date of last period, how many weeks pregnant she was, whether she felt well.

Frightened, she lay down, not sure what was scaring her more—the prospect of seeing her baby on screen, at last, or the fact that she wanted Jamie at her side. She'd anticipated doing this alone. Not telling him. Sneaking in to the appointment after everyone on the night shift had gone and having this moment all to herself. Knowing she would cry. Knowing she would get emotional because finally, *finally* this day had come. The day she would see irrefutable proof that she was pregnant. With a baby she'd thought she would never have.

The technician squirted the gel and applied the probe to Freya's abdomen.

Freya bit her lip. She might have got this all wrong. Perhaps she wasn't even pregnant at all? A false positive? A molar pregnancy? Then everyone could go back to their normal lives. Jamie could leave and go on to another post, or back to his country, and she could remain unchanged on the night shift, revelling in the joy of other people's babies and just imagining what it might feel like to hold her own baby...

The technician was smiling. 'Everything looks wonderful here.'

Freya let out a breath she hadn't realised she'd been holding. 'Really?'

'Any history of multiples in either family?'

What?

The technician turned the screen so that Freya and Jamie could see. There, in black and white, was her womb. Filled with not one but *two* babies, separated by a very fine line which meant...

'Twins? Non-identical twins?' Jamie stared at the screen, laughing with shock and delight.

Freya had to remind herself to breathe. She couldn't quite believe it! Twins? Her grandmother had been one of a pair of twins, but she'd never imagined that this would happen to her. 'Oh, my God...'

'Freya, can you believe it?' Jamie scooped up her hand in his and kissed it, his dark eyes sparkling with unshed tears in the shadows of the room.

She stared at him, seeing his joy, his beaming face, his eyes twinkling in the semi-darkness of the room.

She felt her body flooding with adrenaline. *Twins.* Non-identical twins.

This was crazy. Unbelievable! It was...

She stared at the screen once again. Counted again. Two babies. Growing inside her.

Two.

'I don't believe it.'

The technician continued to make her checks. Measuring the babies, the length of their femurs, checking the Nuchal fold at the backs of their necks.

'Your babies look beautiful. Perfectly healthy and a good size. It probably accounts for all that morning sickness you've been having. You'll get more scans and check-ups due to this being a twin pregnancy, so if you have any problems don't hesitate to shout.' She smiled at them both. 'You ought to go and celebrate.'

Perhaps. But Freya didn't foresee having a party. She liked the idea of keeping it quiet. Just telling family and the people at work. They were the only people she knew anyway.

Jamie probably had loads of people he needed to tell. His family. His staff. His advisors. What would they all tell him to do? He couldn't walk away now, could he? She was carrying *two* royal children.

If she hadn't felt trapped before, she most definitely felt it now.

She began to hyperventilate and felt Jamie's fingers wrap around her own.

'It's okay, Freya. Just breathe slowly. In and out. That's it, slow your breathing.'

She focused on his face. On his voice. On him, her only connection to this world. She felt spaced out, as if she was adrift in a vast universe and he was the umbilical cord connecting her to reality.

He had intensely dark eyes. Eyes she could lose herself in. She had once before and now she needed to again.

Was she about to get swept up into a load of royal political intrigue? Be married and whisked away to live in a desert? Something like that?

How could she continue to live the private life that she loved? Was she about to lose all control over her every decision? Because she wasn't sure she could do that.

This life, her *babies'* lives, were too important. Jamie's demands were not more important than her own.

She'd lost all control once. Had all decisions taken from her. She had lived a life trapped in a hospital, in pain and afraid, with staff all around her, checking on her every hour of the day, waiting on her hand and foot. It had been unbearable. Living a half-life, staring out of windows, watching the world go by and wishing she could be in it. Wishing that the pain would go away, so she could escape...

I won't have that happen again.

Slowly her breathing came back under her control. Jamie was smiling at her, with relief on his face that she was calming down. Sitting up, she pulled her hand from his. She had relied on him enough.

'I'm okay. I'm all right.'

The sonographer passed her a couple of scan pictures. 'Twins can be a bit of a shock. It might take some time to get used to.'

Jamie was watching her, assessing her. He offered her his hand, so she could get up off the bed, but she did it without his help.

She couldn't keep relying on him. He had other commitments. Other duties. No matter what he said their lives were incompatible, and no matter how much she might want something else she couldn't have him and he couldn't have her.

I just need to keep telling myself that.

The rush hour traffic was building around the hospital. The car park was filling with vehicles. Staff were arriving, visitors...

Freya pulled up the collar of her jacket and adjusted her scarf. Aware of too many pairs of eyes all around her.

Jamie stood beside her, gazing down at the scan pictures the technician had given them.

'This doesn't change anything,' she said, hoisting her bag strap firmly into place on her shoulder.

'No?'

'No.'

He stared back at her, frowning, a small divot forming between his dark brows. 'There must be something I can do. To make this easier for you.'

Why did he have to have such a beautiful voice? Deep, slightly accented, smooth and delightful. He was already handsome and charming. Helpful and kind. Did he have to be sexy, too? Couldn't the man have one single fault?

He does. He's royal.

She was struggling not to cry again. Her hormones washed through her with renewed force now that she knew she was carrying twins.

'You could leave. Get a contract someplace else.'

'That's never going to happen. You think I'm going to walk away from you? All three of you?'

With eyes blurred from unshed tears, she glanced up at him and then away as she headed for her car to go home.

'You're under no obligation to be with me, Jamie. I told you that. Why can't you just go? Pretend this never happened? I'll never ask anything of you.'

She heard his footsteps as he hurried to catch up with her. Felt his hand upon her arm, turning her.

'I'm *never* walking away from you. You need to stop asking me to do that.'

She wasn't sure she could do this. How had she got herself into another situation where a man was refusing to let her go? Demanding to stay in her life? It was scary. She didn't want it. *Any* of it! She just wanted to be left in peace. To deal with this alone. Why couldn't she be living her happy dream? The one where she was married and was about to have a family with the man she loved and who loved her and where everything was normal and light and easy? And not terrifying.

'Jamie, I can't be who you need me to be.'

'Who do you think I need?'

'A princess. A queen. A *wife*. Someone who can stand by your side proudly. Someone who can wave to cheering crowds. Someone who can be loved by your people.'

'They'd love any woman I chose to have by my side.'

'Because of their duty?'

'Yes.'

'I don't want love out of *duty*, Jamie. And I could never stand beside you like that. I could never live away from my family. My job. My life. My life and my babies' lives will be *here*. Not in Majidar. You need to accept that.'

She pointed her key fob at her car to unlock it and opened the door.

'You *will* be called at some point to take your brother's throne and be King, so leave me now, leave *us* now and then no one will have to get hurt.' She got in, closed the car door shut after her and gave him one last look.

Did he not understand how much this was hurting *her*? She'd dreamed of this day! She'd never imagined she would ever be blessed by one baby, never mind two, but in that dream of having babies she'd hoped to have a wonderful man by her side too. In her imagination he'd always been a tall, dark and handsome figure, his face blurred. She'd never been sure who he might be. She'd dreamt of a family. Her children, her husband.

Mike had taken that dream away from her the second he'd thrown that acid, but now it was within her grasp again. And it was all wrong.

She wished she could develop something with Jamie, but he had another calling, apart from midwifery.

He was going to be King.

And she could not leave everything and everyone she

knew to live her life beside him. A life of publicity, of always having her photograph taken, with her every choice of clothing or hairstyle criticised and appraised. Her face discussed and talked about in newspapers and on television channels, her relationship with Mike dredged up from history, where she'd consigned it. They'd no doubt track him down in prison, interview him, get the inside scoop on their relationship and publish that too.

A life with Jamie would mean a lifetime of judgement.

All she'd ever wanted was to be loved.

And love did not come from duty.

Jamie pressed his hands against her window and begged her to lower it so he could speak.

She dropped the window slightly and the coolness of the outside air filtered into the car's interior.

Jamie stared at her. 'People are already hurting, Freya. You are. I am. We need to work together to sort this—not just for us, but for our children.'

Her hands went to her belly, protectively wrapping around them. 'They're who I'm thinking of.'

His eyes had narrowed slightly and frustration crept into his voice. '*Are* you, Freya? Or are you just thinking of the man who did that to you? Letting his actions dictate how you think your life must be?'

She bit her lip. Because he was right. Mike—his actions years ago, his attack, her fear—was being allowed to run every decision she made.

But who was Jamie to think he could tell her this? Say it? Confront her with it? As if he had the right?

'I'm their father, Freya. Let me be with my children!'

CHAPTER FOUR

WALK AWAY AND no one would get hurt? Did she think he was made of stone? He already had feelings about this. About the babies. About *her*.

Freya didn't seem to understand that.

He was *already* involved. Already in too deep and he always would be—until the day he took his last breath. These were his *children*!

And she…she was *scared*.

He understood that. What she'd been through… He couldn't even begin to imagine *half* the pain she must have experienced. She must have thought her life was over. Her face ruined. Her life destroyed by what had happened. Had she believed she didn't have a future?

All he wanted to do was help her feel safe. Make sure she was all right. But she seemed determined to keep pushing him away. It was very frustrating and he was trying his hardest not to make demands.

She truly was remarkable. He had nothing but admiration for her. Her spirit, her bravery made her shine from within. She didn't understand that. She didn't realise just how much people cared for her because of who she was. She believed they judged her purely on what she looked like.

She was still beautiful. Imperfections on her face meant nothing. It was who someone was that made them attractive.

Clearly Freya was still bothered by her face and he understood that. Women today were bombarded with messages about what constituted beauty, and it was all focused on outward appearances—being model-thin, having long, luscious hair, drop-dead gorgeous features. Beauty was never seen in acts of charity, or kindness, or caring. No one was ever told that having a good, loving heart was beautiful.

So he would protect her. Care for her as much as she would let him. And hopefully she would begin to let down her walls. To trust him.

He tried to make sure she always had a drink or a snack, as she kept staying in her patients' rooms and not coming out for a break, and he couldn't allow that. She needed to keep her strength up. But when he did these things for her she would give him a look that was almost like fear. As if she was worried about what he might do next. A look that said *You really don't have to do this.*

But he did. Whether she liked it or not they were joined now. For evermore. With or without rings on their fingers.

He brought her mugs of tea. He'd even offered to massage her aching feet once, when she'd complained about them, but all she'd done in response was look at him as if he was mad and then she'd got up to go and do something else. When she should have been resting!

She wouldn't let him in. Wouldn't let him get close.

His security people had told him that after she left the hospital and went home she stayed in. Never went anywhere. Didn't seem to have a life. There had been one visit, where she'd gone to someone's house, but a quick background check had discovered that it was her mother's home. He'd debated about calling in, hoping to meet her mother, but had refrained, not knowing how she'd react to that. If she thought his making her a cup of tea at work was bad, he felt sure she wouldn't want him pushing into her life before he was invited.

The security detail he'd assigned to her reported in every day. It broke his heart that she lived such an isolated life. Was there some way in which he could help her to open up her world? Or perhaps she was happy? Perhaps she was an introvert who enjoyed her own company? He wasn't in any position to judge.

'Would you like to meet me for coffee one day?' he asked her during a break on the ward.

She looked at him askance. 'Why? I see you every day at work.'

He smiled. 'It's different at work. We don't really get a chance to talk. We should be getting to know one another a bit more. We could meet in the open somewhere. In a public place, if that will make you feel better.'

He thought he was suggesting a *good* thing. Neutrality. Safety and security in numbers.

'I was attacked in a public place, Jamie. Surrounded by people. Numbers don't always make you safer.'

No. Of course not. He should have considered that. Freya liked privacy and quietness. She liked being alone.

'Chichester Cathedral.'

She frowned. 'What?'

'Let's meet at Chichester Cathedral. It's quiet, not too many people. There's a place to get coffee. Some grounds to wander in where we could find a private nook.'

'Because you want to talk?'

'Because we *need* to talk. Please, Freya, I beg of you.'

She seemed to consider his proposal. A divot formed in her brow. 'It's still too public for me.'

'Then where? Name it and I will arrange it.'

She thought of her bolthole on Hayling Island. The place she'd gone to after the attack. Her sanctuary.

'There's a path called the Billy Trail on Hayling Island. It starts just after the bridge to the mainland, on your right. We could meet there. I'll bring Rebel.'

Now it was his turn to frown. 'Who's Rebel?'

'My mother's dog.'

He wasn't the biggest fan of dogs, but he could get past that if she could get past her fears. 'Okay. When?'

It was Sunday afternoon, and the sun was burning down through a pure blue sky. He'd had to have the air-conditioning put on full when he'd got into the car because it was so hot. But he was glad the weather was good. He thought that if it had been raining, or bad weather in some way, Freya would have cancelled and they *needed* this. This time together. They needed to know more about one another. More beyond work and pregnancy and past horrors.

He and Freya were from vastly different backgrounds. It was no wonder they were clashing. But they both had the same desire and that was to do the best thing for their babies.

His driver located the small car park just past the bridge. He'd never been this way before, and he'd been positively delighted at the beautiful harbours the bridge had driven them through. The soft stillness of the calm water, the white boats sitting on the surface, the stretch of coastline and beyond, across the water, the views to Portsmouth and the spire of the Spinnaker Tower.

He stood waiting for her to arrive and pretty soon saw her small car turn into the car park. He gave her a smile and a wave. He had butterflies in his stomach! He so wanted this meeting to go well between them. It was imperative that it did so.

His nerves grew worse when he saw her let a large German Shepherd dog out of the boot of her car. For some reason he'd expected something smaller, but Rebel was massive! He was dark with intense eyes, his ears up and alert, ready to protect his mistress.

His mouth dry, he began to walk towards them.

'Hi.'

He stopped, looking down at the dog. Rebel was panting from the heat, but all Jamie could see were rows of sharp white teeth.

Freya had him on a short leash. 'Rebel, sit.'

Instantly the dog sat and looked up to her, waiting for the next order.

He was impressed, but also trying to control the feeling that he needed to bolt. He desperately wanted to run away from this dog, but he had no doubt that it would run after him and pull him to the ground with a well-placed jaw around his arm or leg. Or somewhere worse!

'Are you okay?' she asked.

'Bit nervous of dogs, to be honest.'

She smiled, amused. 'Rebel's all right. You can trust him.'

'Does he know he can trust *me*?'

Her smile broadened. 'We're both still trying to work that out. So, shall we get going?' She slung a backpack over her shoulder and locked her car.

'Sure. How…um…how close should I get to you?'

'Beside me is fine. Don't worry, he won't rip your throat out unless I tell him to.'

'Oh, good. That makes me feel a lot better.'

She laughed. 'Come on!'

Clearly Freya felt at ease with the dog at her side, and he had to admit he really rather liked this relaxed Freya. The dog? Not so much.

Freya looked relaxed in her white tee shirt and blue shorts, sunglasses over her eyes and her hair swept back in a ponytail. She looked fresh and happy, and already he could see a slight swelling to her abdomen. Only three months pregnant, maybe, but this was twins so she was slightly bigger than normal.

Three or four people on mountain bikes went cycling past as they headed onto the path.

'You found the place all right, then?' she asked.

'My driver did.'

'Of course. You have servants. I forget that when I see you at work.'

'Just a driver. Some security. A valet at the hotel. Not much.'

'Not much, huh? You have the entire third floor. I think you have plenty.'

'Just a security issue, that's all.'

'Where are your guards today? Are they lurking behind bushes on the trail? Are they going to walk behind us at twenty paces?' She looked behind them, as if to check.

'Nothing like that.'

He didn't tell her that his security team had already swept the entire five-mile length of the trail. That he had one or two undercover men posing as walkers and another pretending to be a wildlife photographer. The trail passed a nature reserve, so it was the perfect place to hide men in plain sight.

'It must be hard to live a life that's watched over like that.'

'You tell *me*.'

She frowned. 'What do you mean?'

'Don't you think that everyone is constantly looking at *you*? Watching your every move?'

She looked away. 'That's different. That's a perception. Your life is a reality. One you can't escape from.'

'Is that why you don't want to be a part of it? Because people are always watching? Observing? Making judgements?'

'Partly.'

At least she was being honest.

'You don't notice it after a while,' he said.

'I would. I notice everything. Every little glance. Every raise of an eyebrow. Every frown. Every reaction—shock, fear, disgust. That last one I get more than you'd realise. Have you ever thought what that might feel like? To observe someone looking at your face and see that they're disgusted? Of course you haven't. Not looking the way you do. The world is open to those who are good-looking. It's a proven scientific fact. Beautiful and handsome people get better jobs, better pay, more opportunities. Disabled and disfigured people always seem to be at the bottom of the pile.'

'Life must have been hard for you.'

'Must have been? It still is.'

He didn't know how to answer that. He would never know exactly what she had been through. What she still went through, looking in the mirror and seeing a different face.

'But a new phase of our lives is opening up to both of us now.'

She nodded, stopping as Rebel bent his head to sniff at a small post in the ground. 'We have two separate, completely incompatible lives, Jamie. How are we going to manage this?'

The truth? He didn't know. He wanted to be a father to these babies, and to be in their lives, but he would be called upon to rule Majidar at some point and would have to leave this country. He didn't want to leave them behind and she refused to go with him.

He *loved* Majidar. Even though he had left it to come to England and make his life there. It was still his home. It was still the place where his family was. Where his heart was. His people were gracious and kind and understanding, but would they understand when they learned that he had left his children behind? Because he wouldn't. He couldn't get his head around it.

He loved these babies. Already. He'd seen their little hearts beating, had seen them in her womb, two gorgeous little beans that were *his*. He felt he would die for them. Lay down his life for them. Already he dreamed of holding them in his arms, teaching them, playing with them, laughing at their chuckles and watching them grow.

Be a king. Or be a father.

It seemed to be one or the other, and it was an impossible decision to make.

'We *must* manage it. We must find a way.'

'But how?'

He smiled at her. 'Today is a good step forward. We can't afford to shut each other out; we don't have that luxury. I know it's hard for you—hard for you to trust me and let me in.' He paused over his next words, but knew he had to let her know that he *knew*. 'I know what happened to you.'

Freya stopped walking. So did Rebel, who turned back to look at her. 'Who told you?'

'No one was gossiping. I asked. I brought it up. I needed to know why you were shutting me out.'

She started walking again, Rebel loping by her side. 'I see.'

'I don't want you to be frightened of me, Freya. I'm not that kind of man.'

'I can't tell any more. My perspective on men is skewed.'

'Hence the big dog?' He smiled.

She glanced at him. 'Tell me why you're afraid of dogs.'

He thought about why he was afraid, glancing at Rebel's teeth. 'My brother and I were once playing out on the sand dunes. We'd gone out with our father, who was hunting with his falcons and his dogs. We had these big boards—like surfboards—and if we threw them right down the sloping side of a dune we could jump on and surf to the bottom. We were doing that…laughing and joking…having a brilliant time. I'd jumped onto my board and was sitting on it, surfing down the dune, when one of the dogs must have had his hunting instincts activated by our movement and high-pitched cries. This dog—this hound that was almost as tall as I was—raced over to me, and when the board stopped moving it grabbed onto my head, sinking its teeth into my scalp.'

Freya looked fascinated. Interested.

'My father got the dog to stop. It let go and I was rushed to the hospital with four puncture wounds to my skull. After that I couldn't go near any dogs. They made me too nervous.'

She nodded. 'So you know how it feels.'

He looked at her. 'I do. I know you don't know me well enough to be sure I'm not going to pounce, not going to sink my teeth in, but all I can say is I'm not like the man that did this to you. Just like Rebel, there, is probably nothing like the dog that attacked me.'

'You have to trust that.'

'As do you.'

He touched her on the arm, making her stop. Then he sucked in a breath as he contemplated what he had to do. Show her that if he was willing to work past his fear, then so should she. With some hesitation he held his hand out towards Rebel, hoping the dog wouldn't sense his fear. Hoping he wasn't about to lose a chunk of his hand. His heart racing, he watching in horrid fascination as Rebel licked his fingers, then began sniffing the cuff of his shirt.

Jamie knelt down in front of the dog and reached out to stroke it. His arms were trembling, but he was determined to do this. Rebel's fur was soft and thick and, most surprisingly, the dog didn't seem to mind him at all. Slowly he stood up and breathed a sigh of relief, a smile breaking across his face.

'Well, that went better than I'd imagined.'

A small smile broke across her face. 'That must have taken a lot of courage. Were you really that scared?'

'Terrified. But I trusted that I'd be okay. I hope you can do the same with me. Because only then can we get through this. As equals.'

They began walking again, side by side, enjoying the views over the harbour and its old oyster beds, where masses of birds were nesting.

'I'll try. That's all I can do.'

Jamie nodded. 'It's all I ask.'

Freya looked about her, then sucked in a breath and began talking. 'I guess I ought to tell you about him. About Mike—the guy that did this.'

'Only if you want to.'

'I do.'

Freya stooped to undo the clip on Rebel's lead and set him free.

Jamie felt a surge of anxiety, but decided he had to stay calm. She still had control of the dog. And the way the dog kept looking at her, waiting for instruction, showed that she did.

'Mike made me think we were equals. At the beginning. He seemed to adore me. Wanted to be with me all the time. I thought that was just so wonderful, you know? But over time it became insidious, the way he manipulated that. He made me feel bad about going out to see other people. He questioned my clothing. He wanted to know why I needed to wear make-up. Was it for someone else? Was I flirting? I tried to prove him wrong by not wearing make-up, but then he wanted me to cut my hair short. Said it made me look flirty, being so long, that men looked at women with long hair in the wrong way.'

She paused.

'It sounds crazy now, but at the time I was just so afraid of upsetting him. His moods were terrible. We were so good together when he was happy, and I wanted to do what I could to keep him that way. But I refused to cut my hair, so he told me to wear it up, so that it looked a bit less feminine. Less pretty. He began questioning me if I was ever late coming home from work. Who had I been talking to? Was it a man? Didn't I know how scared it made him feel when I didn't come home on time? It was just a part time job at a bar, to help with college fees, but he figured the place was filled with nothing but lecherous guys.'

She paused again.

'I began to realise I had no life outside of college and work. I hadn't seen my family in ages. My friends no longer asked me out. All I did was spend time in the flat with Mike. I was just eighteen. It seemed like no life at all, and I didn't want it to stay that way. It had seemed like a compliment at first, the way he seemed to need me. But I began to see that my life had become a prison. A prison I needed to escape.'

'And he let you go?'

'I waited until he went to work, then packed what few possessions I had and took a bus home to Mum. He went crazy when he came home and found out I wasn't there. Called me on my phone. When I told him we were over there was the longest silence, and then he called me all these vile names, said my life wouldn't be worth living without him, and that if I didn't come back to him by the morning I would regret it.'

'Freya…'

'I thought it was just him letting off steam. I thought he was saying stuff like that because his pride had been hurt. But he really was that crazy. I was shopping when it happened. Out on the high street and suddenly he was there, throwing acid into my face.'

'My God! I'm so sorry.'

'I should have seen it coming. I knew he couldn't let go—knew he was a little unstable. I should have expected it.'

'You can't blame yourself.'

'I do, though. For getting involved with a man like that in the first place.'

'You were just *eighteen*, Freya.'

'I know, but…but I feel I should have had more sense.'

Rebel had been up ahead, but now he came loping back, his large paws pounding the ground. He came running up to Jamie, sniffing around his jacket.

Jamie tried not to freeze. Tried to keep walking. To act normal.

'Rebel, heel!'

The dog left him instantly and went back to its mistress. Jamie breathed a sigh of relief. He understood how hard it was for Freya. She couldn't know. Even if she suspected the worst, she couldn't know if or when it would happen. It was impossible. His own hesitation and fear around dogs was similar, but Freya's fear had to be tenfold. He would do whatever he could to make things easier for her.

'You did what you thought was right at the time, with the knowledge you had. You couldn't have asked any more of yourself back then. Or now, come to think of it.'

'What are we going to do, Jamie? I can't marry you. I can't be your wife and leave everything to go and be Queen in some foreign country. That's not me. That's not what I want from my life. And I can't have my children raised behind walls with security guards for protection. I want them to be free.'

'I know. I understand. I *do*. But I can't leave you behind. A king has to be, above all, a good role model for his citizens. I can't leave my children here and go back to rule as an absent father. But I can't let my people down, either. They'll need me. At some point they'll need me on that throne.'

'We have a stalemate, then.' She pulled a small treat from her pocket and fed it to the dog.

'In the future, yes, but right now we can try and work something out.'

'How do you mean?'

'I might not have to be King for many years. In the meantime let me be with you—and them. Let me be who I need to be. I *have* to be in their lives.'

Could she hear the desperation in his voice?

She looked up at him, considering him, judging him. He knew she was still scared. There was no way that was just going to disappear. But he could see that she was thinking about acquiescing to his request.

'I want my children to know their father,' she said.

'That's good.'

'But I don't want their father running out on them. I won't have their hearts broken, Jamie. I won't.'

'I would never want to hurt them in any way.'

'But it will happen. Eventually. Wouldn't it be easier if—?'

'No.'

He knew what she was going to say. *Wouldn't it be easier for them if they just didn't know about you at all?*

'I can't forget about them. They're here. They're a part of me. They are my sons or my daughters. I can't walk away from that. Could you?'

She let out a heavy sigh. 'No, I couldn't.'

They walked on a little more. An older couple were walking towards them, holding hands, chatting. They looked so comfortable with each other. So safe in their little bubble.

He envied them. Envied them their easy lives.

'I have a responsibility to do the right thing. A father stands by his children *and* the mother of those children. As a man, I have to show them that's what I should do. Take responsibility for my actions. As King, I need to think about my people and how they need a good, strong leader they can respect. But most of all I have to respect myself, and that means doing the best by all of you. That doesn't mean, and nor would it ever mean, walking away.'

Freya nodded. 'Okay. We'll work something out.'

He nodded too, sure they would find a way.

'We will.'

'I've brought you something.' Back at work, Freya stood awkwardly in front of Jamie, holding two mugs of tea.

Jamie put down the magazine he'd been reading and looked up at her in surprise.

'It's tea.' She thrust the mug towards him.

He took it. 'Thank you. That's very kind.'

'It's just tea.'

But they both knew it was more than that. It was an olive branch. A step forward. A slight lowering of the barricades. The walls were still there. Freya didn't know if she would ever be able to trust another man. But she was willing to give him a chance to show her that she was wrong after the way he had approached Rebel. Willing to trust. Being scared, but doing it anyway.

'May I sit with you for a moment?'

'Please do.' He sat up, straightening, and watched her as she lowered herself into the chair opposite him.

'We…er…ought to get to know one another a bit more.'

He smiled, pleased. 'That's a very good idea.'

'Thank you.'

'How do you suppose we do that?'

She wasn't sure. She hadn't thought that far ahead. To be honest, she hadn't thought she'd get past offering him the tea before chickening out and walking away again, but she had done it. And now here she was.

'We should meet outside of work. What sort of things do you like to do?' he asked. 'That don't involve big dogs?'

She smiled. 'I like to read.' Then she realised that they were hardly going to sit and *read* together, were they? 'I don't really have any other hobbies.'

'What did you do when you were little? There must have been something.'

She thought for a moment. 'I loved to swim. But I haven't done that for years.'

'Swimming's very good for pregnant women. We should do that.'

'Oh, I couldn't possibly—'

'I'll arrange for us to have the pool area at my hotel all to ourselves. What day do you fancy?'

Oh. She hadn't thought he would be able to do that. But what did she know? He was a prince—he could probably do anything he wanted. He was right. There was so much they didn't know about each other. But swimming? Wearing just a swimsuit? Was it too late to back out?

'Saturday evening?' she said.

'Perfect. Thank you, Freya.'

'For what?'

'The olive branch.' He sipped at his tea and smiled. 'It tastes lovely.'

She'd had to get herself a new swimsuit, and had bought one online. She'd had to go for one especially for pregnant women, that allowed for a burgeoning belly, and had found a nice dark navy one with a crimson and cream pleat around her boobs.

Trying it on at home, she stood in front of the mirror to see what Jamie would see. She needed to shave her legs, that was for sure. Maybe paint her toenails?

The swimsuit covered her nicely, though, and even coped with her growing breasts without making her look as if she was hanging out of it. So all in all she was quite pleased with her purchase.

It revealed the scars on her neck, though.

She reached to touch the roughened skin where a graft had failed to take and was reminded of the first time she had looked in a mirror after the attack. The doctors had given her a small hand mirror and then left her to look by herself. Even her mum had left the room, giving her privacy for such a moment.

She'd almost not looked. Why had they all left like that? she'd wondered. Was it because the damage was so bad that they didn't want to see her distress?

Lifting up the mirror, turning to see, had been the most heartbreaking moment of her life. Her face had been ravaged by the acid, her nose almost gone. Angry, red, livid skin...

She'd wanted to die. Right at that moment she had thought that life was no longer worth living. That she would never look better than she did there and then. That her life was over at eighteen years of age and that she would now be one of those relatives kept hidden away in a house, never to be seen again.

But time was a great healer. And the body had an amazing ability to repair itself. It had been a long, hard, painful road, but after each surgery, after each debriding, after each skin graft, she had looked into the mirror and seen progress. Incremental progress. The skin had become less angry. Smoother. Flatter. Her nose had been rebuilt, new eyebrows tattooed into place.

Slowly but surely, normality had seemed to be within reach. She knew she would never be perfect again. Never have the face she used to have. But she would no longer look like some kind of monster.

She'd grown used to the scars, but to everyone she met they were brand-new and she still feared their judgement.

Swimming, though… She hadn't done it in years, because she'd been too afraid to go to a public pool. All those people? Not likely. But she had missed it. So much so, she actually felt a small frisson of excitement at the idea of having a pool to herself and just being allowed to float in the water, quiet and serene, without the worry of people watching her.

She knew she shouldn't be so sensitive to that, but she couldn't help it. A person's face was what they presented to the world, and *her* face was different. Not different in that she had too big a nose, or a massive spot on her chin. Her face just had *that look* after all the skin grafts. The hint of something that was awful underneath in the way her top lip was slightly pulled to one side, her nostrils not quite normal.

The thought of returning to the Franklin Hotel caused butterflies in her stomach. The last time she'd been there it had been made clear to her just exactly who Jamie was. This time she already knew. But he would find out who *she* was. And she wasn't used to people probing around inside her life like that.

Suck it up. You're doing this for your babies.

She parked the car and crunched across the stones on the driveway into the entrance hall. Jamie was already there, waiting to meet her, and he surprised her by kissing her on both cheeks.

'I'm glad you came.'

She nodded, trying to make sense—quickly—of how it had felt when his lips had pressed against her face. She'd stopped breathing. Felt hot. Uncertain.

It's nothing. Just get on with it.

But she hadn't been ready for him to touch her face like that. And with his lips. His perfect lips…

'Shall we go through to the pool? I can show you where the changing rooms are.'

Freya nodded hurriedly, glad that she didn't blush any

more the way she'd used to. Following him through the reception area, down a small corridor, through a set of double doors, she was suddenly hit by the smell of chlorine.

It was like going back through time. She'd both forgotten that smell and remembered it intently at the same time. It was so strong! And there was that slight echo in the room, the reflection of the blue water, bouncing off the walls…

'The ladies' changing rooms are off to the right.'

'Thank you.'

Freya headed off to get changed, letting out a strained breath as she got to the changing area.

What was she doing—coming here? Doing this? Was she really about to strip down to a swimming costume in front of Jamie? It was practically like being naked. Naked meant vulnerable, and she didn't like feeling that way.

She sat down on a wooden bench for a moment, to breathe and gather herself.

I'm not doing this for me. I'm doing this for my children, so that when they're grown up I can tell them that I tried my best.

Suitably emboldened, she got up and began to undress. She put on her swimsuit and wrapped herself in a large towel before heading out to the pool.

Jamie was waiting for her. Wearing just a pair of trunks that emphasised his physique. She tried not to stare as she took in his beautiful body. His slightly hairy chest, his toned muscles, his flat stomach and long, strong, powerful thighs…

He was a thing of beauty, with his dark toned skin, whereas *she* hadn't been out in the sun for ages and was milky white, pale, swollen and…

She almost chickened out. Almost turned around to go back inside the changing room saying *I'm not doing this*, but then he smiled at her, padding towards her to take her hand.

'Are you all right?'

She nodded, not trusting herself to speak, fighting the urge to flee, but also wanting to get into that water so very much! She'd missed it. Swimming. Relaxing. Floating in the water with the weight of the world off her body.

'Let's get you in, then.'

He walked ahead of her down the steps, her hand in his, allowing her to slip off the towel and get chest-deep in the water before he turned back to look at her.

She appreciated him being a gentleman like that.

'How does the water feel?' he asked.

It felt wonderful. She felt instantly lighter—her bump supported, the strain off her back—and the temperature was perfect.

'Amazing!' She smiled, treading water and moving her arms.

'How many years has it been?'

'Erm… About twenty years. Maybe more.'

He swam alongside her, dipping his head to get his hair wet.

She glanced at him when he came up for air, and then looked away again. God, the man was sexy, all wet like that! Flustered, she allowed the weight of her legs to drop to the bottom of the pool and stood up. She was feeling strange things happening in her body. Tingling anticipation.

'When did *you* last swim?' she asked, to try and think of anything else but her body's primal reaction to this man beside her.

'Yesterday.' He smiled. 'I always do a few lengths after a shift.'

'*After?* How do you have the energy?'

'I just do. But, then again, I'm not growing babies inside me. How are you feeling?'

'Better now the morning sickness has disappeared. It wasn't too bad. I was never actually sick. But I'm feeling much better, thank you.'

'I'm glad.'

She stared at him for a moment. They were facing each other, about a metre apart, treading water. He looked so relaxed, and she wondered how he could be that way with so many worries upon his broad shoulders.

'How do you do it?'

He frowned. 'Do what?'

'Have those men following you around all the time? Your security? I've noticed I've got some of my own now. They're discreet, but they're there. It scared the hell out of me when I realised I was being followed.'

'I should have mentioned them to you. I'm sorry, I should have thought.'

'You should.'

'You get used to it. After a while you hardly notice.'

'Really?'

'Really.'

'I wonder what they think of all this? Having to follow *me* around?'

'I don't know. They do it because I order them to.'

'To protect me?'

He nodded.

'I don't need protection.'

'Maybe not, but those babies of mine do.' *Duty.* Would it always come back to that? He had a duty to his children, not to her. He *had* to do it, not because he wanted to.

She felt some similarity in her own life. She'd survived because she'd had to. She was trying to let him in because she had to. She owed it to her babies. But was it what she wanted? Yes—in a way. Her desire to be a mother was incredibly strong, and the need for her children to know their father was equally so. Even if she did suspect that at some point he would have to leave them behind.

She thought of women who were married to soldiers. Didn't they do the same thing? Knowing that at some point they might lose their husbands? That one day they just wouldn't come home?

But Jamie wouldn't be dying, would he? He would be choosing his duty, his country, over them.

She turned and began to swim breaststroke across the pool. Jamie swam alongside her. And now that the olive branch had been accepted, now that she wasn't having that knee-jerk reaction to keeping him at arm's length, she was curious about the man whose babies she was carrying. His life. His past.

'Tell me about your childhood. What was it like, growing up as a prince?'

He gave a wry smile. 'It was privileged life—no surprise there. But it was also very difficult.'

'In what way?'

'I was a young boy who wanted to run off and explore. Beyond the palace was a thriving town, and beyond that an oasis. I wanted to go there all on my own, but that was never allowed. I felt my freedom was restricted, and along with my schooling I was given many hours of instruction on politics and court etiquette and council procedures, which was all very dry and uninteresting to a boy who only wanted to be able to go to the falconry or the stables or have friends round after school.'

She tried to imagine him. Tried to imagine her own children having such a life. It didn't sound the best.

'Sounds lonely.'

'I was never lonely—which was half the trouble. There was always someone there, standing in the background, waiting, watching. Once my father had forbidden me to learn midwifery I was very angry for a while, and I would often try my best to evade my guards so I could sneak out of the palace grounds and be free for a little while.'

'Did you manage to do that often?'

He smiled. 'I did—much to their disappointment and anger. But I really felt like I didn't belong there.'

Neither did she belong there. Or her babies. It was part of their heritage, but did they deserve to spend their lives like that? Yearning for freedom and escape? She knew how that felt. She'd been there. Wanting to escape from four walls and having family and doctors constantly watching over her. It had been stifling.

'But you have a wonderful brother?'

'I do. He's only a few years older than me, so hopefully he'll be on the throne for a long time. Who knows? Maybe our children will be fully grown and living lives of their own before I have to return to Majidar.'

She stopped swimming as she came to the edge of the pool and leaned back against it. Wouldn't it be wonderful if it happened that way?

'I hope so, Jamie. I do.'

He smiled, before sinking under the surface and swimming towards her, rising from the depths like a merman, his face right in front of hers. It was unnerving, having him this close. She could see him looking at her, taking in every feature of her face.

'Tell me about *your* childhood, Freya.'

His dark eyes were looking into her own with such concentration. Nervous, she began to talk.

'I've lived my whole life here in Chichester. I was very much a girly girl, playing with dolls and babies. I would line them all up like they were in a hospital nursery, covered with little blankets I'd made myself on my mother's sewing machine.'

'You can sew?'

She shrugged. 'Moderately. Simple things—cushions, blankets, curtains.'

'Go on.'

'I loved to play mum. I wanted a brother or sister desperately, but I never got one.'

It had been lonely, growing up without siblings. At least her twins would have each other. Didn't twins usually have a strong bond?

'I loved to swim. I wanted to have horse-riding lessons, but Mum could never afford it.'

'I have horses.'

She lifted her eyebrows in surprise, smiling. 'You do?'

'In Majidar, yes.'

'Oh.'

'Beautiful stallions. Racehorses.'

'Do you miss them?'

'I'm kept up to date on their progress.'

'But only from afar. It must be hard to be kept from something you love?'

Jamie stared at her. 'It can be.'

She could see him having a proper look now. Seeing the edges of her scars around her hairline. Tracking the damage that must have been done and had been repaired. Realising how many operations she must have gone through to look as she did today.

The intense scrutiny made her uncomfortable.

'Love does strange things to people. Makes them act out of character. Makes them crazy. Makes them not think straight.'

Jamie's hand reached up out of the water and she sucked in a breath as his fingers traced the edges of her face, down her cheek, along her jaw. Such a tender touch—respectful and gentle.

'You're beautiful, you know?'

What?

She hadn't expected him to say that. Never in a million years had she expected to hear *anyone* say that to her. Not the way he had. As if he meant it. He'd not been patronising her. His voice had spoken the truth as he saw it.

Moved to strong emotion, Freya blinked back tears at his words.

'Have I upset you?'

'No.' She wiped her eyes hurriedly and tried to smile bravely, to show him that she was okay. Her mum would tell her she was beautiful, but she'd always dismissed that—mums were duty-bound to say that.

'You're crying.' He reached out and pulled her gently towards him.

At first she resisted. Just slightly. But then she gave in, allowing herself that moment. She rested her head against his shoulder, put her arms around his back, completely in shock that this was even happening. This, she had *not* expected. To be held like this...

'I'm okay,' she said, her face against his wet shoulder.

His hand smoothed down her hair. 'No, you're not. But I'll hold you until you are.'

And he did. They both stood there, in the warmth of the pool, in each other's arms, until the tears dried in her eyes, she stopped sniffing and the water was still, like a pond.

When everything was calm again, and her breathing had settled into a steady in and out motion, she felt him release her.

'We should have a change of scene. Let's go to dinner,' he said. 'Before you get cold.'

And she suddenly couldn't think of anything she wanted more than to sit with him. Talk. This man had been nothing but gentlemanly and kind to her. He'd never shown her pity. Never reacted the way everyone else had.

'I'd love to have dinner with you.' She meant it. Smiled her thanks. And, though she tried her hardest not to look down at his mouth, at those lips that had once brushed her skin in the most intimate way, she couldn't help herself.

She wondered what it would be like to let down her guard completely and kiss him all over again?

The hotel's restaurant was dimly lit, and they were seated in a small alcove near the back, away from prying eyes, where they could pretend it was just the two of them.

From the reception area she could hear the piano being played—gentle, soothing music.

She'd got out of the pool and gone back to the changing room to get dressed on very shaky legs, unsure as to what was happening between the two of them. She wanted to let him in—but just a little bit. To let him know that they could talk about things, discuss the future. But something else seemed to have happened. An anticipation of so much more.

Hope.

Never in her wildest dreams had she ever thought she would be in this position—pregnant, about to become a mother, but also having a man tell her that she was *beautiful.*

It was a word she'd never thought would be used to describe her again. *Brave* got used an awful lot. *Courageous. Stubborn,* maybe.

But beautiful?

She'd stared at the mirror as she blow-dried her hair, focusing intently on her own face, gazing at the façade that it had taken her years to get used to. Inside, she still felt that she looked the way she had before the accident, so every time she looked in the mirror it was a stark reminder that she was different.

She'd tried to embrace that and look forward. Never allowing the melancholy and disappointment to overwhelm her. Never letting what Mike had done beat her down, because then he would have done what he'd set out to do. Never allowing the depression to set in, as it had with so many others affected in a similar way.

She was living the best way that she could. Under *her* rules. *Her* control. And now she was handing some of that control over to him.

She was different now. Not just in looks, but in character. She cared more for the underdogs in society; she listened, empathised, and she worked damned hard to make sure her patients felt empowered and brave and strong. She was their cheerleader. Their support. She knew she could coach women through the scariest moments of their lives, even as they felt they were being split in two, and she knew they *all* had the strength within them to get through it. She gave them everything they needed and asked for nothing in return.

But now Jamie was here and he wanted to pay her attention. He wasn't family, but he was trying to give her everything she needed and a whole lot more besides. He was able, it seemed, to see past the prickly exterior that she had first presented to him. He had pushed it to one side, had powered through, because he was invested in *her* well-being. *Her* thoughts and feelings. *Her* health. *Her* happiness.

And that felt odd. Disconcerting.

Good, but strange.

It had happened at university, too. During her training. Her teachers and lecturers had seen past her face and made sure she qualified, made sure she became the midwife she'd always wanted to be.

Perhaps she needed to give more people the benefit of the doubt?

'I'll have the Caesar salad to start, please, and I think I'll have the pan-seared chicken for my main, thank you,' she said to the waiter from behind her menu card.

'Smoked salmon and the pheasant for me, thanks.'

The waiter disappeared, having removed the menu cards with him.

Freya took a sip of her water. 'You must be used to English food now. Is there anything you miss from back home that you can't get here?'

'You don't serve as much goat as there was back home.' He smiled. 'Or *luqmat al-qadi*.'

She frowned, having never heard of that before. 'What is that?'

'They're like your pastries. A leavened dough that has been deep-fried, then soaked in a very sweet syrup.'

'Like a doughnut?'

'Not quite. My mother made them. Sometimes she would add cinnamon or sweet spices to them. They were out of this world.'

'Your mother cooked?'

'Occasionally. Not as often as she would have liked.'

'My mum likes to cook. She likes to feed people. There's always something on at her house.'

'It was the same at mine.'

She smiled. 'But, to be fair, your house was a palace, so...'

He laughed, good-naturedly. 'True.'

She took another sip of water. 'Is your mother still alive?'

His eyes darkened. 'No. She passed away a few months after my father did. It was a huge shock to lose them both so quickly like that. But I believe she died of a broken heart, after losing my father so suddenly.'

'She must have loved him very much.'

He nodded. 'Al Bakharis love deeply.'

Her breath caught in her throat as she imagined that sort of passion. The depth of love that one person could have for another. It was the type of love she had once imagined for herself. The type of love she had thought she had found with Mike, in the way he had so quickly and deeply fallen for her.

That kind of love was scary. Terrifying. It could totally

condemn you to a future filled with pain, misery and grief. Case in point: Jamie's mother dying of a broken heart. Perhaps love was more dangerous than people realised and they were fools to seek it out? It was best to keep things light. Casual. Even if it did leave you wanting…

'Have you ever felt that way about someone?' she asked.

'Not yet. That kind of love is the kind that stays for eternity. You will always be together, until the end of your days. If I had already found that, then you and I would not be in the situation we now find ourselves in.'

It was a stark reminder of exactly what this was between them.

A *situation*.

That was all. There was no point in reading anything else into it—even if he *had* told her she was beautiful. Even though he had cradled her in his arms until she'd stopped crying. Even if they had shared that one magical night together.

They'd been caught out by Mother Nature and now they were having to deal with the consequences.

That was all this was. Nothing more, nothing less.

So, despite the fact that they were sitting together in a restaurant, having only just a few minutes before shared a most intimate connection as she was wrapped in his embrace, Freya had to remind herself not to get carried away with *hope*. With *possibility*.

But she'd always been a dreamer and it was hard to switch that part of her brain off.

If the accident hadn't happened she would never have been at that charity ball. She would never have had that night with Jamie. She wouldn't be pregnant with twins. But they still would have met at work, and she would still have been attracted to him. The way she was now.

It was hard to tell herself that he probably didn't feel the same way. No matter what he'd said.

Reality hurt when she thought about that. She might have defied the odds and got pregnant, but Jamie was *not* going to be her knight in shining armour and she would do well to remember that.

'Please excuse me a moment.'

She stood, needing to escape to the bathroom for a minute alone—because she could feel tears threatening to fall down her face, and if she cried again he would comfort her again. He would touch her. Hold her. Try to make her feel better. And, despite her best instincts, she realised she *wanted* that.

Even though she shouldn't.

And she couldn't have that.

She stared at her tear-stained reflection in the bathroom mirror.

Why was life testing her so harshly?

CHAPTER FIVE

JAMIE WAS VERY pleased with the way their relationship was progressing. Freya's walls were starting to come down, and now she was letting him sit and talk to her at work. They socialised together sometimes, getting to know one another, and when they went to her check-ups and other appointments with her consultant they asked questions as if they were a real couple.

He'd sat by her side when she'd had her twenty-one-week scan, gripping her hand tightly in his, and they'd both been over the moon when the scan had confirmed that they were going to have non-identical twin boys.

Sons!

That was a big deal for Jamie. He'd always dreamed of having sons and raising them to be good, strong men. Sons to be proud of...sons he would support in their desire to do anything. He would not restrict their lives the way his had been, and if they wanted to become pilots or nurses, whatever their dreams could possibly be, he vowed to himself that he would help them achieve them in any way that he could.

His sons would be his heirs. Heirs to the throne. It was their destiny, but what would they know of it? What would they know of Majidar? With its rolling dunes, its intense heat and its beautiful people. He himself had yearned to leave and live a life he couldn't get there. Should he be the one to tell them that they must follow that path when he didn't want it for himself? Who was he to decide what they should do? He was their father, so shouldn't he want them to be happy more than anything else?

He'd sent news of the babies to his brother Ilias and younger sister Zahra. Both had responded with joy and delight, but both had asked him when he was coming home. With Freya at his side.

It was an awkward question to which he had no answer.

Zahra was already gushing about their wedding and all the things they'd need to organise. How could he tell her that it was probably never going to happen?

So he'd kept silent, swearing them to secrecy in his last email, until he knew what the next few months would bring. He'd used work as his main excuse. Said he was still under contract for another six months, with the possibility of a permanent post, and that he would not let people down when they were depending upon him.

Zahra had emailed back.

Six months? But the babies will be born by then!

It was all so difficult. So confusing. If he'd had his way then he and Freya would already be married. No need for a big ceremony in Majidar...no need to be driven down the streets in an open-topped car, waving to adoring crowds. He would present his marriage as a *fait accompli*. Everyone would just have to accept it.

If only Freya would accept it!

That would be easier, wouldn't it?

He hadn't mentioned it to her for a while, not wanting to raise such a difficult subject again when things between them seemed to be going so well.

When he'd first mentioned marriage he'd done it out of

duty. Done it because of the moral code that told him it was the right thing to do. Not for him, or for her, but for their children. Whether Freya liked it or not, her babies carried royal blood and he would not have them being illegitimate. He hadn't thought too much about whether a marriage between them would work out or not. It just had to be. Details, emotions, feelings—all those could be worked out later, as time allowed them to know each other more.

But now...?

Life was even more complicated.

He liked Freya a lot. He cared for her. And the more he got to know her, the more he realised that if they were to get married then he would have a happy life with her, a happy marriage. He felt it in his bones. She was strong and loving and kind, the bravest woman he had ever known, and he felt proud that a woman like that was carrying his children. What a role model she would be! How much she would love them!

His feelings for her were deepening every day. Each time she laughed or smiled his heart expanded a little bit more. Each time she trusted him with a hint of intimacy—a confession, a secret, a story from her past—his feelings for her grew.

It was confusing. The line between emotion and duty was blending, merging. How could he get her to understand how he felt if he didn't even understand it, himself?

It was the end of November, and at seven months pregnant Freya felt huge. It had been many weeks since she had last been able to reach her own feet, and she thanked the Lord that Jamie, at least, seemed quite happy to lift her feet up onto his lap and massage them for her when they had a break at work.

Her body was protesting. She was knocking back strawberry milkshakes as if they were going out of fashion, and she dreaded to think about how much extra weight she was putting on. But it was all for a good cause, so she was trying to be relaxed about it.

There wasn't long left, and this probably wouldn't happen again, so she was trying to enjoy her pregnancy for as long as she could.

The babies were good movers, kicking and stretching at all hours of the day and night, and she would often sit at work with one hand on her swollen baby, feeling their movements. It was very reassuring.

They were good sizes, too. She and Jamie had attended many scans which had not only marked the growth of the babies, but also the growth of their ever-changing relationship.

She'd started to get the nursery ready at home. Jamie had even come over one evening to help paint the walls and put up some stencils. He'd even climbed a ladder to hang up the new curtains she'd made.

It was almost as if they were a real couple getting ready for their future.

Only without the living together and the sex.

And sex had been high on her mind lately, despite her burgeoning size. It had to be the hormones! She was blaming them entirely as her mind filled with X-rated images of her and Jamie doing really naughty things together.

It didn't help that he was so easy on the eye. Or that he was kind and thoughtful and gentlemanly. Seeing him smile delighted her, and she often found herself reaching out to touch him—a hand on his arm, his shoulder. Touching the small of his back as she passed behind him at work. Just a small contact. But enough to make her desires surge and make her brain remind her of what that one night had been like and how wonderful it would feel to experience that again. To touch him in other places. To have him touch her...

Enough, Freya!

It would never be like that between them again.

Would it?

She blinked, trying to dismiss the thrilling images she'd created, and instead focused on the patient notes she was filling out. Her patient, Rosie Clay, had been progressing through labour quite well until suddenly the baby had started showing decelerations. The infant had gone into distress and Rosie had been rushed to theatre for an emergency Caesarean section. Rosie was now fine, but her baby girl was in the NICU, having aspirated meconium, which meant she had passed her first stool whilst still in the womb.

She dropped the pen to stretch out her shoulders, thrusting them back and trying to roll them. She suddenly felt hands slide down over them.

'Tense?' Jamie asked.

You betcha.

'Yeah, a little. It got a bit frantic in Theatre just now.'

'I heard. The baby's in NICU?'

'A little girl.'

'Little girls are strong.'

She thought of her own babies. Of the struggles they might have in the future together. Alone, without a father.

'So are little boys.'

Jamie's hands felt great, massaging away the tenseness of her muscles, releasing the knots and strain that she'd been carrying all night. She could groan because he was making her feel so good!

'You can stop now.'

She pulled away, not wanting to embarrass herself. Jamie was just doing it out of duty, anyway. She'd accepted that ages ago, and reminded herself daily not to get too carried away with what was happening between them. It was the babies he was interested in. And she was dreaming again. Allowing herself to get carried away with fantasy.

It was her ability to dream and fantasise that had got her through the long, painful days after her attack; it had been the only way she could escape the pain and the four walls that had bound her so tightly.

He settled into a seat beside her. 'Do you need anything to drink? Eat?'

'No, I'm fine, thank you,' she answered, and heard a harshness coming out in her voice that she hadn't intended. But this was so frustrating! Having something so close she could almost touch it. Wanting something—*someone*—so badly, but knowing it could never happen.

'You're sure?'

She nodded, fighting the urge to yell at him, to tell him to leave her alone because that was what he was going to do anyway. At some point. And the idea of it was breaking her heart.

She'd grown to love his friendship, his kindness, his support—even his attentiveness. But sometimes she got angry—mostly with herself—knowing it wouldn't be for ever.

Freya had tried to keep herself distanced from it, but lately it had become nigh on impossible and her hormones were probably to blame for that too! It was as if her body had become conditioned to let him in. To allow him to care for her as the natural father of her children. But she had other feelings developing too, and they were dangerous and stupid!

Beside them, the buzzer rang. Someone required admission.

In the evening, the doors were locked for security, so anyone turning up in the middle of the night, in labour or otherwise, had to buzz to be let in. There was a security camera so the staff could see who was there.

Freya looked at the monitor and its grainy black and

white image. A man stood there, desperately looking up at the camera, wrapped in a coat and scarf.

She picked up the phone to speak through the intercom. 'Hello?'

'My wife! My wife's having the baby!'

'Okay, sir, I'm going to buzz you through.' She went to press the button.

'No, you don't understand! She's having it *now*. In the car! I can see the head!'

Freya glanced at Jamie, who got up at a run and raced down the corridor, grabbing a mobile pack from the supply room as he did so.

'Someone will be with you in a moment. Hang on!'

She knew she wouldn't be able to run like Jamie, but he would need back-up. It was freezing out. And there was a frost.

She got to her feet and moved down the corridor as fast as she could, her feet protesting, the babies kicking at the sudden rush of adrenaline in her system. She grabbed extra blankets and slapped the button release to open the doors, then took the stairs.

It would be quicker than waiting for the lift. It was just two flights.

She held her belly with one hand as she hurried down the stairs, her other hand on the rail, and by the time she got to the bottom she was out of breath and the twins were kicking madly. She burst through another set of double doors, hurried across the lobby and pressed the buzzer for the outer doors, feeling a wall of cold air hit her as she raced outside.

There was a car parked in the dropping-off bay, its doors open on one side—the guy from the monitor was in the front and Jamie was crouching by the back. She could see there was already a little bit of ice forming on the path. She hoped the gritters would be along soon…

'That's it, Catherine, push as hard as you can!' she heard Jamie say.

'What have we got?' She pulled her penlight torch from her top pocket and shone it into the interior of the car.

A woman was lying in the back, her dress up around her waist and her baby's head already born. There was no point in trying to get this patient into a wheelchair and whizzed upstairs now. She was going to have this baby in the car.

'Catherine—thirty-nine, forty weeks' gestation.'

'Okay, anything we need to be worried about?'

'Just the cold.'

'I've brought extra blankets.'

Jamie turned to grab them and laid them over the headrest, so they'd be ready when he needed them. He already had his gloves on, had the kit open, and was ready to clip off the cord.

'Catherine, one more push with the next contraction. I want you to push as hard as you can, okay? Let's get this baby out and safe into your arms.'

Catherine nodded furiously, sucked in a huge breath and began to push.

At first nothing happened, and for a brief second Freya worried about there being a possible shoulder dystocia, but then slowly the baby began to emerge. Catherine sucked in another breath and began to push again, and this time the baby slithered out, crying immediately in protest.

'Well done, Catherine!' Jamie had caught the baby and immediately put it into its mother's arms, grabbing the blankets to drape over them both before he clipped and cut the cord.

'Oh, my God!' Catherine cried, looking down at her baby with love and joy.

'You did it! You gave birth in the car!' cried the new dad. 'The upholstery's probably ruined, but I don't care!'

Behind her, Freya heard the doors open and Mona appeared, pushing a wheelchair. They needed to get the new mum and baby inside so they could do the proper checks and get the placenta delivered.

Jamie took the baby and passed it to Freya, so that he could help get Catherine out of the car, lowering her gently into the wheelchair. She was shivering and shaking, so he wrapped the last blanket around her shoulders.

'Let's get her inside.'

They all hurried into the lobby, and Freya pressed the button for the lift before passing the baby back to its mother.

Catherine gazed into the loving eyes of her husband. 'We have a *son*!'

The man laid his forehead against his wife's and kissed her. 'We do. Well done! I'm so proud of you.'

He turned to look at Freya and Jamie.

'I'm Martin—pleased to meet you.' He shook their hands. 'This little one is so precious to us. He's an IVF baby.'

'Congratulations.'

'We thought we'd left it too late, but now we have him. A son. Thank you all so much!'

'Catherine did all the hard work,' said Freya, and smiled.

The lift doors pinged open and they wheeled Catherine through to an empty room and helped her onto the bed. They injected the syntocinon and the placenta was delivered almost without Catherine noticing as she cradled her little boy.

'Have you thought of a name yet?' asked Freya, who'd donned gloves and was beginning to check it.

Catherine smiled wanly, looking tired. 'Jackson.'

'That's a beautiful name.'

But something was wrong. The placenta was not as it should be. Freya felt the hairs go up on the back of her neck and instinctively knew. Catherine had gone incredibly pale, and now she rested her head back against the pillow.

She caught the baby before Catherine could drop him. 'Martin, take the baby!'

'What's going on?'

Jamie lifted up the sheet and grimaced. 'Haemorrhage.'

He smacked the red button behind Catherine's head and an alarm sounded. Before they knew it the room was filling with people and Catherine was being whisked out on her bed, headed for Theatre. Jamie went with them.

Freya was left with Martin and the baby, in a room with blood all over the floor.

'What just happened?' asked Martin.

'It looks like Catherine is losing too much blood.' She examined the placenta more and realised there was a piece missing. 'Retained placenta. That's why she began to bleed so heavily.' She laid a hand upon his arm. 'They'll look after her.'

'I *can't* lose her. I can't lose my wife!'

'Come and take a seat, Martin.'

She guided him safely to a chair and helped him sit. She needed to examine the baby, but she was very conscious of the fact that Martin would probably be reluctant to hand his son over right now.

'Emergencies can be frightening, but she was in the right place when it happened. If she'd given birth earlier and you hadn't made it here… You did, though. She's in good hands.'

'She'll be okay?'

'Everyone will do their best.'

She couldn't promise him anything. She couldn't tell him everything would be all right because she didn't know. Haemorrhages happened, and sometimes they went badly. The medical team would do everything they could for her.

'I need to check Jackson. I'll just take him over to this cot—is that okay? You can come with me. Watch what I'm doing.'

He nodded and handed her the baby.

Freya took him gently and with the utmost respect. This man had just watched his wife collapse and be taken from him. He felt lost and bereft, and the only thing he had to cling on to with any certainty was his son.

She decided to talk him through it, so he would understand all that she was doing. If he understood what she was doing perhaps he would feel he had a bit of control over *something*.

'First I'll check his breathing.' She looked to Martin to make sure he was listening.

He nodded.

'He cried immediately after birth, and his respiratory rate is good, so he scores two points on the APGAR scale. The scale is out of ten points overall, and the higher the score, the better.'

'Okay…'

'Now I'm going to use my stethoscope to check his heart rate, and this is the most important.'

She put the earbuds in her ears and laid the stethoscope on Jackson's chest. Over a hundred beats per minute.

'He scores two for this as well. His heart rate is *good*, Martin.'

'Good.'

'Next I need to check his muscle tone, and I can see here that he has good active motion, so again he scores two.'

She talked Martin through checking for a grimace response or reflex irritability, and because Jackson began to cry she again scored him two.

'And now skin colour. His entire body is nicely pink, except his hands and feet, but that's normal. His circulation is good, so that's another point. A score of nine. You have a healthy little baby boy, Martin.' She wrapped Jackson up again and handed him back to his father. 'Do you have clothes and a nappy for him?'

Martin thought for a moment. 'Oh, it's all in the car.'

It was important to get Jackson dressed and wrapped up warmly. 'I can go and fetch them for you, if you want?'

'Would you mind?'

'Of course not.'

He reached into his back pocket and pulled out some keys. 'It's all in the boot. The lock release is on the key fob.'

'Okay. I'll do that, and then I'll get you a cup of tea. I think you've earned it.'

'You too, I would imagine.' He looked at her belly. 'How far along are you?'

'Seven months. With twins.'

'Life's about to get crazy for us all, then?'

She nodded. He had no idea how crazy her life already was.

'I'll be back in a few minutes. Any problems, just hit the orange call button on the side of the bed. Someone will come and check on you.'

She closed the door behind her and began to waddle down the corridor once again.

Boy, were her ankles killing her! And what a night shift this was turning out to be! The last time she'd helped deliver a baby in a car parked outside it had been in the middle of summer, when the nights were a lot warmer and they didn't have to worry about tiny babies freezing in the night air.

And this had been her first delivery working with Jamie. Usually they got to work alone, sometimes with another midwife, but she'd not yet had the chance to watch him in action like that. She'd been with him in Theatre before, but that had been different—their patient had been unconscious under a general anaesthetic, because it had been an emergency delivery.

Tonight she'd seen how good he was with a patient. How calm and encouraging. How he'd coached his patient to breathe and push. She could see why he loved midwifery so much, because he'd simply been alive with all that had been going on around him, and even though it had been an unusual delivery, out of the hospital, he had remained cool and in control. Even when the haemorrhage had begun he had worked quickly and calmly.

The lift doors pinged open. She didn't feel like taking the stairs again so soon. She waddled her way across the lobby and opened the double doors to go outside. The cold air hit her again and she glanced down at the keys in her hand to see which side of the fob she needed to open the boot of the car.

She walked straight out, without thinking, onto the pathway, and it happened almost instantly.

Her feet began to slide on the black ice, she lost her footing and slipped and, not having any control over her centre of gravity, she went up into the air backwards, her arms flailing, and landed heavily on the ground, the back of her head smacking hard onto the concrete.

Pain shot through her skull and her back and her belly. She reached up to rub at her head, but felt the world begin to fade and grow dark.

The last thing she saw was the clear dark sky, inky black with shining stars twinkling way beyond her, and then there was the sight of two men in dark suits appearing over her, one reaching into his jacket for a walkie-talkie and saying something in a language she didn't understand.

She closed her eyes and drifted away.

Jamie was relieved. They'd managed to save their patient. Catherine's haemorrhage had been contained, the retained piece of placenta removed and checked. The bleeding had slowed and Catherine's womb had contracted fully. Her pressure was slowly coming back up and her heart rate was getting better.

The surgeons had done it.

He let out a huge sigh of relief and removed his mask and gown, disposing of them in the trash and going to wash his hands, whilst a porter took his patient to a side room for recovery and to be monitored.

It had been touch and go there for a while, he thought as he stood washing his hands. But they had prevailed. *All* of them. Working together to save their patient and give her a chance at life. There was nothing like this feeling in the whole wide world. This miracle they called life. He watched new life coming into the world every day, and it was a privilege to be amongst those who helped women achieve it.

Days like today reiterated for him the rightness of his choice. It had been *right* to leave Majidar, and it had been *right* to pursue this dream of his. Look at what he had done this night. Earlier he'd delivered one baby, safely in a hospital bed, and now he'd safely delivered not only a baby in a car, but a mother too. Everyone in the team had done that.

Outside, he could hear a bit of a commotion. Loud voices. Men. His guards, by the sound of it. What on earth was going on?

He dried his hands on paper towels and disposed of them in the bin. He wanted to see whatever this noise was about, sort it out, and then go check on the new baby. He'd delivered the little boy—it was up to him to write up the notes.

When he pushed through the doors he froze as he saw his security men were on the ward, arguing with Jules. Whatever were they doing in here? Why did they seem so upset? They had strict instructions not to come onto the ward unless there was a just cause.

The only thing he could think of was Freya, but she'd been safe in that delivery room when he'd left with his patient for Theatre, so that left something to do with his brother the King.

Ilias? No, it can't be. He's sick, sometimes, but it can't be now!

Jules threw her hands into the air as the two guards barged past her towards Jamie.

'Jamie, these men—'

'Sadiq? Mujab? What's going on?'

But before they could say anything Jules barged through them and laid a hand upon his arm. 'It's Freya. She's had an accident.'

CHAPTER SIX

IT WAS THE pain she felt first, as she began to become aware of the world once more. Everything felt sore, but the worst thing was her headache. It was as if she had a crown of intense burning fire around her skull. Her mouth felt dry too, and she tried to lick her lips.

'Freya? Open your eyes.'

Jamie.

Jamie was here. Why was he in her bedroom? What had happened?

As she struggled to implement his instruction to open her eyes she began to remember some weird, hazy things.

A woman in a car.

A baby wrapped in blankets in her arms.

The cold.

A set of car keys.

The twinkling stars above.

Two stern-looking men crouching over her, babbling in a language she didn't understand.

And then she remembered.

The black ice.

Slipping on the pavement and falling.

She opened her eyes, struggling to focus, but she could only just make out a face. A man's face. Dark hair and midnight eyes.

'Jamie…'

She saw a relieved smile break across his face and she tried to reach up to touch him, to make sure he was real, but it was as if she was uncoordinated, or didn't have the strength.

'You've had a nasty fall. Knocked yourself out. The babies are okay. You've had a little bleeding, but they're okay. We're keeping you in for monitoring and bed rest.'

Freya blinked as she processed this huge amount of information. 'What? Keeping me in? No.'

She panicked, tried to get up, tried to get out of bed, but dizziness assailed her and she felt his firm hands holding her arms, pressing her down.

'You need to stay in bed.'

'No, I'm—'

'Freya, for once you are going to have to do as you are told!'

And then she heard it in his voice. *Fear.*

He *cared.*

She blinked again and tried to focus on his face, but she just felt so tired. Slowly, inexorably, her eyes closed once again and she drifted off to sleep.

'Concussion?' She stared at Jamie.

'Yes. You're also still bleeding and you have high blood pressure, so you're staying in on bed rest.'

Staying in. In hospital.

Adrenaline was pulsing through her, making her legs twitch. She wanted to run. Wanted to get out of there.

'But the babies are fine, you said.'

'I did.'

'But I need to stay on bed rest? Are you kidding me?'

'What would *you* say to a patient seven months pregnant with twins, who's had a nasty fall, hit her head, has high BP and is bleeding? Would you tell her to carry on, or would you tell her to stay in bed?'

She bit her bottom lip, eyeing the door. He was right, but she didn't want to admit it. She *would* tell a patient in that situation that she needed to stay in. But this was different.

She'd been trapped in a hospital bed before. Lying there, gripping onto the bedrails, whilst a doctor and a nurse debrided the dead tissue from her face. It had felt as if the acid was being splashed onto her all over again. The pain interminable.

Being back in a hospital bed, being told she had to stay there, was making her feel trapped. Claustrophobic. As if she couldn't breathe.

She turned away, upset but not wanting to let him see her cry, her gaze falling on the fruit baskets and the balloons filling her room and all the cards on the windowsill that sent best wishes from her work colleagues and her family.

It was all terribly familiar. She was unable to move, feeling terrified and afraid. Her own life was out of her control. In the hands of doctors.

How had she forgotten what that felt like?

'I'm not sure I can do this,' she whispered.

'You have to.'

'You can't make me. I can discharge myself.'

'You'd have to get past the guards I'll put on your door first.' He raised an eyebrow. Daring her to challenge his authority.

She stared at him. He'd never ordered her about like this before. Never challenged her.

She baulked at his attempt. 'You wouldn't…?'

He leaned forward over the end of the bed. 'Try me. I've let you do this your way ever since day one. I have acquiesced to your wishes and tried my best not to upset you. But, damn you, Freya, if you get out of that bed and endanger yourself and those babies then, so help me, I will not be held responsible for my actions!'

He meant it. Every word.

She crossed her arms and looked away.

Again her life was being taken out of her control by other people. She had vowed never to let that happen to her again. This was *her* life and she wanted to be the one in charge, making all the decisions.

However, she had no doubt that he would post guards on her door, and then everyone would know who Jamie was. And as soon as that little nugget got out her life would most definitely not be her own. There would be reporters and gossip and her happy, quiet little life, hidden away on the night shift, would be destroyed.

'Fine.'

It wasn't fine. Far from it. But this wasn't just about her any more. She wasn't in this bed alone. She had two babies to think of.

He stared hard at her, his hands on his hips. 'Fine?'

'I'll stay in bed.'

'Good.'

'But on one condition.'

There was that eyebrow again. Wary. 'Yes?'

'Someone brings me a goddamned strawberry milkshake!'

There was the ghost of a smile and then he bowed, almost to the floor. 'Yes, Your Majesty.'

Freya was a cranky patient. Short on temper, irritable, bad of mood. Nervous.

But didn't they say that medics made the worst patients?

'I know it's difficult, but you need to try and relax,' he'd told her.

She'd glared at him. 'How can I? When being here reminds me of what it was like before?'

He'd placed his hand on hers. 'I know. But this is different. No one is going to hurt you now. I won't let them.'

She'd had another scan, and the babies looked fine. The consultant believed the bleeding was coming from a small lesion on her cervix, but it was nothing sinister. They'd tested it and believed the lesion had occurred as a result of her fall. The pressure of two babies on her cervix as well as the severity of the impact of her hitting the concrete had caused a small tear.

He'd given her books to read, had brought delicious yet healthy treats, and he would often sit with her, slowly massaging her feet or her shoulders as she tried to relax.

His favourite moments were spent watching her as she read. The small divot that formed between her brows, the cute way she sometimes bit her bottom lip, the way she would hurriedly turn the page, as if she just couldn't wait to find out what would happen next. Those were the moments when she forgot where she was.

She looked up at him and caught him staring. 'What are you doing?'

He smiled. 'Looking at you.'

Freya frowned and smiled at the same time. 'Well, don't.'

'Why not?'

'It's weird. I don't like people looking at me.'

'No, and you don't like people making assumptions about what happened to you. You don't like people showing sympathy. Was I doing *any* of those things?'

She looked as if she was thinking about that. 'I guess not.'

'Well, then, I'll continue to look at you.'

'But why?'

'Because I like doing it.'

It was true. He did. She was such a complicated person, prickly when scared, but fascinating. And she really was beautiful. Outwardly and inside. Her scars—shocking because of how she'd got them—were totally a part of her character. Who she was.

'But why?' She really sounded confused.

He sighed. 'Does it ever occur to you that you might be worth looking at?'

Her eyes clouded over. 'No.'

'Well, then, you're wrong.'

'Are you sure *you* didn't get the bump on the head? Perhaps you should be lying here instead of me?'

'Perhaps I should be lying *next* to you? Beside you?'

That stopped her from speaking. She immediately looked down at her book, tried to read on, but he could see that she wasn't taking anything in.

Eventually she looked up at him, exasperated, and said, 'You can't say things like that, Jamie. It's not fair.'

'Even if it's true?'

'Even if it's true. Even if you did want to be lying here next to me you shouldn't say it—because then I start to get the feelings, and I don't want to get the feelings, because some day you're going to leave. You'll leave us, Jamie, you *will*. You can't deny that.'

No. He couldn't. She was right. One day he would get called back and then what? If he tried to start a relationship with this woman it would always be there, hanging over them like a swinging blade, ready to fall down and sever them in two. Was that fair? On either of them? On the babies?

'I'll go and make us some tea.'

He got up and slipped from the room, his mind dark with thoughts of ascension to the throne and responsibility and living a life behind walls. Never to enjoy himself again. Never to deliver another baby.

Away from Freya and his sons.

He fought the urge to punch a wall. It was all just so maddening! He'd fought to get access into her life, which she had finally given, and they were becoming used to one another, liked one another—but for what?

Either way, he was going to lose someone or something.

Majidar, or Freya and the babies.

Or maybe he'd just lose himself?

'Mona, please stop fussing.' Freya laid a hand on her friend's as she continued to fiddle about with Freya's sheets.

If she was going to visit, she'd prefer it if her friend just kept her up to date with what was happening on the ward, had a cup of tea with her and chatted. Not fussed about like an old mother hen.

'I can't help it.'

Freya smiled. 'Sit. Eat one of these.' She passed over a box of chocolates that her mum had brought on her last visit. 'They're truffles.'

'Oh! Okay.' Mona took the box.

'The praline one is nice.'

Mona checked to see which one that was, and then popped it into her mouth and began to make appreciative sounds.

'Told you.'

Freya lay back against the pillows and turned away from the bright light pouring in through the window. It made a pleasant change from the dark, grey wintry days they had been having recently. Life was passing her by and she was still stuck here.

'I got the Christmas decorations out just now. I'm going to pop them up later.'

Freya frowned. 'It's still November.'

'It's never too early.'

'I beg to differ.'

'Well, *you* would. You've always been a Grumpus around Christmas.'

Mona was wrong. Freya loved Christmas. But these last

few years she'd begun to resent it. Everyone she knew was married or in a relationship, or had kids, or both, so they had a reason to enjoy Christmas. They were with their loved ones. They were making memories. For Freya every Christmas was spent with her mum, and though she loved her mum it wasn't what Freya wanted.

She had big dreams of what Christmas should be. Of a Christmas morning on which she could sit and watch her children open their presents with squeals of delight. Of a festive season during which she could go out and build snowmen and have snowball fights, visit Santa in his grotto, go to see a pantomime.

Her mum was great company, but she didn't want to do any of those things. She liked a quiet, understated Christmas, where her only concern was whether the turkey would be cooked and whether they'd finish eating in time to watch the Queen's Speech. Then she'd fall asleep in her chair, until Freya woke her later in the evening to see if she wanted a mince pie.

'Wait 'til next Christmas. You'll have twins!' exclaimed Mona.

Freya nodded. But would she be alone with them? Or would Jamie be there? How was she going to cope with raising two babies? She would have to brave *everything*. Living during the day time. Seeing all those people. Changing her shifts at work because the hospital nursery only took children during daylight hours.

Her whole life was going to change.

It wasn't meant to have happened like this! She was meant to have been *happy*! Thrilled that she was having children. She *was* thrilled, but it wasn't turning out to be the fairy tale she'd imagined it would be.

'Are you and Jamie spending Christmas together?'

'I think he's working.'

'But he'll have *some* time at home. Are you going to do anything special?'

'I don't think so. I'll be at Mum's, as usual, I guess.'

'You aren't spending *any* time together?'

This line of questioning was making her feel very uncomfortable. 'He hasn't said anything.'

Mona handed her back the box of chocolates, looking sceptical. 'Is there something you're not telling me, Freya?'

'Like what?'

'About Jamie? Who were those men in suits? They looked like bodyguards.'

She hurried to try and put Mona off the scent. 'Oh, I don't know. Just some guys who were passing, I think.'

'Well, for guys who were *just passing* they hang around a lot. And they talk to Jamie a lot.'

'He's probably just thanking them.'

'He's not some secret undercover boss, or anything?' Mona grinned. 'Because if he's secretly the CEO of the NHS then I think we need to enlighten him about a few things.'

Freya laughed. 'Jamie? No!'

'I just think it's strange, that's all. They even wear those earpiece things…like Secret Service guys.'

Thank goodness she didn't blush as she'd used to. 'Really? That's weird. But, no, Jamie is just a midwife. Honestly.'

Mona nodded, watching her. 'Okay.' She got up and went to the door, put her hand on the handle. 'You know, I still don't understand why you two aren't together. You obviously slept together, and you seem to get on. So what's keeping you apart?'

Freya shrugged. 'He's a temp. He'll be leaving soon—there's no point.'

'But Sarah from HR told me that they've offered him a permanent post, which he's accepted.'

That was news to Freya. Why hadn't Jamie told her? That he was planning on sticking around for her and the babies?

'I didn't know.'

'It's clear he has feelings for you.'

Her smile was tinged with sadness. 'For the babies, not me.'

'You really think that? I've seen the way his eyes shine when he talks about you. The way his face lights up.'

'He talks about me?'

Mona nodded. 'Frequently. He *cares* about you. You must see it.'

She cared about him, too. Probably more than she should. But she'd been holding back. Afraid of showing any of it. Alone in the day, she dreamed about what it would be like to be with him, and at night her dreams were filled with his smiling face and his steaming hot kisses.

No wonder she woke up cranky. She couldn't have what she wanted the most. Was afraid to let herself have him in case she lost him.

'It's complicated.'

Mona laughed. 'When isn't it? Look, I've got to go, but he'll be in later. Do me a favour and be nice to him. He's doing his best, but you're a bloody expert at keeping people at a distance. Let him care for you, Freya. He's not Mike.'

No. She knew that.

'It's difficult.'

'"*'Tis better to have loved and lost, than never to have loved at all.*" Who was it who said that? Was it Shakespeare?'

'I never was any good at English.'

'Me neither.' Mona opened the door. 'But we're very good at chemistry!'

And she gave Freya a tiny wave before she headed off to do her shift.

Freya lay there on the bed, thinking over all the things her friend had said. Jamie was staying on permanently. He had feelings for her. She had feelings for him. The babies would be here soon.

We could be a family.

If she were only brave enough to let it happen.

Was it better to love someone and then lose them than not to love at all?

It sounded to her like devastation. And Jamie's mother had died of it.

Could she let her babies grow to love their father in the knowledge that he would desert them at some point? And would her babies one day leave her too?

But the temptation to give in, to try it, to accept the love and care that Jamie clearly wanted to give her, was extremely potent. The proximity of all that imagined happiness was intoxicating.

If she gave herself the chance to explore that happiness, to cast all her concerns to one side and just live in the moment with him, what would that be like?

Her heart soared at the idea. At the hope. At the possibility of such happiness.

Didn't she deserve it?

No matter how short-lived?

Jamie opened the door to Freya's room and stopped, frozen in place, when he saw how she looked.

Out of bed. Getting dressed.

Smiling. No. *Beaming.*

'What's happened?'

'I've been told I can go home and start my maternity leave. As long as I rest.'

He frowned and went to the end of her bed, picked up her chart and began to read it. 'The bleeding's stopped?'

'For almost a day now.'

'And your blood pressure is down?'

'Almost to normal levels. I can get out of here. You've no idea how much I've longed to hear that.'

'Well, I know how much you've been bugging your consultant about it, so I have a fair idea.'

He smiled. These last few days had been hard for her.

'All this bed rest… I could have done it at home in the first place. There was no need for me to have taken up a bed.'

'There was *every* need. Here, I've brought you a milk-shake.' He passed her the drink he'd bought from the café downstairs. 'Why don't you sit down? I'll do your packing for you.'

She held up her hand. 'No, thank you! I don't need you seeing all my knickers and things.'

He smiled, picking up a pair of unflattering maternity pants. 'Why ever not? I've seen—no, *tasted*—what's underneath.'

And then he grinned, because he saw how flustered that comment made her.

She snatched them from him. 'I haven't been allowed to do anything for myself for days now. At least let me do this.'

'Okay.' He sank onto her bed and watched her busily pack her holdall, the excitement in her eyes at finally being able to leave the hospital almost palpable. 'I hope when you get home you do actually rest.'

'I'm fine. I've been discharged. There are things I have to get done. The nursery isn't ready and—'

'Then I'll help you. Tell me what needs doing and I'll get it sorted.'

She stopped to look at him. 'How will you have the time? Now that you're a *permanent* member of staff? Yes, I know about that. Why didn't you tell me?'

'I was waiting until I'd actually signed the contract.

Which I did about twenty minutes ago. So here I am. Telling you. Don't change the subject.'

'I'm not.'

'You did. Now, what do you need help with in the nursery?'

'I've ordered two cribs, which are going to be delivered, and some furniture—all of which will need building.'

He nodded. 'I'll do it.'

'I can do it. I'm not helpless.'

'I know you're not, Freya, but you are still meant to be resting.'

'Don't I get *any* say in this?'

He thought for a moment, then smiled. 'No.'

She smiled back. 'You're infuriating, you know?'

Jamie nodded, happy to be so if it meant she was taking it easy. He had no doubt that if he let her go home without supervision she'd be up ladders and cleaning and painting and building wardrobes and putting herself straight back into a hospital bed. He couldn't allow that to happen.

'How are you getting home?'

'Mum's coming over on the bus, then we're using my car to drive back. It's been in the staff car park ever since my fall on the ice.'

'Okay.' He knew her mum would take good care of her. 'I'm on shift now until seven, but I'll pop round straight after—see what needs doing and formulate a plan.'

'You don't need to babysit me.'

'I know.' He stood up and dropped a kiss onto her cheek.

She looked a little startled. 'I'm a grown woman.'

He smiled again, as his mind handily provided him with flashbacks to that steamy night many moons ago. 'I *know*.'

'Stop it.'

'What?'

'Remembering what we did.'

'I'm not allowed to remember?'

'Not that, no.'

'Why?'

'Because of the way it makes you smile. The way you look like you hope it will happen again.'

He stood up and stepped between her and the holdall. 'Would that be a bad thing?'

She was breathing heavily, and licked her lips. She tried her hardest not to look at his lips, but failed.

'Yes.'

'We wouldn't know unless we tried.'

She licked her lips again, bit the lower one and then looked away. Then back again.

'I'm on bed rest.'

'We could be in bed.' He smiled.

She swallowed. 'Please don't, Jamie.'

'Why?'

'Because we *can't*!'

'Who says?'

'The consultant. He said no sex.'

Well, wasn't *that* interesting? Freya herself wasn't saying no. She wasn't turning him down because *she* didn't want to, but because it was a strict order from her consultant.

He smiled, feeling a swell of joy not only in his heart, but elsewhere too.

'I can wait.' He paused to stare at her, then laid his hand on her arm, stilling her, drawing her close. 'Won't you give us a chance to be together?' he whispered.

Her eyes looked up at him, full of conflict, yearning and desire.

Until he bent his head and kissed her.

CHAPTER SEVEN

HIS LIPS WERE SOFT, gentle. It was the most tender kiss. As his lips met hers it was as if the world slowed. Everything around her faded into nothingness, and all that mattered, all she could feel, was his lips pressed against her own. She forgot her scars, forgot her fears.

Tenderness. Heat. Her heart racing inside her chest… pounding away within the cage that contained it.

He's kissing me!

She'd thought about what it would be like to kiss him again, without hiding behind masks and anonymity.

She knew him now. Knew who Jamie was. *What* he was. He'd become her friend as well as her colleague, and somehow, without her realising how, he had wormed his way into her affections. She cared for him. Worried about him. Feared for their future.

And she had wondered what it might be like for them both if their lives were different. If he weren't heir to the throne of some faraway kingdom, and if she weren't the woman who hid behind the scars on her face.

And now he's kissing me.

She felt herself sink further into his embrace. Felt her body press up against his. God, she needed this! Needed *him*.

Freya had never imagined losing herself to something so wonderful as this.

But it felt so right. It felt so *good*.

She was almost dizzy with all the sensations running rampant through her system, with all the emotions she was experiencing. What was it doing to her blood pressure?

I need to breathe.

She pulled back, looked at him, her eyes dazed with confusion.

'You kissed me.'

'Yes.' His eyes shone darkly, with a heat in them she had never noticed before.

'Why?' It was a whisper.

'Because I needed to.'

'Needed?'

A smile. 'Wanted.'

'Me?'

Another smile. Broader this time. 'Of *course* you. When will you start to believe that?'

Her words caught in her throat for a moment, a painful lump of disbelief that she had to swallow down, blinking rapidly to stop the tears from falling.

'I see you, Freya. Who you are. I see the woman who stands before me today and she's the bravest, strongest, most wonderful woman I know.'

'I don't…'

'You keep comparing yourself to who you used to be. I don't know who you used to be, or what you looked like before, and I don't need to know. That was the past. What matters is the present, the *now*, and the woman before me is beautiful. She is caring and loving, fragile yet strong and courageous. As beautiful on the inside as she is on the outside. That's who I see.'

He tucked a strand of her hair behind her ear.

'But…'

'No buts. No whys or maybes. Just accept it. Can you

accept the fact that I have feelings for you and that I'd like us to be more than just friends?'

It was everything she could possibly want to hear. Everything she's thought she'd never hear. And here he was. This man. This drop-dead gorgeous, handsome *prince* was saying it to her!

And suddenly she felt afraid. Afraid of what it all meant. If she accepted it—if she let him in—then wouldn't she be making herself vulnerable all over again?

But she was teetering on the edge of a giant abyss and she wanted to fall for him. Wanted to believe so much!

Her heartbeat pounded in her ears. She felt hot and dizzy with it all. But she wasn't ill. Just lovesick. And she wanted that happiness, even if it was just for a short while. She'd accept it and have him for as long as she could have him.

'I can.'

Hesitantly she smiled at him, watching as his face lit up.

He let out a heavy breath and beamed at her, before pulling her back into his embrace. 'Then let's get you safely home and we'll take it from there.'

It was strange to be back home. Her mum put on a pot of decaffeinated coffee to brew. Freya sat on the couch, her feet up, cradling her mug.

'I think Jamie and I are going to give things a go.'

It felt odd to say it. *Jamie and I.*

Her mum smiled at her over her own mug. 'Really? Oh, I'm so pleased to hear that. I really am.'

'We don't know what's going to happen, but we're going to take it a day at a time. It's all we *can* do, really.'

'Stop downplaying it, Freya. You're already making it sound like it's doomed before it starts.'

'I'm just being realistic.'

'No, you're trying to protect yourself before you get hurt and it won't work that way. If you are going to give it a try with Jamie then you've got to be in it wholeheartedly. One hundred per cent. Not with one foot already out of the door.'

'You think that's what I'm doing?'

Her mum put her mug down and came over to sit beside her. Took her hand in her own. 'I know that's what you're doing. But Jamie's different. He's honourable and kind and I think he cares deeply about you. You can't play with his feelings because you're scared. Be in it totally, give everything of your heart, one hundred per cent, or don't give anything at all.'

Tears began to sting her eyes. 'I want to be with him.'

'Then do it.'

'But what if—?'

'No what ifs, Freya. No fear. You are having two babies with this man, and whether it works or not he will be in your life until your last day on this earth. So make it work. Give him your whole heart, not half of it.'

The tears began to fall. 'I think I might love him.'

Her mum was tearing up too.

'Then you both have my blessing.'

She leaned forward and kissed Freya on the cheek, then pulled her into a hug.

Casey Benson looked calm. She was sitting in her hospital bed, serenely tapping a message into her mobile phone. But then again, Jamie mused, Casey had been through this three times before. She was an experienced mother.

'Hi, Casey. I'm Jamie, and I'm going to be your midwife today.'

She turned and smiled, her smile freezing slightly when she saw him. 'I get *you*?'

He nodded. 'You do.'

'For when I give birth?'

'That's the plan!'

'Oh.'

She looked a little perturbed, and he wondered if she was feeling uncomfortable at having a man deliver her child.

'Is that all right?'

'Yes! Course it is, it's just…'

'Yes?'

She blushed. 'You're very attractive.'

Well, that was very flattering, but he didn't understand why that should be a problem.

'An attractive man down at my—' She stopped and blushed again. Her face going very red.

He tried to change the subject, feeling amused. 'Are you here alone today?'

'I always do this alone.'

He saw on her file that she was married. 'Is your husband at work?'

'You could say that. He's in the Antarctic.'

'Oh, really? Doing what?'

'He's part of a research team studying the biodiversity of a special organism, or some such thing. He hopes to be back when this one is about two months old.'

'No other family who can be with you?'

'There is, but I'm happy to do this myself. It never takes long—they usually pop out after an hour or two. I'll be home in a few hours.'

'Who's babysitting the others?'

'Mum is. She's not very good with blood and gore, but she's an absolute whizz with spilt milk and baby dribble, so she's keeping an eye on the troops.'

'Glad to hear it. So it's just you and me, then. Unless you'd like a chaperone?'

She smiled at him over her mobile. 'Just you and me is fine.'

Casey had been right. She did labour easily. Though her contractions were showing up good and strong on the trace she remained calm, breathing easily through each of them as she leaned over the back of her bed, her knees on the mattress.

'You're doing brilliantly, Casey.'

Casey beckoned him over. 'Come and join me for a selfie. Otherwise no one is going to believe I had *you* deliver my baby.'

He capitulated, and put his head close to hers for a photo, smiling as the camera on her phone clicked the two of them together.

'You still all right with just the gas and air?'

'Absolutely!' She settled back on her haunches whilst she waited for the next contraction. 'Still all systems go here. Though, if I'm honest with you, I can't believe I'm back here, doing this again. I swore the last time that Benji was going to be my last baby, yet here I am.'

'Does your husband get to come home often?'

'Every six months. He gets home for about four weeks and then he goes off again. And obviously, because we haven't seen each other in all that time, we're very keen to see each other as much as we can, if you get my drift, and that usually results in me peeing on another of those ruddy sticks. Mind you, I love being a mum. I love all my kids—we have such a great time.'

'Do they miss their dad? What with him not being around?'

'Of course they do! They play up every now and again, but don't all children? They know their dad loves them, and that he's off doing some very special scientific work, and it's good for them to see that their dad is dedicated and works hard for a cause he believes in. It's good moral grounding for them.'

'It must be hard for him, too. Being away from his children?'

She nodded. 'It is. But he absolutely adores what he does,

and I don't think he could be away from them unless he did. Why would he lose all that time he could have with them if he was stuck somewhere hating what he did? No, it's good he has that passion. Do you have kids?'

He smiled. 'I have two on the way.'

'Twins, huh? Wow. But I imagine you'll be the same. You must love what you do? Because when they're born… when they're finally here and you hold them in your own arms…you can't imagine spending any time away from them. Missing any of it. Not unless you love what you do.'

He nodded. She was right. He wanted to spend as much time as he possibly could with his babies when they came. And if at some point he got called away to be King of Majidar that would be his crisis point.

Because he could *never* imagine himself wanting to do that. Could not imagine himself being stuck inside a glittering palace, getting bogged down in politics and laws, stuff he didn't care for, when instead he could be with his children. Doing a job he adored.

Majidar was never meant to be his. Ilias should have had his own heirs. He was a midwife. It had always been his calling. His vocation. He'd never wanted to rule, but it was the family he had been born into. And he felt a responsibility there, too.

The people of Majidar expected him to be their next King. And he knew, because it had been reported to him, that his people were *proud* of him for following his passion, for working far away from them in another country, bringing life into the world. But they knew he would come back. They *expected* him to come back.

But he wanted to be with his children. And Freya.

Unexpectedly, he had built a life here. Was putting down roots for the first time ever. And it was exciting and thrilling and the most terrifying thing he had ever done.

But it also felt like the *right* thing.

Knowing he would have to leave at some point, knowing he would have to walk away from them, was killing him inside.

Casey pulled herself back up over the bed railing and began to breathe heavily. 'Okay, let's do this.'

'I'm ready when you are.'

Casey gave birth to a healthy seven-pound, four-ounce baby girl that she called Francesca.

Jamie escorted her through to Postnatal for a little while and, as she'd predicted, waved her on her way home a few hours after that.

She'd given him a lot to think about, and he wondered if she'd made light of her situation at home. It had to be hard for her, living as a single parent, with her husband away for long periods of time.

Would that be Freya's life too? Stuck here in England alone? Knowing that he was away, and knowing that he'd put his *duty* to his country before his duty to his own children?

Casey was able to do it because she knew her husband was passionate about what he did, and she valued the life lessons she could show her children—that their dad was working hard at something he believed in. That he was doing it for *them*.

Would Freya be able to say the same to their two boys? Jamie *did* believe in the honour and privilege that it would be to sit on his country's throne, but would he be able to like himself for doing something he didn't actually want to do? Forcing himself out of duty?

He arrived at Freya's flat bright and early, knocking on her door and waiting for her to answer.

She opened it and he held up his box. 'I've brought tools.'

She smiled at him. 'Milkshakes or chocolates are my preferred gifts.'

'Maybe, but milkshakes and chocolates can't build bedroom furniture, can they?' He stepped past her, then stopped, turned, smiled and lowered his head to kiss her. 'Almost forgot this part,' he whispered, his lips closing over hers.

He'd missed her. Even more so since spending time with Casey. He felt the need to be with her. Her and the babies. Whilst he could. Her lips were full, soft and warm. She was comforting to him. It made him feel good just to be with her, and already he could feel his cares and worries being soothed away.

He wanted more. Could feel his body awakening to her touch, her presence. But more was forbidden. Which made the idea of it all the more desirable, and he had to pull back, bite his lip and just look at her with adoration and maddening frustration.

'Has everything arrived?'

'It's all in the nursery, awaiting your attention.'

'Good.'

She stared back at him, licked her lips, and he tracked every motion. The way her tongue swept over her lips, wetting them, leaving them glistening, before slipping back into her mouth.

'Can I make you a drink?'

He let out a sigh, imagining what that tongue could do to his body. 'Tea, please.'

He watched her head off to the kitchen and forcibly pushed aside his very sinful thoughts of all the things he wanted to do to her. That would have to wait. They had time. Time, at least, was on their side.

'I thought it might snow.' He followed her and watched her make the tea. 'They've forecast it in the paper.'

Freya laughed cynically. 'Let me tell you something about England, Jamie. They *always* forecast snow. They give us dire warnings every year, but we never get it. We can barely manage a frost down here, near the coast. It's very disappointing, actually.'

He smiled. 'This time last year I was working in Edinburgh, and we had snow. First time I'd ever experienced a heavy snowfall and it was wonderful.'

'Well, you'd better keep a hold of that memory, because you probably won't get it again.' She handed him his tea, smiling. 'Shall we get to it?'

'I'd love to. But apparently there's furniture that needs building.' He smiled.

She smiled back. 'That's what I meant.'

'You can supervise. And pass me things.' He pointed at her. 'No heavy lifting.'

Freya saluted him. 'Yes, sir.'

'Orders from your consultant.'

'I get it—don't worry. Are you sure you don't want something to eat before we start?'

He turned to look at her, devilment in his eyes. 'Freya, what I want to eat is, unfortunately, not on the menu at this moment in time.'

The instructions for the two cots seemed to be written in gibberish, and the pictures showing where to place the locking nuts didn't seem all that clear either. It took over an hour to do the first cot, through a process of elimination, but by the time he'd started the second he actually felt he knew what he was doing.

Freya sat beside him in a rocking chair, reading a book about what to expect in the first year of their child's life. She looked so cute, rocking away, one hand resting on her ample stomach, intensely concentrating on the words. He sat and watched her for a moment, quite unable to believe that this was his family now.

'Good book?'

She closed it and wiggled her eyebrows. 'Scary book. There seems so much to watch out for and worry about.'

'Like what?'

'Like colic, whooping cough, vaccinations and sterilising everything to within an inch of its life! What if they choke on something? What if I wean them too early and it does them more harm than good?' She let out a sigh. 'Being a mum seemed so much easier when it was just hypothetical.'

He could see that she was feeling nervous and needed reassurance. 'We'll be absolutely fine. We can do this. Thousands do.'

'And thousands of parents end up in A&E with their babies—we both know that. They get gastroenteritis and need rehydration drips and monitoring, or they swallow some coin or a marble or a little toy gun—I don't know, *something*—and they need an operation.'

He went to kneel beside her and took her hands in his. 'We can't protect them from everything.'

'But we're their parents. We're meant to protect them from things that will cause them harm!'

'You can't protect them from illness. Germs will get in no matter what you do. And, yes, they might swallow something they shouldn't. I believe I swallowed a small plastic camel when I was two years old, but here I am, absolutely fine and without trauma to my system. It's okay to worry, Freya. It's part of being a parent.'

'But I never thought I'd get the chance at this and now I am! And it's getting closer now, and I'm just worried that I'll get it all wrong!'

'Every mother worries. This is natural. Let's focus our energies on things we can control—like baby names, for instance. Have you had any thoughts on what you might want to call them?'

She let out a sigh and he saw a small smile begin to

emerge as she focused on happier things. 'I quite like the name Samuel.'

He mused on it. 'Samuel MacFadden. That sounds like a good strong name.'

She smiled. 'Samuel Al Bakhari. I'm going to give them your surname.'

He sat back on his heels, pleasantly surprised. And honoured. 'You are?'

'And I figured if you let me pick their first names, then you could pick their middle names. Something Arabic? So they get a name from both our cultures?'

'Wow... I don't quite know what to say.' The gesture meant a lot to him.

'Just suggest some good names!'

He smiled back at her, stroking her beautiful face and staring into her eyes.

They decided upon Samuel Dawoud and James Kadin.

'Good, strong names.'

'For good, strong boys.' She rubbed her tummy. 'They'll be here soon.'

He squeezed her hands. 'And we'll be ready for them.'

Once the cots were up, and Jamie had powered through constructing a wardrobe, a baby-changing station and a set of drawers, Freya cooked them both something to eat.

It was wonderful to have Jamie there with her, now that she was determined to step forward into the future with him at her side, instead of fighting him every inch of the way. Watching him work on the bedroom furniture, seeing how careful he was, how focused, making sure everything was put together correctly and securely, made her feel warm inside.

'I can't wait to see them in those cots.'

She smiled. 'Me too.'

'Can't wait to see their little faces. Hold them. Love them.'

She knew exactly what he meant. She felt it too.

Passing him a bowl of pasta, she sat down on the couch opposite. 'Thanks for today, Jamie. It feels good to see the nursery taking shape. Makes me feel like I'm a bit more prepared.'

'I'm glad. I'd do anything to make this easier for you.'

'It must be difficult for you too. Not knowing what's ahead?'

He nodded. 'I don't want to screw this up. Us... The twins... Majidar...'

'I never wanted to come between you and your country, Jamie. You have to know that.'

'Of course I do.'

'I just feel like...'

'Like what?'

'Like I'm making you choose. And I know I won't win.'

He put the pasta down. Sat beside her. Kissed her on the forehead. 'This isn't your fault. You're not making me do anything I don't want to.'

'But you have a responsibility to your people. A million of them. I'm just one. Soon to be three. I can't compete with that. I don't want to think of the day when you'll have to make that decision.'

His eyes darkened as he felt her pain. 'I don't want to leave you. You know that?'

She nodded.

Jamie let out a heavy sigh. 'We can't worry about that yet. It could be decades away. Let's consider brighter, better things.' He thought for a moment. 'What do you want to do over Christmas?'

Christmas? She hadn't really thought about it. She'd figured she'd be spending it in the normal way. 'I'll be at my mum's house.'

'I'm scheduled to work over Christmas. The afternoon shift from two p.m. But I wondered…well, I *hoped* that maybe we could spend the morning together?'

'Oh… Okay… Well, why don't you come to Mum's? It'll give you both an opportunity to get to know each other a bit more and we'll get to share the day together. We eat at midday, so you'll get lunch.'

He smiled and nodded. 'Sounds good. I'd love that—thank you.'

'I'll let Mum know there'll be an extra mouth to feed!'

Freya felt good about that. This would be her last Christmas without children. Maybe next year she and Jamie would be living together? Inviting her mum over to their place? Cooking for her instead? And there would be the joy of watching the babies rip open their presents. Would they be toddling by then? Crawling? Making mischief between the pair of them? Babbling away in their own little twins' language?

The idea of it made her smile. Made her feel warm and happy. Her future with Jamie might be uncertain, but whilst he was here they would make good memories together. Memories they would both cherish. Every moment would be precious.

Life was changing—and for the better. She couldn't quite believe she'd resisted this so much! Look at how well she and Jamie got along! All she'd needed to do was give him a chance. Give *them* a chance. And, even though she still felt apprehensive about the future, everything was looking much brighter now.

Maybe they *could* do this?

Together.

'We're going out.'

Freya frowned at Jamie. She'd just opened the door to him, expecting to invite him in for them to spend the evening together the way they usually did—watching a movie, eating popcorn, that kind of thing. She hadn't been expecting to go out, and she was wearing jogging bottoms and a maternity tee shirt that was having difficulty stretching over her twins-filled abdomen.

'What?'

'I've arranged something special. Just for you. So get dressed—we're heading into town.'

'Into town? Oh, no, I really don't think that I could—'

He pressed a finger to her lips, silencing her with a smile. 'Trust me.'

Freya stared back at him. Going into town was not her favourite thing. She'd done it a few times after the attack. It had been part of her therapy—heading out with her counsellor to show that she was okay being around crowds of people.

She'd been in a crowd of people when Mike had thrown the acid at her. It had happened in town. On the main street. He'd been lucky it hadn't hit anyone else and scarred them too. For a long time she'd been afraid to go out. Had almost become agoraphobic. Her counsellor had worked on exposing her gradually, getting her back out into the world.

It had been a long, difficult road, but one she had accomplished with much pride, even standing in the very spot on which the attack had happened, her eyes closed, breathing everything in—the familiar sounds of people all around her, the faint music from a clothing store playing far away, a busker a little further along, the aroma of freshly brewed coffee, the ringing of the church bells, the hustle and bustle of life all around her.

She'd done it. It had been fine. Until she'd opened her eyes.

Then she'd seen it. The stares of people passing her by. Had watched them notice her scarred face, seen the looks of repulsion, the pity, the sympathy, the recognition of who she was—that girl from the news who was attacked.

Her counsellor had told her not to worry about other people's reactions, but that had been easy for her to say—she hadn't been the one with a ruined face. It had been horrible to be looked at so differently.

Freya had always been pretty. Had always been aware that people looked at her with appreciation. That they'd wanted to know her, be her friend. She'd never had to try too hard with her looks, hadn't needed loads of make-up or anything like that. A natural beauty—wasn't that what everyone had said?

It had been torture to see that change. To look in the mirror and see what everyone else saw. Her face told her story. Her past relationship, her pain, her journey to recovery. Every operation, every painful skin graft—all there on her face for the world to judge. She would always be 'the acid girl'.

It was easier not to expose herself to people like that. To work nights, to order online, to keep to her small group of family and friends and the patients she saw on shift.

She had to admit that her patients had all been fine with her. No one had reacted with shock or pity. One or two had asked her what had happened, but the majority had decided it wasn't any of their business and hadn't asked at all.

Perhaps she needed to let the rest of the world have that chance?

'What have you got planned?' she asked nervously.

'It's a surprise.'

'I don't like surprises. Besides, I'm meant to be resting,' she added, trying to use her pregnancy as one last grip on the door.

'I've taken all that into consideration.' He stepped into her flat and closed the door behind him. 'Now, go and get dressed.'

'Jamie, the town…for me, it's—'

He pulled her towards him and held her tightly. 'I know. I *do*. But we won't be going anywhere near that part of it and I'll be with you every step of the way.'

What had he got planned? She didn't like surprises. Surprises were bad news.

Reluctantly she rummaged in her wardrobe for anything that might fit her and found a pair of maternity jeans and a pink hoodie that said *I'm Doing Nine Months Inside*.

Then she brushed her hair, put it up into a ponytail, added a bit of mascara to her lashes and some lip gloss, a quick spritz of perfume and stood in front of the mirror. Psyching herself up for this 'surprise'.

When she was ready she headed out, grabbing her handbag. 'Will I do?'

His face lit up in a smile. 'You look perfect.'

'Where are you taking me?'

'I told you—it's a surprise.' He got her coat and helped her put it on, slipping her arms into the sleeves, and then grabbed her long, woolly scarf and wrapped it gently around her neck, before dropping a soft kiss on her nose.

She followed him down to his car and he opened the door for her, closing it again once she was safely inside.

Butterflies gathered in her belly as he drove her towards town. They could be going *anywhere*. To do *anything*! She was meant to be resting—which was why Jamie had been spending every spare moment with her when he wasn't on shift. How he got any sleep and managed to function, she had no idea, but he must be power-napping or something, because he always seemed wide awake when he was with her.

And she liked it that he was spending this time with her. It was good for them. Snuggling on the sofa, holding hands, each kiss he gave her heartfelt and meaningful, warming her, making her feel safe and secure and loved.

Oh, there'd been times when she'd wanted a whole lot more! But they were both on strict instructions. No sex until the babies were born! And, as they were determined to keep the twins inside her for as long as they could, they were both being extremely diligent about that rule.

Jamie drove them through the streets towards town, and Freya had to admit it looked really pretty at night. The Christmas lights were up, adorning most of the streets in the city centre, Christmas music was being played, and everyone seemed to be in a happy, relaxed mood. Perhaps everyone was feeling goodwill to all men?

Jamie parked in a small service road to the rear of one of the big shopping centres.

Where on earth were they?

Jamie got out, walked around the outside of the car and then opened her door. 'Madam?'

She smiled nervously. 'Where are we? What are we doing?'

'I need my guys to watch the car, so I've parked here; it means my security looks a little less conspicuous. And I think you'll find that we'll be met in just a moment.'

He pressed a buzzer beside a set of double doors and instantly they were opened by a woman wearing a pretty blue dress and a name tag that read *'Michelle'*.

'Mr Bakhari? Miss MacFadden? Good evening and welcome to The Nesting Site.'

The Nesting Site? She'd read about that store in the local paper when it had opened up a few years ago. It was a stylish baby store, selling everything from plain muslin squares right through to the most hi-tech buggy anyone could possibly hope to purchase. It was exclusive—and a bit pricey, too. She'd heard some of her patients, when they'd come in to give birth, talking about browsing there, just to look at the beautiful things.

'I have a lift on hold, waiting for us.'

Michelle stood back to let them in and Freya breathed in the woman's perfume as she passed her by, feeling completely underdressed in her jeans and hoodie. She leant in towards Jamie for security and comfort, and felt better when he took her hand in his and give it a squeeze.

Michelle was looking at her with a polite smile. 'How many months are you?'

'Seven and a half, but it's twins, so…'

Michelle nodded, as if she understood perfectly. 'I had twins. One of each. Do you know what flavours you're expecting?'

'Two boys.'

Michelle smiled. 'Two princes. How wonderful!'

Freya looked at Jamie in shock. Did this woman know *who* and *what* Jamie was? She'd thought he didn't tell anyone that. But Jamie just smiled enigmatically at her and said nothing.

The lift doors pinged open and Michelle invited them in to the amazing store.

Freya sucked in a breath at all the beautiful things she could see—cribs with white lace curtains, the most beautiful rocking chairs, baby clothes in all manner of colours and designs, from plain white with gold embroidery through to brightly patterned Babygros in pinks and blues and the palest of palettes.

Michelle indicated a large reclining chair, stuffed with cushions, for Freya to sit down upon—which she did, wondering just what was about to happen here.

'I've arranged for us to have the store to ourselves, and for personal shoppers to bring us anything we wish to see. We don't have any clothes yet for the little ones, and I'd like us to get a few things.' Jamie smiled and squeezed her hand once more.

'Jamie, you didn't have to do this. I could have ordered online, like I always do.'

'I thought it would be better to see the items in person, before we buy. And I know you don't like crowds, so we have the place to ourselves. Now, what sort of thing should we look at first?'

'How about their going-home outfits?' Michelle suggested, snapping her fingers at some staff who must be were hidden away beyond Freya's eyeline. 'Would you like some tea? I can have a tray brought in.'

She almost felt dizzy with the possibility of it all.

Was this what it felt like to be a princess?

A princess in a hoodie and jeans...

CHAPTER EIGHT

'JAMIE, THIS FEELS WEIRD.' She leant over to whisper to him.

He smiled at her. 'Why?'

'All these people running around after me. Fetching and carrying. It's not right.'

'It's what *you* do when you're at work. Don't you look after your pregnant mothers? Fetching them cups of tea? Getting them epidurals or pethidine or gas and air? Don't you rub their backs and mop their heads with cool flannels when they need it? Hold their hands?'

She could understand his point. But that was different, surely? That was her *job*. Her patients needed her to do that because that was what she was trained to do. It was what she was there for.

'It's what they're here for, Freya,' Jamie said, echoing her thought process. 'It's what they're paid to do.'

'It just doesn't feel right to be on the receiving end of it, that's all.'

'Enjoy it whilst you can. When Samuel and James get here you'll look back on this moment and wonder why you didn't take full advantage of getting to put your feet up for a short while.'

She smiled as she imagined her babies in her arms. Who would they look like? Would they be dark-haired, like Jamie? Or blonde, like her? Would they have his intense midnight-dark eyes or her blue ones? Would they be happy, giggly babies? Or cry all the time with colic?

It was getting so close now, and she couldn't wait to hold them in her arms. To feel their little bodies snuggled up close to hers. She was looking forward to breastfeeding, if she could, although she worried about producing enough milk for both of them. She knew her body was designed to produce as much milk as the babies needed, but she couldn't stop worrying. Fretting about this and that. All the *what ifs* and all the horrors that might befall them.

She knew it was a normal part of being a new parent. She and Jamie were about to take on a huge responsibility and that they, more than anyone else, had uncertain futures.

I can't think about that now. I told myself I wouldn't.

The personal shoppers arrived, pushing a small clothes rail from which hung a plethora of baby clothes on tiny hangers. She went through them one by one, holding them, touching them. Laughing and smiling with Jamie as they imagined their sons dressed in each item and cooing over the small size of each piece.

She picked out baby vests and Babygros, tee shirts and tiny pairs of trousers. There were the most gorgeous pairs of baby shoes and trainers, pure white scratch mitts and the cutest knitted hats that looked like raccoons and foxes. She chose them both a winter snow suit, and picked out towels with white stripes that were adorned with tiny white sheep, and a gorgeous set of soft cherrywood brushes for their hair.

Michelle suggested a range of handmade bibs that were more like neckerchiefs, and then they moved on to car seats, and a double buggy that they both practised putting up and collapsing down. Freya chose a V-shaped pillow to assist with breastfeeding support, and a cute bedroom thermometer that looked like an owl. Plain and patterned fitted sheets and cellular blankets went onto the purchase pile. Then there were all the toys—teddy bears and rattles and soothers.

As each item was scanned Freya began to feel a little queasy. She saw the total totting up but, glancing at Jamie, she saw he was totally unfazed and realised that cost was not a concern for him. How nice it must be, she thought, not to have to worry about the pennies.

'And where shall we deliver this?' Michelle asked.

Jamie gave them her address and arranged a time for delivery tomorrow, promising Freya that the men would bring everything up to her flat and pack it away for her, so that she didn't have to do a thing.

'Oh, no—I'd like to do it, if that's okay.' She very much wanted to go through everything by herself. Sorting out where to put the clothes and how to organise everything in the wardrobes that Jamie had put up the other day.

'Just the clothes,' Jamie agreed. 'You're meant to be resting.'

Michelle escorted them back through the store, down into the lift and back to their car, waving at them as they drove off, with a big smile on her face.

'Well, if she works on commission I think we've just bought enough to give her the rest of the year off,' Freya joked.

Jamie laid his hand on hers. 'Did you enjoy it?'

She smiled. 'I did. You were right—it was lovely to actually see the items in person, rather than online. Some of those clothes were just so *dinky*!'

He laughed. 'They were, weren't they?'

Freya out a long sigh. 'So, are we going back home now?'

'I thought we could go and get something to eat, if that's okay?'

She thought of the crowds, and her mood dipped slightly. 'What did you have in mind?'

'How about pizza?'

Oh, yes! 'You read my mind.'

Jamie parked the car by the marina and left the engine on, keeping them warm as they ate their pizza. The boats were lit with security lights and bobbed about on the gently rocking waves as the wind whipped across the bay, biting at any exposed flesh on passers-by.

'Thanks for tonight, Jamie. It was amazing—it really was.'

'Once you got over what it felt like to be looked after for a change?'

She laughed. 'I guess.'

He peered out of the window. 'Still no snow.'

'I told you.'

'Yes, you did.' He wiped at his mouth and fingers with a napkin, before closing the lid on his pizza. 'That was delicious.'

'The pizza? Or me being right?'

He smiled at her. 'Both. And I wouldn't have it any other way.'

Wouldn't he? She knew this situation wasn't ideal for either of them. They both wanted the same things for the years ahead. They wanted to stay here in England. But he knew he would have to leave at some point. To be King. It was a dark thought that cast a long shadow over both of them.

'I'm sorry, Jamie.'

He turned to her and frowned. 'For what?'

'For not being able to leave here. For not agreeing to be your wife. I know it's me that's making this difficult for you and that if I just changed my mind then everything would be okay.'

Jamie shook his head. 'I would never force you to do anything. *Never*. I love the fact that you have been honest with me.' He took one of her hands in his and kissed the back of it. 'You were true to yourself. You told me the truth and I appreciate that. It makes what we have all the more special.'

She squeezed his fingers. 'What *do* we have, Jamie? Sometimes I'm not sure of anything.'

'We have a promise to be there for our children together, as much as we can be. To love them, and each other, until we can no longer do so.'

And each other? What did he mean by that? That he loved her? Or that the babies would love each other? That they would have a loving family? What he'd said was ambiguous. It could mean anything. And, although she was desperate to know whether he loved her, she felt at that moment that she couldn't ask him. The words were stuck in her throat.

She nodded. 'I don't want them to miss out on anything.'

'They won't.'

'I don't mean we should spoil them. I mean...' She looked away, out across the bay, past the boats and out to sea, where God only knew what was waiting. 'I mean that they should know just how much they are loved, by *both* of us. Even if one of us isn't there.'

'They will.' Jamie's voice was deep and full of emotion.

She loved it that he cared about this as much as she did. That his love for their babies ran as deeply as hers. Desperately she wanted to grab his hands and beg him never to go. Never to leave them. But she knew she couldn't ask him that. He had a duty. Over a million people would need him one day.

She couldn't make him choose between Majidar and her! He would always resent her for making him do it. So she knew that one day he would have to leave, and the idea of that, as her babies' birth grew closer, was beginning to break her heart.

Her feelings for Jamie had changed and grown. Especially over these last few weeks. Why did they have to be in this situation? Why did he have to be born to such a duty? Why couldn't he just be a midwife? Some random guy whom she'd met one day?

Why did he have to be a prince? Heir to a throne?

Why would she have to break her own heart one day and let go of him?

It wasn't fair.

Christmas morning arrived in the middle of a downpour.

Freya would not let the rain sully her day. It didn't matter. What mattered was that today was a day for family, and that for the first time in for ever she wouldn't be spending it alone with her mum. Jamie would be with them, arriving mid-morning, having lunch with them, before he had to leave for his shift at the hospital.

She hoped he'd like the present she'd got him. It had taken her ages to find something she thought he might like. What did you buy a *prince*—a man who could buy anything?

In the end she'd been rather sneaky, asking the security guys who followed her to get her a picture of Jamie's most successful racehorse so that she could have a painting done. One of her patients was an artist, and she'd commissioned her to do it.

Freya had to admit the painting looked amazing. Jamie's horse, Pride of Jameel, was a magnificent-looking animal, and Susie had painted the stallion standing tall and proud on a sand dune, his black coat gleaming.

As a little something extra—something silly—she'd got him a pair of teddy bears that played a recording of their twins' heartbeats when their bellies were squeezed.

'Merry Christmas, Mum!'

'Merry Christmas, Freya!' Her mum turned and blew her a kiss before turning her attention back to the frying pan. 'Full English for you?'

'Erm...just bacon and eggs, please.'

'What time are we expecting your young man?'

'Around ten, I think.'

'You've told him we don't open our gifts until after lunch?'

Freya nodded.

'And he's okay with turkey?'

'Yes, Mum.'

'What about the sausages? They're pork.'

'If there's anything he doesn't want he'll just leave it.'

'I don't want to offend him.'

'You won't, Mum. Honestly.'

'It's such an important day. I wouldn't want to ruin it.'

She helped her mum prepare all the vegetables, peel the potatoes and baste the turkey, which was already in the oven. The kitchen was filled with succulent aromas as they made the bread sauce, the cranberry sauce, and her mum's special stuffing. In the background Christmas carols played from the radio, and Freya realised as she sliced and chopped that she had never felt happier. It was Christmas, she was going to be a mother, and she had a man in her life whom she loved.

She'd fought it. Oh, how she'd tried to fight it! But she had to be honest with herself and admit the truth. She loved Jamie. He'd made it impossible for her not to.

Part of her still couldn't quite believe she had made herself that vulnerable again, but the other part—her love for Jamie—kept telling her it didn't matter, because she felt sure he loved her too and that he would never try to hurt her the way that Mike had, that by opening her heart and allowing him in she was not going to get burned this time.

There was only one way Jamie could hurt her, and that was by leaving, but she was being optimistic and trusting in what Jamie had said. They might have *years* together yet. Samuel and James might be grown men before he got called back to Majidar, so why waste all that time being lonely and miserable when they could be together, happy and loved?

The doorbell rang, breaking her thoughts, and instantly a smile lit her face. Wiping her hands on a tea towel, she went to answer the door.

Jamie stood on the doorstep beneath the shadow of a large black umbrella, holding a small sack of Christmas presents in his other hand.

'Merry Christmas!'

He smiled and stepped forward, planting a kiss upon her lips that made her hungry for more. She could have stood there all day, kissing him in the doorway, if it hadn't been for her mum coming to the door.

'Well, let the poor man in, Freya—it's bucketing down out there!'

'Something smells good.'

'It's your lunch. I hope you're hungry?'

He met her gaze. 'Starving.'

Freya could have melted there and then. The heat between them had been growing uncontrollably, and it was a terrible struggle not to let things advance between them physically when it was what they both wanted.

'Come on through. I'll make you a cup of tea.'

'Nope.' He took the bag of presents back from her. 'I'll make the tea. You put your feet up. Just show me where to put these and I'll get right on it.'

Freya showed him where to put the presents and then allowed him to settle her down on the couch, lifting her feet onto a foot rest.

He leaned over her, his hands either side of her, his face close to her own. 'I've missed you.'

'You saw me just yesterday.' She smiled, glancing down at his soft, sultry lips.

'And I missed you the second I left. I'm so happy to be here with you today. You have no idea.'

How was everything going so right for her? How was she so lucky? To have this—Jamie, the babies, Christmas, the *future*. Just a year or so ago her future had seemed quite lonely, but now...now she had everything she could possibly want. Perhaps it *was* her turn to be happy. She'd had what felt like a lifetime of pain, disappointment and grief. Her luck was turning at last.

Jamie slid onto the couch next to her and she rested her head against his strong, broad shoulder. She sat there feeling content. *Happy*.

CHAPTER NINE

'YOU'VE NOT GOT long now. Just a few more weeks before those babies arrive. What are you planning on doing once they get here?'

Freya frowned at her mum. 'How do you mean?'

'Well I know you're getting the flat ready, and the nursery is all decked out, but do you have any plans to move in together?'

Freya looked at Jamie, unsure. They hadn't talked about this.

'I'd be lying if I said I hadn't thought about the future, but I don't want to push Freya unless she's ready,' Jamie answered diplomatically.

It was scary. Terrifying. But she said it anyway. 'I might be ready.'

He raised an eyebrow, smiling. 'Really?'

'I'll need all the help I can get when the twins are born, and it would make sense, wouldn't it?'

Freya's mum was looking between them. 'What a romantic you are, Freya! You could sound a little more enthusiastic if you're asking him to move in!'

If she'd been able to blush properly she would have. Instead she looked at Jamie uncertainly. 'I'd love you to move in. If *you're* ready?'

Did he know how much it was taking for her to say this?

Jamie put down his knife and fork, dabbed at his mouth with a napkin and then got to his feet, walking around the table to kneel by her side. He took her hand in his and kissed it. 'I'd love to move in.'

Freya's mum clapped her hands together in excitement. 'Oh, yes! What a merry Christmas it is, indeed!'

Jamie embraced Freya in a quick hug, kissed her on the lips and then went back to his seat. 'Let's have a toast.' He raised his glass of juice and waited for Freya and her mum to do the same. 'To moving in and to bright futures.'

'To moving in and to bright futures!'

Their glasses clinked.

Freya had got her mum a scarf, hat and mittens set, along with a couple of books she wanted and some Belgian chocolates to satisfy her sweet tooth.

In return she'd received a gift voucher, some perfume, a new pair of pyjamas and a book in which to record all the twins' milestones as they grew.

'Thanks, Mum.'

'You're welcome, love.'

'Your turn, Jamie.'

Her mum had bought him a bottle of aftershave and a jumper, which he immediately tried on and declared that it fitted perfectly.

'Thank you, Mrs MacFadden.'

He handed Freya's mum an envelope, and when she opened it she realised, to her immense delight, that she'd been given a pass for a spa day at the Franklin Hotel.

'Jamie, that's brilliant—thank you!'

'After all your hard work in the kitchen today, you deserve it.'

'Open this next.'

Freya passed Jamie her present. The painting of his favourite horse, wrapped in bubble wrap and Christmas paper and tied with a huge, sparkly silver bow.

Curious, he began to unwrap it, struggling a little with all the tape Freya had used, until eventually he turned it around to see what it was.

'Freya, that's just *gorgeous*! It looks like Pride of Jameel.'

'It *is*!'

She laughed at the pure delight and amazement on his face, pleased that she could make him so happy—the same way he made *her* feel. This was what it was all about. Moments like these. When you could make the person you loved feel joy.

'How did you manage it?'

'Well, seeing as you've insisted I have bodyguards follow me around, I put them to actual work and told them to get me a photo of your most beloved horse.'

'It's amazing!' He kept admiring it, turning it this way and that to catch the light and admire new aspects of the painting. Then he put it down and kissed her. 'Thank you.'

'There's this, too.' She handed him the wrapped teddy bears.

He opened the gift, smiling when he saw it was two honey-coloured bears.

'Squeeze their tummies.'

He did, and his face broke into a huge smile when he heard the babies' heartbeats, which she'd had recorded at one of her antenatal visits.

'Samuel and James. I'll treasure them. Always.'

Freya felt she could burst with happiness! She hadn't been sure how he'd feel about the gifts, but she was thrilled with how much he liked the painting of his horse. It meant so much to her that he did.

'There's only two gifts left. Both for you, Freya.' Her mum smiled, passing over the gifts.

They were both small boxes. Jewellery-sized boxes. The type that rings came in...

Feeling nervous, Freya accepted the first one and began to unwrap it.

She'd been right. It was a small, red velvet box, shaped like a heart.

What if he was going to ask her to marry him again? Here and now? What would she say?

Sucking in a deep breath, she pushed open the lid.

There, nestled on a cushion of dark blue silk, was a pair of beautiful earrings. Silver, each encircling a beautiful jewel.

'They're platinum, and the jewels are black diamonds. The largest I could find.'

'They're beautiful!'

'Put them in, Freya,' urged her mum.

Part of her felt relief that his gift wasn't a ring. But there was still that second box. There could be a ring in there. It wasn't over yet.

She smiled nervously and put in the earrings, which both her mum and Jamie admired.

'They look beautiful on you, love.'

'Diamonds for my diamond.' Jamie smiled.

She leant over as much as she was able to and kissed him, meeting his gaze and holding it, trying to tell him without words just how much he meant to her and how frightened she was by his next gift.

It had to be the ring in that box, didn't it? And she wanted to say yes, but how could she? When the worst happened and Jamie got called back to Majidar she would have to go with him if she were his wife. It would be expected. But if she said no then she'd be ruining this beautiful day and breaking both their hearts, when right now they were both so happy.

Why had he done this? *Why?*

She felt a small surge of anger inside, irritation flooding her that it was all about to go wrong. She was about to feign a headache, or something, when the front doorbell rang.

Her mum frowned. 'Who on earth could that be? It's Christmas!'

'I'll go,' Jamie said, getting to his feet.

But Freya, feeling the need to escape the anticipation of what was in that tiny box, laid her hand upon his arm, stopping him. 'No. I'll go. You two have been looking after me all day—I need to stretch my legs for a moment.'

It was an excuse, but a welcome one, whoever it was. She just needed time to try and think. To try and decide what to do.

More than anything she would love to be Jamie's wife. To stand by his side with their babies as part of a loving family. But she knew she couldn't put herself under that much scrutiny. The world's press would have a field-day.

'Just coming!' She waddled down the hallway, exhaling loudly as she approached the door. She had no idea who it could be.

Standing before her was a man wearing a long white robe and a traditional *keffiyeh* on his head. He looked sombre, and bowed slightly at her appearance. 'Madam Mac-Fadden. My name is Faiz and I am the personal emissary of His Majesty King Ilias Al Bakhari. It is imperative that I speak with his brother, Prince Jameel.'

Freya froze for a moment as she took in his appearance and his message. Personal emissary? Why would Jamie's brother send a message on Christmas Day? It could hardly be a festive greeting. She was sure that they didn't celebrate Christmas over there in Majidar.

'An emissary?'

Faiz bowed again. 'Time is of the essence. If I may be allowed entry to speak with My Prince?'

Freya blinked rapidly as her brain raced through a thousand and one possibilities. Numb, she moved back and said nothing as Faiz stepped inside and past her.

'Who is it, Freya?' she heard her mum call from the room where moments ago everything had been perfect.

A chill crept over her as she began to suspect the reason for Faiz's visit. No. It *couldn't* be that. Could it?

Fighting back tears, she followed Faiz to the living room, where he stood just inside the doorway.

Jamie had got to his feet, his face stoic and ashen. 'Faiz?'

'My Prince. I must speak with you privately.'

Jamie glanced at her. The briefest eye contact. He must have seen the horror on her face before he looked away again.

'Anything you have to say, Faiz, can be said in front of everyone here.'

Faiz gave her a considered look, then nodded. 'Your brother has been taken ill. He is in hospital and it is imperative that you return to the kingdom.'

'Ill?'

'It is believed that His Majesty has suffered a stroke.'

Jamie stared at the floor, his body tense, his fists clenched at his side. 'Is Jasmeen with him?'

'The Queen has not left his side.'

'So you need me to return?'

His voice was thick with emotion, and more than anything Freya wanted to go to him and put her arms around him and comfort him, but her own grief kept her glued to the spot.

Jamie was leaving.

Now.

She wasn't ready. She wasn't ready to let him go! They'd only just started to be happy. They'd only just decided to be together. This wasn't fair! What about the babies? It was so close to her due date…he'd miss seeing them born!

'Jamie?' Her voice croaked in a painful whisper of grief.

He couldn't look at her. He just kept staring at the floor.

'Faiz? Are you absolutely sure that I must return?'

'I am not to return without you.'

Her mum hurried over to her and draped an arm around her shoulders. She turned into her mum's body and began to cry.

Behind them, she heard Jamie dismiss Faiz. 'Give me a moment.'

'Yes, My Prince.'

'Freya?'

She couldn't look at him. It hurt too much. She just clutched her mother harder.

'Freya? Please...'

Her mother released her and stepped away. 'I'll be in the kitchen.'

Freya folded her arms around herself and stared at Jamie through her tears. 'You can't go!'

'I must.'

He stepped forward and reached for her, intending to hold her, but she couldn't bear the idea of him touching her. If she let him hold her then she would never let him go.

She stepped back. 'Don't.'

'I never expected this. We were meant to have years...'

'But we both knew that it would happen one day,' she threw back.

'I'm so sorry. I never wanted this.'

She couldn't say anything. Words were not enough to express how she felt right now.

He looked remorseful. 'I could be back in time for the birth. Ilias may recover.'

'He might. But I can't compete with a million people who need you. And that's how it should be. The needs of a million people outweigh my own. You have to go. I understand.'

'I want to stay.'

'But you *can't*!' Her voice broke. 'We knew this day would come. We were fools to think we could cheat it.'

'There must be a way?'

She nodded. 'There is. Accept your fate. It's always been there for you. Coming to England, meeting me…it could never stop that wheel from turning.'

He looked hurt. 'You know that I would stay if I could?'

She nodded, fresh tears running down her cheeks.

'You'll keep me informed?'

She frowned. 'How?'

'I'll leave my men. They can get messages to me.'

'No, Jamie. Take them all with you. Leave nothing behind.'

'I'm leaving *you* behind.'

She stared directly at him, through her tears and her pain. 'Exactly.'

He shook his head. 'I can't believe this is happening. Do we have to end this? Now?'

'We do. Because I can't live a half-life, Jamie. I've already done that for far too long…hiding from the world, living in the shadows. I've got to live for me now. For my children. And I deserve—*we* deserve—a happy, full life.'

'I can't walk away from my children.'

She winced. So he *could* walk away from her?

'But you will, Jamie. You've already made your choice. You've been called and you're going and you *should* go. Your brother is sick—has had a stroke. You need to see him, just in case his condition does not improve. You will be called upon to rule the country in his stead, and if he does not recover you will rule permanently. By going now you're choosing Majidar over us—as it should be. It's your duty.'

'You truly are the bravest woman I have ever known.'

She swallowed down her pain. 'You need to go now. Just *go*, Jamie.'

He looked away, his gaze taking in the twinkling Christmas tree, the wrapping paper discarded on the floor, the presents, the painting of his horse. And the small gift that she still had to open.

Jamie picked it up and held it in his hands. Staring at it for a moment, twisting it this way and that. Then he put it in his pocket, bent to pick up the teddy bears and gave her one last look.

'I love you, Freya MacFadden.'

She stared back, her heart breaking at this one last message, more tears falling freely down her face. 'And I love you, Jameel.'

And he went.

He turned his back and disappeared through the doorway.

Grief and pain tore sobs from her as she sank to her knees on the floor.

And on the television was the Queen, in her annual speech, talking to the nation. She focused on the Queen's face. A monarch addressing her people. Her whole life committed to her country.

How had she ever believed she could come between a man and such a love?

The house on Hayling Island had been closed up for a while.

Freya went through it, opening windows, letting in the aroma of the sea air despite the winter cold.

She turned up the thermostat on the central heating, made herself a mug of tea, and then stood outside on the small balcony and looked out to sea.

It was very still, calm, as if it was waiting for something. Grey-green, dully reflecting the grey sky above.

Down by the water she could see a dog walker, wrapped up in a thick jacket, throwing a tennis ball for three small dogs that chased after it happily.

This was what she needed—calm. The relaxed, unhurried way of life here, where no demands could be made of her and where she wouldn't have to find a brave face when inside she could feel herself crumbling.

She and Jamie had had their time cut short. Much too short. Both of them had believed—hoped—that they would have years…decades, perhaps. She'd begun to believe that her two sons would have a father. A great father. One who would adore them, teach them, raise them to be good boys. Good men.

Only now she would have that task alone.

What would she tell them about him? And when? As they got older they would begin to understand what a prince was, what a king was. Would they want to go to him?

She toyed with the idea of going with them one day. But she could only foresee agony in doing so. Meeting Jamie after many years… What if he had moved on? Married, as a king would be expected to do? What if he had a new family? Would she be welcomed in Majidar? Or spurned? Would Samuel and James always be known in Majidar as the King's illegitimate children?

And if they did visit there would always have to be another goodbye, and it wouldn't just be Freya who would be distraught afterwards it would be the boys, too, and *she* would be the one who would have to deal with the fallout. She would be the one to pick up the pieces of her children and slowly put them back together again.

Perhaps it might be best not to tell the boys who their father was? But the idea of lying to them, of manipulating the truth, made her feel sick.

What to do?

This was why she had come here to Hayling Island. To get some space. To think clearly. Not to see the nursery every day and be reminded of the ticking of the clock. She had mere weeks left of her pregnancy, and as if in reminder of that she felt her first Braxton Hicks contraction.

A tightening of her belly. Her body preparing itself for the battle to come.

She rubbed her hand underneath her bump and breathed through it. There wasn't any pain, just a tightness, her belly going hard and rigid before slowly softening and relaxing again.

'I'll always be here for you,' she said to them, before going to close all the windows she'd opened. so she'd feel the benefit of the central heating.

She wanted to go down to the water, to walk along the beach and feel that sea air invigorate her lungs.

She grabbed her coat, hat and scarf and wrapped up well, then opened the door and stepped out, locking up behind her.

As she turned to begin her walk she felt something touch her cheek. Then her nose.

She looked up and saw that snow was finally beginning to fall, and it pained her to know that he was missing it.

'Oh, Jamie…'

Security guards lined the floor of the private hospital in which his brother the King lay. Escorted by Faiz and his own personal assistant, Rafiq, Jamie strode down the corridor towards his brother's room.

He had been kept informed throughout his seven-hour flight back home on the Bakhari private jet. And the briefcase of documents awaiting his attention on the plane had reminded him of the life he had left behind when he'd first come to England.

He was trying his hardest to remain stoic, but his mind was a mess. He'd left her behind.

I left her behind!

Freya and his two babies. His sons. His heirs.

My heart.

But duty had called him and he felt helpless to try and

fight it. He would never be the same again now that he'd been ripped in two.

Part of him hoped that when he walked into that hospital room and saw his brother lying in a hospital bed Ilias would open his mouth to speak and smile, maybe hold his brother in greeting, give him a hug, pat him on the back and say, *Welcome home, brother.*

That would be the best solution for them all.

His duty, his future, hung over him like a guillotine. He hated to refer to his noble duty in such a way, but it was how it had always felt to him. He'd never asked to be royal, never asked to be born into such a family, and being King had *never* interested him. Not once.

Leaving his country, his family, and flying thousands of miles away as a young man had taken a lot of courage, but he had followed his heart and done what he'd thought was right.

He came to his brother's room and placed his hand upon the door. The doctors had informed him that Ilias appeared to have a blood disorder. They weren't sure of it yet, but they were running tests.

He hoped they would learn what it was soon. So his brother could be treated and recover as quickly as possible.

He opened the door.

CHAPTER TEN

THERE WERE MONITORS sounding out the beats of his brother's heart.

He is alive.

But then he saw him—pale and wan against the hospital pillows, with his wife Jasmeen dutifully by his bedside, clutching his hand.

The shock of seeing him looking so ill stopped Jamie in his tracks.

'Jameel? You're here!' Jasmeen let go of her husband's hand and came over to embrace her brother-in-law.

'How is he?'

'The doctors say he is stable…but I have never seen him like this before.'

'Nor I.'

Jamie took a seat by his brother's bed and took hold of Ilias's hand.

'Ilias? It's Jameel. I'm here. I've come home.'

'He sleeps deeply since the stroke. It's like he has a tiredness that cannot be quenched.'

'Can he speak yet?'

'Sounds, but not words. It distresses him greatly. He tries to write, but he is right-handed, so it takes a while to read his words.'

Jamie squeezed his brother's fingers and felt tears sting

the backs of his eyes. But he refused to cry here. Crying would be an admission of just how out of control he was, when he was desperately clinging to the one bit of hope that he still had.

'Ilias?'

His brother moaned and then began to blink, looking about him to find the source of his brother's voice.

'Nurgh...'

Tears appeared in Ilias's eyes when he saw his brother, and Jamie leant forward to kiss his brother's cheeks.

'I am here, brother. I am here.' He held his brother's face in his hands, touching his forehead to Ilias's.

His brother signalled for his writing pad and Jasmeen presented it to him.

I'm sorry you had to come home.

Jamie read the tight scrawl and smiled. 'Don't be sorry. You couldn't have known this was going to happen.'

You're about to become a father.

He nodded, thinking of Freya and her huge belly, of his hand resting on her abdomen, feeling the boys kick and stretch inside. He'd left them. Left them behind. Maybe never to see them again.

The ache in his chest was palpable. 'Yes.'

I did not want to do this to you.

'It's not your fault, brother. None of this is. I am just so grateful that you are still alive. You must fight hard, Ilias. Fight hard to get better.'

He turned to look at Jasmeen.

'Has he seen any physiotherapists yet?'

'They come three times a day.'

Ilias began to scribble again.

I don't think I can remain King like this.

Jamie's stomach dropped like a stone. 'You don't know what the future holds.'

Jasmeen gave a weak smile. 'The doctors hoped that his speech would be back by now, and though the weakness on his right side has yet to improve they hope with time that it will get a little better. But they are unsure of a full recovery.'

Jamie thought about what that meant for a moment. 'I see.'

'I have been talking to Ilias, Jameel. We have talked long and hard and taken everything into consideration. Ilias loves Majidar and its people so much—he believes it needs a strong leader. Right now he does not feel that that is him.'

Jamie shook his head and tried to implore his brother. 'It *is* you.'

'He wants to abdicate.'

Jasmeen's words dropped into the room like a grenade.

Abdicate? *Abdicate?* But if Ilias abdicated that would mean that he...

Jamie stood up and began to pace the room, coming to a stop by the window to stare out, far and wide over the desert in the distance, on the outskirts of the city. Freya was so far away.

'Nurgh...'

Jamie's eyes closed at the sound of his brother's voice. He felt awful. Pathetic. Thinking only of himself when his brother was in such distress and pain! What sort of man did that make him?

He turned to see that Ilias was holding up his writing pad. He read the words.

It doesn't have to be you.

It was New Year's Eve and the snow had been falling for a few days now. Thick, heavy flakes, tumbling silently, covering the world in a white blanket of softness.

It made everything look beautiful, but it had certainly put paid to Freya's ideas of getting some walks in. All the heavy rain there had been before the snow meant that there was a thick layer of ice beneath it, so the pavements and roads were treacherous.

The weather forecasters predicted more heavy snow and informed people that they should not travel unless they had to. Gritters were out, trying to line the roads, but they were fighting an endless battle.

Freya stayed in the small house, drinking lots of tea and eating plenty of warm, buttery toast in front of the log fire, flicking from channel to channel on the television to try and find something interesting to watch.

Today she'd found a few films and had settled in to watch those, aware that her Braxton Hicks contractions had been coming a lot more frequently just recently. This morning they had begun to start hurting, and every now and then she'd find herself having to stop and breathe, clutching onto the back of the sofa or a kitchen unit.

She dutifully called her mum and told her she was fine.

'I'm so worried about you, stuck out there with all this snow. What if you go into labour?'

'Then I'll call an ambulance, Mum. Stop worrying, I'm fine. I've got a few weeks left.'

'Two weeks left, Freya. *Two weeks*. Those babies could come any time.'

'Well, I *am* a midwife, Mum, so I'll know what to do.'

She managed to get her mum off the phone eventually, sighing heavily, and decided to run herself a bath.

A soak in warm water helped soothe her troubled nerves, and she was soon settled back on the couch with a nice cup of tea.

A sudden pain, low in her belly, had her gasping, and she had to reach under her bump to rub at her abdomen. Slowly the pain eased and she lay back again, wondering if she'd sat down awkwardly and maybe pulled a muscle?

But the pain was gone now, and she felt confident that she'd know if she was really in labour.

On the screen, a newsflash came up on the local news to say that most roads in the area were becoming inaccessible and it was recommended that people did not drive anywhere unless it was absolutely necessary.

She glanced out of the window. The snow was still falling and there were drifts right up to the ledge.

She'd never known it to snow like this before. Not down here. Not by the coast, where you'd imagine there'd be enough salt around to prevent it. But there it all was. A thick white blanket. Would it snow like this next year? Would she be able to let the twins out in it? See the wonder on their faces?

The thought made her smile—a smile that soon faded when she got another pain.

Oh, God. Is this it? Is this labour?

All her bravery, all her bravado because she was a midwife, went out of the window. She suddenly realised just how *alone* she was here, how isolated. And if she needed to call an ambulance would it be able to get here?

There was only a single road on and off the island, connected to the mainland by a bridge. What if that was blocked? Impassable?

She hauled herself up and began to breathe through the panic, pacing back and forth.

*Okay...okay. This could just be early labour, and I'm a
first-time mother so my labour could be hours yet. Plus,
it could still die down. There's nothing to say that these
pains will continue.*

But they did. Every eight minutes she got a pain, and
as the hours passed they increased to every five minutes.

She picked up the phone, but the line was dead. She
scrabbled in her handbag for her mobile and dialled 999.

'Ambulance, please.'

She was put through to Control and gave her address
and situation. The guy on the phone told her that someone
would be with her as quickly as they could, but because of
the snowfall their ambulances were busy elsewhere. She
was to try and find someone to be with her, so they could
call again later if she needed to deliver at home.

Panicking, she put down her phone and began to think.
Who could she get to help her? These properties were
mostly summer holiday lets, and it was New Year's Eve!

A knock at the door had her struggling to walk over to
it. Whoever it was, she would tell them what was happening. See if they could help her or if they knew someone else
who could help. There were first responders on the island,
surely? Perhaps they could get to her? She knew they didn't
usually attend labouring women, but when needs must...

She grabbed hold of the door handle, turned the key and
yanked the door open.

And there—shivering, wet, and very, very cold-look-
ing—was Jamie. His face was red and glistening, his hair
flattened by snowflakes.

Hesitantly, he smiled. 'I told you it would snow.'

'Jamie?'

'The one and only. Can I come in? Only I've been trudg-
ing through snow for the last couple of hours.'

'How did you know where to find me?'

But before he could answer another contraction ripped

through her, and she gasped and let go of the door to bend
over and put both hands on her knees to breathe through it.

'Freya? Are you in *labour*?'

She couldn't answer him for a moment. The contraction had completely obliterated her ability to talk whilst it
was going on. The most she could do—the *only* thing she
could do—was remain upright and breathe.

When it receded, and when normal thought and the real
world returned, she stood straight again and looked at him
with tears in her eyes. Her heart felt overwhelmed with relief and love for this man before her.

'For about four hours now.'

'*Four hours?* Why didn't you call for an ambulance?
Stranded out here like this!'

'I did. They don't know when they can get to me. Apparently they're busy.'

He rummaged in his pocket for his mobile. 'I'll get
someone here.'

He tapped at the screen and then held the phone to his
ear, shouting instructions in Arabic before snapping it shut
again.

'I've got a paramedic being choppered in.'

'A helicopter? In this? How did you know where to find
me?'

'There's a GPS tracker on your phone.'

'What?'

'They all have them. Don't worry—I didn't place some
secret bug in it, or anything. I'm not that kind of guy.'

Another contraction began to build. 'Oh, God!'

She turned to lean against the stairs and felt Jamie's
hands hold her steady and rub the small of her back. When
it was done, he guided her back to the lounge so she could
sit down.

'That last contraction was about a minute and they're
coming fast.'

'You don't need to tell *me* that. I'm the one having them.'

'We need to prepare. Where are your towels? I'll put on some hot water, and we'll need scissors I can sterilise for cutting the cord—just in case.'

'Wait a minute. You can't come sweeping in here like a white knight. You need to tell me what's happening. How's your brother? Are you King?'

'Ilias has Von Willebrand's disease. He's being treated for it. The stroke has caused deficits, which hopefully will improve over time, but he has decided to abdicate, feeling that it's in the best interests of our country to have a ruler in full health.'

'He's *abdicated*? Can he do that?'

Her abdomen tightened with another vice-like contraction.

'*Ohhhhh...*'

She leaned forward and gripped the sofa, her eyes tightly shut as the feelings within her body overwhelmed her. Pain. Intensity. Breathing was the only thing she could manage for sure.

She felt Jamie take her hand and she gripped his fingers tightly, squeezing the blood from his digits. 'Oh, I think I need to push.'

'I'll need to check you first. Can I do that?'

She nodded quickly and removed her pyjama bottoms and underwear, wincing at the dying pain in her belly.

'I'll wash my hands. Do you have any gloves?'

Freya pointed into the kitchen. 'Beneath the kitchen sink are some latex gloves. Mum uses them for when she has to touch raw meat.' She tried to laugh, recalling her mother's squeamish nature.

'I'll be back in a moment.'

She lay back on the couch and wiped the sweat from her forehead.

Jamie was back. But how? If Ilias had abdicated, didn't

that mean that Jamie was now King? *Why* had he returned?
Had they allowed him some kind of compassionate leave
to be with her for when the babies arrived? So he could
see them and *then* leave? She hoped not. Because even if
that was good for him, it would be doubly difficult for *her*.

Having him here, holding her hand, mopping her brow,
seeing the joy and love on his face as he looked at his sons
and then having to wave him goodbye again... *No.* She
couldn't allow that. She wouldn't survive it. The birth would
be hard enough without being deserted right afterwards.

Jamie came back into the living room wearing a pair
of latex gloves. 'Right, let's take a look. Has the contraction gone?'

'Yes. But maybe you should leave, Jamie?'

He looked up at her, confused. 'Leave? I just got here—
and I don't think there's anyone more suitably qualified to
help than me right now. I don't think I'll be fetching your
elderly neighbour from next door, who needs a magnify-
ing glass to read the evening paper.'

Now it was her turn to frown. 'Does he? How do you
even *know* that?'

'I have *people*, remember? I'm going to examine you
now. Try to relax.'

She lay back, opening her legs. 'Why does every man
say that when he has to do an internal? Perhaps if men
had a vagina they'd realise exactly how hard it is to *relax*!'

'Good point.' He smiled up at her. 'And good news.
You're fully dilated. You can start to push with the next
contraction.'

Freya's eyes finally began to leak tears of relief and happiness. 'I can?'

'You can.'

Jamie removed the gloves, pulling them inside out before discarding them in a small wastepaper bin. Then he
pulled another pair from his pocket.

'Now—quickly—where are the towels kept?'

I can push. They'll be here soon. Samuel and James.

'Upstairs. Second door to the left is a small airing cupboard.'

'Don't do anything exciting without me.'

He kissed her on the cheek and raced upstairs and she watched him go, shocked by the feel of his kiss still upon her skin.

He seemed okay. He seemed as if he was in control. Was he really? Or was this all a front?

She still didn't know what was happening. Still didn't know whether he was staying. The hope that he might stay was building much too quickly, and she was struggling to fight it down, because she really wanted him to stay with her.

But reality told her that if Ilias had abdicated then Jamie was soon to be King, and he was only here on loan. His country had claimed him. And the knowledge of that was destroying her.

She began to cry.

Why was he doing this to her? Why had he come back and made her think there was hope? Made her think there was a chance for them still? It wasn't fair. Did he not know how hard it had been for her after he'd left the first time? If he did know then he wouldn't have done this.

She heard him come running back down the stairs and he appeared at her side with a huge pile of towels.

'You need to go.'

He frowned. 'Don't be ridiculous. I'm not going anywhere. What kind of man would I be to leave you in this state in the middle of a white-out?'

'A man with principles. I can't have you here, Jamie. Not like this! Not knowing you're going to leave me again!'

Another contraction hit and she heard nothing as his words faded beyond the pain she could feel surround her whole body. She sucked in a breath and, remembering all the advice she gave to labouring mothers, tucked her chin into her chest, curled around her baby and pushed down into her bottom.

It felt *good* to push! Excellent, in fact. There was almost relief there, because now she wasn't a passive observer of her pain, letting it roll over her in waves. Now she could do something about it!

She pushed against it, shoved back, using the pain of the contraction to start moving and birthing her babies.

'That's it, Freya! You're doing really well! Keep pushing right there. That's *it*!'

She let out a breath, then immediately sucked in another and began again. She managed two more huge breaths and two more pushes before the contraction died down and she could breathe properly again.

'Freya…' He took her hand and made her look him in the eyes. 'I'm not going to leave you. Not tonight. Not tomorrow. Not ever.'

Not ever?

'But—'

Another contraction began. *God, they're coming thick and fast now!* But she knew that was good. This was what was *meant* to happen.

'I can see a head, Freya! You're *doing* this! You're really doing this!'

When it was over, she reached down to touch the head of her first son and gasped when she felt it. 'Oh, my God!'

'With the next contraction his head will be born. Okay?'

She nodded, sucked in a breath, and began pushing again as the next contraction built.

'Keep pushing! Keep pushing! That's it—just like that. Now, stop! Pant it out!'

She panted, huffing away like an old-fashioned steam train, and then Jamie was telling her to give one last push.

She felt her son slither from her body and into Jamie's safe, waiting hands. He lifted Samuel up onto her belly. 'Here he is!'

'Oh, Jamie!' She grasped her son, her darling Samuel, ignoring all the stuff he was covered in—the white vernix, the smears of blood—and cried again out loud when her son opened up his lungs for the first time, letting out a long, strangled cry. 'Oh, he's so beautiful!'

He was. He was a good size—between six and seven pounds, she estimated—and with a thick, full head of dark hair like his father.

Jamie draped a couple of towels over his son, so he wouldn't get cold, then tied off the cord with string and cut it with the scissors he'd sterilised in a bowl of steaming hot water.

Then he looked at them. With *such* pride. 'I'm so proud of you.'

Freya beamed at him as she cradled her son. 'I can't believe he's here.'

'Safe and sound.'

'Thanks to you.'

'Thanks to *you*.'

She smiled and reached for him, so that he would lean forward and place a kiss upon her lips. A soft, gentle, reaffirming kiss. And then he stooped over his son's head and laid a kiss on his son's head, too.

'Oh, my! I can't believe this has happened so quickly!' She looked at him. 'And you're here! And you can *stay*?'

He nodded, smiling. 'I can stay.'

'How?'

'Ilias told me that I didn't have to take the throne. That my sister Zahra wants to do it. She's a good, strong woman. She's always wanted to get more involved with the running of things and she's a good choice. The people will look up to her.'

'But I thought you *had* to do it?'

'So did I. But what kind of King would I be? With my people knowing that I had deserted my own two sons to sit on the throne? Knowing that I had left behind the woman I loved? Above all, my people would want me to be happy— as my brother Ilias wanted me to be happy by letting me come to England in the first place. He knows my life is here now, as do my people. They will understand. And Zahra is much loved. She will make a fine monarch. A brilliant one.'

He could stay? For good? With her and Samuel and James and without any possibility of his desertion hanging over them?

Another contraction began to make itself known. 'It's starting again…'

'Do you want me to take Samuel?'

'Please. I don't want to squash him.'

She passed her firstborn safely over to Jamie and began to breathe through the contraction. Jamie would need to check her first, before she began pushing again. To make sure James was in a good position.

He checked her and smiled. 'He's head down. He's right there, Freya.'

'Okay. I can do this again, right?'

He smiled back at her. 'You can do *anything*!'

She had to believe him. Had to believe that she could give birth again even though she felt exhausted after delivering Samuel.

Hunkering down, she began to push.

It felt a little easier this time. She pushed and pushed, and before she knew what was happening the head was delivered.

'One more push and it will all be over.'

'I hope so!'

She gave a quick glance to Samuel, lying on the floor beside Jamie, wrapped up in towels, resting from the trauma of being pushed through the birth canal.

She'd often wondered if babies cried because of the pain in their skull bones, overlapping to fit through, or whether it was just the shock of all the tiny alveoli in their lungs suddenly inflating for the first time. Maybe it was both?

But Samuel was here and he was safe, and he had a mother *and* a father, and of course she could do it again.

She sucked in a breath.

'That's it, Freya! Push! Harder!'

From somewhere she found a reserve she hadn't known she had. Whether it came from the knowledge that if she just did this one last push, as hard as she could, it would all be over, or whether she really did have that endless supply of energy distinctly found in women giving birth she didn't know. But she found it, and she used it, and she pushed with all of her might.

James was born. Into his father's hands and then up onto her stomach, the same as Samuel had been.

Crying with relief, she held him weakly, glad the pain was over, overjoyed that her babies were finally here, safe and well.

And Jamie...? Jamie was here to stay, it seemed. They could have the future that both of them wanted.

With the cord cut and the placentas delivered, Jamie sat himself next to her. They held a baby each. From above they could hear a helicopter, looking for a suitable place to land.

She smiled at her babies' little faces, gasping with delight at each tiny noise, each little snuffle, each beautiful yawn.

'Look at them, Jamie. They're so beautiful.'

'How could they not be with a mother like you?'

She smiled and leant her forehead against his. 'You're truly here to stay?'

'I'm here to stay. If you'll have me, of course.'

She turned to look at him. Looked deeply into those midnight-black eyes of his. Of course she wanted him! It was what she had always wanted but had been too afraid to admit, because she'd always thought he would have to desert her.

But that threat was gone now.

'Can I ask you something?'

She waited for him to look at her. He was still gazing at his sons with such love.

'Of course you can. You can ask me anything.'

'Will you marry me, Jamie?'

His gaze locked with hers and a delighted smile appeared upon his face. 'Yes. A thousand times, yes!' He leant forward until their lips touched.

Closing her eyes in exhausted delight, she kissed him back, pouring every ounce of her love for him into it. Oh, how she needed this man! She'd never known what was missing from her life. She'd convinced herself that her life was fine, hiding herself away on the night shift, pretending she was doing herself a favour.

That hadn't been any way to live. And Jamie had seen that. Known that. He'd looked beyond the mask she was wearing and called her on it. Not allowing her to get away with it.

He'd made her into the woman she'd been *before*. The woman she'd thought she would never be again.

'I love you, Jameel.'

He stroked her face. 'And I love *you*.'

EPILOGUE

MAJIDAR WAS MORE beautiful than she could ever have imagined. A vast desert kingdom, filled with a thriving populace that had roared and cheered their delight at Jamie's return for a two-week visit.

She'd been nervous. All those people! And she had taken Jamie from them. She had stopped him from being their king.

But the people were thrilled to have her there. They waved and smiled, and small children brought her bouquet after bouquet, which she passed back to the bodyguards who escorted them on their tour wherever they went. Everyone had treated her with deference, and she did not doubt their love for her as Jamie's wife.

Now, as she stood on the palace balcony, looking out across the oasis beyond, she felt Jamie's arms come around her from behind.

'How do you feel?'

She smiled and laid her head against his shoulder. 'Loved.'

'I told you they would all love you.'

She turned to face him, to look deeply into his eyes. 'But to be loved *this much*... I never would have thought it was possible.'

Jamie smiled back and lowered one of his hands to her slightly rounded abdomen. 'When should we tell them?'

She was pregnant again. This time carrying only one baby. She hoped it might be a girl, but she didn't really mind.

'Let's do it tomorrow. Let's tell the whole world.'

She knew it would be all right.

He smiled and pulled her towards him.

* * * * *

LET'S TALK
Romance

For exclusive extracts, competitions
and special offers, find us online:

JOIN US ON SOCIAL MEDIA!

Stay up to date with our latest releases, author news and gossip, special offers and discounts, and all the behind-the-scenes action from Mills & Boon...

 millsandboon

 millsandboonuk

 millsandboon

might just be true love...

MILLS & BOON
True Love
Romance from the Heart

Celebrate true love with tender stories of heartfelt romance, from the rush of falling in love to the joy a new baby can bring, and a focus on the emotional heart of a relationship.